Beyond Sin

Beyond Sin

Emma Louise
Jordan

POOLBEG
Crimson

Published 2009
by Poolbeg Press Ltd
123 Grange Hill, Baldoyle
Dublin 13, Ireland
E-mail: poolbeg@poolbeg.com

© Emma Louise Jordan 2009

Typesetting, layout, design © Poolbeg Press Ltd.

1 3 5 7 9 10 8 6 4 2

A catalogue record for this book is available from the British Library.

ISBN 978-1-84223-399-3

Typeset by Patricia Hope in Sabon 10.2/14
Printed by
Litografia Rosés, S.A., Spain

www.poolbeg.com

About the author

"Emma Louise Jordan" is a Poolbeg Crimson pen name for Emma Heatherington. Emma is a freelance PR and lives in the village of Donaghmore, Tyrone, with her husband and three children.

Coming soon: *Playing the Field* by Emma Heatherington (Poolbeg Press, September 2009)

Acknowledgements

Writing *Beyond Sin* was both a stimulating and exciting challenge – one which certainly allowed me to step out of my comfort zone as a writer.

The idea for the story came to me as I pondered the hysteria that often comes with a family wedding and the pressure for everything to be absolutely perfect as the big day comes around – and what might happen when the ugly side of real life gets in the way of the celebrations and things go horribly wrong.

For listening to my idea and for giving me the opportunity to bring it to life through the Poolbeg Crimson range of fiction, thanks to Paula, Niamh, David and all at Poolbeg Press; to Gaye Shortland whose eye for detail made my story much more concise and even better than I hoped it would be; and to my very supportive and enthusiastic agent, Ger Nicholl, who keeps me on my toes with her extensive knowledge and her honesty.

Thanks to all of the Irish bookshops for their help in promoting my novels, especially Easons at Rushmere (Craigavon) and Sheehy's in Cookstown for local support.

For encouragement and sharing each step of my writing career and for their continuous belief, thanks to my good friends – Kathryn, Ann Marie and Grace at the B.E.A.M Centre and Seán and all at Bardic Theatre Group in Donaghmore.

Thanks to Margaret for being there every step of the way.

To my husband Dalglish, my children Jordyn, Jade and Adam, my dad Hugh and all my friends and family who continue to cheer me on in this writing life – thank you all so, so much.

For Dalglish

"Who can say, 'I have kept my heart pure; I am clean and without sin'?"

PROVERBS 20:9

Chapter 1

Wednesday

"What do you think, Mum?" asked Andrea O'Neill, tilting her head to the side in front of the mirror.

Ella watched her daughter as her shoulder-length black hair tossed across her shoulders and rested on her fine collarbone, skimming her delicate, fake-tanned skin. "Huh?"

"Off the shoulder or on the shoulder . . . like this? Gosh, I really can't decide . . ."

Ella stared outside into the dark July drizzle that looked more like a winter's day than a summer morning.

"Mum! Earth to Mother!" called Andrea again, her tone more pinched now.

It was the worst summer in fifteen years, the weatherman on the news channel had said. Ella truly hoped he was wrong and that the sun would come out before Saturday. The Infant of Prague would help, she was told. Yes, she would place an Infant of Prague in the

1

window – an old Catholic belief that claimed an innocent-looking statue had the power to influence the weather.

Despite her doubts about religion, when there was an event as important as her younger daughter's wedding Ella would take her chances and give it a go.

"*Mum*!"

"I have told you at least twice already, love," said Ella, going to where her baby girl was to-ing and fro-ing in front of the full-length mirror. "Keep it *on* your shoulder. And, believe me, you don't have to try on your dress every day. It's beautiful. You're beautiful."

She kissed her daughter on the cheek and Andrea wiped the pale pink lipstick mark off her face.

"And, Mum, this rain! Jesus!" she moaned.

"The rain will go," said Ella. "The rain will go by Saturday, even if I have to climb up there and stop it myself!"

Andrea gave her mother a smile and turned her back to be helped out of her dress. "Well, if it doesn't go away, then *I'm* going to go around the bend. And I'm going to be late for my make-up-trial appointment if Jessie doesn't show up soon." She rambled on as her mother unzipped her long ivory gown. "Why does she always have to be running behind for everything? She'll be late for her own funeral, one day, I swear she will."

Ella laughed and she had to agree. Her older daughter Jessie was always chasing her tail but she gave everyone such entertaining excuses that they always forgave her no matter how many minutes she kept them waiting.

"She'll be here. Don't worry."

"Well, if she doesn't, I'll never forgive her. This is the most important week of my life. I want everything to be perfect."

Ella watched how Andrea put her wedding dress back on the hanger and zipped up its protective cover, pure pleasure on her face at its sheer beauty and all that it represented. Then she glanced at the bedroom window again and her mood darkened when she saw that the summer rain had not yet subsided. Money could let her buy Andrea the most beautiful dress, hire out the most desirable venue, choose the most exquisite flowers but all the money in the world couldn't help fix the weather.

"Why don't you get dressed, love?" she said. "So that you're ready when your sister arrives?"

It was a command more than a question but Ella knew she had to be firm and practical as Andrea had been known to blow her top at the slightest bit of panic or delay. The days that followed would be extremely trying on the whole family if Andrea's recent mood-swings were anything to go by.

Like an obedient schoolgirl, Andrea reached up into the top of her wardrobe and fished out a pale pink shirt, then teamed it with her new indigo jeans and silver pumps and sat in the window seat that on a good day gave a wonderful view of Glencuan, the border town she had been born and reared in – a town in which her family owned most of the land and buildings that gave it its picture-postcard character.

Ella came to stand beside her daughter. "Cain Daniels is a very lucky man," she murmured as she stroked her hair. "A very lucky man indeed."

Ella had been lucky in life too. With Jessie happily married to David, a police detective, in her grand house only a mile down the road and Andrea's wedding just around the corner, the only one of the O'Neill children who had yet to settle down was the precious only son of the house. Young Ryan was a chip off the old block and hopefully would, in his own time, grow into the fine businessman that his father had groomed him to be. Her husband, Tom, was an influential man in the widest of circles. A self-made millionaire, he was a generous, old-school type who strongly believed in looking after his own, especially his immediate family.

"Now, love, you have about twenty minutes and then you'll really have to get going if you want to make your appointment for ten thirty," said Ella. "Can I get you anything while you wait for Jess? A cup of tea?"

She sensed Andrea's patience was wearing thin and as always she felt the need to subtly play referee between her two daughters.

"No thanks, Mum," said Andrea. "I'll phone the beautician and tell her we're running late. But next time I get married, remind me never to rely on my only sister as my Matron of Honour."

"Oh darling, I'm sorry about this. Did you try calling her again? I'm sure she's on her way." She squeezed Andrea's shoulder in reassurance but she shrugged beneath her touch as expected. When Andrea was in a mood . . .

"I have called her at least ten times now and her phone is going straight to voicemail," Andrea groaned and hugged her knees, checking her nails as she did so.

"She'll be here," said her mother.

Andrea leaned against the window and stared outside, quietly singing a chant that she and her sister had repeated down the years on days like this: "*Rain, rain, go to Spain, never show your face again! Rain, rain, go to Spain, never show your face again!*"

Ella threw her eyes up and left the room. Her daughter might not want or need a cup of tea but she was parched. As soon as Andrea and Jessie left, she would take an hour to herself, perhaps read for a while and then enjoy a quiet early lunch before preparing for the rest of the day's activities.

She walked down the staircase and into the kitchen, sensing she was in for a very trying few days ahead and, although she cursed herself for thinking so, she really believed that the sooner this wedding was over and done with, the better. Jessie looked and was acting like a nervous wreck and Andrea was wound up as tight as a spring.

Ella couldn't shift a niggling worry that something about this wedding was just not right at all.

No, she couldn't wait until the wedding was over. Then this family tension might subside again, her heart rate might slow down and life just might get back to normal.

Andrea sighed and stretched her legs out on the window seat, letting her finger follow a tiny river of rain that flowed down the pane of glass.

She felt like crying enough tears to match the rain that lashed down outside. Why did God have to do this to her? Didn't he know how important her wedding day was?

Her dress was stunning, her flowers were magnificent, the hotel, the menu, the entertainment and most of all her gorgeous groom were all just wonderful but the bloody rain just wouldn't stop.

"Please!" she said to the heavens and she thumped the window.

Of course, on Jessie's big day the year before, the sun had been splitting the trees and the sky was a turquoise shade of blue. Her dress had been bought a mere six weeks before her wedding and she only decided three days before to arrange a video-recording of the ceremony, but on the day itself it all went like clockwork. It was breathtaking.

Where Jessie was concerned everything was always 'breathtaking' or 'amazing' or 'wonderful' and her easy-going manner and 'come what may' attitude to life was just so goddamned perfect! That was how everyone viewed her. Isn't Jessie so beautiful? Isn't Jessie so lucky? Doesn't Jessie always come out on top?

When Jessie arrived at a party the room would light up. She could always be relied on to lift your spirits. She could never do any wrong, despite the fact that she was always late. Oh yes, Jessie was just so good at everything!

Her poor husband David had been as white as a sheet on their wedding day when she hadn't turned up twenty minutes after she was due to and Andrea had felt

6

so sorry for him as he stood clenching his hands together and glancing behind him towards the door. His family and friends from England, all twenty of them – quite a pitiful turnout compared to the extended O'Neill clan – had been most bemused by this Irish easy-going manner in comparison to their stiff-upper-lip way of doing everything on time.

Andrea was not going to do that to Cain. No way.

She wouldn't keep him waiting for a second on their big day – nor the three hundred friends, family and media personalities who had been lucky enough to receive an invitation to Castle Bromley on the Fermanagh border on Saturday.

Andrea would be exactly on time. Just as the village clock struck noon she would be there and she had made sure all of Ireland's media had been informed of that.

Andrea O'Neill wasn't going to waste one second of her wedding day. This was something she had dreamed of since she was a young child and it was going to be just as perfect as her sister's had been, if not more so.

If only it would stop bloody raining.

Chapter 2

Jessie O'Neill-Chambers stared at the note in front of her and reminded herself to breathe. She leaned on the worktop and tried to focus her eyes on what lay before her, convinced that if she read David's note again the words would magically change before her and he would suddenly be there, wrapping his arms around her and saying it had all been a big fat joke.

His handwriting was scrawled across a sheet of lined paper which was torn across the top, as if it had been a whimsical decision even to write it in the first place.

He didn't mean it. He couldn't.

She read it again and every word stung, almost burning her skin, and yet it felt as if her blood had frozen in her veins.

She hadn't meant for him to go. Yes, she had said so but she hadn't actually meant it, had she? She meant that she simply needed more time to sort out her mind, to sort out her life. She had made mistakes but the world was overtaking her and she needed time to think, to clear out her sins and to start again. She didn't want him to leave.

But he had left her just as she had asked him to. Had done as she wished. Just as he always did.

And he had told her so in a note.

She had no idea what to do. She had no idea where to go. What would she say? Andrea was getting married on Saturday for Christ's sake and there was so much to organise, so much to do and now this!

She lifted David's empty coffee mug from the island centrepiece in her kitchen. Then she ran the water and it pumped out in giant splurges, scalding hot with steam billowing so it fogged the window until she couldn't see outside. She wrung out a cloth under the water, ignoring how it burned her hands, and squirted kitchen cleaner heavily around the room despite the fact that the granite worktop gleamed from the weekly polish her cleaner had given it the day before.

She had to keep moving or she feared she might collapse but, even now amid her shock and panic, the back of her mind buzzed with the practicalities of everyday life that had led to her feeling so claustrophobic and so squashed into a world she felt she didn't belong to any more.

Why was she still thinking of the overflowing in-tray in her office that bulged with information on her forthcoming law case?

Why was that face still etched in her mind, a reminder

of her dirty secret that had led to her feeling on the brink of insanity?

Why was she cleaning the already sparkling worktops?

She had ruined everything and her husband had left her after only eleven months. She had ruined her own life and was teetering on the edge of destroying the lives of a few other loved ones very soon.

Jessie thumped the worktop so hard her wrist cracked. She let the pain of it pierce her heart, cradled it in her other hand and slid down the side of the kitchen cupboard until she met the floor, where she cried and cried until she made herself sick.

"What have I done?" she cried. "Oh God, what have I done?"

She got up and vomited into the sink, rinsed it off and cursed her very existence. Who was she? She didn't know any more. Had she really turned into a nasty, evil cheat who had been living a lie? Her guilt was eating her insides, gorging on her, reminding her at every turn of the wrong that she had done. She slammed closed the blinds when she caught a glimpse of herself in the kitchen window, not wanting to look at her gormless reflection.

Then she splashed her face with ice-cold water, tied back her hair and walked outside into the pouring rain.

"I'm really, really sorry," said Andrea to the beautician. "Something has come up at home and we won't be able to make our appointment."

She held out the phone, not wanting to hear the

backlash she would get for cancelling a double appointment at such short notice.

"Well, if you really must know," she said, interrupting the flurry of words that spun down the line, "my sister is being a selfish bitch. It's her fault not mine."

"Andrea!" said Ella from the adjoining room.

"Yes, of course, I will pay you in full! In fact, I'll be over to you right away. Yeah, I know, I know. Goodbye."

She hung up the phone with a bang, almost knocking it off the stand in the hallway and resisted the urge to scream in bad temper. She should have taken the appointment up herself and left Jessie to her own devices. She should have known that something would go wrong. Nothing ever went to plan in Andrea's life. Why would her wedding plans be any different?

Her mother was standing at the kitchen door, a tea towel over her shoulder, her arms folded and her lips pursed.

"You really are overreacting here, Andrea. I'm sure there is an explanation –"

"Oh, surprise, surprise!" said Andrea and she pushed past her mother into the kitchen and lifted her handbag from the dresser. "Stick up for Jessie, as bloody usual! Just as I expected."

Ella followed Andrea through the kitchen.

"But don't you think we should call at the house and check that she's all right? I mean, I know Jessie can be late but she wouldn't let you down like this. It's not like her to be this late. Could she be – could she be in some sort of trouble?"

"Dunno, don't care," said Andrea. She had no room for worry just yet. She was seething at her sister's irresponsibility and sick and tired of her selfish behaviour of late. "And yes, it *is* like her. She's been acting like a real weirdo all week and I'm afraid if I see her now I might say something I'll regret. If there's one thing I don't need right now, it's a blazing row with my so-called Matron of Honour."

She watched her mother desperately scramble for excuses, her eyes darting round the room.

"It's just that – I know Jessie has the worst reputation for timekeeping – but, well," said Ella, "she should have been here almost an hour ago. That's not late, that's . . ."

Andrea grunted and grabbed her car keys from the kitchen's dresser drawer. "That's just taking the fucking piss?" she said.

Ella marched after her daughter.

"Don't you dare speak to me like that, Andrea! If this is how you're going to behave at every little bump in life, then you have a very long and stressful rocky road ahead! You know that Jessie would never let you down on purpose."

"I know. I'm sorry, Mum," said Andrea, rubbing her forehead. "Look, I suppose I could call to her house if it makes you feel better."

"That's more like it."

"But she'd better have a whopper of an excuse for this because I now have to go and pay The Beauty Box sixty feckin' quid for absolutely shit all!"

Ella winced as the door slammed. Her daughter's Mini Cooper roared down the driveway.

She pulled out a chair and sat down, then stood up again and wiped her hands down her Cath Kidson apron. She loved that apron. It was a birthday present from Jessie back in February and she adored its floral patterns and bright colours.

"It reminds me of a summer's day," Jessie had said when she presented her with it on a cold, bleak winter morning and it had cheered Ella up no end.

Jessie had always chosen birthday presents so carefully for her, whereas her son would present her with a hasty garage bouquet and a box of Milk Tray. The same bunch from the same garage every single year and it always made Ella chuckle when she saw him balance it all in his arms as he dismounted from his motorbike. Andrea, bless her, was always full of great intentions but never came up with the goods until the next occasion, like Mother's Day or Easter when she would go totally over the top to make up for missing out first time round.

But Jessie had always been so reliable. A little bit late, sometimes, but she would never let you down. It was just that she was always so busy and had so much to juggle in her mind.

Ella felt the flurry of anxiety simmer inside and she practised her deep-breathing exercises, just as Dr Pat had shown her how to do when she felt an attack coming on.

Perhaps Jessie had just lost track of time or had the wrong day marked in her overflowing diary? She was more than likely buried in that darned O'Donnell case that seemed to be causing her all sorts of problems these days.

Breathe in, and out . . .

She tried to remember her last conversation with her eldest child. What had they discussed? How was her form? She had been anxious this week. A bit off, she had said. Tired too.

Breathe in, out, in, out . . .

Her mind was too confused now to recall the precise moment she had last seen her daughter but she remembered Jessie had dismissed any signs that she hadn't been herself, changing the subject when Ella said she looked pale and withdrawn and that she was much quieter than usual.

Tense, then relax – tense, then relax . . .

She could hear Dr Pat's soothing voice reminding her how to control her worries. She counted her breaths and emptied her mind as he had taught her, closing her eyes and shutting out her thoughts, but then she opened her eyes to check the clock and, realising how little time she had to prepare for her guests who were due to arrive in from London that evening, her heart began to race again. She was a way behind now in her preparations.

Tom had insisted his only sister Lily and her boys stay at the family home over the course of the wedding. After all, they had enough spare bedrooms to cater for an entire army, he'd reminded her. Not that Ella minded at all. Lily was a godsend and a breath of fresh air and they knew each other inside out. If anyone could take

Ella's mind off her unexplainable worry about this wedding, it was Lily.

Ella's quiet morning had turned into a mini-drama and now it was time to eat on the go and get on with preparing light snacks for her guests' arrival.

She folded a row of filo parcels and placed them on a baking tray, then finished off her home-made mini pizzas and whipped some cream for the profiteroles in the fridge. Lily had insisted that she and the boys would have dinner in the city on the way through but Ella wanted to be sure that her fridge was well stocked with nibbles. And she knew the first thing Lily would appreciate on arrival would be a full glass of gin and tonic topped with ice and a slice of lemon.

She forced herself to hum along to the music on the radio and concentrated on her future son-in-law's voice as he broadcast a string of music requests and birthday greetings. Cain Daniels had a charm to his voice and Ella listened as he chatted to listeners who were equally miffed at the summer storm, and well-wishers who called in to wish him luck for the wedding, and fans who blatantly begged him not to break their hearts by tying the knot. She barely noticed the time tick by, though she was conscious of a long stretch of unbroken music before Cian's dulcet tones flooded the airwaves again with more requests and his daily competition.

Ella took the smoked salmon from the fridge and laid it on the worktop. She selected a sharp knife and began to cut the fish into small slices, trying all the while not to worry about Jessie's whereabouts.

But then she paused, sat down and scrolled through her mobile phone until she came to her daughter's home number.

She would call her once more and Jessie would answer her phone this time and her excuse for letting her sister down so badly would be perfectly viable. Yes, she would explain that she had been desperately distracted in her office and apologise and come over straightaway to make things up with her sister.

But the phone rang and it rang and it rang until David's familiar, throaty voice kicked in with a deep London accent that made many local women go weak at the knees.

"Hiya, you've reached David and Jess. Well, it's actually David, obviously, but you know what to do. Er, leave a message . . ."

Ella smiled to herself despite her fears. David was always so chirpy, so happy, no matter what time of day or night it was and his voicemail message reflected his bouncy personality to perfection. Jessie had fallen for him in a far-fetched belief that he was like Hugh Grant, but then that was typical of her eldest daughter. For all her brains and worldly experience, she would have fallen for any story if it was told to her in the right way, especially where a handsome man was concerned.

"Hey there, Jess and David, it's just Mum," said Ella to the answering machine. "Listen, Jess, I'm a little bit . . . look, just give me a call as soon as you get this, won't you, darling? You, er, must have forgotten about Andrea's make-up appointment this morning and I just want to

16

warn you of the inevitable world war that is about to break out. Andrea is spitting feathers. Call me soon. Bye."

She hung up and then rang Jessie's mobile number straightaway but, just as Andrea had told her earlier, it went straight to voicemail. Either Jessie was on a very long call or she had let her battery die.

"Jessie, call me. Where are you? Nothing's wrong, don't panic but I'm just wondering where you've got to today. You and Andrea had plans. Just give me a call when you get this."

Ella felt her heart race and she told herself to settle down. She was often mocked by family members about her great obsession with knowing almost every move her three children made, of smothering them with affection and at the same time making blatant excuses for every minor blip they made along the way.

When young Ryan crashed his car just a week after he passed his test, Ella found reasons for his carelessness and thanked the Lord her baby boy hadn't been hurt. She knew the entire village was whispering about her, saying she was in denial that her boy could do anything but good, and that he was too young to have such a sporty, brand-new vehicle in the first place.

When Andrea got engaged at nineteen to a Mr Bad Boy from the wrong end of town only eight weeks into their so-called relationship, Ella put on a positive front to the world, while every night she prayed and pleaded that her daughter would see sense. And she did eventually.

And then there was Jessie. Cardboard cut-out, angelic Jessie who could simply do no wrong in her mother's eyes. It was a classic case of blind, unconditional love which had engulfed a younger Ella O'Neill when she gave birth to Jessie in a local hospital at a time when she and Tom lived an altogether more modest life in a terraced flat on the outskirts of Belfast city. No matter how wrong and foolish a young girl she had been in the past, the birth of her first daughter had given her the greatest opportunity to live again and look to the future with her wonderful husband.

Although she denied it in her heart, Ella's whole person swelled just that little bit more when she was with Jessie – such a warm, loving, pleasant child who had grown into a modest and beautiful young lady.

But as her three children grew older, through their teens and now in their twenties, Ella's worries grew too and lately she found it desperately hard to control the deep agony she felt and the fear that something would happen to them.

A key turned in the front door and Ella shot up from the kitchen chair. She tidied herself, took a deep breath and pretended to be busy with the smoked salmon she had been working on before her worried mind had urged her to make a call to Jessie.

"Jessie? Is that you?"

"No, sorry, it's just me," said Andrea, bounding into the kitchen. She slammed her keys on the table and folded her arms in exasperation. "I can't find her. I checked the house and her garden and I even rang

David but he didn't say much – just that Jessie would be in touch eventually. What the hell is she playing at? It's after one now. Where the hell is she?"

"*What* did David say? That she would be in touch eventually? What does that mean? What is going on? I'll phone him. He'll tell me."

"No, Mum. Just leave it. They've obviously had some petty row. Oh, why does this have to happen now? Why is she doing this to me? We have so much to organise and I would really appreciate her help right now."

Ella paced across the floor and physically shook herself in a bid to make her mind see sense.

"Andrea, love, I know you're upset about the make-up appointment. But let's think for a minute. Let's just think about –"

"How could she do this to me?" Andrea ranted on. "This is the most important week of my life and she just decides to disappear when I need her most!"

"Did David say anything else? Did he *say* they had a row?"

Andrea didn't even hear her. "When she was getting married I was like her shadow in the days running up to the wedding. I had to run here, there, fetch this, collect that, leave this to the hotel, give opinions on that! All I want is the same bloody attention from her and she couldn't give a shit!"

Ella bit her tongue. Andrea always compared her life to Jessie's and it was sometimes hard to swallow. She had often tried to give Andrea some extra attention, especially as a young child, to make her feel her sister's equal but it never worked and sometimes it made Ella want to scream. Middle-child syndrome at its very worst.

But she could say too much now and cause even more problems. There was no point falling out with Andrea in the midst of all this but once Jessie turned up, as she would, of course, she would gently remind her younger daughter that the world unfortunately couldn't be called to a halt just because she was marrying Cain Daniels in a few days' time.

There was obviously a perfectly acceptable explanation for this. There had to be.

"Think, Andrea," she said, rubbing her forehead which was by now beginning to throb. "Think of when you last spoke to her. Did she mention any worries she and David had? Or hey, how about Maria – have you tried phoning Maria? She's probably out for coffee with Maria and talking about –"

"Mum, stop making excuses for her! You always do this!"

"I'm not. I'm simply –"

"Look, we agreed that she would call here and we would go for the appointment together and she knows I was really looking forward to it. But obviously she wasn't looking forward to it that much. Obviously she couldn't give a toss about my plans."

Andrea's phone rang from her handbag and both women jumped for it at the same time, but it stopped just as Andrea's hand found it amongst a host of wedding brochures and trinkets that would have filled a small filing cabinet.

"It's just Cain," she said and dropped it back into her handbag. "I'll call him back."

Ella's face fell. "Well, go ahead. Give him a call."

"It's okay. I just wanted to find out why he was off air earlier. He seemed to be off for ages."

Ella put the smoked salmon back into the fridge – she could attend to it later. "Yeah, I noticed that too. Look, I'm going for a short lie-down."

"Right. If Jessie calls I'll come and get you. That's if you don't hear me screaming at her first."

Chapter 3

Jessie blessed herself and left the church through the back door, hoping that no one had recognised her as she prayed in the far corner, huddled up in self-loathing and pity. She'd been there for almost two hours now and she couldn't think of any more prayers to be said. They often mocked her at home for her religious beliefs and the way she turned to God at every hurdle she faced but she got great comfort from her faith and it helped her find answers to issues in both her personal life and her turbulent career.

She wandered through the windy streets of the village, past the school and the post office, then off the main road and up the driveway to her parents' house.

Stopping at the top of the driveway, Jessie pushed her soaking hair out of her face. She knew she looked a sight but she didn't care right now. She had been wandering around the park before finding solace in the church where she had battled deeply with her conscience. Now she was cold and damp and tired and was longing for some of her mother's home comforts.

"Home sweet home," she mumbled. Her mum's car was parked in its usual place and Andrea's was haphazardly abandoned at the top of the drive.

Andrea. The wedding. It all flashed through her mind. Oh shit! The beauty appointment! Shit, shit, shit! She had totally forgotten. Oh crap, this was a nightmare! Andrea would go mental and she didn't have the energy for arguments.

Jessie slunk into the kitchen where her sister was sitting, curled up in a ball on an armchair and flicking absent-mindedly through television channels.

"I am so, so sorry, Andrea. Really, I am. I can explain."

"You'd better," said Andrea. She didn't look up.

"Look, I was halfway down the motorway when I remembered about our appointment and my mobile went dead and, oh, please let me make it up to you?"

"The motorway?" said Andrea. She shot up from the chair. "Where the hell were you going to, Jess? We had an appointment. For my fucking wedding day, in case you forgot! This is really important to me."

Jessie avoided her gaze.

"And look at the state of you! What is going on? You look like you've been dragged through a ditch. What the hell is the story here, Jess? I think I deserve to know."

"You do," said Jessie, her eyes glazing over as she stared at the tiles on the floor. "You do deserve to know.

23

You deserve to know everything." Jessie felt as if her insides were on fire. You deserve better, she wanted to tell her sister. You deserve the truth and when I get the strength I will tell you. But she couldn't find the words right now.

"Well, how about you spit it out then?" said Andrea. "You've been acting really weird with me all week. Tell me. Tell me now!"

Ella burst into the kitchen at the sound of raised voices, just as Andrea had predicted.

"Jessie, what is going on with you? Where have you been? You look dreadful," cried Ella.

Jessie's heart jumped with guilt and fear. No matter how she tried, she knew she wasn't ready to air her dirty linen to her family and knew that if she did it would open a whole can of worms that would tear them all apart. She sighed and pushed her hair back, holding her head to the side in her hand.

"I, well, I had to meet David to give him his phone, you see. He had forgotten it this morning so I arranged to meet him on the motorway. About halfway to Belfast. The appointment totally slipped my mind. I'm so sorry."

"Halfway to Belfast?" said Andrea. "You just decided to drive halfway to Belfast and not tell me? Thanks a lot, Jess!"

"Andrea, please!" said Ella. "Calm down!"

Andrea's fury was having no effect on Jessie – if Andrea knew the whole truth, a make-up appointment would be the least of her concerns.

"You know how dangerous it would be for his mobile to get into the wrong hands in his line of work," she said, twisting a napkin in her hands, "and he was in such a panic to catch his plane that I just dropped everything and then –"

"You didn't say he was going away."

"I didn't know."

"So you gave him his phone? He didn't mention any of this when I spoke to him earlier. He said you would turn up 'eventually', whatever that means," said Andrea.

"What? Well, yes, I . . ." Jessie was too tired for this. She might have known her sister would be like a dog with a bone. She should have known she wouldn't believe that she would let her down over a stupid mobile phone. Why hadn't she just said it was an unexpected work call that had kept her late? Yes, a call from the O'Donnell case that she had been waiting on. That would have been so much easier.

But Andrea was on a roll now. "You're lying! Mum, she's lying!"

Jessie glanced from Andrea to her mother. She'd only had seconds to come up with her excuse so she hadn't decided on what the finer details of the story would be.

"Well, I don't know what David meant by 'eventually' . . . he must have just meant I was on my way back . . . and I don't know why he didn't tell you about the phone . . . he was in a hurry."

She was a poor liar and she knew it. Quite ironic, really, considering her occupation. But twisting the truth in the courtroom was one thing, lying to her family was a whole different ball game.

"You should have called us, honey," said Ella. "We were very worried."

"I couldn't call. I'm sorry. Like I said, my own phone was dead. Can't we reschedule? There's still time. Surely there's still time?" Jessie felt the hole she was digging become deeper and deeper but her brain was so clogged she couldn't think straight at all.

"No, we can't bloody reschedule," said Andrea, "and no, I'm not buying your stupid excuses at all, Jessie!"

Jessie felt like throwing something at her and telling her to wake up and see the big picture but, of course, none of this was Andrea's fault. Andrea was the victim. Andrea was the real victim and it was so hard to keep the truth from her. She longed to tell her but it would kill her. It would really kill her.

"Look, I said I'm sorry, Andrea. I'm really sorry but there's been a lot going on and my head is bursting with –"

"Oh, boo fucking hoo! We all have a lot going on right now. You can't use your work life as an excuse forever, Jessie." Andrea was close to tears again. "I won't argue with you about this now, but maybe some day you just might take your head down from the clouds and think of someone else rather than yourself for a change!"

Andrea ran from the kitchen and slammed the door, reminding Jessie of earlier years when the girls were stroppy teenagers and they would argue over everything from homework to soap-opera storylines. She would always have given in to Andrea's demands because, like her mother, she much preferred a quiet life to raising a row over something trivial whereas Andrea had taken her much more fiery temperament from the O'Neills.

But on this occasion, Jessie could sense that Ella agreed with Andrea's right to be angry. Her mobile-phone story was totally unconvincing.

She felt her mother's stare as she poured herself a glass of milk from the fridge and her heart sank when she realised Ella could see how much her hands were shaking.

"Jessie, what's going on?" she asked. "I know you've been crying."

Jessie shook her head and gulped down the cool white milk.

"Yes, you have, Jessie. Come on. Tell me the truth. Is it David? Have you had a row?"

Jessie didn't answer and avoided eye contact with her mother.

"Jessie?"

"No, Mum, I'm fine. We're fine. David was called away on police business and I was just a bit upset, that's all."

"But when did this come about? You didn't say."

"Because I didn't know, Mum." She felt her face burn. She hated all these lies. "It was a last-minute trip they sprang on him and I was annoyed that he didn't have any notice so we could get used to the idea. That's all. He'll be back on Friday."

She could almost hear the days tick by in her mother's head.

"Friday?" said Ella. "But Friday is the day before the wedding. He won't have much time to join in with all the events we've planned. We're having a family barbecue on Friday."

Jessie put her empty glass in the dishwasher and turned her back to her mother to help her continue with her fabricated story.

"Exactly," she said. "That's why I'm so upset. I really wanted him to be here and I was angry with him. I got sidetracked, that's all. The delights of being married to a detective, I suppose."

Jessie felt her mother's arm around her and she relished her light squeeze, but winced knowing she had made such a mess of her marriage. She wanted to hug her mother tight and let the truth spill out but she couldn't tell anyone yet. She really couldn't.

"Well, why don't you go upstairs and explain that to your sister?" said Ella. "I'm sure David's speedy departure will justify your scatterbrain actions this morning and perhaps you can spend the evening here with us?"

Jessie breathed out and held the back of the kitchen chair for support. Her emotional state was draining her entire body and the battle to hide her true feelings was wearing her down.

"That would be nice," she said. "I'm sorry, Mum."

"I know you are," said Ella. "But, as a punishment of sorts, you can hang around and help with the chaos that's about to descend on our household when Lily and

28

the boys arrive. That will take your mind off marriage and all its worldly troubles."

Jessie's guilt heightened as she absorbed her mother's unconditional support.

"It's a deal," she said and she left the kitchen to go upstairs to find Andrea.

As she took each step towards the first floor of her family home, her body ached in warning of just how uphill her struggle would be to try and appease her baby sister. She had to be strong right now. Her own life was ruined but she couldn't tell Andrea the truth.

Even if it was the right thing to do.

Chapter 4

Ella hummed to herself as she worked around the kitchen, glad that the row between her daughters was on the mend.

"A black and white bird regarded with suspicious awe," said the radio presenter on the early-evening quiz show. It had just gone five thirty and Tom was due home. It was Ella's favourite time of day.

"Magpie!" she said aloud and listened intently for the next question.

The panic from earlier had simmered down and she realised she was beginning to relax into cooking dinner and the fact that her entire brood would be home to enjoy it. Then the party would really begin. Lily and the boys were due to arrive in a few hours' time and Ella couldn't wait to see her sister-in-law.

She poured herself a glass of chilled Sauvignon Blanc and turned the radio over to Classic FM to reflect her newly found peace of mind as she prepared the evening meal in her very own haven. The music soothed her weary mind and she concentrated on the positives in her life, just as her doctor had taught her to.

Here she was, just days before another great big family occasion when all her sisters and brothers, nephews and nieces, in-laws and friends would gather from all corners of Ireland and further afield to celebrate a most wonderful occasion.

Lily would fuss over everyone, her cousin Jeff and his family would constantly admire everything they loved about Ireland, especially Glencuan town, and Tom's heaps of cousins would turn into the von Trapp family for the weekend with each of them taking turns on the piano for a good old sing-along.

These were good times, thought Ella, and because the good times in life – the really good times – were few and far between, she would make herself absorb every second of this wedding and the build-up to it.

"Something smells good."

The back door closed and her husband's arrival interrupted her faraway thoughts.

"Oh hi, love. Yes, it's curry," said Ella. "Jessie is here so I thought I'd change the menu. You know how she loves a curry."

Tom's familiar evening routine began. He laid his briefcase on the dresser, much to his wife's mock frustration, and she lifted it off immediately and put it out of her way.

Then, just as expected, his evening newspaper was

thrown on the table and his jacket strewn over the back of a chair. Then he lifted the lid from a steaming saucepan and took a peep into the oven, ready for his evening meal as if he hadn't seen a bite since breakfast.

Tom O'Neill was a creature of habit and Ella liked it that way. It gave a great sense of security to know that at the same time each evening her husband would come home and they would chat about their day over dinner while listening to their children's stories of work life and all the challenges it brought.

"Good day at work?"

"Not bad," said Tom. "Same old, same old really. I'll be glad to have a few days off for the wedding."

He wrapped his strong arms around her and kissed her cheek as she stood at the cooker.

"What on earth was that for?" she asked.

Contentment was one thing but outbursts of affection weren't Tom's usual way, especially after a long day's work.

"Can't a man greet his wife with a kiss any more?"

He swayed her gently in his grasp to the sounds of Bach in the background and she turned and looked up into his handsome face which she still found so attractive even after almost thirty years of marriage.

"Of course, he can," she said, pulling back from him in mock annoyance. "I have no problem whatsoever with a man greeting his wife with a kiss. This man, on the other hand, should do it more often."

She gave him a playful swipe with the tea towel and he pulled her into his arms once more. Then he stopped.

"Hey, what's that I hear?" he asked, cocking his head to one side.

"What? Bach?"

"No, it's . . . could it possibly be laughter?"

"Oh, yes. I suppose it is. Thank the Lord."

"But I thought you said I'd be coming home to World War Three between our daughters? I had my combat gear all prepared, too."

He lifted a wooden spoon and held it up, eyebrows raised threateningly in mock battle.

"It did look that way earlier I can assure you," said Ella. "It really did."

"Well, thank the Lord for small mercies, that's all I say!" he laughed. "At least we can have dinner in peace."

His laughter irritated her slightly but she shared his relief. A bad atmosphere between family members was always discouraged as far as possible in their household.

"They've been upstairs reminiscing for ages now," said Ella. "It's like they're teenagers again, all whispers and giggles and playing songs from the early nineties. Have to say it all sounds like great fun. I only wish I had time to join in."

Tom rummaged for his reading glasses in his briefcase, eventually finding them in his jacket pocket.

"You worry too much. I knew they'd be as thick as thieves again in a matter of minutes," he said. "They always are after a row. You panic if either of them as much as sniffles."

Ella wiped her hands on her apron. Her panic

attacks had worried Tom so much that lately she had been hiding her anxiety from him as far as possible.

"I know I do, I know. But that's a mother's prerogative, isn't it?" she said. "But you know how worked-up Andrea can be, all fire and brimstone and 'poor me' and 'Jessie this' and 'Jessie that'." She knew Tom was biting his tongue but she continued. "Then, when Jessie explained that she had missed the appointment by accident because she'd been so upset with David having to leave on business again so swiftly, Andrea understood. And the rest as they say is history. And as you say, thank the Lord."

Tom flicked his newspaper back and looked over the top of the broadsheet.

"Hold on," he said. "Andrea understood? Are you sure she understood, or are you trying to convince yourself that she did, just for a quiet life? I hope you weren't taking sides, love."

"No, I wasn't. She understood. We all do."

"Mmm . . ."

"You know it's hard for Jessie that David is away from home so often and it's usually at the drop of a hat, not to mention all that damn secrecy that comes with –" her voice dropped into a whisper "– with him being a flaming-well cop in this town. It's very hard for her. She was so annoyed today, poor thing."

"But the war is over now," said Tom, and he settled into his evening paper again.

"Yes, it's all sorted now," said Ella and she went back to the cooker to stir her curry that was bubbling now on the stove.

She hummed aloud to the sounds from the radio and put the finishing touches to the dinner setting for five. Ryan would be home soon and she would call her girls down from upstairs just like she would have done when they were younger and all in her care.

"Hungry?" she asked her husband and she danced back towards the cooker.

"Starving," he replied.

"Good. It's almost done."

She stirred quickly, admiring her culinary efforts as the rich smell of chicken curry with peas, onions and mushrooms filled the kitchen. She tasted a spoonful from the pot and her contentment warmed her body as much as the food did.

It tasted delicious but, best of all, it warmed her heart to know that it was Jessie's favourite.

Jessie was exhausted when she and her sister arrived downstairs for dinner moments later. Her insides churned with the thought of the secret she was hiding and the smell of food from the kitchen made her feel ten times worse.

Being an actor and a liar was hard work and she hated it.

"You two sound like you're having fun," said Tom, hovering around his wife like a hungry wolf and waiting for dinner to be served.

"We have had fun," said Andrea. "In fact, we've now agreed that we'll do our own make-up on Saturday after all."

"Really? I'm sure they would fit you in if you asked them to," said Ella. "God knows you two give them enough business all year round."

"No, sod the missed appointment!" said Andrea. "We've had some experimental runs this afternoon, so that's us all sorted."

Jessie painted on a smile for her father's peace of mind and took her place at the table beside her sister.

"We could open our own beauty parlour now with all our new-found experience," she said. "Of course, it turned out so well that Andrea just had to try on her dress again to make sure that it looked all right."

"Oh, Andrea!" said Ella and she scooped a dome of rice onto her husband's plate. "You'll wear it out at this rate."

"No, you're right, love," said Tom, knife and fork poised. "Get your money's worth out of it, that's what I say. Try it on to your heart's content because after Saturday it will never be on your back again. And Lord knows I paid enough for it!"

"Good point, Dad," laughed Andrea. "Hey, on that subject, did you ever get around to selling yours like you planned to do, Sis? I think you're mental to do such a thing."

Jessie deliberately dropped her fork on the floor. She couldn't cope with any mentions of her own marriage or anything associated with it. In fact, she detested any talk of weddings at all, but she had to put up a front for her sister's sake.

"Of course not," she muttered as she bent to pick it

up. "That was just a silly notion that has worn off a long time ago."

"Oh, that's good."

"So, Dad?" said Jessie, trying desperately to shake off her despair and put on a brave front. "Do you have your Father of the Bride speech off to perfection yet, or do you need an extra last-minute rehearsal with the rest of us as your audience?"

Tom pushed back his shoulders and tucked into his curry. "Don't you worry about my speech, my pretty ladies. I have it all under control. And speaking of Ryan, where on earth has he got to this evening? Is he going to grace us with his presence or do I get to eat his share of dinner too?"

Ella placed Ryan's dinner carefully in the oven, took off her oven gloves and made her way to the table, but Ryan's bike engine roared to a halt outside the moment she sat down.

"Speak of the devil," she said and stood up again with a sigh. "I knew that would happen."

"No, Mum," said Jessie. "Sit down and have yours. I'll get the son and heir his feast."

Her mother smiled gratefully. "Thanks, love."

The atmosphere shifted when Ryan O'Neill entered the room with his usual swagger of confidence and boyish good looks. With long muscular limbs and cropped sandy hair, he looked more like an all-around American jock than a twenty-two-year-old Irishman who preferred biking, rock music and dissecting movie scripts to doing a day's work in his father's construction firm.

"Ah ha, I knew it!" he said sarcastically as he entered the room. "Jessie Time is Curry Time!"

"You really are so clever," said Jessie and she laid her kid brother's dinner down at his place at the table. Ryan was always teasing her about being the family favourite. She only hoped she had the strength to play along with him now as the irony of her guilt ate her insides.

"Well, it's true," he said and his tone was caustic. "No offence, Mum, but do you see Andrea and me getting such special treatment around here? Oh, no, no, no! Only Mrs O'Neill-Chambers fits in that category! Little Miss Perfect!"

The way he spat his words nudged everyone's mood and Andrea exchanged bewildered glances with her parents.

Jessie stuttered and attempted a joke to lighten the mood. "Got out of the wrong side of the bed, little brother, or is it girl trouble?" She knew the moment she said it that she had simply fed his mood.

"Trouble? I thought that was more your camp?"

Tom O'Neill swallowed his food and eyeballed his son. Ryan would start a row in heaven at the best of times and, with the rumblings of a row having brewed earlier in the day, Tom was not going to let the boat be rocked again.

"Well, son," he said with a grin, in a bid to lighten things, "all we need now is for you to find a lovely girl and walk off into the sunset with her – and I promise you, when you call around here for dinner, your mum will rustle up your favourite Cowboy Supper especially for the occasion each and every time."

"Aaah," said Andrea, brushing her brother's spite off as the playful joke she hoped he had intended it to be, "Wee Ryan and his Cowboy Supper!"

"Do you remember how he used to love it?" said Jessie. "He would have eaten it every –"

"Shut the fuck up, Jess!" said Ryan with a glare in his eyes that shook everyone present. "Just shut up."

"Ryan!" said Tom. "Watch your mouth!"

"I'm kidding," said Jessie, putting her hands up and looking at her father in appreciation of his support. "It was only a joke. Take a joke, Ryan!"

She pushed her curry around her plate, then nibbled some though it felt as if she was swallowing nails. Her hands shook as she scraped her fork along the plate.

"So, what time are our guests arriving?" asked Andrea, feeling the need to break the silence that followed. "I'm really looking forward to seeing Aunty Lily and our cousins."

"At eight," said Ella who was relieved and pleasantly surprised at her younger daughter's quick distraction to defuse Ryan's taunts. "They're having dinner first in Belfast. I'm sure she can't wait to see you too, love." It stuck in Ella's gut that what would normally have passed as some friendly banter between siblings had turned into a very unusual and tense situation. There was suddenly an atmosphere that hung like a dense cloud and Ella had no idea why. She continued, determined to brighten the mood, "Mind you, with Aunty Lily you would normally hear her before you see her. Isn't that right, Tom?"

Andrea giggled at the thought of Lily's hollering tones which could be heard from the far end of the Irish Sea if you listened for it. Lily was the life and soul of every party and she herself even joked about her distinctive, almost squawking voice.

"Now, now," said Tom. "Poor Lily isn't here to defend herself so as her brother I'll have to do so in her absence. She has the voice of – well, she has the voice of an angel!"

Ella smiled as Andrea and Tom laughed – she could feel her whole body relax again.

"Here, have some wine, love," said Tom and she gratefully held out her glass. He clinked his glass with hers and took a sip of his drink. "Do you know, since this is possibly the last family meal we'll have round this table before our baby girl flees the coop, I feel a toast coming on."

Andrea's smile lit up the room. "Ah, that's so sweet! Thanks, Dad."

"To Andrea and Cain!" said Tom. "Here's to a long and healthy, happy future together! If you're as happy as your mother and I have been, that's as much as I can ask for."

Ryan casually touched his glass to Andrea's but ignored Jessie's efforts to join in. He was deliberately ignoring her very presence and she could feel it like a rash creeping over her entire body. She glanced at her brother and, as she had imagined, he was staring at her, his mouth twisted in disgust. It was as if the two of them were in a different zone to the rest of their family. Was it a zone of truth, wondered Jessie, and her heart raced at the very possibility.

"Do you know something?" Tom said with a grin, now oblivious to the dagger looks that passed between his son and his eldest daughter. "We really should have eaten outside this evening under the canopy."

"But it's lashing outside," said Ella. "It may be summer but it's like a swimming pool out there!"

"Exactly," said Tom. "And if this is what our summer is going to be like, then so be it. I say, let's ignore the rain and eat alfresco under the cover of my new toy – I mean, my new remote-control canopy."

"You are absolutely right, Dad," chirped Andrea, her mood lightening further much to Ella's delight. "Come on! Grab your plates and glasses and let's move outside. Maybe it will make the rain go away."

"Okay, okay, but you're all raving mad," said Ella and she, Andrea and Tom began to gather up their plates and cutlery.

Ryan was shovelling his food in haste while staring across the table at his eldest sister.

"Where's your husband?" he asked, pausing to take a sip of his own wine. He gulped it and smirked, awaiting her answer, but Jessie avoided his eye.

"Oh, David's away on business," said Ella, jumping to her daughter's defence. She didn't want David's absence brought up again when things were just starting to go well. "He'll be back on Friday."

"Friday? Really –"

"Yes, he'll be back on Friday," said Jessie and she matched Ryan's stare. "He's on police business."

Ryan took another drink and then scraped the remainder of his food from his plate onto his fork.

"I was just asking," he said. "Just wondering, that's all."

Ella gathered her belongings and made her way outside, leaving her children to follow. Tom was already there, fiddling with the canopy and in sheer determination he finally pulled it into shape, having given up on the remote-control feature.

Jessie and Ryan squinted and stared at each other across the table as they lifted their own plates and cutlery.

"Would you two mind?" said Andrea who had come back in to collect the rest of the condiments from the table. "What the hell is the attitude for, Ryan?"

"Attitude? Do I have an attitude? I was just asking after Jessie's husband, that's all."

"Oh, come on, you two! This is supposed to be the happiest time of my life. I'm getting married in three days. Drop it, whatever your problem is!"

Ryan shrugged and lifted his plate from the table, then flung it onto the draining-board on his way past. It crashed into the sink and smashed into smithereens.

"Ryan!" called Tom from the other side of the open patio doors, in the way he would have chastised his son when he was a teenager. "What the hell are you playing at? Clear that up and get out here immediately!"

"Okay, okay," said Ryan. "I'm coming now."

He made his way outside to join his family on the ornate metal patio set which had been painted and glossed in time for the wedding but which to date had sat under the protective ceiling of canvas.

For a while, the only sounds were the clinks of cutlery and the odd compliment on the delicious food but despite Ella's efforts to maintain a family atmosphere, conversation was strained.

"Did you have a good day at work, son?" said Tom.

"Not bad."

"Jessie, you look strained," said Ella. "Are you feeling okay?"

"I'm fine, Mum."

Ryan continued to answer questions with short answers no matter who spoke to him and Jessie was uneasily quiet.

It was just after six, following dessert and before coffee, when Jessie decided she couldn't take any more tension and announced she was leaving.

"Oh, come on, love!" said Ella. "It's not often we are all together like this. And Lily will be here soon and you know how your cousins love to see all of you. Please stay for another while!"

"I can't," said Jessie. "I'm sorry, Mum, but I really do have a few things to clear up for work. I have to finish my research on the O'Donnell case if I want to enjoy my wedding anniversary next week."

Ryan scraped his chair back along the stone paving so that it made Ella's skin crawl. Like nails on a blackboard, it interrupted the conversation and drew attention once again to his funny mood.

43

"David taking you somewhere nice?" he asked, sitting back in his chair, his arms folded.

"We're going to Sligo," said Jessie, biting her lip. "Next Thursday. I'm really looking forward to it. So is he."

Ryan spat out a callous laugh. "He is? Funny he didn't mention it to me this afternoon."

Jessie's face paled as silence swept through the entire family group.

"This afternoon?" asked Andrea. "But didn't you say he left on business this morning, Jessie?"

Ella prayed that Jessie had a decent explanation but she felt the embers of a row had been stoked already.

"He did. I have no idea what Ryan's problem is this evening but it seems to be directed at me. Look, I'm sorry, Mum, but I really have to go. Dinner was lovely. Thanks."

She quickly kissed her mum on the cheek and then kissed her father who was sitting there, taking everything in.

"Jessie, are you hiding something from us?" said Tom. "And you, Ryan? I think it's time you two told us exactly what is going on. You've been at each other's throats all evening, sniping at every turnaround. What is it?"

But Jessie couldn't answer.

She just grabbed her keys and handbag and ran into the rain towards her car.

Chapter 5

Aunt Lily and the boys arrived just as the dishes were cleared and although she had been looking forward to their arrival, Ella had a lump in her throat that wouldn't subside.

"I hope you're hungry again," she said to Lily when she greeted her at her car with a hug. "I have enough food here to feed a small army."

Lily put up her umbrella and stood arm in arm with her sister-in-law as her family climbed out of the car. The boys opened the boot and lugged out a host of suitcases and then hauled hangers and coats from the back seat.

"Well, you now have a small army at your service," said Lily's eldest son, Declan, who was looking as handsome as ever. At twenty-seven to his younger brother's twenty-five, he had inherited the same dark brooding looks as the O'Neill girls. "We boys will soon eat you out of house and home – though all we've talked about is going for a few pints and a round of golf with Uncle Tom if the rain clears."

"It's so good to see you all," said Ella and she held Lily tight, her soft skin smelling so familiar and reassuring.

"My goodness, that's a welcome and a half," said Lily. "But it is great to be back. It really is good to have my best friend and my brother under one roof. Who'd have thought, eh? And now we've years of weddings and babies to look forward to."

Lily was wonderful easy company and, having been reared in modest upbringing with Tom as her only sibling, she had no airs or graces. She felt that coming to stay with her brother and his family was much more satisfying than being cooped up in a posh hotel during any of her visits home to Ireland.

If anyone would lift a moody atmosphere, it was Lily.

"Come on, everyone," said Tom. "Let's get inside before these two start talking about university days and about Lily's skills as a matchmaker. We'll never get them stopped."

They made their way through the door and into the shelter of the O'Neill home, out of the blustering rain.

"So, where is the beautiful bride to be?" asked Lily as her son Joseph tugged her larger-than-life suitcase into the impressive hallway. "And the bridesmaids? Where is all the hustle and bustle that we witnessed last time around for Jessie's wedding?"

Tom and Ella glanced at each other, both wondering what to say.

"I'm afraid our welcoming committee scattered just minutes ago, Lily," said Tom, taking his sister's case from Joseph's struggling grasp.

"Yes, just minutes ago," said Ella.

She gave Lily a 'don't ask' look and gratefully accepted a huge bouquet of tulips that Declan was almost smothered with as he squeezed through the front door, laden also with his own case and a few outfits on hangers that undoubtedly belonged to his mother.

"Where is my favourite cousin?" asked Declan. "I thought she would have been here with open arms as always?"

"She just popped back home for a while," said Ella, knowing instinctively that he was referring to Jessie who would normally have come bounding down the driveway to greet her cousins on their rare trips to Ireland.

"And Andrea?" he asked, more out of politeness than anticipation.

"Oh, she's on the phone to her beloved," said Ella. "She won't be long. We weren't expecting you for another while. I take it Joseph was driving?"

"You are absolutely right," said Lily, unravelling her light scarf from around her neck. She let out her trademark throaty laugh. "I thought I'd left my cheeks in the back seat we were going so fast. And it's not my face I'm talking about!"

"Mum!" said Joseph, greeting his aunt with a kiss and his uncle with a strong handshake. "At least wait until we get our first home-cooked meal before we lower the tone."

"Oh, I can take it," said Ella, delighted that Lily had lightened the heavy mood that had hung over them like a fog since Jessie's swift departure and Ryan's disappearance on his motorbike. She was genuinely embarrassed that her children were absent for their aunt's arrival from England.

The boys were shown to their rooms by Tom and their hearty chuckles could be heard from down the hallway as they joked and laughed about Declan's way with women and Joseph's bad luck of recent years.

Ella led Lily into the kitchen where the strong smell of rich curry still lingered and poured a long, cool gin and tonic with Lily's trademark two slices of lemon and extra ice. She smiled as Lily licked her lips and took the glass with both hands.

"You are a saint and I love you, Ella Foley," she said, referring to Ella by her maiden name as she always had since their first encounter and when she moved round the room a waft of her sweet perfume filled her friend's air. "An all-round saint! I hope you're joining me for one."

"You bet I am," said Ella. "Gosh, it's so good to see you!"

"And you. I just can't believe how quiet the house is. It's not normal Not that I'm complaining, mind you, after being hauled around Belfast for over an hour!"

"I know," said Ella. "I'm sure you know the city inside out, but your boys love it so much."

"They do. They often say they feel more at home over here and I can see why."

They sat back on the cane furniture and listened to the rain.

"Ah well, it looks like we might be having a quieter evening than what we'd originally planned," said Ella. "I feel so bad the kids weren't here to greet you."

"Stop fussing, Ella!" said Lily, taking another gulp of her drink. "You know what my two are like – they'll get over it!"

Lily gave her heart-lifting laugh again and Ella tried her best to chuckle along.

"Well, Tom has planned a boys' night out down at the golf club so you and I can have a good old girly chat with Andrea and catch up on all the news."

"And Jessie, of course," said Lily and Ella did her best to keep up appearances. "I can't wait to see my gorgeous goddaughter."

"Yes, and Jessie too." Ella sensed that Lily could see right through her and in a way she was longing to let off some steam to someone she loved and trusted so much.

"Jessie is joining us, I hope?" said Lily.

"Of course. She's just . . . well, you know how busy she and David are these days. It's a wonder how she manages to squeeze us all in." Ella looked at the floor as she spoke and then took a long breath.

"Oh, spit it out, El! Is there something wrong or is this just your normal pre-wedding jitters?"

Ella remained quiet, fighting back tears of worry which she knew were inflamed by the wine and the rush of the day, but Lily gave her a playful nudge.

"Come on!"

"Oh, please tell me that I'm imagining things, Lily, but I have a feeling there's something not right with Jessie. Tell me I'm overreacting as always."

Lily gave Ella a light hug and let out another of her loud laughs. "You? Overreacting? Never!"

But Ella didn't stir. "I know, but . . ."

"What on earth do you think could be wrong with her? Jessie has everything. A gorgeous, attentive husband, a loving family, a beautiful home, a top-notch job and the world at her feet. What on earth would she have to complain about?"

Ella shook her head. Part of her told her she was overreacting but she had to get a second opinion. "She just seems distant, nervous even. And she and Ryan are at loggerheads over something that I know nothing about. It's just not right. Something's not right."

"In what way?"

Ella shifted in her seat. "Well, today she missed a beauty appointment she and Andrea had made weeks ago and then made up some feeble excuse about having to meet David with his mobile phone. Then she and Ryan were griping at each other – well, Ryan was griping at her like I've never witnessed before and she left in a bit of a state. Plus David's away on business and she's upset about that and –"

"Ella, Ella, Ella! You really are a bit of a drama queen! But if you think something is wrong, just ask her."

"I did. But I think she's covering up."

"Well, then, tell her that's what you think. Tell her

50

you don't believe her. You know Jessie. She's like your carbon copy. She'll tell you everything. She always does."

Ella blinked back tears. Everyone was nervous. Everyone was tense. It was last-minute jitters, she reminded herself. A Mother of the Bride was entitled to a degree of nerves before her daughter's wedding.

"You know, you're right," she said. "I bet she'll come sweeping in here as large as life any minute now and I'll feel like a right old fool. They always say I fuss too much. Okay, I'll pull the brakes on it."

"That's the spirit," said Lily.

"Now, let's go and find Andrea. She can't talk to her lover boy all evening when she has guests to attend to."

Lily and Ella found Andrea in her room arranging piles of photographs which were strewn across her double bed.

"Oh my goodness, Aunt Lily, you're here!" she said. "Mum, you should have told me they had arrived! I am so glad to see you! Where are the boys?"

Andrea fell into Lily's arms, nearly knocking the older woman down with her heartfelt enthusiasm.

"Off drinking with your dad by now, I hope," said Lily, delighted to finally see one of her nieces. "You know what boys are like, all testosterone and attitude. It's so good to have some female company for a change. Now, tell me all the gossip in Glencuan. What's the buzz around my favourite little Irish town?"

"The gossip is I'm getting married!" said Andrea,

almost dancing with delight. "Me. Getting married! Can you believe it?"

"And to a radio star too," said Lily. "I've told all my friends at the bridge club and my Declan showed me how to listen to Cain's breakfast show online. He sounds like a real hunk! I can't wait to meet him in the flesh."

"Oh, he is!" said Andrea, handing her aunt a recent photo of Cain with her on their last holiday. She was tanned and toned and her hair was shorter then and Cain was looking great, as always. It was one of her favourite pictures.

"What a dish he is too! Is that Jessie in the background? Oh, and there's David. Oh, yes – this is in France?" said Lily. She always kept totally up to date with all of her nieces' antics.

"Yes, these are from when we all went camping in May," said Andrea, handing her aunt a small bundle of photos from the same collection. "Jessie packed in work for once, I closed up the bookshop and we all headed off for a wild long weekend. And wild it was, I can tell you. Maybe it was a little bit too wild but something to tell the grandchildren about, as they say. I'll tell you all about it some day when Mum isn't listening."

Ella tutted, took the photo from Lily and studied it hard.

Jessie and David were in the background of the photo all right, but they didn't look like a couple who were enjoying a wild weekend as Andrea had described it. While Andrea and Cain looked as if they were having the time of their lives, Jessie looked removed, vacant even, and David was staring at her, almost coldly. They certainly didn't look like a young pair of newly weds in the first flushes of married bliss.

"Mum, should I show Aunt Lily my dress?" asked Andrea. "I would love to hear what she thinks. I bet she'll love it."

"No way!" said Ella, handing the photo back to her daughter. "I'm sure Lily wants to wait and see you in your finery on Saturday. You'll end up ruining that dress if you keep this up."

"Exactly," said Lily. "Don't go spoiling the surprise, love. I'd rather wait to see you in it on Saturday."

"Ah well, it was worth a try," said Andrea. "I just can't stop staring at it."

"And I'm sure you'll look like a real princess," said Lily. "Now, tell me all about the bridesmaids. Are they happy with how their dresses turned out? Your mother told me about the little one throwing a strop about the colour."

"Oh, that was Cain's niece, Donna," said Andrea, gathering up the photos and bundling them back into a coloured shoebox. "She has the most beautiful red hair which contrasts – she says clashes! – with my choice of colour for her dress. In any case, it was too late to change it. I think it looks gorgeous on her but she's always shooting her mouth off about it. She's a bit spoilt anyway – even Cain says so."

She lifted the box of photos but it slipped from her grasp and the photos spilled out onto the floor.

"Gosh, trust me! I'm all fingers and thumbs these

days," she said, bending down to pick up the bundle of memories she had so carefully gathered. Lily and Ella helped her, resisting the urge to look at each photo one by one as they did so.

"You'll have to get a nice album for those," said Lily. "Then you can look back on your courtship when you're a cynical old goose like me and remember how good you once had it."

Andrea laughed and stacked the photos into a neat bundle.

"I don't ever want to be cynical about marriage. What did you teach us, Mum? Marriage is for life, forever."

"Yeah, right!" said Lily, rolling her eyes. "Never say never, I say. Marriage is forever until reality comes and bites you with its fangs. But don't listen to me. Tell me all about Cain. I can't wait to hear how this whirlwind romance started."

Andrea brightened immediately. "I wouldn't call it whirlwind. We've been together for eight months now!"

"Well, it must have been a whirlwind romance since we haven't even met him before!" said Lily. "Come on, tell me all about it!"

Sitting cross-legged on her bed, Andrea launched into a description of her wonderful fiancé.

Ella's relief was tangible at Lily's insistence on changing the conversation to a more cheery topic. There was nothing that pleased Andrea as much as a conversation about Cain, who was North FM's most popular presenter and the number one housewife's favourite throughout

Ireland. There wasn't an event or ceremony that he wasn't invited to, and in between radio shows he spent numerous evenings every week acting as compère at fashion shows, charity events and awards ceremonies.

RTÉ had tried to poach him on numerous occasions and the bosses at BBC had hinted that in the near future Cain would be offered his very own television-presenting job. The future was bright for Cain Daniels and Andrea was so excited to be part of it.

"Are you sure you want to hear all this?" asked Andrea. "Mum is so bored with me gushing all the time."

"It's fascinating! You do like to surprise us all, love."

"You can say that again," said Ella and she fidgeted with the bottom of her blouse.

Andrea had surprised them all right, but then nothing Andrea had ever done was by half measures. This time though, Ella hoped she had got it right. Cain Daniels seemed like a true gentleman and so far he had managed to keep Andrea's fiery temper and sometimes demanding ways under control. His city background complemented her 'live life to the full' attitude and Ella was glad that her younger daughter had finally met her match.

But it was only a few months ago that Cain had been formally introduced to the O'Neill family and Ella wondered if this was all too much too soon.

Andrea had just fulfilled her dream of opening a bookshop in the nearby town of Drumfee and, with a little bit of financial help from her father, she had transformed a fairly modest shop unit into a hive of activity and had attracted some of Ireland's more popular fiction writers to attend talks and seminars in the cosy den that she had extended on the back of the unit.

From an early age, Andrea had known exactly what she had wanted from her life. She would open her own bookstore that would match her personality to a tee. She would bring the experience of buying books to the traditional mode of a library-style treasure-chest of knowledge with cosy corners for a sneaky read and a magazine archive on subjects that ranged on everything from gardening to architecture. And that's exactly what she did. So far, it was working out very nicely and had acquired quite a cult following.

So, while Jessie turned her hand to representing some of the Irish border's petty criminals in the courtroom, Andrea wiled her days away tending to customers who wanted to find a first edition of Dickens or a box set of *Harry Potter*.

The opening party of Haven bookshop had a guest list which read as a who's who of Ireland's media. Television presenters and models were drafted in, courtesy of a quiet word through Tom O'Neill's business contacts, to see Ireland's bestselling novelist, Rita O'Riordan, officially open the doors to the shop. Haven had been kitted out with only the best traditional interior design that brought every book lover into their own little corner of heaven.

Like most of the invited guests, Cain Daniels had been instantly smitten, both by the genuine character of the shop itself with its nooks and crannies and topic-led shelves with floor cushions and fresh coffee, and by the effortless charm and confidence of the lady behind the entire Haven concept. This was not a money-making device. This was a dream job for a young lady who had everything else she needed in life presented to her on a plate, thanks to her wealthy father.

Cain Daniels, having tried in vain to satisfy his longing to converse with Andrea amidst the hubbub of the launch and the constant flashing of cameras from the *Tatler*, had returned to the shop the next day with a truly unique and challenging request.

"Well, I was chatting with Mrs Bradley from down the road who was looking for a gift for her son's return to college life . . ."

Ella was listening politely from the foot of the bed, despite having heard the same story recited to everyone and anyone who asked how Andrea met the man of her dreams. It made her heart glow to see her daughter so happy, despite her own reservations about too much too soon.

"He strolled into the shop and fumbled around through the gardening section until Mrs Bradley had left. As he lifted gardening books out, one after the other, I took the opportunity to figure out where I had seen him before, and then when I finally did recognise him, I mustered up the courage to make some light conversation."

"Sounds romantic already," said Aunt Lily and Andrea beamed. "So, what did he say? Did he ask you out straight away?"

"Well, he seemed to be really shy at first which is *so*

not him at all. And then he introduced himself and when he said his name I blurted out to him how much I loved his breakfast show and how Jessie and I would always talk about his discussions of the day, which believe me are wide and varied, sometimes to the point of idiocy, but entertaining nonetheless. Jessie is such a fan and that was my first thought – that I couldn't wait to tell her he had come back after the launch event!"

Lily and Ella smiled knowingly at each other.

"So, he asked me then if I had any books on motoring in the 19th century. The very look on my face must have given me away. Here was a man I had listened to first thing every morning for the past, I don't know, two years and he had an interest in the history of motor cars! I pretended to look it up on the computer when he burst out laughing and said it was the first topic that had come into his head and the real reason he came in to the shop was to ask me out to dinner."

"Oooh, and I take it you said yes?" said Lily, mesmerised by the picture she had in her head of her niece's first meeting with this local celebrity.

"Like hell I did!" laughed Andrea.

"Do you honestly think she would give in so easily?" asked Ella, smiling at her daughter. "I don't think Andrea has ever agreed to a date on a man's first request."

Lily laughed, remembering some of Andrea's early encounters with the opposite sex and the random decisions she made, often turning down the most eligible men in the North of Ireland in favour of the most eccentric characters you could imagine.

"I forgot about that. Well, that makes it more interesting. So what did you say to the poor guy?"

Andrea poised herself. This was her favourite bit.

"I said, ahem . . . I said that he had to choose a book for me from my entire collection in the shop and if I read it and liked it, I would join him for dinner the following Friday."

Lily whooped with joy at her niece's determination. Any other young woman would have jumped at the chance for as much as a conversation with such a handsome, successful man but Andrea had chosen to throw him a challenge.

"So, go on. What did he choose? I take it you liked it, anyhow?"

"Well, he spent, I swear, at least an hour scouring the shelves and it was almost lunch-time when he finally came into the den at the back of the shop where I was dressing the room for a school creative-writing class. He tapped me on the shoulder, handed me a book and turned and left me standing there without even saying a word."

"What was it?" asked Lily. "What did he choose?"

Andrea glanced at her mother with a grin and paused for effect.

"I read the title and it said: *Hollywood Wives* by Jackie Collins!"

Lily's face fell and Ella burst out laughing at the disappointment in her poor sister-in-law's eyes. She had seen the same reaction in everyone who had heard of how Andrea fell for her knight in shining armour.

"Jackie feckin' Collins! Jackie feckin' Collins!" said Lily. "I would have thrown it straight back! Whatever happened to *Wuthering Heights* or *Pride and Prejudice*? What did you do?"

"I laughed," said Andrea. "I laughed and laughed and laughed and then I ran out onto the street and called him back and shouted 'To hell with Friday! Let's go to dinner tonight!' And the rest, as they say, is the future!"

Lily let the humour of the story sink in and then she nodded furiously.

"You know," she said, joining in now with Ella and Andrea's laughter. "I think you two will have a very long and happy future together. Fair play to him is what I say. Fair play! He caught you hook, line and sinker from day one."

"He sure did," said Andrea, a glazed mist now coming over her eyes. "And now I'm going to be his wife. Sometimes I can't believe just how lucky I am. Oh, Mum, Aunt Lily! I am so, so happy!"

Andrea's tears of laughter turned sentimental and she found a tissue from her sleeve, carefully dabbing under her dark eyes so as not to ruin her make-up.

"Come on now, ladies," said Ella. "I think I hear someone home. Let's hope Ryan has made it up with Jessie by now so we can all enjoy the wonderful days ahead until we see you becoming Mrs Cain Daniels!"

The three women pulled themselves from the bed and were still laughing when they got to the top of the stairs.

Then Ella stopped dead and let out a scream.

"Oh my God, Andrea! Oh my good God!"

Andrea's laughter trailed off and then it turned into a piercing cry.

Her dress. Her precious wedding dress had been cut to pieces and was strewn all over the stairs and landing of her home.

Chapter 6

"My dress! Oh Mum, my dress! No!"

Andrea dropped to her knees and hysterically began to gather up clumps of fabric from the floor.

"Mum!" she cried. "Mum, tell me this isn't happening! My wedding dress! How did this happen? Who would do this to me?"

She clutched the banister with both hands, shreds of silk and balls of antique lace on her lap, hot tears now causing dark heavy streaks to stream down her cheeks and onto the high-pile carpet.

Ella tried to add it up in her head. How could anyone have taken the dress? They had been in the house all evening. Andrea had tried it on when Jessie had been around earlier. No one had been upstairs since, had they? How could this have possibly happened?

Refusing to believe it, she stumbled past Andrea who still lay sobbing on the floor and raced back into her daughter's bedroom. She flung open the wardrobe doors where Andrea's beautiful hand-made gown had hung for almost three weeks now and scrambled through coats and jackets to find it.

Her heart leapt when she came across its pale-pink protective cover and she unzipped it to the floor.

Then her hand met her mouth.

There, hanging in its place was a grey, withered, raggy dress that had been chopped and was stained all over with huge damp marks from top to toe. And scrawled in what looked like lipstick on the inside of the wardrobe door were the words '*Don't Marry Him*!'

She stifled a scream. Who would do such a thing? And only days before the wedding? What did all of this mean? What was going on?

Grabbing a damp facecloth from the en-suite, Ella frantically wiped off the text on the inside of the wardrobe and shoved the ragged dress to the back of the closet until she had the opportunity to make sure it would never be found. She ran back onto the landing where her daughter had been helped now onto her feet by Lily, who couldn't hide her own trauma at the horrific scene she had witnessed.

"I'm so sorry, love," said Ella, hugging her baby girl. "I don't know how. I don't know why. But we'll fix this. We'll get this all sorted. Don't you worry about a thing, I promise."

A door opened across the way and Ryan walked out of his bedroom door, rubbing his eyes and stretching.

"What the hell is all the noise about?" he asked,

scratching his sleepy head. "Jesus, what happened here?"

Ella's head spun towards him and she felt her stomach sour as she patted Andrea's damp hair.

Had Ryan been in his bedroom this whole time? She was sure he had left on his bike after Jessie's swift departure only an hour ago. A chill ran through her and she urged the notion that flashed through her mind to go away. Could her son possibly have done this to his own sister? Was he capable of such a horrendous action? No, no, no, she told herself. No.

"Just leave us alone, Ryan," she said, hoping that if he was out of her sight the very notion that he had done this would be out of her mind. "Go and get your father quickly so we can try and get this sorry mess sorted out."

"I must tell Cain!" said Andrea.

A minute later Andrea was sobbing down the phone to her fiancé as her mother and aunt gathered up the lumps of cloth that had just hours earlier formed the dress of her dreams. A dress she had shopped hours and hours for. A dress that she had tried on first out of at least twenty others. A dress that she went back to time and time again because she just knew it was the one for her.

"I don't know what to say, babe," said Cain. "I'm horrified. Who was in the house when it happened? Did anything seem out of sorts?"

"No, it's been just a normal evening really apart from Aunt Lily and the boys, and I had tried the dress on earlier when Jessie was around and we were planning our make-up and –"

"What? Jessie was around? Today?"

"Yes, why?" asked Andrea. "What difference does that make?"

"I thought you said she had gone walkabout this morning and you were mad at her?"

"I *was* mad at her but we got it sorted."

"My God, you were fit to be tied when I spoke to you last. You don't stay angry with Jessie for long, do you?"

Andrea realised that Cain had a lot of catching up to do on the day's events. When she had last spoken to him, Jessie was still missing in action and she was spitting blood.

"Yeah, well, it turns out she and David had a bit of a row because he had to go away on business at the last minute again."

"Oh," said Cain. "Well, let's decide what we can do in just two days to get you a new wedding dress. I'm sure I know someone who can help. Don't worry, baby, I'll get this all fixed for you. We still have time and I promise you we'll find out who is out to ruin our day."

Andrea crossed her legs on her bed which she feared she might mould into if she kept spending so much time sitting on top of it. Who could have broken into her room? It must have happened when they were having dinner, or out on the patio. Someone was incredibly jealous of her position and it chilled her to the bone.

There was a knock on the bedroom door and her father popped his head around it.

"Cain, I'll call you back in a few minutes," said Andrea. "Daddy has just come into the room. He might have some news already."

"But I hate leaving you like this. Should I come around?"

"No, no. I'll see you tomorrow. Just please tell me what I'm going to do!"

Tom O'Neill gestured at Andrea to hand him the phone before she hung up on her fiancé.

"Cain . . . Yes, it's really terrible. It's a horrible thing to have happened. Look, I've been thinking long and hard about this and I'm sure you'll agree if this was leaked to the Press we might be doing exactly what the perpetrator wants."

Andrea couldn't believe her ears. The Press? Who the hell cared about the Press?

"Now, I suggest that we keep this to ourselves for as long as we possibly can," said Tom. "We don't want to draw any unnecessary attention on you or Andrea and turn the wedding into a media circus that would distract from all the hard work Andrea – well, both of you have put into this wedding. What do you think?"

Andrea looked up at her father in horror. Was he planning to let whoever had broken into her bedroom and dumped her wedding dress all over the family home get away with it? Just to avoid any Press coverage!

"Daddy, please! We have to find out who did this to me," she said. "Someone was in our house! Someone is out to destroy my wedding day!"

Tom held up his hand for Andrea to be quiet as he

listened to Cain's reaction. He nodded and Andrea sobbed until Ella tiptoed into the bedroom as if she had been listening all along from the other side of the door. She closed the door gently behind her.

"Hush, baby," she whispered and sat alongside Andrea who was on the verge of hysterics. "Please, Andrea. Let your dad and Cain deal with this. We all need to put this behind us until after the wedding and then, I can assure you, we will find out exactly what is going on. We will find out exactly who did this to you."

Andrea rocked now in her mother's arms and sobbed like a baby. Her wedding day was already ruined. There was no way it could go ahead when her precious dress had been mangled to a pulp.

"Think who it might be," said Ella. "Is there someone you know who, I don't know, may envy your relationship with Cain?"

Andrea grunted. "Envy?" she spat. "Well, I could think of at least half a dozen girls who have called me names in the street, who have mailed Cain and phoned him at the station begging him not to get married – but they are just crazed fans, I'd say. I don't think any of them would go this far."

Ella shrugged. She thought it was a fair possibility.

"Thanks, Cain," said Tom. "I'll call you later for an update. Good man."

Tom hung up the phone and sat down on the edge of his daughter's bed, rubbing his knees. He had rarely been in this room since Andrea was little, when he would have told her a bedtime story or tucked her in when she was feeling poorly or checked under the bed for the bogey man when she was frightened and other usual night-time routines. As she had grown up into a feisty teenager, signs like 'No Boys Allowed' were pasted on the door and now that she was in her mid-twenties, the room was more of a retreat to his girl than ever.

Who would have invaded her space in such a horrific way? He dreaded to think of the possibilities.

"Now, love," he said, "Cain says he has a good friend in the bridal business he knows through the station. He says you know her. Bernice?"

"Yes, Bernice Bradshaw," nodded Andrea. "I know of her. Everyone does. She's an ex-girlfriend of his. How wonderful!"

"Well, it's going to be a real rush to get something you like or that lives up to your own dress, so it's all we can think of at the minute. Is that okay, love? Unless you have any other suggestions?"

"Yes, like call the police?" said Andrea. "Find out who was in my bedroom? Oh, I'm even beginning to suspect my cousins! This is ridiculous."

"Andrea! That's enough," said Tom. "You can't point the finger at our guests! And anyhow they were with me. Look now, Cain says he might have one or two angles on who might have done this that he would like to try and get his head around before we jump to any conclusions."

Andrea straightened up now and her eyes widened.

"Who? Tell me who he is thinking of."

"I don't know – but let him work on it, love. Your

fiancé is a very well-known popular man in this area and whoever destroyed your wedding dress is probably linked to how well-liked Cain is."

"And what am I supposed to do in the meantime? Just wait until something else happens? Until someone else breaks into my bedroom?"

"No, of course not," said Tom. "Let me call our security people and we'll arrange extra staff around the house until the wedding is over and, Ella, maybe you could get this Bernice person's number and have her here in the morning first thing?"

"Okay. The sooner the better," said Ella.

"I'll entertain Lily and the others and make sure we give the dressmaker the space she needs," said Tom.

Andrea nodded and her mother stood up, brushing her clothes down with her hands in a gesture that marked the end of the conversation.

"Now, remember," said Tom, "we want to keep this as discreet as possible. No one else will know of this except those who already do. That's the three of us and Aunt Lily. Not another soul, do you hear?"

Ella stood up but remained silent, letting the man of the house declare his rules on protecting his brood.

"Not even Jessie?" asked Andrea. "Or David? David will know what to do. We could call him and ask his advice?"

"No. Not even Jessie," said her father and he turned towards the door. "And definitely not David."

"But David might be able to help?" said Andrea. "I mean, in his line of work . . ."

"No! Not a word and I mean that. Not until I say so."

Andrea lay down on her bed and Ella followed her husband quietly out onto the landing.

So that was that, thought Ella. Every scrap of the desecrated wedding dress had been gathered up and all was quiet, the commotion of the evening having been swept under the carpet.

Only three people knew about it, four including Lily. And then Ella remembered.

Ryan did too.

Ella drew a deep breath and felt her head begin to spin as she swallowed her secret on her way down the stairs.

She would keep it all to herself like she was told to. Not a word would be said.

Not a word.

Chapter 7

Thursday

Bernice Bradshaw followed her friend Cain Daniels' car through the automatic gates and up the winding driveway that led to the magnificent O'Neill homestead at the ungodly hour of six thirty in the morning. Her tummy rumbled and she hoped that whoever was in charge of catering in this magnificent manor had been informed of her visit.

She fixed her lipstick in the rear-view and flicked back her white-blonde bob, then stepped out of the car and approached the back entrance of her new client's home.

The house had an unusually shaped, modern design but was beautiful nonetheless and was no doubt the envy of many a humble neighbour from the nearby village it looked down upon. It jutted out in opposing angles, with huge clear-glass panels that were more like doors than windows and Bernice guessed that one day about twenty-five years ago this house had been every architect's biggest fantasy.

She felt hot and sticky after the thirty-mile drive from Belfast city and although she was ever so slightly aggrieved to be called upon at such late notice, she hoped that she could do something to help her good friend. And he was a very good friend.

Yes, Cain Daniels had been so useful to her down the years, introducing her to friends in high places and ensuring that she had all the right contacts in her little black book since she started out just over seven years ago. All in return for the odd night of passion – even in recent months when the silly cow he was engaged to was too caught up in books or family stuff.

Bernice still found him to be shit hot, if she was forced to admit it, even if he was stupid enough to get married.

Thankfully for Bernice, weddings had come swiftly back in fashion and she had quickly made a name for herself, mixing in the highest media circles and having classy representation at all the best fashion shows and in all of Ireland's glossy magazines.

She had originally been extremely offended that this poor little country rich girl, Andrea O'Neill, with her media-friendly sullen beauty, her big fancy home and her eccentric way of spending her time in a bookshop just a few inches from her own backyard, hadn't come to her in the first place to design her dress.

No, Miss O'Neill had insisted, much to Cain's embarrassment, to go her own way and ignore any suggestion of designers or styles and had been quite intent on doing everything for their big day just as she had wanted it. No wedding planner, no PR, just her way or no way.

Poor Cain didn't know what he was letting himself in for, so they said. And now, just because the original designer had made some cheap last-minute muck-up, Bernice had been pulled in to clear up the mess.

Oh, but she would make sure Daddy Big Bucks would pay up for this one, that was for sure, and the media mileage she would get out of this would be huge.

She would insist that every press release issued on this wedding by Cain's radio colleagues carried her name and though making a dress fit for this princess might mean she would have no sleep for the next forty-eight hours, she would make enough money out of it to allow her to sleep for the next six months if she chose to do so.

"So, you must be the blushing bride," she said, extending her fine, porcelain hand to Andrea's lightly tanned one when they reached the doorway.

It was raining lightly and Bernice prayed her styled bob wouldn't turn into a frizz in front of Cain Daniels.

"Andrea, this is my good friend, Bernice Bradshaw," said Cain. "This has all been quite emotional for my fiancée as I'm sure you can imagine, Bernice, but I know she's in the best hands now."

Andrea forced a grin, knowing that 'Bernice' had nothing only big fat pound-signs in her eyes at this present moment. Ah well, she thought, beggars can't be choosers.

"I can't thank you enough for coming to see me at such short notice," she said. "Hopefully it shouldn't be too painful. I know exactly what I want."

I'll bet you do, thought Bernice and she accepted Andrea's invitation to come inside.

"Yes, I've brought the material your mother spoke to me about and I have a car boot full of accessories and suggested patterns," said Bernice, following Andrea and Cain into a huge modern dining-room. "Now, this room is ideal. I feel inspired already."

"Great," said Andrea. "Do you mind if we get started right away?"

Bernice gave a pinched smile and her tummy let out a growl.

"After coffee?" said Cain with a flashy smile. "I know. Why don't you ladies get acquainted and I'll order some breakfast, then leave you both to it?"

"Now, that would be perfect, Cain," said Bernice. "We don't need you to come in and see our grand designs and ruin the big surprise. That would just be all the bad luck in the world, now wouldn't it?"

She let out a cackle and Andrea gulped back her dislike for the girl who was about to save the day, quite literally.

Jessie awoke from a fitful sleep and let her senses come to. She sleepily reached for the clock and then threw her head back down on the bed when the dramatic turn her life had taken washed over her tired mind.

David was gone. And she knew in her heart that he was never, ever coming back.

She was glad she had stayed away from her family home the night before, allowing Aunt Lily and company get settled without having to face all the usual questions about wedded bliss.

Her sister's wedding was the last thing she could think about at the present moment but she knew she would have to force herself out of bed, into the shower and paint on a happy face to match the joviality that no doubt was going on just down the road. She imagined the scene – a direct copy of what had gone on over breakfast last year when the first of the cousins had arrived. Mum would be fussing one hundred times more than she normally did, making sure that Lily was getting enough to eat and that the boys weren't bored despite the fact they were both well into their twenties.

Dad would be showing off in front of his new audience, challenging everyone to a game of golf – even in the rain – or a cross-country run along the back fields and Ryan would be taunting his cousins about their non-existent love lives or else dodging everyone's company for fear of being asked to do something useful.

And Andrea. Well, Andrea, right now, would probably be wondering where her big sister was and why she wasn't there to share in all of the excitement.

Jessie's heart sank but, as much as the image of abandoning her sister pained her, she couldn't keep up her façade for much longer. She couldn't go on denying to her family that her marriage was over. She couldn't go on pretending that she as wholesome as they thought she was. She couldn't go on lying to her sister like this, using the pressures of her job and that of her husband's for her avoidance of the truth: the truth that she was about to let her sister make the biggest mistake of her life.

Her family would smell a rat when David didn't come home tomorrow as she had said he would, and Ryan seemed to know more than he should already about the whole situation.

She reached her hand over to David's side of the bed and stroked his pillow. She could still smell his shampoo from when he had arrived back from swimming the night before he left. Jessie had left a note for him on the kitchen table, directing him to where dinner could be found in the oven while she buried herself in the latest turn of events in the O'Donnell case upstairs in her study.

He had arrived home full of chat and fun, playfully tugging at her to come away from her desk. He had begged her to join him for dinner, to share a bottle of wine and relax for just one evening. To switch off the computer and to put away her files, but she had refused, as she always did when working on such a big case.

Eventually his mood had changed. He had become fed up with trying to humour her.

"You don't have time for anyone in your life," he had said, pausing at the doorway. "Except for your precious work and your family, that is."

Jessie had sniggered in disbelief. "What the hell is that supposed to mean? Are you jealous of how much I love my family? Is this your next excuse for an argument?"

"It's like being married to the Mob," he said, leaning on the doorframe. "Your sister needs you, you jump. Your mother, the same. I just think you should create a bit of distance, that's all. Then maybe you'd have a bit more time for me."

Jessie had looked at his pitiful face but instead of following him downstairs, instead of giving him half an hour of her time, she had shrugged and turned her attention back to the O'Donnell case. Representing a man who most of the county wanted dead was no mean feat, but Jessie knew it was just the type of case she needed to cut her teeth on and make her mark in the world of Irish law. Like the rest of the local population, David believed that Jack O'Donnell was a ruthless thug, but to Jessie attempted murder was attempted murder and she had to rise to the challenge of prosecuting the gang who had tried to kill him.

She had known exactly what David was getting at, though, when he said she was giving too much of her time to this case.

He wasn't just saying that she had no time for him, but that she had no time for making him a father, for expanding the Chambers family and for giving him the son or daughter that he so yearned for.

She couldn't deny it.

At this moment in her life, she wasn't ready for a family, with the pressures of her job and the recent torrid distractions that had come her way.

She longed for breathing space, for time to think, for time to find out what exactly she did want from her life, and David's gentle persistence had made her dig her heels in even further against the subject and further out of his reach.

Then in the heat of a ridiculous argument she had asked him to leave and now she was paying the price that deep down she knew she deserved.

She dragged herself out of bed, her conscience now too heavy to let her lie down and rest for much longer.

She stepped into the shower and let the hot steamy water run off her face, down her shoulders and onto the stylish floor tiles she had carefully chosen to match the en-suite's adjoining bedroom. Next to that was her study and on the other side was what David had hoped would be a nursery.

That must have been the real reason he left, she told herself.

He could blame her involvement in the O'Donnell case. He could issue her ultimatum after ultimatum about standing back from it before she got herself into real danger.

But the truth was, David longed for a baby and she didn't. There was no way that he could have known of anything else, was there? Was there? Then Jessie recalled Ryan's accusing face from earlier and her stomach churned once again. She ran to the bathroom and was violently sick.

"So, can I come in?" asked Ella, knocking lightly on the dining-room door. She pushed the door with her elbow, balancing a tray of coffee and muffins in her hands, and made her way into the most underused room of her magnificent home.

"We're almost there," said Bernice, leaning away from Andrea to view the dress as she put in the final pins, a rather endangering needle clamped between her lips. "Well, we're almost past round one, I suppose."

"Any news?" asked Andrea and her mother caught her drift instantly.

"Not a thing," she said. "All's quiet and your dad has taken your cousins to the North Coast for the day while Lily is having a mid-morning nap, so we have the place to ourselves."

"And Ryan? Where is he?"

Ella found herself startled at the sound of her son's name. "Oh, he's away with them too. He's following them on the bike. He says he loves the road up to the coast. It's perfect for biking, or so he says."

Bernice stood back in admiration of her speedy efforts and spun her model around. Andrea was now pinned into a real-life version of what just two hours ago had been a rough sketch on paper of Andrea's original dress.

Andrea had barely spoken throughout the procedure, despite Bernice's persistence in questioning her on her luxurious lifestyle, province-wide famous bookstore and forthcoming marriage to the devilishly handsome Cain Daniels.

Some girls had it all, Bernice had mused, resisting the temptation to prick this spoilt little diva's perfect skin as she worked.

"I didn't realise you had a brother," she said with a

wry look. "All this time in your company and I thought it was just you and Mummy and Daddy. Is he single?"

"And a sister. *Ow!*" yelped Andrea. "Careful! Yes, he is single but he's too young for you."

"Sorry," said Bernice and she tacked the side of the luxurious raw silk up the side of Andrea's slender hip. "Oh, yes, that's right. You have a sister. How could I forget? I've seen her around. It's Jessie, isn't it?"

"Yes. It's Jessie. Any word yet from her this morning, Mum?"

"No, nothing," said Ella who was lingering at the window, looking out at the dark, almost wintry morning that reflected how she felt inside. "No sign of her at all. In fact, I'll go and give her a call right now. I think it's about time I had a good long chat with her."

Jessie flicked her phone on to silent mode as she entered the chapel doors. It was cold inside, colder than normal, and she shivered under her light clothing. She hadn't eaten all morning and her body felt empty, almost soulless with lack of food, yet full of remorse.

She dipped her hand in the holy-water font and shivered at its cool marble touch.

Just under twelve months ago she had stood at this same doorway, taking deep breaths and wondering if she was about to make the biggest mistake of her life by committing to 'till death us do part'.

She had always been married to her career and even as a teenager she had questioned her honesty when it came to relationships.

"You're just a perfectionist, too hard to please," her mother once told her. "There's no such thing as the perfect man. They all have flaws. We all do."

Now, one year on, Jessie still wasn't sure if she had ever loved David as she should have, but the dilemma to stay with him or not was now out of her hands.

She wandered down the dark brick-red tiles of the church aisle, trailing her hands along the shiny pews and breathing in the still air. An elderly lady grasped rosary beads and chanted prayer in the front row, but apart from her whistling whispers, the place was silent.

Jessie blessed herself and slipped into a pew near the back of the building and knelt down on the cold wooden ledge, dropped her head and gloried in the soothing silence.

"*Hail Mary, full of grace . . .*" she prayed and then continued, though she was unable to concentrate on the words that normally meant so much to her. She shivered, then closed her eyes and let the thoughts in her mind swirl around like a spinning top. The last twenty-four hours twisted and turned and she rubbed her temples, urging all of the confusion she felt to leave her weary body.

She thought of the O'Donnell case that had occupied her every minute since she took it on six months ago: a classic drug war that had ended in the attempted murder of baron Jack O'Donnell and a trail of deceit which had so far led her to dangerous people who were too close to her own doorstep for comfort. She spent hours upon hours delving deeper and deeper into the heart of the case, searching for information and building a prosecution case on behalf of a man who in most people's eyes didn't deserve it.

She knew she was at risk, she knew that it was almost tipping over the verge of danger but this was the biggest case of her career and she was determined to find justice for Jack O'Donnell, even if it did put her own life on the line. But was her obsession with representing this worldly criminal worth threatening her marriage? Or her judgement? Or her sanity?

She thought of David and of his frustrations with her of late, of how he had become last on her list, after her career and her precious family.

But David's job had its downsides as well as hers. As one of the North's top detectives, he spent a lot of his time away on missions that were so secretive even she didn't know his destination for most of the time.

Their paths had first crossed when he was sent to a neighbouring town on one of his private investigations and Jessie now realised how ironic it was that the secrets and undercover behaviour that had intrigued her about David in the first place had helped to drive them apart before the wedding cake had gone stale.

Then there was her sister's wedding. Her baby sister whom she loved and adored, who was enjoying all of the fuss that Jessie had avoided and whom she had let down so badly the day before and whom she had upset because her brother seemed to want to pick a fight at the wrong moment. She should tell Andrea the truth, she knew she should, but it would ruin her. It would ruin all of the O'Neills. Christ, but she could hardly look at Andrea's sweet face. It took all her strength to keep the truth from her and every day she would ask God to guide her to do the right thing. To keep her silence and continue living a lie, hoping that things would work out for the best, or risk the ruination of her family.

Ryan's behaviour was most worrying of all. She only had one brother and, despite her love for him which ran deep and loyal inside her, of late he was trying to make her life a misery. What did he know? Could he see inside her mind and feel her unnerving, heart-wrenching guilt that was tearing her life apart and keeping her awake at night? Did he know of her terrible secret, a horrid, sickening reality that was haunting her until it was close to driving her out of control?

She clenched her hands more tightly and dropped her head, begging God for forgiveness, pleading with him to help her release the devil from inside her. She had always been such a good girl and in everyone's eyes she still was.

Everyone's eyes, apart from her own, that was. When she looked in the mirror she could see the truth seeping from her eyes and she could read it written all over her face. She could feel it in her hands right down to her fingertips, she could see it in her reflection on shop windows, she could hear it in her voice every time she spoke.

Dirty, rotten, angry, life-changing guilt. God but she was sorry!

Her train of thought was interrupted with a shuffle from the pew behind her. She ignored it at first and finished her prayer, locked in a moment of confession and a mission to cleanse her soul.

When she couldn't stand the flashbacks in her head any longer, she stood up and genuflected towards the altar, then turned around to see Father Christopher Lennon, Glencuan's new parish priest, sitting in the row behind her.

She smiled at him and sat down again, soothed by his presence, aware of his capacity for unconditional judgement and forgiveness.

He was only a few years older than her, she guessed, which was much, much too young to be a priest in this town. Glencuan was more used to pensioners in the pulpit than gorgeous young men who could make women fall to their knees at the sound of his voice. But Jess saw him differently.

"Nice to see you again, Father," she said eventually and she meant it. She longed to be cleansed again, for him to help release her sorrows and get her life back on track. He had been so good for her of late with all his gentle words of wisdom and understanding.

"So, you've given in to my advice then at last?" he said in his charming Cork accent, and she turned around in the pew to face him. His teeth were perfect, his lips a pale soft pink that almost bled into his sallow skin. "I told you a few quiet moments in here might help you get your head around things."

"You were right," she whispered, conscious of the old lady at the front of the church who was shuffling in her seat, obviously aware of a conversation going on in the house of God. "You were right about a lot of things, Father."

Father Christopher sighed and glanced at the floor. Then he lifted his head to meet hers. "We all go through extremely hard times in our lives, Jessie. Just remember that. I'm really glad you confided in me."

"Yes. I know. I'm glad I did too."

What was it about him that made her feel she could tell him anything in the world? He was a priest, yes. He was up on a pedestal to many, but to her right now he was just a friend. He was just a man who listened to her and who reassured her when she needed him. And most of all, he was a man who couldn't tell a soul of her secret. He couldn't judge her, couldn't shout at her, couldn't tell her she was making a mess of her so-called life. He knew it all and yet he spoke to her as if she was as pure as she had ever been. She knew a lot of this came with the territory – after all, in this liberal age he was trained to be gentle in the confessional – but she felt he genuinely didn't see her for the person she really was.

"I suppose I should probably get going," she murmured and she stood up, adjusting her jacket around her waist. "I think I'm all done for now. Like you said, talking to God every day really helps. I hope it can show me the right path to take. I really do appreciate your advice. Thanks again, Father."

She noticed how his black eyes looked sad for her and, beneath his handsome and astute exterior, she suspected he had troubles of his own.

"That's what I'm here for," he smiled. "It will get

better, you know it will. Don't go down over this, Jessie. You made a mistake. Everyone does."

She broke eye contact, then shuffled past him, out into the centre aisle.

"Thanks, Father," she whispered. "You're very kind. You're a wonderful man and you've been most helpful to me. I will always remember that."

She walked away but as she did she could sense rather than hear him following her. On the way through the stone porch, she paused to dip her hand in the holy-water font and blessed herself again slowly, giving him time to catch up on her.

"Jessie?"

His black vestments looked strange on such a young man, so formal and authoritarian.

"Yes, Father?"

"How about you walk back to the Parochial House with me?" he said, his voice louder now that they were almost outside. "We could have a coffee? Talk more? I'm all finished here for now and you look like you could use a friend. I'm worried about you."

"I – I really should get going," she mumbled. "My mum will be going crazy with worry by now. I haven't checked in at home in, well, in almost fifteen hours and that's enough to send her into a blind panic, believe me."

Father Christopher smiled back at her and nodded. "That's okay. If you're sure. I'll see you for the rehearsal then?"

She looked at him in question before the huge reality of what he spoke of registered in her brain.

"The rehearsal? Oh, of course," she whispered. She took a deep breath and pictured the wedding rehearsal in her mind. Then she thought of her sister's gleeful face, her brother's sudden silent hatred for her, her absent husband, her discerning parents, her sin . . .

She walked back towards him as a shower of rain broke out from the heavens. He looked up at it, spatters of rain falling on his face.

"Actually, you know, a coffee would be really good right now," she said, pulling her hood over her head.

"I think so too." He smiled back at her and they hurried through the church gardens, past the old gate lodge that nestled against a dry stone wall at the edge of the grounds, then through a gap that led to the Parochial House.

"Jessie! At last! I've been so worried about you."

Ella left the cooker and embraced her daughter. She felt as if she hadn't left her kitchen in days and she could feel the exhaustion creep up on her. "My goodness, you're freezing cold! Where have you been?"

"I – I just went for a walk, that's all," said Jessie. "I just had to clear my head. I'm fine. Really I am."

Ella could see a distant torture in her daughter's eyes and it stung her to the core. She looked blank almost and so pale that her skin was almost transparent.

"Jessie, I know you're in some sort of trouble," she said. "This is not like you to keep disappearing like this."

Jessie sat down in her father's armchair by the Aga and Ella knelt down by the side of the chair.

"Mum, I do not keep on disappearing!" she said. "I am just busy at the minute, that's all. I have a lot going on."

"Like what, love? Please tell me *what's* going on? What's going on that has you so distracted from the things and the people you love the most? I know this isn't the real you. Tell me!"

Jessie shook her head and fidgeted in the chair. She felt like a wounded schoolgirl who was sent home for being bold in class.

"It's nothing, Mum. Really, you don't have to worry."

"Is it David? Is it work?"

"No."

"Is it the O'Donnell case? Maybe you should slow it down a little. Maybe David is right in saying that you're into it too deep?"

"David is *not* right about this case. It's very important to me."

"More important than your marriage? Than your health?"

Ella held Jessie's hand and tilted her chin upwards. Her skin was so white. A wave of nausea flooded Ella's insides.

"Jessie, are you sick? Oh please, don't hold it back from me! Let me help you. Tell me."

"No, Mum, I'm definitely not sick," said Jessie and she smiled lightly in reassurance. "Definitely not sick."

"Pregnant, then? That would explain all these changes in you of late. Have you checked? Maybe you are, maybe –"

"Mum, stop!" said Jessie and she stood up from the chair, pulling her hand from her mother's warm grasp. "Please, stop fussing! You're always fussing over me like I'm a child. I'm not a child any more."

"I'm just trying to find out why you're in such a terrible state. You're avoiding us all, you are quiet and you –"

"Mum, this is Andrea's time. Fuss over Andrea, not me! I'm sick of this! I'm sick of everything!"

Jessie's words stung and Ella was taken aback at her untypical tone.

"Jessie, please!"

"No, Mum! I mean it! Just leave me alone!" Jessie shouted, running outside into the rain. "That's all I want! Just leave me alone!"

Chapter 8

As Jessie pushed open her own front door, she shoved a heap of mail with it. Not able to cope with its reality and its signal of normal existence, she bundled it on to the hall table together with her handbag. Then she flung her coat on a hall chair and made her way into her state-of-the-art kitchen that had once given her so much pleasure with its stainless-steel and cherry-wood décor and its cool cream walls.

Everything looked exactly as she'd left it that morning.

The cloth she had scrubbed the worktops with still lay there from the day before, wrung out so tightly it reminded her instantly of the pain she had felt on discovering her marriage was well and truly over.

David's cup still sat on the draining-board and the wooden Venetian blinds on the two large windows – one to the back and one to the side of the house – were still closed. Everything looked the same.

Everything looked the same, but what was different was the smell.

She tried to ignore it at first but then it swept through her nostrils again and she ran to the living room, desperately trying to follow the distinctive faint stench of cigarette smoke.

David had come home. He had changed his mind.

"David! Where are you?" she called, pacing around the bottom floor of her house, opening and closing doors through empty room after room.

And then she pounded up the stairs, calling his name.

"David, are you home?" she shouted across the landing. The bedroom door was closed but she listened and heard the shower running from the bedroom en-suite and her heart settled.

Maybe everything was going to be okay. Maybe the scare she'd had was just a kick in the right direction for her.

She sat on the top stair and breathed in and out, in and out, thanking God for giving her a base of sanity, a chance to make things better before it was too late.

Father Christopher had been right. Yes, she had made a mistake, but then again, everyone does. She would put the past behind her and make more of an effort with her husband. Yes, that would fix things. Well, it might be a start. She would drop the damn O'Donnell case if it was too much for David to bear. Hell, she would even consider having a baby in the not too distant future. Well, she would at least talk about it.

She would clean up her act and accept the forgiveness

of God as a means to move on. She would make her life work again.

Millions of thoughts and hopes raced through her mind as she sat at the top of the stairs.

Her husband was home. He was having a shower. Things would be back to normal in no time.

She walked back downstairs into the kitchen and opened the blinds at the back of the house, in a bid to grab the last chance of daylight.

Then she flicked on the kettle and opened the fridge, lifted out a bottle of cold white wine and popped the cork, filling two large glasses with the cool, clear liquid to welcome him back. David had always said it was little things like that that he loved to come home to.

She would make his welcome home extra special. Perhaps she would even cook something. Her freezer was full of culinary delights he had gathered up every time he went to the supermarket.

Yes, she would show her husband she was making more of an effort to meet him halfway. She wouldn't give up on her marriage without knowing that she had given it a one-hundred-per-cent chance of survival and that was exactly what she was going to do from now on.

She went to the sink and rinsed out the dishes that had lain there for almost two days now. Pouring a generous blob of washing-up liquid into the sink, she let the bubbles froth and the warm water fill the cups and splash off the cutlery that had long waited for this moment.

From now on, she would revel in the simple things in life. Things that she had let pass her by, that's what

Father Christopher had told her to do. She had become too caught up in chasing rainbows that would never truly satisfy her, and now it was time to address the change in focus and attitude.

She pulled open the blinds above the sink and smiled to herself as she let the warm water soothe away her troubles and ease her conscience clear.

It wasn't until she was drying off her hands that she glanced out the window and her rosy dreams evaporated in an instant.

She held the towel in a tight grip. David's car wasn't there. If David's car wasn't there, then there must be something wrong. Had he had an accident? Was he home only because of car trouble and not because he wanted to start again?

She hurried into the hallway and stopped at the bottom of the stairs.

"David!" she called. "David? Where is the car?"

There was no reply.

In the distance she could still hear the hum of the shower from the bedroom. It was dropping down dark quickly now and she flicked on the hallway lights. Was he there at all? Had she left the shower running all this time herself? No. She wouldn't have.

Besides, now she could hear another muffled sound from upstairs. Voices. The TV? Or did he have his phone on speaker?

She started up the stairs and as she went her steps slowed, her greatest fears storming towards her as the sounds became clearer and clearer.

Voices, yes, but also screams of pleasure and sounds of ecstasy.

"That's so good! Yes. That's how I like it. Yes."

Jessie stopped at the top of the stairs.

"More! Don't stop! Please don't stop!"

"Oh Jesus," said Jessie and her skin turned to ice as she recognised her own voice issuing from the bedroom.

She knew at once what she was listening to. It was a recording of her and her adulterous lover and someone was playing it loudly to let her know that her every move had been secretly recorded for all to see.

She heard footsteps – real footsteps – and then the gasps and cries of ecstasy were cut off, together with the shower sounds. But the footsteps continued, heavy on the wooden floor in her bedroom.

Dizzy, she stumbled down the stairs, into the hallway and towards the door where a large envelope on the hall table caught her terrified eye. There was no address on it, no stamp, just her name in large bold letters in a hand she didn't recognise: **Jessie O'Neill**. And in brackets the word 'slut'.

She grabbed the letter and her handbag, ran outside into the evening mist and jumped into her car. There was a light on in her bedroom now and she wanted to scream with fear. She rummaged in her handbag for her car keys but in her haste she couldn't find them. She tipped the contents of her bag onto the passenger seat. Make-up, receipts, her purse, random pieces of jewellery, a pocket-size perfume – but no car keys. Shit!

She had run outside in such haste that she had forgotten her car keys, her phone and her coat but there was no way she was going back inside now.

She could see his shadow now, walking back and forth in her bedroom. Who was it? Who was in her house? Who was taunting her like this?

Someone wanted her to suffer for her actions and she was so, so frightened.

She stuffed everything back in her bag, including the horrible letter, and jumped out of the car. She glanced left and right, barely recognising her surroundings such was her deep confusion. The street was silent apart from a dog barking in the distance and she heard a door slam shut in a house further down the road. She began to walk swiftly, not looking behind her, and then increased her pace to a light run and eventually into a sprint as the fear mounted and mounted but she had no idea who or where she could run to.

She had always been so aloof with her neighbours, always kept her distance so much that she couldn't just turn up on their doorstep now and air her dirty linen to them on their first encounter.

She turned the corner that led into the main street of the village.

She was caught. Her sordid actions had been recorded and no matter who it was in her bedroom, she knew they were determined to let her know that she had been found out in the most frightening, threatening way.

She paused to catch her breath when she came to the

centre of the village, glancing back in the direction of her home, up on a height just like her parents' house, but at the opposite end of the village boundaries.

What would her family say? How could she ever stop her mother's obsessive fussing over her at every turn if she told her someone was stalking her? There was no way she could divulge the truth to them but the truth was catching up with her so fast it was suffocating her.

There was only one person she could talk to about this. There was only one person who understood her right now. She looked back up at her beautiful home – her home that was now so stained with sin and bad memories – and then she ran for her life in the direction of the only person in the world she trusted.

Jessie lifted the huge brass knocker of the Parochial House's black shiny door and knocked, then waited for Father Christopher to answer. She tapped her feet and knocked on the door again, glancing around her to make sure no one was watching. She knew this was crazy, to land on a priest's doorstep, but he had been genuinely concerned for her earlier. He could see how tortured she was. He had talked her through it before, had given her hope. He'd said, "If there's anything I can do, just ask." Well now, Jessie was asking. She just hoped no one would see her at his door. There was one sure thing about Glencuan – if someone had idle gossip to spread, they would do so in a heartbeat and the sight of a distraught married woman at the priest's door would surely spark rumours among the townsfolk.

"Hello, er, Miss O'Neill, isn't it?"

Oh crap. This was all she needed. Rosie Sheehan.

"Yes . . . em, I need to speak to Father Christopher, please," said Jessie, her voice quivering in fear and impatience. She had no time for small talk with the village gossip who also happened to be the priest's housekeeper.

"Father Christopher?" asked Rosie, her silver head cocked to the side, correcting Jessie for using the priest's first name.

"Erm, I mean Father Lennon. Is he in?"

She composed herself so as not to appear too desperate. The last thing she needed was for Rosie Sheehan to smell a rat.

Rosie stood aside and gestured for Jessie to enter the plush hallway.

It looked different now – almost homely and welcoming in comparison to how cold and vacant it had seemed when she had first entered its doors as a bride-to-be last year, or on her introductory meeting with Father Christopher only a week ago.

"Just take a seat in the drawing-room and I'll give him a shout," said Rosie, opening the door for Jessie to go inside. "I do believe he is getting changed so he may be a moment or two. I don't imagine that he was expecting a visitor at this hour."

At this hour. It was barely past nine for goodness sake!

Jessie did what she was told and waited in the adjacent drawing-room where a small fire was glowing in the hearth, despite the time of year.

As well as feeling different, this house had a completely diverse style to it now that Father Christopher had made his mark. Gone were the gaudy curtains, the green floral woven three-piece and the lacy tablemats on dark furniture that had been there the week before. Instead, there was a new brown leather sofa, a large matching floor cushion and much more pleasant oak coffee tables scattered around the room, all complemented by smart bookcases and soft lighting.

"I'll just be a second, Jessie," Father Christopher called from the hallway and Jessie felt more relaxed already. "Can Rosie get you anything? Tea? Coffee?"

Jessie breathed deeply at the now familiar, soothing sound of his voice.

"I'll just have a glass of water, please," she said, knowing that she could hardly ask for a stiff brandy on this occasion, although that was exactly what she needed.

Rosie shuffled into the drawing-room with a glass and a jug of water on a tray which she laid down on the coffee table in front of Jessie's armchair.

"Thank you," said Jessie.

"Not long now to your sister's big day," said Rosie, holding her veiny hands on her hips. "I hope everything is going to plan?"

"Yes, yes, it is," said Jessie as she poured herself a glass of water.

"Apart from the weather," said Rosie. "You can do nothing about the weather, unfortunately. That's one thing money can't buy."

"No, it can't," said Jessie, recognising the woman's quip. "Unless you jet off to sunnier climates, that is. But yes, all is going to plan."

"Good. All arranged for the service then? Father Lennon has a very different style to Father Jones, you know."

Jessie felt like she was in a quiz show. She wasn't the type to be rude but Rosie's inquisitive way of sucking information from her was getting under her skin.

"I'm sure," she said. "Ah well, you know what it's like, all go in the last few days!" A thought struck her. "I'm in charge of the readings. I just want to see Father Lennon to make sure I've chosen the most suitable ones."

She thought that answer would feed the woman's curiosity, but Rosie wouldn't let it go at that.

"Fussy, is she, your sister? I'd imagine so. It would be nothing but the best for you O'Neill girls."

Jessie clasped her hands tightly and counted to five, an old trick she often practised in the courtroom, and then flashed a smile.

"No, she's not fussy at all in fact," she said, knowing the grin she wore was so exaggerated it was obviously false. "She's very relaxed and very excited too. We all are."

"Good," said Rosie and she glanced around the room and lingered a bit more. "Father really shouldn't be much longer. Like I said, he wasn't expecting visitors so forgive the delay. I'm sure he'll have you sorted with whatever it is you need him for in no time."

At that, Father Christopher burst into the drawing-room, full of smiles and looking totally different from how Jessie had ever seen him before.

He wore a black round-neck T-shirt and matching loose trousers. Still all in black, granted, but without his clerical garb he looked remarkably, well, human. His hair was wet too and he smelled of sandalwood and jasmine when he walked past Jessie to the sofa opposite.

"Miss O'Neill has some changes to discuss with you regarding her sister's readings for the wedding, Father Lennon," said Rosie disapprovingly and she sat protectively on the end of his sofa. "I did say you weren't expecting anyone."

Father Christopher laughed. "Now, Rosie, you know my rules. I never turn any of my parishioners away, day or night!"

Despite his words, Jessie felt her face flush. She looked at Father Christopher and his housekeeper as they sat in unity in front of her and a voice of reality boomed in her head. She felt totally out of place.

Rosie was right. What was she thinking, sitting here at this time of night when her family were just around the corner? Why did she think that a man she had barely known for seven days, priest though he was, could help her with her problems to this degree?

She had taken this too far. She had completely misjudged his kindness. Familiarity breeds contempt and all that. She had to go.

"Look, Father, I'm really sorry for disturbing you. It was just that I was passing through and I thought it would be better to have the readings sorted for Andrea – you know, just another thing less to worry about – but I can call back at another time."

She stood up abruptly but Father Christopher held a hand up and said, "No – you don't have to go. I can sort this for you now, no problem. In fact, Rosie was just leaving before you arrived so I will just see her out."

Rosie's eyes darted from one to the other. "What? Oh, oh . . ." A pinched look of embarrassment swept over her face. "Well, yes, I suppose I'm still not quite used to Father Jones being gone. His ways were so different."

"Now, now, Rosie, don't be like that," said Father Christopher, standing up and waiting for Rosie to move.

Rosie got up. "Well, he was very strict about appointments and he liked to be in bed by nine on week nights. Don't worry, Father. It will just take me a while to adapt to your routines. I'll get there."

Father Christopher smiled back at Jessie as he escorted Rosie out.

"I lit the fire but maybe I shouldn't have," she muttered as they left. "Father Jones loved a fire in the evening, no matter what time of year it was. Let it go out if you want, Father Lennon. Don't mind me . . ."

"No, no, it's lovely. I'm most grateful, Rosie."

Jessie sat down and waited. She heard them say goodbye in the hall, then the front door closed and Father Christopher was back in the room with her.

She gulped, avoiding his gaze. In a way, catching him like this, in his comfortable clothing, freshly showered and looking more like a movie star than a priest was a lot to take in. It was like she had caught him naked.

"So . . ." he said, taking a seat on the sofa again, "tell me, what are the changes you'd like to discuss about the readings?"

Jessie looked up and caught the ironic look on his face.

A smile flitted across her face. "I'm sorry," she said.

"For?"

"Well, I'm sorry for turning up like this and now that I have I feel so silly. God knows what Rosie thinks is going on. I'm sure it looked very strange to her and I know what the people of Glencuan think of me and my sister as it is."

Father Christopher sat forward, his hands clasping his knees. "And how might that be?"

"Spoilt, rich, that we think we're above everyone else. But it's not like that, really it's not."

He sighed and then finally spoke. "Look, Jessie, I know you're going through a very hard time at the moment and I will do anything I can to help you, but you must be careful . . ."

"It's just that I was so scared and I didn't know where else to go."

Jessie picked up her glass of water and gulped some down.

"What are you scared of, Jessie? You have to let go of your guilt. You have to move on. You have great faith. Indulge in your faith and God will forgive you. You will forgive yourself."

"I can't! That's what I'm trying to tell you. Someone is playing with my mind and they won't let me forget! Someone was in my house tonight. In my bedroom. Someone was running my shower to make me think it was David! Someone has . . ." Jessie knew she was shouting but she couldn't stop. She ripped the envelope from her coat pocket and flung it on the table in front of her. "Someone has sent me hate-mail from *inside* my house! How the hell can I move on when this is going on? How can I celebrate my sister's wonderful big day when inside I'm falling to pieces with guilt and these threats? You are the only one who can help me. You are the only one I can talk to. Please."

Father Christopher got up and took the envelope. He held it, staring at it, turning it over and over in his hands.

"Have you read this yet?"

"No. I haven't even opened it. I'm too afraid."

"May I?"

Jessie nodded.

He went to the sideboard, lifted a letter-opener from the drawer and tore the envelope open.

Jessie watched as his eyes scanned the white piece of notepaper that he took from inside the envelope and she felt her breathing gather pace as she saw the look of concern in his face. His hand rose to his chin as he read and then he crumpled the letter into a ball and stuffed it in his pocket.

"Father, why did you do that? Show it to me! What does it say?"

"Jessie," he said, looking into her eyes which were spilling over with fear, "apart from me and all that you've told me, who else knows what has been going on in your life over the past few months?"

She shook her head, her voice shrill and exact. "No one. No one could possibly know. No one at all."

"Are you sure?"

"Yes."

"Think about it, Jessie. Are you one hundred per cent sure that no one knows what you have told me about you and that spineless drop-kick who calls himself a man? Think carefully."

He walked towards the corner cabinet and lifted a bottle of brandy. He poured two large glasses and walked back towards her.

"No," Jessie admitted as she took the glass from the priest's hand. "I suppose I'm not one hundred per cent sure at all. In fact, I have a feeling my brother might know quite a bit more than I want him to."

"Your brother?"

"Yes. My brother. But Ryan wouldn't do this to me? Would he?"

"Ryan for a song! Come on, love!" said Aunt Lily as wedding guests gathered in the formal sitting-room of the O'Neill mansion. Lily was balancing a gin and tonic in one hand and a canapé in the other. "I can't believe how quiet you all are! We need Jessie here to perk this party up a bit."

Tom O'Neill stood up, took centre stage on the huge

chenille rectangular rug that covered almost the entire wooden floor and tapped his glass.

"Here, here!" he said, raising a glass to his visitors. "As always, my sister Lily is absolutely right. This is the most sombre pre-wedding party I have ever been at and I demand that we liven things up right now! Come on!"

The twenty-plus crowd cheered with delight and raised their glasses to some light relief from the suffocating intensity of the room. It was a segregated crowd, with huddles of relatives and friends scattered around the vast interior and only Andrea, Tom and Lily making an effort to blend things together.

"Well said, Dad!" said Andrea, and she draped her arm around her father's waist and gave him a cuddle. "I agree with Aunty Lily. Come on, Ryan. Give us a song!"

Ryan gave his sister a warm smile and raised both hands in surrender.

"Okay, okay. It's time for the brother of the bride to make his pre-wedding speech." The room fell silent. "I just can't believe my big sister is getting married and I have to say I don't like it one bit."

Aunt Lily coughed and Andrea shifted uncomfortably.

"It's not that I despise Cain. I just don't think he is good enough."

Some of the guests tittered, thinking he was making a tasteless joke, but members of the immediate family knew better. Ryan's behaviour of late had been erratic to say the least and when he'd had a few drinks, his loose tongue was more like a loose cannon.

"I think I'll take over right now," said Tom, lifting

the bottle of beer from his son's hand. "I don't think our guests need to hear of any sibling rivalry."

"No, no, Dad! Let me finish!" Ryan addressed the guests again. "When I said I don't *think* Cain isn't good enough for Andrea, I was wrong. You see, I *know* that Cain isn't good enough for her. Full stop."

Andrea was numb. What was he doing? Trying to humiliate her? If this was a comedy attempt, she wasn't getting the joke.

Ryan lifted his guitar and strummed a chord. "You should see all of your faces right now! If you'd just let me finish –"

"Enough is enough!" said Tom sternly.

"If you'd let me finish! What I *mean* is that no one will ever be good enough for Andrea in *my* eyes."

"Aaw," said Aunt Lily and she took a large gulp of her drink. "You've always been incredibly close, you two!"

"Yes, we have," said Ryan and he strummed the guitar again. "That's why I hate to see her go."

Andrea felt her eyes burn and her body relax from the spasm it had gone into when Ryan began his speech. For a second she had feared that he was out to disgrace her, but now she knew he meant well.

"Now you all know how Andrea and I used to pretend we were in a rock band when we were younger?" he went on.

"Ryan!" said Andrea and she playfully slapped his arm. "Don't you dare!"

"Oh, but I have to! Well, everyone thinks that I'm the only musical one in the family. We have so many great memories of singing together as we were growing up, but then Jessie would wave an exam result around and steal our thunder, but that's another story."

Andrea could sense the discomfort in the room. Sharing Ryan's company was like being on a rollercoaster ride this evening.

"Well, Andrea and I used to sing lots of cheesy eighties and nineties music but, among all of our poor choices in music, this was one of the better tunes. It's her favourite."

Ryan lifted his guitar and strummed a few chords as Ella entered the room and sat quietly beside her husband on the arm of his chair. Andrea noticed the memories in her mother's eyes as Ryan sang the opening lines of REM's "Daysleeper".

Andrea felt so uneasy. Where was Jessie? There was something going on but it was all top secret, or so it seemed. Andrea knew that by not telling her they were just trying to protect her from any more annoyance in the last few days before the wedding. Had they told Jessie not to come, because of the tension with Ryan? She had to admit the atmosphere was somewhat easier without her.

Ryan finished the song to rapturous applause and Andrea's heart warmed as the atmosphere heated up and the party mood filled the room.

"Wonderful, Ryan!" said Aunt Lily. "Just wonderful as always."

Andrea really did wish Jessie was with them and that this unexplained tension could be lifted as soon as possible but she wasn't going to raise the subject at the moment. Her wedding dress and the trauma over keeping everything so secret had almost broken her but Bernice, as much as Andrea didn't like her, had made almost an exact replica of her original.

No one could tell the difference. No one would have to know of the intruder in the house who slashed her dress. Aunt Lily had never mentioned it since, Mum and Dad were totally hushed about it and any time she tried to bring it up with Cain he abruptly changed the subject.

But whoever it was who was out to ruin her dreams would never win. No one would torment her into stalling her wedding plans. Oh no. Andrea O'Neill was going to marry Cain Daniels and no one was going to stop her.

"I can't call David from here, Father," said Jessie, her hands now shaking despite the warmth of the brandy. "I've left everything at home. My car keys, my phone, my very sanity. Oh, I hope my office door is locked! Could someone be trying to scare me off the O'Donnell case? You know how a lot of locals are opposed to my involvement?"

Father Christopher paced the floor.

"Jessie, your husband is a policeman. There is a stranger in your house. You have to tell him. Tell him now. Or else call the police at the station. You have to."

Father Christopher felt frustrated. Helping out someone like Jessie with marital problems was one thing, but he didn't want to get involved in the O'Donnell case, especially when it had got to the stage of house break-ins. From what Rosie had told him, it was a messy, long-running feud that was far from over and Jessie was destined to get her fingers burnt, according to many villagers.

"I'm afraid to tell him. I'm afraid to tell his colleagues. What if they found that horrid recording? David would be devastated."

And you're afraid your marriage would be wrecked beyond redemption, thought the priest.

"Could it be an enemy of Jack O'Donnell?" said Jessie.

"No, to be honest, I don't think it is anything to do with O'Donnell. Not from what the note said anyhow, but perhaps, just to be sure, you should rethink your position on that case. Your life and sanity are more important than your job." Father Christopher rubbed his forehead. "But someone knows about your relationship and they care enough about it to have collected their dirty evidence. Look, it's obvious that this is all one big scare tactic which has got out of hand. You have to tell the police and I suggest you start with your husband."

Jessie looked at him with childlike eyes that were full of fear. "And tell him everything? As in *everything*?"

"Yes, Jessie. For your own sake I think you should come clean," said the priest. "Like I said, if there is someone snooping around your house it's dangerous for you to be there on your own. Call your husband and tell him that much at least. Then, if you want, let the rest come out eventually. Because, believe me, it will!"

Father Christopher handed Jessie his landline handset and sat back down on the sofa opposite her.

"But I don't know what to say. Where do I start?"

"Just tell him what happened this evening. Ask him if he was home and then explain that someone has managed to find their way into your house. He's a detective, for crying out loud! If he can't find out what's going on, then no one can."

Jessie lifted the phone and dialled her husband's mobile number. Just as she expected, it rang until it went to voicemail. David never answered calls from numbers he didn't recognise.

She took a long breath and then spoke.

"David, it's me. Look, I really need to talk to you. It's urgent. Something has happened. Please take my calls. David, I'm frightened and I'm sorry. I'm not at home but I'll call you again later."

She quickly hung up and let the phone fall on her lap.

"He is angry and bitter. Imagine how he'll feel when he finds out the truth. Oh, what am I going to do, Father? Where am I going to go?"

She could see Father Christopher weigh up different options in his head and he rubbed his temples. To think that this time last week she barely knew this man, this stranger in town, and now here she was having spilled her heart out to him and totally depending on him to get her out of her sorry mess.

"Don't you have a friend you can trust with all of this? Someone not connected to your family or to David?"

Jessie shook her head. "My best friend Maria is on holiday until Sunday. And I wouldn't trust any of my work colleagues nor would I know them well enough to land on their doorstep with all of this baggage. I'll have to go back to my mum's, I suppose. Put on a brave face. Again."

The priest sank the remainder of his brandy. "I'm not sure about that, Jessie."

"But I don't have a choice, do I?"

"You're in no fit state to keep this all to yourself. How could you possibly hide this anguish and fear from them when it's so fresh in your head? Someone has been watching you. Someone is following you. Are you going to tell your parents at least that?"

"No. No way. It would push my mum over the edge and I can just imagine Andrea's reaction. I'd really be accused of stealing her limelight then, wouldn't I? Gosh, if she ever found out the whole story . . ."

"Yes, I can see that, with the wedding the day after tomorrow, you don't want to raise any alarms. It wouldn't be fair on Andrea, would it? Like you said, you don't want to take away the attention from her."

Jessie bit her lip and felt her eyes well up again. This was a total nightmare. She thought for a moment.

"Or I could stay here?" she said, her dark eyes pleading with her only friend in the world at the moment. "I'll stay out of your way. I'll leave at first light."

"No, Jessie." He shook his head ruefully.

"Please."

111

"I'm sorry, you can't. And where would you go tomorrow night and the next? Someone would find out and then your problems would be doubled. As would mine."

"Well, then, what else do you suggest?" said Jessie. "Maybe I should just go home and face up to the maniac who broke into my house and walked around my bedroom and did God knows what else earlier? What the hell am I supposed to do!? Tell me and I'll do it!!"

Jessie's breathing increased rapidly and she broke down into uncontrollable sobbing on Father Christopher's new sofa.

He got up and handed her a tissue and she wiped her face, staring at the floor as the tears refused to stop flowing. She was so frightened and so confused. Who could she turn to if he turned his back on her now? She couldn't go home to her parents and ruin Andrea's pre-wedding celebrations. She knew that by staying away she was hurting her family so much but if they knew the truth it would be ten times worse and, he was right, she couldn't trust her current state of mind to keep it to herself any longer.

The guilt was eating her insides like a cancer. Every moment of every day it had haunted her since it began two months before and now it was all well and truly coming to a head. She needed someone to guide her, to tell her what to do. In the space of a few days she had lost her husband, she was on the brink of losing her family if the truth came out and now she feared she was on the verge of losing her mind.

"Okay, okay," said Father Christopher. "You can stay here. But on one – no – actually, two conditions."

"What are they? I'll do anything for you to help me. I'll stay out of your way. It's just for one night."

"Just listen to me, Jessie. First of all, you need to phone your mother and let her know you're safe. And secondly, promise me that you'll never tell a soul you stayed here. My career as a priest would be in ruins if this got out. And your reputation would be in tatters."

"Okay," said Jessie. "Okay, I promise. I'll never tell a soul. Thank you so much, Father. Oh, thank you so, so much!"

Ella was so tempted to slip off to bed. Her eyes were heavy and sore and she really needed to lie down.

It was well after eleven now and the revellers in the sitting-room didn't seem to want to go home. The drinks were flowing and Ryan was in full entertainment mode with his guitar but she was exhausted after the entire day's activity and her acting skills had been tested to the limit over the past few days.

"Tired, love?" asked Tom when he followed her into the kitchen.

She had curled herself up into a ball by the Aga, a warm mug of cocoa in her hand and her shoes kicked off beneath her. She was past caring about being rude and anyhow, no one would even have noticed she had popped out for a moment.

"I'm knackered, Tom," she said, lifting her cheek to receive his kiss. "It's been a long day and I'm terribly worried about Jessie. I really did think she'd be in touch by now."

"Oh, Ella, don't fret, pet. You know she and David have obviously hit a bit of a rough patch and I'm sure the last thing she wants to do is put on a jolly face in front of everyone as they whoop and cheer about the joys of married life when her own is a bit off at the moment."

Ella sat up straight. "Oh, so I have to put on the jolly face for her then, is that it? I'm feeling the pressure too, you know!"

Tom paused. Was his wife actually resisting doing something for her precious daughter? There was a first time for everything.

"Ssh," he said, pulling over a chair. "You know, you have always held that girl of ours in such high regard, Ella, but guess what? She's as human as the rest of us. She's not Superwoman, she's not invincible, she has flaws and weaknesses just the same as you or me or Andrea or Ryan. You have to take the rough with the smooth sometimes, and Lord knows Jessie hasn't given us too many rough moments in comparison to her siblings, has she?"

Ella sipped her cocoa and shook her head. "No, she hasn't. I think that's why her behaviour is rattling me so much, Tom. I've never seen her like this before. You have to admit it, Jessie has always been so selfless, so quick to help others in need and now, when she needs someone she closes us all out. She said she wants to be left alone. That's just not my Jessie."

Ella looked around the kitchen, anxious that none of her guests should come in and hear her spilling out all her inner worries.

"Be strong for her, Ella. That's all you can do. We all have to be strong for Jessie as she rides out this storm with David. It's probably nothing serious, just a bit of a blip now that the honeymoon period is over."

"You think?"

"Wait and see. He's due back tomorrow and by Saturday they'll be all smiles in their finery at the wedding."

Ella relaxed once more. "Gosh, I really hope you're right."

"I bet I am." Tom took her dainty hand into his and looked her in the eye. "But in the meantime, we also have two other children to be strong for too, okay? Andrea is as high as a kite over this wedding, and Ryan, well, he needs a good toe up the behind from time to time but we'll get him sorted out once this is all over. And he's in his element in there, strumming along to the dulcet tones of his drunken aunts and uncles."

Ella managed a giggle. Her son really could be a tearaway at times, but he could be so much fun, especially at family occasions. 'Ryan for a song' was a famous request in their family and it always reminded her of the good times. Then the awful vision she had of him ruining his sister's dress flashed into her mind again and she lost control once more.

She felt her head go into a spin again. Her hands began to shake in a mixture of temper and frustration.

"There's something going on, Tom. You can pussy-foot around this all you want but I know there's something not right."

"Keep your voice down, Ella. Please!"

"No, I won't keep my voice down! I have had enough of this. Someone had better tell me what is going on before I shout it from the rooftops. First Jessie's behaviour and disappearing acts, then Ryan's weird accusing looks at her and then Andrea's dress torn to ribbons! What is it? Who is out to ruin our family?"

Tom put his arms around his wife's heaving shoulders and hushed her, constantly watching the door as he did so. He didn't mind dealing with any problem thrown in his direction, but he had one rule – private matters should be kept private and that's the way they would be.

"Don't worry. Please don't worry, Ella. I am taking care of everything. You've had a lot to deal with over the past few days but it's all under control now. You know the doctor said you can't let yourself get worked up over things like this. It's not good for you."

He led his wife out into the hallway and up the staircase, then into her bedroom.

"But I'm so afraid, Tom. I'm so worried about this wedding. Something doesn't feel right. Someone –"

"No one is going to hurt you nor will they hurt my children. I am totally sure of that. Now get some sleep and I promise that tomorrow everything will be all right. I promise."

Chapter 9

"So, go on. What did she say?"

Father Christopher was waiting on Jessie when she finished her phone call to her parents' house.

She felt embarrassed now and slightly uncomfortable, knowing that she was truly overstepping the mark by asking to stay at the Parochial House but she really didn't have too many other options.

She felt that she had found a friend in Father Christopher. Being a solicitor on the O'Donnell case had shut her off from so many people and it frightened her now to think that in an hour of need like this, she had very few to turn to.

"My dad answered," she said. "There's a full party going on in the background so I just asked how everyone was and I told him that I'd be there in the morning. I said I felt a bit sick. He didn't say much but I just know Mum is in full worry mode at this stage."

"But I bet you feel better already for having spoken to him?"

Jessie sat down on the sofa and flicked through a religious magazine that lay in front of her, not seeing the words or pictures as she turned the pages. "I do." She put the magazine back. "I really do. Look, Father, I can't tell you how much I appreciate this. I know I'm putting you under great pressure and you hardly know me at all, but –"

"I do know you. And for some unknown reason I trust you not to tell of this. I know you are desperate and you need a friend right now. I really wouldn't have let you stay unless I trusted you wholeheartedly."

Jessie was startled at this. She looked across to where he sat, and she thought again of how out of place he looked in this grand house, despite the modern touch-up he had attempted with his redecoration.

He was so young – well under forty – and so handsome that sometimes she found herself staring at him, taking in his skin-tone, his black hair that ruffled into a staggered line on his forehead, and the breathtaking smile that he wore every time he greeted her. He had been blessed with features that any woman would have swooned over and during the past few days Jessie wondered if this was part of the reason she had been able to confide so much in him. Would she have been able to tell old Father Jones her troubles?

No, she told herself. Father Jones was an elderly man with staunch traditional views. She trusted Father Christopher and felt a connection with him because he was nearer her age and more open in his views.

"You have a lot of respect in this town," said Jessie, in a tone of soft reassurance. "I won't deny that your arrival shook us all up a little but you seem to have settled in well."

He smiled. "Really? So who or what were you all expecting then? An ancient, flaking old cleric? Or a whiskey-guzzling Father Jack type?"

"Yes," laughed Jessie. "A bit of both maybe. Someone like that would have been more expected than someone like you."

They looked at each other in silence and Jessie scrambled for words.

"Can I ask you something?" she said.

"Of course. Ask away."

"Why did you decide to become a priest, Father? I mean, it's hardly in the top ten career choices for young men from Cork, or young men from anywhere for that matter nowadays, is it?"

He stood up walked to the drinks cabinet where he poured himself another drink. He didn't answer and again Jessie felt the silence uncomfortable.

"Oh, I'm sorry," she said. "I didn't mean to get so personal. Really, you don't have to answer that. I shouldn't have asked."

"No, that's okay," he said. "I don't mind. Believe me, I've been asked much worse. It's a long story."

"Well, I'm not going anywhere," said Jessie.

It was after midnight when the party began to settle and Andrea stifled a yawn.

"Thanks so much, Ry, for all your help tonight. I really appreciate how enthused you are about my wedding."

"My pleasure," he said. He laid his guitar carefully in its carry-case and clasped it at the sides.

He could be such a good brother, thought Andrea and she leaned across and kissed his hair.

He took her hand and gave it a squeeze. "I know how much this means to you, Andrea."

Andrea waited for the 'but'. She knew it was coming.

"Go on, out with it! You think I'm rushing things too, don't you?"

Ryan leaned the guitar-case against the sofa and sat down beside it while Andrea lifted glasses and empty bottles at speed. She was so fed up with her family's last-minute 'what-ifs' about her goddamn wedding. Why couldn't they all just be happy for her? Her mum was fretting about Jessie, her dad was putting up a front and Jessie and Ryan were at loggerheads. It just wasn't fair and she felt like throwing a childish strop with all of them.

"I just want you to be happy, that's all . . ."

"But I am happy!" she said.

"I don't think you are. How do you know that Cain is the one for you when you've only known him five minutes? I just – I'm just not sure – that you know what you're getting into. This is for life, Andrea.

"Don't you dare throw up my first engagement! I swear, if you do . . ."

Ryan held his arms out in defence. "I have no

120

intention of bringing that up. It's just that you're so rash sometimes. As much as I adore you, I'm worried that you hardly even know this man. We hardly –"

Andrea's blood was pumping now. "I love Cain! Why can't you all see that?" she shouted over him. "I am so happy with him. He makes me happy. What more can I say? How can I prove it to you all?"

Ryan was jolted but determined to persist. Andrea was well known for her ability to whip anyone's butt in an argument by simply raising her voice louder than anyone else and getting into such a state that the other person eventually couldn't listen to any more, but he had a point to make and he was going to do so.

"How?" he asked. "How does he make you happy?"

"Oh my God, who are you? Jerry fuckin' Springer? What do you want me to do? Give a detailed analysis of every way my fiancé pleases me? No way!"

Ryan stood and joined in with the clear-up. Somehow, he felt he could talk to his sister in a more reasonable way if he met her eye to eye, not that it was possible with the way she was scurrying around the huge sitting-room in bad temper.

"No, I don't want every single detail, thank you! I'm just wondering if you know enough about him, that's all. It seems like he was barely around five minutes and next of all you're sporting this huge rock on your finger and all you can talk about is your wedding. Excuse me if I find this all a bit mental!"

"Well, excuse me for getting excited about the biggest day of my life!" said Andrea, plumping cushions with such force she feared she might puncture one. "I think you are all jealous, that's all."

"What? Jealous of what? Jealous of *you*? Christ, you sound like Jessie!"

"Jealous of Cain and me! You and Jessie are jealous that my future husband is so fantastic and successful and jealous of the wonderful lifestyle I have ahead of me with him!"

Ryan grunted. "You think you have?"

"No, I *know* I have. You are so jealous because you can't seem to find yourself a girl who will put up with your big butch biker friends or your nerdy movie-geek mates!" Andrea was on a roll. "I mean, what or who are you to criticise me for any decisions I make in my life? You don't even know what you want to be when you grow up and you're only two years younger than me!"

Ryan could feel his temper pump through his veins. He didn't want to lose it with his sister but she was pushing him. He could say so much that would bomb all of her hopes and dreams but he had promised himself he wouldn't – but, boy, was she pushing all the right buttons!

"You're just like Jessie underneath it all, aren't you?" he said. He was right in Andrea's face now, and his temper was broken so far that he couldn't hold himself back, spitting saliva as he spoke every word. "Trying so hard to please Mummy and Daddy in everything you do!"

"No, I don't!"

"Oh, you do, Andrea! You're so desperate to be

exactly like Little Miss Perfect that you've rushed Cain 'Radio Man' Daniels into taking you up the aisle because you are shit scared that if you don't, in no time he'll move on to someone just that bit brighter, just that bit more beautiful, just that bit more successful than you!"

"Like who?" yelled Andrea. "Like *who*?"

"Like your fucking big sister! That's who!"

Ryan had said too much and he knew it. Too much for now, that was. He lifted his guitar-case and ran up the stairs, slamming his bedroom door so hard that he woke everyone in the house but Andrea didn't notice.

She sat alone, clutching a handful of empty champagne glasses in the middle of the living-room, praying that Ryan had had one too many and that he would take every one of his words back in the morning.

Yes. It would be all right. He would take it all back and everything would be all right in the morning.

Jessie and Father Christopher sat in the kitchen now, still talking over coffee despite the fact that it was almost two o'clock in the morning.

Jessie had listened to his every word and he hers. Every phrase he uttered, she asked him for more. Every scenario she spoke of, he dug deeper and deeper.

She could feel his eyes burn into her as she told him of growing up in such a privileged, wholesome background and of how it sometimes made her yearn to break free and rebel, but that it was never truly her style.

"I tend to leave that sort of reaction to Andrea and Ryan," she said, realising, of course, that her actions of late were as against the rules as everything her brother and sister had done in their lifetime. "I just contradicted myself there, big time, didn't I?"

But Father Christopher shook his head. "You made a mistake, Jessie. You were caught up in a moment and you saw him in a different light. You were vulnerable to him and you were weak, but you know that now."

For the past two hours she had almost forgotten her terrible sin, talking about her happy childhood and her fond memories of holidays abroad, of caravanning in Donegal, of exotic school trips and of all the wonderful family occasions her parents made sure were celebrated with such love for their children.

"Yes, but I have never done anything like that in my life, Father. I've never been unfaithful in any relationship I've ever had. I've never even as much as looked at another man and then he came along and I couldn't control myself. It was like I was a different person. I feel so dirty. I feel so sick . . ."

He sighed. "And where is he now, eh? Do you think he ran to the nearest priest he could find, begging for forgiveness and wanting to be absolved for his sin? Or is he happy to put it down as a bit of a bumpy patch in an otherwise very smooth relationship that just lost its way temporarily?"

Jessie shrugged and gripped her hands together. "Well, it's obvious he isn't as cut up about it as I am. In fact it's probably something he's proud of, but then, maybe that's a male thing. Just another trophy, just another box ticked, another notch on his bedpost. Typical man."

Father Christopher raised an eyebrow. "We're not all lust-filled, amoral animals, you know," he said, sitting back in his chair.

He looked genuinely hurt and Jessie couldn't help but giggle.

"I didn't mean you, silly!" she said. "How on earth could I have been talking about you? You're a priest! You're practically a saint!"

"So because I'm a priest, I'm not a man, then?"

"No, I didn't say that," said Jessie. "No, Father, that's not what I meant. It was supposed to be a compliment, of sorts. Please don't be offended."

Father Christopher dropped his head in hands and ran his fingers through his black hair. He stayed like that for a few moments and Jessie reached across and touched his arm.

"Father, you are one of the finest men I've ever met. My God, I'm sure every woman who comes your way thinks the same."

He gently moved away from her touch.

"What I was trying to say was that I would never put you in the same league as Cain Daniels with all his glitzy charm and empty promises. He fooled me, Father. He lured me into a situation that I never, ever want to experience again. He has almost ruined my life and now I have to watch him walk up the aisle on Saturday and pledge his undying love for my sister. It will kill me to sit there and say nothing but it's what I have to do. It's what I have to do. It's like somewhere inside of me I'm holding on to this hope that Cain will tell me it was all a silly mistake and that he completely loves Andrea. That it was all just a lust-filled first encounter when we were on holiday that happened a second time when it shouldn't and that it will never, ever happen again."

Father Christopher yawned, covering it with his hand. He wasn't used to such late nights and he was already thinking of all he had to do the next day – morning Mass, attend the sick, visit the local primary school. He was relaxed in Jessie's company but he had a job to do.

"Jessie, listen to me. You have to choose what is right for your sister and what is right for you. If telling her now is out of the question, then you have to make a decision not to tell her ever."

"I know. But if I don't tell her now and he does it to her again, with someone else, then I've deceived her even more. My feelings don't come into it. I have sinned against my husband and against my sister. I don't matter any more."

"I think you're an incredibly brave woman, Jessie. And I'm glad you trust me enough to tell me your troubles. I just hope I can help you through these difficult times."

"I'm very lucky to have found you," she said. "You're a great friend and I would never get through this without you."

"You can rely on me, Jessie," he said softly.

Seeing he was looking very tired, Jessie got up, tidied away their glasses and wiped around the kitchen.

Father Christopher gave a more deliberate yawn this

time. "Well, now that the mutual appreciation society meeting is over, I'd better call it a night," he said, getting up, and Jessie laughed.

"I really enjoyed the company," she said.

"Me too. Goodnight, Jessie." He walked to the door and stopped. "Jessie, I'm sorry to mention it again but . . . please don't let anyone know you've been here. I would get into so much trouble. And so would you."

"Of course, I won't," she said without turning around from the sink.

He nodded, then slipped off upstairs.

Chapter 10

Friday . . .

Andrea's phone bleeped for the third time that morning from the side of her bed. She reached out and checked her messages which she knew in advance would all be from her fiancé.

"Hope you slept well, Miss O'Neill! Tomorrow you change your name! Love you!"

She flicked on the radio and closed her eyes as she listened to her husband-to-be on his morning programme.

"Yes, your good wishes are just flooding in this morning here at North FM and I have to say a really big thank-you to all of you very kind listeners who have sent cards and gifts to the station for my beautiful fiancée and me."

Andrea warmed on hearing his velvet tones but then her mood sagged when she remembered the events of the night before. She lifted the duvet over her head so that the sound of the radio was muffled.

"Andrea and I are so excited about tomorrow," said Cain in his perfected radio accent, "and hey, it's my last day on here for a whole month as we jet off on Sunday to Fiji for a long and well-deserved honeymoon. I'll be thinking of you all! It may be raining outside but here's a nice sunny tune to get you all in a summertime mood . . ."

Cain's voice trailed off to make way for an upbeat summer anthem and Andrea lifted the covers back as the memories of her row with Ryan came back to her bit by bit.

She'd had two, no, three generous glasses of wine last night and her head was throbbing now. Ryan had had quite a few too, so she really shouldn't be too concerned, should she? After all, she was well known to be much more highly strung when she'd had a few and Cain often warned her how she shouldn't take things that people say so personally after a glass or two of wine.

Nonetheless, Ryan's comments had cut her to the core. Was he really insinuating that Cain had his eye on her older sister? Her older married sister whose wedding had been only the year before? No, that was absolutely ridiculous and Andrea would just put it to the very back of her mind.

It would explain Jessie's weird behaviour of late, though. She sat up in her bed and fiddled with the duvet cover, a comforting habit she had developed as a child and one which she often reverted to when she was tired or worried or just thinking about something in her own little dream world.

She thought of Jessie and Cain and of when they were last in the same company. It was ages ago, perhaps the week after they came back from holidaying together. There was nothing between them at all. She would have picked up on it so easily. Jessie wouldn't do that to her. Neither would Cain.

But Jessie had really let her down this week. They had talked about spending so much time together as they prepared for the wedding, but there had been no girly days out, no long lunches when they chatted furiously about the future and what it might hold. No pamper days or afternoons at the spa in Donegal like they had dreamed of when Andrea first announced her engagement.

Yet Andrea had done it all for Jessie the year before. They'd driven to the coast one day and sat in the car on Portstewart beach eating ice cream and toasting Jessie's future as the wife of the very handsome Detective Inspector David Russell. They'd booked an all-day seaweed treatment at the new spa in Enniskillen and they'd laughed and laughed when they remembered little incidents from their childhood days when they would dress up as brides and use their mother's best jewellery as their engagement rings.

Andrea had wanted it to be so special for her sister and it had been so. But now, here she was one year on, pondering her own wedding day as the rain pelted down outside and her brother taunted her into wondering whether she was doing the right thing.

The most hurtful thing of all was that her sister, her

precious only sister whom she had idolised all her life, had totally abandoned her.

Perhaps she could call her and say so. Just have it out and express her disappointment at her behaviour and her strangely selfish ways. She lifted her phone and pressed on Jessie's number. Yes, she would tell her once and for all how she was sick of her always hogging the limelight, ever since they were children on every damned occasion.

Fucking voicemail! That was another new habit her sister had. She never answered her calls any more. What the hell was she up to?

Andrea flung herself back onto her pillows and stared at the ceiling. It was one day before her wedding. One day. She should be on top of the world right now but instead all she could do was think about her bloody sister and long for her to turn up and be happy for her.

For just once she wanted to be the belle of the ball.

Yes, Jessie and David were having trouble so early in their marriage and it frightened Andrea. How can you know someone inside out like that and pledge to love them forever and then have doubts so soon? Perhaps she was incredibly naïve. Perhaps she believed in people too easily. Her mother always said so.

She shuddered when she recalled her disastrous first engagement to Dan Edwards from the other side of Glencuan. His family were a bunch of lazy layabouts who thought they had won the lottery when Dan arrived home with Andrea sporting an engagement ring. It wasn't until three months later that Andrea finally realised that Dan, with his long greasy hair and ill-fitting clothes, had as much in common with her as he had with his pet pig. She had dumped him on the spot and run back into the safe arms of her parents who as always had picked up the pieces and never mentioned his name again.

Now she was just one day away from marrying Cain Daniels and it was a match made in heaven – even her father had said so. Cain was a true romantic – a ladies' man, yes, but Andrea knew that behind his charm and flirtatious ways, he only had eyes for her.

Look how he had pulled out all the stops to have the dress of her dreams restyled in record time. Listen to all the loving requests and messages he was reading out for her on his live radio show. See how jealous all of her circle were when they saw her on his arm.

To hell with her family and their doubting ways! To hell with her selfish older sister and her weirdo brother who couldn't have the grace to be happy for her. To hell with whoever had ruined her dress and tried to shatter her wedding plans!

Andrea O'Neill had found the man of her dreams in Cain Daniels and she couldn't wait to be his wife.

Jessie's eyes opened before her brain clicked into gear and she gasped for air, not knowing where she was for a minute.

The room was incredibly old-fashioned with its high bed and spring mattress and shiny mahogany wardrobes with brass locks that had keys fitted in them. The curtains were floral and the walls were magnolia and on the table opposite her was a huge statue of St Martin that was giving her the creeps.

She sat up on the bed and tried to avoid the long gaze of the statue ahead of her. The black face of St Martin was looking at her accusingly, like she had no place in this house.

Father Christopher had given her a T-shirt to wear in bed and she felt guilty undressing in front of so many holy pictures and rosary beads and, only for the few glasses of brandy she had taken, she knew she wouldn't have slept at all.

A light knock came to the door and she paused, holding her dress from the day before across her chest.

"Father?" she said.

"Just checking you're awake, Jess," he said from the other side of the door. "I'm just back from Mass – you were sound asleep before I left."

Jessie gasped and looked around the room for a clock. "What time is it?"

"It's just gone nine thirty."

She stuffed her arms into her dress and pulled it over her head. She had so much to do! She had to get home and get organised for the wedding. But how?

"Father?" she called again and this time he opened the door.

He covered his eyes playfully with his hands. "Can I look?"

She pointed to St Martin and the holy pictures. "Well, all the rest of them in the room have had a good look, so you may as well," she laughed. "I'm kidding. It's okay, I'm fully clothed."

He stood awkwardly on the threshold of the door, then stepped in and leaned against the wall.

"You really could get me into a lot of trouble, Jessie."

"I'm already in enough trouble, don't you think?" she said, squashing her feet into her shoes. "Has it stopped raining?"

"Afraid not," he said.

"Good. Then less people will see me. I'll slip out the back way, down by the gate lodge and through the churchyard." She looked at him and then away again. "I'm really grateful for all of this, Father. I don't know what I would have done without you." She dropped her head.

"Chin up, Jessie! Come on. You have a lot to do today, remember? Contacting your husband might be top of your list?"

Jessie pursed her lips and then stared out the window. "You know, Father. I'm not sure about that. I'm not so sure it is top of my list."

"What? Why do you say that? I thought you wanted David back? To start again? You said you'd made a mistake. Have you changed your mind? Do you love Cain Daniels? Is that it?"

Jessie inhaled deeply and fixed her bracelet onto her wrist.

"No, of course not! I can barely look at him. All he stands for repulses me to the core but, like I said, I'd be willing to overcome it all if I thought he truly did love my sister and that he would change his ways. But do I love David? That's the most frightening thing of all, Father. I'm not sure if I want David back. I'm not sure of anything any more."

Chapter 11

It was later that morning when Father Christopher made his way in through the doors of the O'Neill home for the first time and he gasped at its splendour. No matter how much he had heard about this magnificent home, it couldn't have prepared him for the luxury and extravagance it displayed.

A huge central oak staircase dominated the hallway and the pale gold wallpaper oozed wealth and grandeur. Family photos were tastefully placed on a side table and on the main wall. He stopped to take them in. There was one of Andrea as a teenager striking a model-like pose, a more recent, professional black and white one of Andrea with Cain on their engagement, a sultry-looking Ryan on his first motorbike, Jessie on her wedding day and another with her entire family, Jessie's graduation from law school, her high school formal in a black velvet dress . . . in fact, he couldn't help but notice that the photos of the truly stunning Jessie outnumbered the others at least two to one.

Now he could really sense her fear of letting her family down. She really was the apple of their eye.

"Do you come from a big family, Father?"

Andrea O'Neill was smaller than her sister, not as fine-featured but striking nonetheless. He told himself not to fall into the trap of comparing the two. He sensed there was enough of that already.

"Er, no," he said, looking just a little flustered. "Just me and my mum."

"Cork?" she smiled at him.

"Yeah, Cork," he said, rubbing his hands and Andrea wondered why on earth such a handsome young man was so nervous.

"Come in and have a drink," she said and she led him into the kitchen. A few last-minute guests had arrived but somehow she sensed their frivolous festivities in the sitting-room would make him even more uncomfortable.

She watched as he took in every detail of his surroundings. Of the tasteful décor, of the warmth and love that oozed out of every crevice in the house. There was a sadness in his eyes as he absorbed it all.

"You are a very privileged family," he said with a sigh that took her aback.

"Privileged?" said Andrea, bemused. "Yes, I suppose we are. I'm sure you've seen all sorts of homes in your career. Some perhaps who are not as happy or lucky as we are?"

He'd been given a lifeline and he grabbed it. "Yes.

That's exactly it. Lucky. There are some families who have it very hard indeed. Very hard."

Andrea waited for him to speak again but he didn't. He just lifted a photo of Jessie and David from the table, stared at it for a few seconds and then set it back in its place.

"So," said Andrea, feeling ever so slightly nervous as the hours ticked past to her wedding day. "Why don't you come inside and meet the rest of the family. I believe you've already had the pleasure of my father's company on more than one occasion?"

He followed Andrea down the long hallway that led to the family kitchen. A strong smell of home baking filled the air and the sound of laughter overflowed down the corridor.

"Indeed I have. At a few committee meetings here and there. I like to meet some of the main movers and shakers in my parish when I start in a new area and your father's name was first on everyone's lips. He's done very well for himself."

Andrea glowed with pride as she walked towards the kitchen door. "Yes, he has done very well for us all. Like you said, we are a very, very lucky family."

Tom O'Neill almost jumped from his seat when he saw Father Christopher enter the room. He extended his hand as he approached from the far side of the kitchen and shook the young priest's firmly with a friendly pat on the back.

"We're delighted to have you in our home, Father. You're very welcome. Here, have a seat."

"Thanks for the hearty welcome, Tom, but it's literally a flying visit. I am just popping in on my way past so I won't be staying."

Andrea pulled out a chair from the kitchen table and watched as her Aunt Lily and her mother exchanged playful winks at each other in admiration of the very handsome priest.

"Introductions aside now, Father," said Tom after giving a brief rundown of who was who, "can you do anything about this terrible weather we're having?"

He let out a guffaw and Andrea rolled her eyes.

"He's a priest, Daddy. Not a flaming magician!"

Father Christopher looked slightly uncomfortable with all the attention and he shifted in his seat.

"I'm so delighted you're marrying us, Father," said Andrea. "No harm to old Father Jones but he did ramble on a bit. I'm sure your marriage ceremonies are much more pleasant than his!"

Now it was Ella's time to interrupt. "What Andrea means, Father, is that it's wonderful to have a lovely young man like you in our parish. You really have caused quite a stir around here." Ella almost bit her tongue when she said it. The young priest's arrival had sent her into quite a fluster.

"Ah, and here he is, the Prodigal Son!" said Tom as Ryan burst through the back door, his leather jacket thrown over his shoulder and a shiny black helmet in his hand. "Ryan, come and meet Father Christopher."

"Hi," said Ryan and he nodded in the priest's direction. "Mum, have you seen my bike polish? I just bought a new can but it's not in the garage."

Tom was aggrieved by his son's poor manners but he was determined not to let it show. "He's a very busy young man, our Ryan," he said and Aunt Lily gave out one of her trademark laughs.

"Yes, he sure is," she said hastily when she belatedly realised what Tom was trying to do.

"So, that's all of you then," said the priest and they all nodded and looked at each other with pride. "I was just remarking to Andrea how lucky you are to have such a precious, loving family."

"Jessie!" said Ella suddenly. "How silly of us! You haven't met Jessie yet!"

"Actually, I . . ."

"Andrea, go get your sister," said Tom. "She's in the sitting-room entertaining some of her cousins with a game of Scrabble. She's a wonderful girl, Father. We're very proud of her. We're very proud of all of them."

Father Christopher tried to speak again but he didn't need to as Jessie walked into the kitchen before Andrea had a chance to move from her seat.

"Mum, we need to – oh, hello Father," she said, fixing her hair behind her ear, and she blushed noticeably.

"This is Father Christopher Lennon," said Tom, his eyes bright with pride. "Father, this is our eldest girl, Jessie."

"We . . . em . . ." He didn't know how to react as he felt all eyes on him. It almost seemed that with Jessie they felt they had saved the best to last.

"Lovely to meet you, Father," said Jessie and she extended her hand.

"And you too," he said and glanced around to see that everyone, as he expected, was still staring.

"Jessie's a solicitor," said Aunt Lily. "She's destined for very high places – isn't that right, Jess?"

Jessie gave a coy smile.

"So, what time is David due home, Jessie?" said Ryan as he breezed back through the kitchen, his can of bike polish in his hand. "You did say he was due back today, didn't you?"

The family's stares veered in Jessie's direction and she felt her face flush.

"Er, not until later. Tonight, in fact. It will be late but he'll be home in time for the wedding and that's the most important thing."

"Excellent," said Ryan and he marched out through the back door with a laugh. "I can't wait to see him."

Ella carried a pot of tea to the table and Jessie helped her with cups and saucers, her hands shaking all the time, while Andrea laid out a feast of cakes and buns that made everyone's mouth water.

"I hope this isn't all for my benefit," said Father Christopher, feeling the pinch in the atmosphere. "I need to watch the old calories, you know." He accepted a cup from Ella with gratitude.

"Or maybe it's for my benefit?" said Cain Daniels and Andrea jumped from her seat to greet her fiancé at the kitchen door. "Sorry, I did knock but no one heard," he said, his flashy grin almost lighting up the room. He kissed Andrea's cheek and then, like a true expert communicator, focused directly on who he perceived to be the most influential person in the room. "And you must be Father Lennon?"

Father Christopher stood up and greeted Cain Daniels with a wary handshake. "And you're the, er, nervous groom-to-be, I assume?"

"It's Cain – Cain Daniels," he said, flitting back into his polished radio voice. "It's good to finally meet you, Father, and no, I'm not a bit nervous at all. Why would I be nervous when I'm marrying the most beautiful girl in Ireland?" He cuddled Andrea close by his side and gave her another kiss on the forehead. She wrapped her arms around his waist and gazed up at him.

"Thank you, honey," she said. "You always say the nicest things. Come and sit down. I'm sure Aunt Lily won't bite."

"You never know!" said Aunt Lily when Cain followed Andrea over to the corner of the room where she was sitting on the two-seater sofa. Cain playfully snuggled up beside her much to her mock delight and Andrea perched on the arm of the sofa.

"Oh, if only the rain would go away," sighed Andrea. "What on earth will we do if our wedding day is as horrible as today?"

"Believe me, babe, if there was anything to be done about the weather, I'd do it for you," said Cain and he placed his hand on Andrea's thigh but his eyes followed Jessie who had diverted to the sink and was washing dishes that had just been taken from the dishwasher only moments before.

"So are we still all set for a rehearsal at the church at three?" said Father Christopher.

Andrea's face lit up. "Yes, of course. We'll probably arrive just before that to get a feel for the place, won't we, Jess?"

Jessie spun round from the sink at the sound of her name. "Huh?"

"I said we'll be there before three? For the rehearsal?"

"Oh, yes. Of course," said Jessie. "We'll be there well on time."

"I can pick you up at your house," said Cain. "And then we can get Andrea here on the way to church? The rest of the gang are meeting us there."

"No, it's okay," said Jessie abruptly. "I can drive myself."

She caught Father Christopher's eye and could sense his discomfort. Having Cain and Andrea in the same room was highly stressful.

"In fact, Dad," she added, "you could come in my car too."

Tom nodded. "That's fine, Jessie. That's what we'll do." He turned to Cain. "And the best man and company, they're coming from Belfast?"

"Yes," said Cain. "They'll be there for three. It's all organised. It shouldn't take long though?"

"No," said Father Christopher. "I won't keep you more than half an hour. Now, let's pray the weather picks up a little. This storm is bound to subside for tomorrow."

Cain Daniels' very presence was getting under his skin. Jessie was right. He oozed confidence and charm but there was something false about him that the priest sensed the moment he walked into the room. Be careful not to judge, he reminded himself.

"Let's hope it settles soon," said Tom. "The Farmers' Forecast said to expect some light drizzle, but then who knows? Anyhow, we won't let it dampen our spirits, will we?"

"No, we won't," said Andrea.

"Well, I really just wanted to call and wish you the best of luck," said Father Christopher, standing up. "And here's hoping the weather picks up for you all." He walked over to the sink and placed his cup into the water where Jessie's hands were immersed, then giving her arm a light surreptitious squeeze in support. Then he turned and said, "I'll see you at three and we'll take it from there."

"But, Father, you didn't even have anything to eat!" Tom protested. "And Cain has only just arrived. Really, you must stay a bit longer. For lunch?"

Father Christopher glanced over at Cain and Andrea and shook his head.

"I'm sorry, Tom, but it really was only intended to be a flying visit. I've a lot of paperwork to do and then the rehearsal at three, of course. Thanks, anyway. You're very kind."

Tom and Ella walked the young priest to the door and Jessie followed them, delighted to have an excuse to leave the kitchen.

"Jessie," said Cain Daniels to her on her way past.

She stopped and painted a bright smile on her face before she looked his way.

"Yes, Cain?" she said, her insides sour at the very sight of him.

"You look good," he said. "As always."

Jessie felt her face burn and she thought she saw Andrea flinch at Cain's usual charming comment. She always joked how she was used to his charismatic ways with every female who turned his way, but for the first time Jessie sensed Andrea's annoyance as she fidgeted with her skirt.

"David home yet?" Cain asked, rubbing his hand slowly up and down Andrea's arm. "I hope he makes it in time for tomorrow."

Jessie felt her blood run cold. His sleazy stare made her skin crawl and she longed to spit in his perfectly groomed face.

"No," she said. "David is not home. Not yet. And yes, he will make it on time. For tomorrow."

Chapter 12

After Father Christopher had left, Jessie ran up the stairs and locked herself in her childhood bedroom where she sat huddled on her old rocking chair trying desperately to decide how she was going to get through the next few days without telling her family, and most of all her sister, the truth.

Her bedroom looked exactly as it had before she left home for university over ten years ago. An Oasis poster still hung, though frayed around the edges, on her bedroom door and the heart-shaped cushions she had collected as a young teenager were neatly arranged in the huge window seat that shared the same wonderful views of Glencuan as her sister's room did just next to hers.

She lay down on the double bed and stared at the ceiling to gather her thoughts. How could she stomach watching her sister marry someone who was so wrong for her? How could she save face when she had played such a guilty role in his downfall if she told Andrea the truth? And who on earth was snooping around after her, taunting her and scaring her with their secret notes and invasion of her own home?

As much as she longed to stay in the cocoon of her bedroom with her mother and family downstairs, she knew she had to face the music at some stage. All of her belongings for the wedding were at her marital home and she would have to take the chance and go and get them, no matter how petrified she would be in doing so.

She looked out the window to see the rain had somewhat settled. Yes, she would brave it because she had to. No one was going to keep her out of her own house without a fight on their hands.

"Mum, Andrea, I'll be back soon," she called from the hallway, hoping for a quick getaway but, as she expected, her mother came out after her to quiz her on her whereabouts.

"Why do you have to leave so early, love? I thought you'd stay for lunch?"

"I need to go and get ready for the rehearsal."

"Well, Daddy is going to barbecue this evening. You did remember about the barbecue, didn't you?"

Jessie looked outside to where the flowers bowed their heads, dripping with the afternoon's rainfall.

"I know, I know, the rain, but he insists," said Ella and Jessie threw her eyes up in jest.

"Well, I'm just popping home to get things ready for the rehearsal and for David coming home," she lied, "and I need to get all my stuff organised for tomorrow. I'll be back, I promise. Not for lunch, but for the barbecue this evening. I wouldn't miss it for the world."

She could hear Cain and Andrea laughing from the kitchen and it crawled under her skin. No one would ever know how she longed to scream at that smarmy bastard to stay away from her sister. His roving eye would never leave him and Andrea deserved so much better.

"Okay, then, but do you want me to drive you?" asked Ella. "I don't understand why you walked all this way in the first place. It's not your form."

"No, no!" Jessie said, laughing. "I just fancied the walk, Mum. You know, just to clear my head after burning the midnight oil with – well, with the case. I'll be back after the rehearsal. Promise."

She kissed her mother on the cheek and set off down the winding driveway, her heart thumping in her chest.

She was scared to death of going back to her house for fear of what she might find this time. Whoever knew of her brief fling with her sister's fiancé wasn't going to let her forget about it.

She suspected her brother was involved but no matter how taunting and nasty he was to her of late, there was no way she believed he would be so malicious as to write her hate-mail and break into her home and record her like that.

On the other hand, perhaps her stalker was someone who disagreed with her representing Jack O'Donnell. There was no doubt about it, O'Donnell was a man who had many enemies and there were very few locals who'd want to see whoever tried to get rid of him punished.

Someone had been watching her very closely, that was for sure, and it gave her the creeps. She'd read up before on people from her profession who had found themselves under scrutiny when the public didn't believe in the characters or causes they defended in court.

She walked through the village with her head down, dodging people's glances and avoiding unnecessary conversations with gossipy neighbours, until she reached her house on Slater's Hill.

The house looked lonely, sad even. She stopped and let her eye run along the whole of its exterior.

She pushed the door open slowly.

"Hello?" she called into the hallway. The house was eerily silent. "Hello?"

She crossed the threshold, her heart thumping in her chest so hard she could hear it. She closed the door behind her. Slowly, she walked into the kitchen, looking behind her after every other step in case her stalker approached her from behind.

The kitchen had been tidied.

There was a fresh smell of pine floor cleaner. Her phone and her car keys lay side by side on top of the freshly washed surface of the furthest worktop. She walked towards them, wondering if it would make her feel any more secure if she grabbed her phone and keys. She quietly slipped her belongings into her handbag and tiptoed across to make sure that the patio doors were locked. Then, her hands trembling, she made her way into the sitting-room.

It too had been cleaned to perfection. Gone was the newspaper that had lain there on David's favourite armchair for days now.

But she noticed that a photo of them on holiday, smiling and waving to the camera, that had been positioned pride of place on the mantelpiece looked like it was in the wrong place.

She walked towards it, perspiration bleeding through her palms as she opened and closed her hands in anticipation. It had always been her favourite photo of them, taken in much happier times – her arms wrapped around David's shoulders as she peeped at the camera from behind him while he held onto her hands with both of his. She lifted the picture and gasped as something stuck in her finger. She pulled her hand away and a fine sliver of glass fell onto the mantelpiece.

She sucked the blood but it was too late. A drip had made its way onto the white rug below her. She hardly noticed. All she could see was how the protective glass on the photo frame had been shattered and the photo carefully propped up and placed not too far from where she normally liked it to sit.

She looked closer at the photo only to see it had been torn down the middle and a fine gap sliced between the two of them, separating them in a bold statement.

Jessie covered her mouth in an urge not to be sick.

Was David himself playing games with her mind? Had he found out about Cain and was he trying to punish her for being a cheat?

"Jessie!"

Jessie screamed and then stifled the noise that spilled from her mouth.

She swung around to see Charlotte, her young cleaner, standing in the doorway with her rubber-gloved hands on her hips and a cleaning rag hanging from her apron.

"You scared the heart out of me, Charlotte!" said Jessie, clutching her chest now. She fell onto an armchair and concentrated on getting her breath back. "Oh my God, you scared me! How long have you been here?"

"About half an hour, I guess. Is everything okay? You weren't expecting me today?"

Jessie rubbed her head as the room came back into focus. "Friday. Of course, I'm sorry, Charlotte. I'm a bit . . . Well, things are a bit crazy with work and the wedding as you can imagine."

"I'm sorry if I scared you but I didn't hear you come in. I was . . . I was in the en-suite and the bedroom door was closed."

Charlotte was looking distinctly nervous and Jessie hastened to reassure her. "Of course. Never mind."

She by now felt like hugging the younger woman. Despite her shock, she was so relieved at having company in her house. She urged herself not to sound too frantic when she spoke.

"Charlotte, would you mind coming upstairs with me so I can pack a few things?"

Charlotte looked taken aback. "Look, is everything okay, Mrs Chambers? You don't look well."

"I'm fine. I'm just – well, I've had a lot of pressure due

151

to work. I'm staying overnight at the hotel after the wedding reception – we all are – but things have been so frantic lately I haven't had a chance to pack. I thought you might help me pick out some clothes for the following day?"

Charlotte's young face lit up. "Oh, Mrs Chambers, I'd be delighted! You have such wonderful clothes. I will help you, of course."

Jessie was already climbing the stairs, too afraid to look up in case her intruder had left her another note or clue to a recent visit. She wondered was she becoming increasingly paranoid but the evidence was there – like the note that Father Christopher had protected her eyes from seeing. She certainly hadn't imagined that.

"Charlotte?" asked Jessie when they reached the top of the stairs.

"Yes, Mrs Chambers?"

"I'm just wondering . . ." Jessie stopped on the landing and turned to the girl. "It's no big deal but – the photo on the mantelpiece of David and me? Did you accidentally . . .?"

"No, no, no, Mrs Chambers, I have no idea what happened to it. I swear to you I did not break your photo frame. It was like that when I arrived." Charlotte's eyes darted around the landing where they stood. "In fact, Mrs Chambers, there were a few things out of place when I arrived here today. I was quite uncomfortable when I came upstairs and . . . and when I went into the bathroom . . ." Her voice trailed away as Jessie had turned and disappeared into her bedroom.

She followed and found her sitting on the edge of the bed.

Jessie felt dreadful. The room began to spin and she could feel a cold sweat resting on her forehead. She felt so alone, so unsafe. Who was trying to get to her like this?

"Like what, Charlotte? What did you see? What else was out of place? You have to tell me."

Charlotte's glanced around the bedroom, rubbing her hands together and Jessie knew the girl was feeling some of the same fear that was by now pumping through her veins.

"Well," said Charlotte, her voice settling into a nervous whisper, "it was the en-suite. There was something strange there . . ."

"Just tell me, Charlotte!" screamed Jessie and then she took a deep breath. "I'm sorry. I'm sorry. Just tell me."

Charlotte sucked her bottom lip. "Well, when I went into the bathroom, it said . . . it said . . . Something was written in lipstick on the bathroom mirror. I cleaned it off. It was horrible."

Jessie felt shivers prickle across her shoulders. "Something? Charlotte, what was written there? Don't worry – I can handle it. Tell me what was written on the bathroom mirror."

Charlotte looked down at the cream carpet, clearly embarrassed, and frightened at the same time.

"It said . . . 'Scum-loving slut'. But I just wiped it off. And it was on the wall in the shower as well. On the tiles. So I wiped that off too. And then I ran downstairs and there you were. I didn't know what to say to you . . ."

Jessie wiped her hands across her black trousers and rocked back and forth on the edge of the bed. 'Scum' was the term used repeatedly when locals spoke of O'Donnell, and 'slut' implied that she had been caught out with Cain. She was terrified and confused, but there was one thing she knew she could do that might help her.

"Hand me the phone from the bedside locker, please," she whispered to Charlotte who brought her the cordless handset.

Her mind raced as her fingers slipped off the digits when she tried to dial the number. This was something she should have done weeks ago. This was something her husband had told her to do at the very start. At least it might be a step in the right direction, even if she was on the wrong track as to who was after her. She couldn't attract this trouble any longer. It was unfair to the people she loved the most and her worst fear was that her mother and father might be a target next.

"Good morning, Angela," she said, holding her hair back from her face and taking shallow breaths. "It's Jessie."

"Ms O'Neill, good morning," said the chirpy receptionist. "How can I help you? I'm afraid the boss is out of the country until Monday and is unavailable for mobile transfers. Can I help?"

"No, er, look, I'll explain to him on Monday. I'm phoning to say I am no longer in a position to act as prosecutor in the investigation of the attempted murder of Jack O'Donnell. You can take this as an official notice of my stepping down from the case. Please pass on the message to whom it may concern, straightaway."

"But Ms O'Neill, the O'Donnell case is due in court in just over a week. Are you sure? Can I ask why?"

"I'm sorry, Angela, but that's all I can say. All of my files will be handed in on Monday and I'm sorry for any inconvenience caused. I have to go. Goodbye."

Jessie hung up the phone and wept with relief, tears dribbling down her face. She felt better already, as if some of the heaviness had left her weary, crushed mind.

"Mrs Chambers, what is going on? Is there anything I can do?" asked Charlotte. She gave Jessie a glass of water she had poured from the en-suite sink, fearing that otherwise Mrs Chambers might faint and she really wouldn't know how to handle it.

Jessie shook her head and with trembling hands clung to the glass, gulping the water.

"I'm okay," she said between sobs and she concentrated on taking long, slow, deliberate deep breaths. "Please, Charlotte, you mustn't tell a soul about this. I mean it, not a word . . ."

Charlotte wasn't convinced. "But shouldn't you tell the police?" she asked, her voice rising into a frantic tone. "What about your husband? Does he know? I don't like this, Mrs Chambers. Not one bit. I really think you should!"

Jessie looked up at Charlotte seriously. "Just listen to

me, Charlotte. You mustn't say a word about this. Not to anyone," she whispered. "Now, we will pack my bags for the wedding very quickly and then we will both leave this house together. No one needs to know this happened. I can sort this all out for myself, okay?"

"Okay," said Charlotte and she opened the sliding wardrobe doors and began to help Jessie pick out her clothes.

Tom O'Neill loved to entertain and this impromptu barbecue with his family was exactly his type of occasion. He wore full cooking gear and wheeled the gas barbecue under the canopy to protect it from the light drizzle that refused to subside.

"Do you think there could possibly *be* any more rain left in the sky?" asked Andrea, handing him some tongs.

"It looks to me like it's spitting out the last few drops, honey," said Tom and he put his arm around his baby girl. "Don't worry. You're going to have a wonderful wedding day tomorrow, rain or no rain."

"Thanks, Daddy. And thanks for keeping spirits up at the rehearsal. At least you believe in my wedding."

Tom stood back and frowned. "And what's that supposed to mean? I hope you're not thinking about the dress, are you? I thought we were never going to mention that again?"

"No, well, yes. I'm thinking about who would have wanted to hurt me so much and there was such a horrible atmosphere at the rehearsal and then there's what Ryan said . . ."

156

Andrea stopped. This was silly. It was the night before her wedding and she should be having the time of her life.

"What did Ryan say?" asked Tom. "Come on, you have to tell me now."

"Well, he'd had a few drinks last night as you know, and he sort of implied that I had rushed into things with Cain."

Tom laughed and turned over some skewered kebabs on the grill. "That boy is a rascal at times. Who the hell is he to be dishing out advice on relationships? The only love of his life is that damn bike of his, so don't you worry about Ryan, love. Do what's right for you."

Andrea rubbed her temples and her father gave her a hug. "You're right, Dad. I'm just a little super-sensitive at the moment. There's been a lot going on."

"It will be fine, baby. It will all work out just fine. I'll make sure it does."

Jessie had overwhelming flashes of regret now for crying in front of her cleaner. She hated herself for letting her guard down in front of a virtual stranger and it stung her to the core to let Charlotte know of her weaknesses. Her human side had always been one she revealed only to close friends and family and lately she had managed to block even her nearest and dearest out, transforming herself into a steely solicitor who kept her private life just so.

The wedding rehearsal had been quick and as pain-free as Father Christopher could possibly have made it and she had gone straight back to her house, determined not to be frightened out of her own home.

She sat curled up on the sofa now, clutching her knees, and looking around the room. She wondered if it all was just a fantasy fairy tale from the start with David. Everything had been so perfect for so long – he was the most endearing man she had ever met and fussed over her every move.

She had had the wedding day of her dreams and a luxurious home that was effortlessly acquired with Daddy's all-embracing assistance, and a career to die for which was going upwards at a speed that was almost breathtaking. Her mother was always on the sidelines, cheering her on and encouraging her with lashings of praise and unconditional adoration, and when she and her sister stepped out for an evening they were snapped by photographers and featured in the most-read social columns.

Everything had been so wonderful, yet so absolutely out of her control. And now, in the space of four days, it had become like a whirlwind, spinning her into a blind panic as she watched everything she once took for granted fall apart at the seams.

With Charlotte gone, Jessie's house felt so empty again. It was a beautiful home located on the outskirts of the village on a two-acre site, on land that had been earmarked for her many years before when she was more interested in dolls' houses than building her own home.

Her neighbours barely saw her come and go, which

Jessie knew had fuelled rumours of her elusive lifestyle around the village. She heard them whisper – some called her a snob who believed she was above her station with her glamour and riches, while others stared with deep envy or admiration when they caught a rare glimpse of the dark-haired eldest O'Neill girl.

But Jessie's house helped to protect her fiercely private lifestyle and had been built exactly to her specifications, with David remarking only when he felt it was necessary. This was very much an O'Neill project and David knew that if his opinion was welcome it would have been asked for. And Jessie had done a fantastic job on the entire design and build of her hilltop hideaway. Forever practical, she had worked with a well-known, Dublin-based architect to create a tasteful contemporary two-storey home with special features that gave it a unique voice of its own.

The cream marble fireplace with its deep mantelpiece had always been her pride and joy but now, as she stared at it, instead of the rich centrepiece she had searched high and low for to complement the airy freshness of the front-facing room, the shattered glass on the smashed photograph was the only thing she could see.

The huge en-suite adjacent to her bedroom had been a must, with its double sink and power-filled jet shower and a bathtub fit for two and cool blue walls that reminded her of the sea. It had excited her so much when it was first fitted out and painted and she had found little trinkets in all corners of Ireland to complement and warm its aquatic tones. Now, when she thought of this room, she could only imagine her intruder running his hands over her property, probing through her possessions and taunting her by invading the most private space in her home.

Even her hallway haunted her – a magnificent entrance which she had insisted on being wide enough to host a huge piece of modern art blasted in reds and golds and greens that she had picked up on her worldly travels during her well-deserved gap year across Europe and America. Now it seemed intimidating and the life-size mirror that dominated its far side made her feel she was being watched every time she walked past it.

Everywhere seemed different. Every room was intimidating. Every room held a trace of the prowler who had entered her house and examined every corner of it, leaving subtle hints along the way that only a careful owner like Jessie could see.

She knew she should call the police. That would be the most sensible reaction to her fears. With her involvement in the O'Donnell case, threatening behaviour like this towards her would be expected and surveillance would be on her in a heartbeat.

But in her heart she knew it was nothing to do with her job. She could resign from every case in the country and it wouldn't make one iota of difference. Someone out there knew of her affair with Cain Daniels, someone knew of her resounding guilt and terror of being found out and they were playing dangerous, destructive games with her mind.

The telephone in the hallway rang and Jessie froze, listening to its repetitive *hum-hum, hum-hum.*

She felt her muscles clench and she waited, too frightened to answer it in case it might be another clue, another message that she didn't want to hear. Another cryptic code from her stalker who was trying to force her into confessing her sins to all.

The answerphone kicked in and Jessie waited to hear her caller's voice, praying it would be a sincere call and not a prank that she wasn't in a fit state to deal with. She listened to David's recorded greeting, asking the caller to leave a message and her heart sank.

"Oh, David, I'm so sorry!" she said aloud, rocking back and forth in her chair as she waited for whoever was on the other end of the line to respond to his gentle voice.

"Jessie, hi. I, well, I got your message . . ."

Jessie raced for the phone. It was him.

"David! Oh my God, I've been . . . oh, David, I'm so glad to hear from you! Where are you? When are you coming home? What's this all about?"

"You know what it's all about, Jess. And no, I'm not coming home. I can't."

Jessie felt tears prick her eyes. She didn't deserve him. She had lied and cheated and she shouldn't beg him to come home just to make her feel safe and to save face with her family. But she needed him now. She needed someone.

"But you can't just disappear like this! Where are you?"

David didn't answer her and she could sense him inhaling his cigarette at the other end of the line. She

161

thought of the cigarette smoke and the sense of him being there the day before.

"People disappear all the time, Jessie. Hey, I might as well have disappeared months ago and you wouldn't have noticed. I can't cope with it any more. I can't cope with you any more."

Jessie sat down on the wooden floor, one hand gripping the phone and the other wrapped around the leg of the hall table. She shivered, despite the longed-for ray of sunlight that beamed through the enormous stained-glass feature that surrounded the front doorframe.

"You couldn't cope with me?" she whispered. "Was it O'Donnell? I've dropped everything to do with it, David. Just today. I walked away from it."

"You what?"

"I rang today and told them I have to walk away. You were right. I was way in over my head. I'm not up to such a high-profile case. I'll walk away from crime and concentrate on family law like before. It's more my thing, perhaps."

"But, Jessie, it's not your thing. You're so passionate about what you do and I'd never deny you that."

"But, like you said, it was dangerous. I was obsessed. I –"

David interrupted her. "You've become a different person lately, Jessie," he said softly. "You've become so blinded by ambition that I was, well, I am, merely a stepping stone to your success."

"David, that's not true!" Jessie tried to defend herself.

He continued, determined to get his point across. "On paper we were a great match and for a long time I really did believe we were good together, but now it's dead. It's gone."

Jessie felt her breathing going shallow and the walls closed in, suffocating her and mocking her for being so foolish with her young marriage and a life that most women only ever dreamed of.

For the first time since David left, the finality of it all began to sink in and the fear of being alone choked her from within. She had destroyed everything and David had left her without even knowing the full story.

She hadn't meant to hurt him as she so evidently had, but though her head throbbed and her sorrow was physically agonising, she knew in her heart that this chapter of her life was over. She had ruined it all and she would never forgive herself.

"David, I am so scared. I'm so scared, David." She meant it in more ways than one. She was frightened of the future – the long-term future without her husband to lean on – and she worried about what awaited her just around the corner. She would lose a lot more than her marriage if anyone found out what she had done. "I don't know where to go or what to do. What have I done to my life? I don't know who to turn to."

She shuffled back into the corner of the hallway, seeking comfort in the walls around her. She was terrified now.

"I'm sorry, Jessie. It's not me you're looking for. I was never the one you wanted. I know that now and I've decided to move on."

"But, David –"

"Goodbye, Jess. I'll sort out all the legal stuff next week when you recover from the wedding."

Jessie felt a rush of energy race through her veins. She couldn't let this happen. She was in a strange place emotionally. She had to shake this off. She had to fight for her marriage. It was all she had to cling to.

"David, don't do this to me. I'll try harder. I know I've done wrong by you but we can fix this! Please let me try to fix this!"

There was a brief silence and then David whispered to her, sorrow rasping his throat, "You can't, Jessie. It's too late. Just face it. You never loved me like I loved you. I can't live like that any more. Goodbye."

Chapter 13

It was only sixteen hours now until Andrea would walk up the aisle in St John's Church and she couldn't contain her excitement. Cain had said his farewells to her just after six, declining Ella's offer to stay for tea and insisting he had to make it back to Belfast to spend time with his parents and prepare for the big day ahead.

Things were looking up on the weather front, he had told them on good first-hand information from the radio station's weather forecast, and he had left the O'Neill's home vowing to have an early night and wake up refreshed and ready to ensure that all his guests had the time of their lives.

Andrea had spent the most glorious evening with her fiancé, taking a drive down to the Bromley Castle to deliver the wedding cake and their luggage for their impending honeymoon. They would leave in a blaze of glory the following afternoon.

"I can't wait to make you my wife," he had whispered to her at the door of her home before he left. "We have such wonderful times ahead."

Andrea thought her heart was going to burst with love for this man who had come into her life only months ago and she could barely remember a day without him since then. He was part of her now and she couldn't help but glow at the thought of waking up beside him in their new home in the city when they returned from their well-earned break in just three weeks' time.

Now she was looking forward to a relaxing few hours with her family, making last-minute plans and going over the finer details even though it was already so well planned she didn't need to give any of it a second thought.

Aunt Lily and her family had retired to the second sitting-room for the evening in a bid to give the O'Neills a chance to savour their time together as planned and requesting only that Jessie would pop her head in to say hello when she came around later.

The family were gathered around the patio set, nibbling at the remainder of the chargrilled steaks and kebabs that Tom had so proudly prepared, when Jessie finally arrived, looking dishevelled and distracted, much to Andrea's frustration. Her hair was unwashed and her face tear-stained and just as Ryan had predicted earlier, there was no sign of David.

"We've kept you some food," said Ella, who looked almost as distressed as Jessie did at the sight of her eldest daughter.

"It's okay, Mum. I'm not hungry."

Jessie pulled out a chair, avoiding eye contact with anyone and Ryan let out an exaggerated yawn that demanded everyone's attention.

"Oh, come on!" he cried when he felt their eyes bore through him. "How long is this circus going to continue? Spit it out, Jessie. I think it's time you told everyone the truth. Where's your husband?"

Jessie looked bewildered, exhausted even, and Andrea felt her heart drop down to her toes.

"Yes, Jessie," she said. "I think you need to tell us. This has been going on for too long."

But Jessie didn't answer.

Ella fetched a blanket from indoors and placed it around Jessie's shoulders.

"We're very concerned," she whispered. "Tell us, love. We only want to help you if we can."

Jessie stared at the ground and Andrea wanted to shake her. She could feel her temper rise at how pathetic her sister looked, all forlorn and weak with her father's arm now around her and her mother's pitiful, nervous glances into nowhere.

"Aren't you going to speak, Jess?" she said. "Aren't you going to try and put us all out of our misery here? You have made this all very miserable for me, that's for sure!"

"*Your* misery?" said Ella, jumping immediately to Jessie's defence. "Your sister is in trouble so this is hardly *your* misery, Andrea. It doesn't have to always be about you!"

Ryan guffawed and shook his head. "Here we go again!" he said. "Poor Jessie! Oh, don't worry about anyone else, Mum. As long as Jessie is on top of the world, then it will keep spinning around. As long as Poor Jessie wears a smile on her face, then we will all just plod along wearing our own masks of delirium. I've had enough!" He slammed his fist on the table so that the cutlery and plates rattled together.

Andrea could see Jessie's shoulders heave beneath her father's grasp and she battled to control the anger that surged from within her entire body. "And so have I! I can't stand this any more. This is my wedding and all you have done, Mum, is pussy-foot around *her* all week while I have been going through hell and having to hide it all!"

"Andrea! That is enough!" said Tom O'Neill. "Don't speak to your mother like that and, Ryan, don't you even think about going anywhere!" His face was red with frustration and he eyeballed all of his family who drank in his every word as always.

Ryan, who had planned on leaving the scene, settled back in his seat. When Tom O'Neill raised his voice, everyone listened.

"But it's not fair, Daddy," said Andrea, fighting back her own tears as Jessie wept like a baby in front of her. She felt like a child again too. "Why does it always have to be about *her*?"

"That is not true," said Tom. "Well, not in my eyes, anyway."

Ella raised her chin and met her husband's gaze.

"But in my eyes it's different, is it?" she said, her voice breaking under the strain.

"I didn't say that."

"I am simply concerned about my daughter's wellbeing," said Ella. "Seeing her like this is tearing my heart open and you lot are inhumane if you aren't in the slightest bit worried about anyone only yourselves and the cotton-wool life you have become accustomed to!"

Andrea pursed her lips and caught Ryan's eye. He looked like he was threatening to burst with an answer that would cut everyone to pieces and she could see him fighting with himself to hold back.

"Cotton-wool life?" he said eventually. "Cotton-wool life is absolutely right! But I didn't ask for this. I didn't ask to be the local rich kid who everyone hates because I don't fit in with ordinary people around this place. I didn't ask for this silver spoon that has been shoved down my throat and, most of all, I didn't ask to be treated like I'm last in the queue for any airtime in this family!"

Ella walked over to her son and for the first time in her life, she lifted her hand and slapped him in the face so hard her fingers stung.

"You wouldn't know what it's like to have a hard life if it slapped you in the face!" she said and she walked towards the doors that led back into the family kitchen.

"Stop it! Stop it now!" screamed Jessie. She threw off the blanket her mother had placed on her and stood up, her shoulders hunched and her face wet with tears that she no longer felt any more. "Andrea is right! Ryan is right! This is my fault. It's all my fault and I'm sorry."

She broke down again in convulsions and stood in the centre of the patio, wiping her eyes and shaking her head. Ella came back outside and quietly approached Jessie.

Andrea glared at her sister. This was the most disgusting, selfish scene she had ever witnessed and one she would always remember.

But Jessie was admitting at last to overshadowing her and Ryan, only this time it was not for her good behaviour. Jessie had fucked up somewhere along the line and Andrea couldn't help but gloat as she awaited the sad story that was to come.

"I'm sorry, Andrea. I'm sorry for not being with you this week and I'm sorry if it seemed that I was getting more attention from Mum than you have been."

Everyone waited for her to get to the crux of the matter.

"David has left me," she said. "My marriage is over."

Ryan broke into applause and then stopped when his father pointed his finger in his direction.

"Ryan!" he said. "What the hell is that reaction all about?"

"It's about time she admitted it, that's all," said Ryan.

"You knew?" said Jessie.

"Hold on! What do you mean David has left you? When? How?" asked Tom.

170

"He's gone," mumbled Jessie and then she took a deep breath and said with more confidence, "For many reasons, we both realised that we have come to the end of our relationship . . ."

Ryan chuckled. "For many reasons!"

"After one year?" said Tom and he gave out a nervous laugh. "After one fucking year? How can you decide that a marriage is over in just a year? This is a joke, Jessie. It has to be."

Jessie didn't even wait to think about what she might say next. Like a pressure cooker, it began to spill out.

"The real joke is that I never should have married him in the first place! Not so soon anyhow!"

Everyone fell silent at Jessie's stark admission. Her words spat at them in an accusing tone and she looked at each of her parents in turn.

"I made a mistake," she said more quietly. "I wasn't ready for marriage and all that comes with it and before I knew it I was caught up in all the fuss of setting a date, booking a hotel, arranging a honeymoon, reading about it in the paper and the pressure was on from that moment."

Ella looked away. Had she pushed her daughter down the aisle to satisfy her own desires of the huge white wedding she had never had?

"A long engagement would have suited me just fine for a while. I'd have liked to have taken my time. I'd have liked to have planned my wedding my way. Hell, a ceremony on a faraway beach would have been more pleasant but, before I knew it, I was choosing curtains

171

for my house and kitchen tiles and deciding on nursery colours and now I just want to scream! It's not me. It's just not me, not yet!"

Andrea was gobsmacked. The golden child who had everything laid down for her, peppered with rose petals and tied with a bow if she wanted it that way, hadn't really wanted it all in the first place.

"And so you've decided to announce all this to perfectly match in with my wedding day? Did you ever stop to think it might have waited?"

"Andrea, I said I'm sorry! I know it is all so poorly timed but it was out of my control. David left me on Wednesday. That's why I missed our appointment and I have been in turmoil since. I know I'm backtracking here when I complain about getting caught up in things but I don't want the same thing to happen to you."

Andrea sat up straight, her face flushed now with temper. Was Jessie insinuating that they had anything in common on this matter? Was she suggesting that she had merely been caught in a romantic whirlwind that would settle within the guts of twelve palsy months!

"You are such a bitch," she said, shaking her head in disbelief. "Just because your marriage fell apart at the seams because you were so goddamned selfish, you think mine might too? I don't believe you!" She looked at her father who sat with his head in his hands. "Dad? Can't you support me in this?"

"Do you know what I think?" he said, rubbing his temples, his jaw tightening as he then ran his hands through his silver-grey hair. "I never thought I'd say this, but I have never heard of anything so ungrateful or pathetic in all my days. First Ryan complains about being the poor little rich kid, and then you, Jessie! You can't even work on your marriage because you've decided one year down the line that all the privileges and luxuries that were so lovingly given to you weren't what you wanted after all! I'm baffled. I'm disgusted and baffled at all of this."

Andrea knew she was next.

"And what about you, Andrea? Is Jessie right? Are you sure this is what you want? Because if you're anything like your sister, maybe you feel you are being forced into all of this marriage malarkey." His tone was dripping with sarcasm and his voice was bitter. "Because one thing is for sure – I don't want to be sitting here in one year's time hearing the same fucking nonsense from you!"

Andrea had never seen her father look so weak in all her life. He was deeply hurt and she hated her sister for it.

"Like I said, Daddy, I don't feel the same at all. I know you have always worked hard for us and I appreciate all of it. If my sister and brother are too tunnel-visioned to see that they make their own decisions in life, then that is their own problem."

Ella sat in silence, rubbing her thumbs together, obviously bewildered at the scene that was unfolding. This was meant to be such a happy time but instead her precious family was falling apart. They'd had plenty of rows down the years, but nothing as close to the bone as this before. She could feel her heart race and her breath quicken.

"Well, at least one of my children has the grace to show some maturity for the loving family life they have been reared in," continued Tom. "As for you two, I'll speak to you about this after the wedding. Until then, I don't want to hear a word from either of you. Now, go and freshen up and we'll all have an early night. I think some of us have some long, hard thinking to do."

Tom left the table, his head hanging low with disappointment and Ella placed her hand on Jessie's, much to Ryan and Andrea's disgust.

They left one by one and entered the house, leaving Ella and Jessie alone, sitting on a shared summer seat, the rain dripping in the background and the evening sun setting on another day.

Chapter 14

Saturday

Andrea prayed her eyes wouldn't tell of her lack of sleep on the eve of her wedding. It was only 7am and the butterflies in her stomach were having a party at her expense.

She checked her phone and just as she had hoped and expected, she had a message from Cain declaring his love for her and how he would make her the happiest woman in Ireland. Her heart warmed and she glanced up at the sky from her bedroom window, acknowledging at last that her wedding day wouldn't be the blue-skied dream she had longed for.

She could hear the hustle and bustle downstairs and her sister's footsteps coming towards her bedroom.

She checked herself in the mirror and then turned to admire her wedding dress which she had laid out on the bed, ready for her to step into in just a few hours' time. No one would ever know it was a replica of her original gown and that was the way she would keep it. It was time for her to put the past in the past and look forward in earnest to her new life as Mrs Cain Daniels.

"Knock knock!" said Jessie and Andrea was relieved to see her sister smiling as she entered the bedroom.

"Hi, Jess," she said with a mirrored smile.

"I'm so sorry about last night," said Jessie.

"Me too," said Andrea and she walked towards Jessie and gave her a hug.

They stood together, entwined for longer than they realised and when Jessie finally let go, Andrea could see the tears well again in her sister's eyes. This was going to be a tough day for her to get through without David but Andrea knew she was trying her best to fight through her emotions.

"I bought you something," said Jessie and she reached into her oversized handbag and produced a small box, gift-wrapped in silver paper with a scarlet bow. "I hope you like it."

Andrea sat on the edge of the bed and Jessie sat beside her, eagerly awaiting her response just as they would have done on birthdays and Christmas when they exchanged presents.

Andrea tore off the paper, glancing at her sister in anticipation, and revealed a small white wooden box. She lifted the lid and a ballerina popped up, then the tinkling sound of music filled the air to the tune of *Swan Lake*. Andrea gasped in delight and then they both sat in silence, listening to the beautiful sound of the trinket box as it brought them both back to happier times in their childhood.

"Where on earth did you find this?" said Andrea, wiping a stray tear from her eye. "It's just perfect."

"I've had it for ages," said Jessie. "I dragged David around every corner of Galway one weekend until I found one exactly like you had when you were little."

Andrea put her head on Jessie's shoulder, closed the lid on the box and then opened it again to hear the music once more. They both watched the tiny plastic girl, with her dark hair tied back in a bun and her pretty net dress, move around in circles to the girls' favourite ballet tune.

"I can't believe you did this for me, Jess," she said. "It just makes everything better, you know."

She could hear Jessie breathing beside her and she closed her eyes and listened, feeling comfort, hope and sorrow for her sister whose own marriage and dreams of happiness slipped away just as she was beginning hers.

"I want you to know something," said Jessie. "I want you to know something before we go any further with what today might bring."

Andrea sat up, her dark eyes fixed on her big sister, not knowing what was to come. "What do you mean by that?" she asked, puzzled.

"No, no, relax," said Jessie, holding Andrea's hands. "I know I've been a selfish bitch all week. I know you feel I have taken the limelight from you just like you always feel I have. But I want you to know that this is going to be your perfect day and I will make sure it all goes exactly to plan. Nothing is going to happen to ruin this for you. You deserve to be happy and, if Cain is what you want, then I am happy for you too."

Andrea walked to her dressing-table and put the ballerina trinket box beside a framed photo of her siblings, then turned towards her sister.

"You say that like you think I'm making a mistake, Jess. What do you mean if Cain is what I want? You know he is all I've ever wanted. You're making me question all of this. What are you trying to tell me?"

Jessie shook her head. "No, I'm saying you deserve to be happy and I'm asking you to forgive me."

"Forgive you for what? For being upset this week that your husband has left you? My God, what type of hard-nosed bitch do you think I am?"

Then what Ryan had said to her flashed into her head. She saw images of Cain and Jessie and she forced them from her mind, not wanting to even contemplate that she was always going to be second-best to her sister in everything she tried to do.

"I'm just telling you I'm sorry," said Jessie. "Just remember that. I'm so, so sorry."

Jessie rushed to Andrea and buried her face in her shoulder. She sobbed like a baby and Andrea felt her hot tears soak her neck.

"It's true," said Jessie. "You've always had to live in my shadow and I just wish I could go back and make it all different. I'm sorry for always making you feel you were the awkward middle child and for making you crave Mum's attention every day of your life. I'm sorry

178

for everything. I need you to forgive me. Please, Andrea!"

Andrea rocked her sister in her arms and then wiped away her tears. Jessie had never done this before. She had always been so aloof, untouchable almost, and now here she was begging for forgiveness for all the years of Andrea's inadequate feelings. For the first time, Jessie was asking Andrea for help. She couldn't turn her away. She would never turn her sister away.

"I forgive you," she whispered. "For whatever memories of incidents you are rolling over in your mind right now, I forgive you."

She waited until her sister's sobs subsided and then she pushed her shoulders back and fixed her hair behind her ears.

"Oh, and I almost forgot. I have something for you too."

Jessie wiped her eyes. "What? You really shouldn't have."

"Oh, it's just a little keepsake for being my maid of honour. I'd like you to wear it today."

Andrea reached for a long slim rectangular box and lifted from it a delicate, ruby-encrusted silver bracelet. She held up her sister's arm and clipped it onto her wrist and they both stood in admiration, absorbing the precious moment between them

"Now, what do you say we get this party started?" said Andrea, knowing there were too many emotions flying around the room. "We have a wedding to prepare for and I call first in the make-up chair."

"That's okay with me," said Jessie with a smile. "This is your day. You can be first with everything from now on."

It seemed like most of Glencuan had travelled to see the glamorous O'Neill wedding that morning. The dull grey sky and odd drizzle of rain hadn't dampened the villagers' spirits as they gathered at the gates of St John's to catch a glimpse of Andrea and her family, not to mention the list of celebrities who were rumoured to be in attendance.

Cain and his three groomsmen arrived first to the applause of the gathered crowd and they stopped for photos with awaiting fans, before making their way inside to meet the official photographer and media personnel lucky enough to be granted an interview with the man many believed to be Ireland's hottest broadcaster of the moment.

A silence fell on the crowd moments later when the black stretch limo sailed through the gates and Jessie and a small army of bridesmaids were chaperoned inside from the rain by an umbrella-bearing team of suited ushers.

The girls looked breathtaking in long scarlet gowns, a colour which was particularly striking when teamed with Jessie's raven hair, and they each carried a bouquet of seasonal flowers in reds with dark green foliage.

But the crowd saved their biggest applause for Andrea who arrived in a tasteful Bentley decked in red ribbon. She was the epitome of grace and glamour in her ivory gown which her chauffeur dutifully tended to so as not to allow one speck of rain touch it as she dodged the weather and made her way inside the church.

"No more tears," whispered Jessie to her sister and she adjusted Andrea's veil as they waited for the church choir to give them their entrance cue. "You are the most beautiful bride I have ever seen."

Andrea nodded and smiled and then Tom O'Neill gave his daughter his arm and they made their way up the lengthy aisle to a sea of sighs and camera flashes as the three-hundred-plus congregation stood up and showed their appreciation of the blushing bride whose outstanding beauty took their breath away.

Andrea clasped her father's arm and focused on Cain who stood in the distance, awaiting her with a broad grin. He looked confident and cool and his reassuring presence made Andrea relax and enjoy every part of this wonderful moment.

She spied her brother and her mum in the second pew. Ella, of course, had tears in her eyes and Ryan gave her a wink of approval. It was only Father Christopher, looking slightly out of place on the altar, who unnerved Andrea when she looked his way. He seemed jittery and distracted and then, for some reason, looked searchingly at Jessie who walked a few steps ahead with the other bridesmaids.

She saw Bernice Bradshaw – a last-minute guest on Cain's insistence for the way she managed to make Andrea's dream wedding dress in record time and was sure she looked ever so slightly bitter.

She turned her attention to Cain again as she drew

closer and closer to the top of the aisle to the sound of Mendelssohn's "Wedding March" and then she left her father's side, took Cain's hand, walked to the altar and prepared to take her vows.

Andrea just knew that, as she had planned, this was going to be the best day of her life.

The difficulty with weddings and family fallings-out is that they are so hard to disguise, thought Ella, as she plodded through the day, wondering about everything from Jessie's breakdown to her husband's grief and disappointment to Ryan's sporadic outbursts and Andrea's future with Cain which gnawed at her like something stuck in her throat.

As her baby girl vowed to love Cain for rich or for poor, in sickness and in health, the tears that Ella shed weren't those of an emotionally happy mother, but instead those of a mother who couldn't get her head around the niggling doubts she felt about the whole scenario.

Perhaps it was Jessie's marriage that had spurred her feelings on. She really couldn't recall Jessie having had any doubts whatsoever, but then she would barely have noticed as she was so busy making phone calls to florists and visiting designer bakeries and negotiating with the harpist and the swing band and the DJ.

Andrea was right, of course. No matter how hard she tried, Ella couldn't have the same enthusiasm this time round and it was all down to that underlying feeling that something just wasn't right.

Yet, in the back of her mind, she hoped that Cain and Andrea might just prove everyone wrong. That for once, her nerve-racking, mind-boggling mother's instinct was wrong.

God, she really did hope so.

Chapter 15

Jessie glanced around the hotel reception area for Father Christopher.

Her feet throbbed and her head spun from the effects of the wine that had been served at dinner. Her dress was beautiful and Andrea looked like a movie star, but the deep sickening feeling she got every time she looked in Cain's direction almost made her faint.

It had been a big fat mistake and one he would regret for the rest of his life, he'd said, when they bumped into each other earlier after the formalities had all taken place. She meant nothing to him and never had. It was just a fling that she'd have to get over.

But that wasn't all he said.

"If you as much as breathe any of this to Andrea, I will make sure your life is made a misery," he had hissed. "In fact, your life won't be worth living if anyone ever finds out, okay?"

"What the hell does that mean? What, are you going to bump me off, is that it?" The wine had given her a sense of Dutch courage and she was fit for his taunts and insults.

"Well, the way I see it, Jessie," said Cain, laughing out loud as he spoke so as to divert any attention from the intensity of their secret conversation, "if anyone finds out, I can walk away. I love Andrea and I don't want to lose her, but if it comes to the crunch, I can be the bad guy. I can be the cheat, the malicious bastard who fucked around with two sisters. But what does that make you? My family will forgive me and mop up my tears and I can move on. But you? Who would ever forgive you when you tumble off your pedestal? Your whole life would be a pure misery. The adulteress, liar, scheming bitch who couldn't keep her hands off her sister's man. The future doesn't look too bright, does it? Now, keep your fucking mouth shut or you're the one who will have blood on your hands."

In response, Jessie splashed her glass of red wine so that it spilled right down his crotch, muttered the word "Bastard!" and then made her way to the bar where she sank three shots in a row to numb the pain and guilt she was feeling, not to mention the sickening regret and hatred she felt towards the man she would forever have to call her brother-in-law.

Of course, she had contemplated telling her sister the whole truth the night before when tempers were frayed but fear had stopped her. Now she was glad she hadn't said a word when she listened to Cain's malicious threats.

185

Her father couldn't even look her in the eye as things stood and as for Ryan . . . well, she was convinced he knew more than he was letting on. He had sat in the corner for most of the afternoon, gulping bottles of lager, and Jessie hoped and prayed the alcohol didn't loosen his tongue again.

"Father!" she said, when she finally spotted Father Christopher who was surrounded by a gaggle of her old aunts, all asking him more questions than a chat-show host would have, and smiling through their dentures up into his handsome face.

He excused himself immediately and walked to Jessie's side, his face lighting up as he approached.

"Thanks for rescuing me," he whispered, gently ushering her to a nearby table by the crook of her arm. "How are you holding up? You look good."

Jessie swallowed hard and nodded. Seeing him had made her feel better already. He made her feel so safe. "I'm getting through it. Don't suppose you fancy a few shots at the bar? I know how you're partial to the odd brandy and I could do with a drinking buddy."

Father Christopher let out a laugh and their eyes met for a second, then he looked away. "I wish I could," he said.

"I really can't thank you enough for being there for me," said Jessie and she rested her hand on his arm just for a brief moment. "I couldn't have got this far without you, you know that."

Father Christopher gently pulled away from Jessie's touch and waved at a few of his elderly admirers as they shuffled back into the main hall where the dancing was about to begin.

"That's what friends are for," he said and he signalled to a waiter. "A glass of sparkling water, please. What will you have, Jessie?"

Jessie swirled the remainder of the rich, bloody wine in her glass and downed it. "A glass of red wine would be lovely."

Father Christopher hesitated, sensing that Jessie had had enough to drink already. "Would you like a coffee too? I think I'll have a coffee."

Jessie cackled and swayed slightly. "What are you now, my keeper?" she said. "Cut the coffee. Have a brandy."

"No," he said. "A wine then and a sparkling water will be all."

The waiter left and Jessie linked the priest's arm. Again, he subtly moved from her grasp.

"Jessie, I'm going home soon. Are you sure you'll be okay? You seem to have had a lot to drink."

Despite the fact that the alcohol had numbed her senses, Jessie knew she had overstepped the mark by physically hanging on to him.

"How do you think I've got through today?" she whispered. "If I didn't have so much wine, I'd have crumbled. I am falling apart, Father. I am this close to telling Andrea. This close."

Father Christopher waited to respond as the waiter brought their drinks.

"It's too late, Jessie," he said. "You know you

should have told her before the wedding. It was a case of speak now or forever hold your peace. You can't tell her now. You'll have to hold your peace."

Jessie nodded at him and then gave a false smile to her fellow-bridesmaid Donna, Cain's niece – the little redhead who didn't like the colour of her dress – who stood across the room staring her way.

"D'you know what, Father?" she said when she looked back his way. "I'm so glad I know you."

"Really? Where did that come from?"

"Well, you always say the right things. Just when I think I'm going to fall apart, you bring me right back again."

She could have sworn she saw him blush beneath his swarthy complexion.

"So, you don't think I've gone all preachy on you with the 'forever hold your peace' advice?"

"I like preachy," she said. "Listening to you and asking for God's help, with a little bit of alcohol thrown in for good measure are the only reasons why I've got through the past few days."

Jessie meant what she said and he knew it.

"God will always answer your prayers if you believe He will," he said. "You're right to keep the faith. If you ever feel like things are creeping up on you again, ask Him for help and it will come."

"Whoah, whoah, whoah!" said Jessie, taking another huge gulp of wine. "Don't *overdo* the preaching. Quit while you're ahead, Father!"

She was glad when Father Christopher took her joke on the chin.

"Well, you started it," he said.

Jessie lazily blinked her eyes as the warmth of the alcohol made her whole body feel pleasantly fuzzy.

"You have propped me up when I was at my lowest ebb," she said, "and I will never forget you. Please, no matter what happens, tell me you will never forget that."

Father Christopher looked more serious now. His beautiful face creased into a frown and he looked at her as if there was no one else in the room.

"No matter what happens? You sound as if you're going somewhere when you say that, Jessie? Are you?"

"Who, me?" said Jessie and she gave his hand a squeeze, then let go when she realised the barman was casting strange glances at the handsome priest and the beautiful bridesmaid locked in such an intimate conversation. She downed her wine and stood up. "The only place I'm going is on to the dance floor. I'll see you later for a sneaky brandy, my friend. I'm fine now. Thanks to you I'm just fine."

She leaned forward to kiss his cheek, the wine rushing through her veins making her feel warmer and happier than she had felt in a long time and then she disappeared through the function-room doors, leaving Father Christopher feeling bemused.

"Tut-tut, Father," said the cheeky young barman as he walked past balancing a tray of drinks in one hand. "Lipstick on your collar and all that! I wouldn't blame you, mind. She is one hot bit of stuff!"

Father Christopher's face reddened with anger and

189

embarrassment and he knew right then he had to fight against his growing closeness to Jessie once and for all. He pushed through the mingling crowd, said a few muffled goodbyes, ran for his car and quickly drove off. He still hadn't recovered his equilibrium when he reached Glencuan almost two hours later.

The rain had continued to pour down, despite Cain's reassurances the night before, but apart from that everything else about the wedding so far had gone exactly to plan.

Tom was putting on a wonderful act, being the perfect host, and Ryan was staying out of everyone's way. Andrea looked radiantly happy and Ella hoped that this could be a new beginning for her family. They would get through this bumpy period in their life. Every family had their ups and downs, didn't they? This wasn't the worst thing that could happen. Jessie would pick up the pieces of her life and would find the path she wanted to go down and Ryan would accept all the wonderful things he had ahead of him and embrace them with gratitude and good faith.

She patted a seat beside her for Lily to join her. Lily and her family had been having a ball all afternoon, oblivious to the goings-on of the past few days.

"I just love Irish weddings," Lily said, and she plumped down on the chair which was draped in white linen and tied with a huge blood-red bow to match the bridesmaid dresses. "We Irish are the best at letting our hair down. There's no place like home!" Lily laughed and clicked her heels together.

Ella gave her a hug. "You know, you always cheer me up, Lily. I just wish you could be here more often. Tom does too."

"Don't be going all mushy on me now, Ella! It's about three hours too early for that. Believe me, in a wee while I'll be declaring my undying love for you and my brother but don't believe a word of it. It'll be just the wine and the merriment of the occasion!"

Lily knocked back the dregs of her wine and the waiter filled it back up again right on cue.

"It's been a wonderful day, hasn't it?" said Ella, smiling as Lily checked out the waiter's fine physique.

"It sure has, and bar staff like that make it all the more wonderful in my eyes!"

Ella was convinced by now that a sensible conversation with her best friend was out of the question. She glanced around the magnificent ballroom of Bromley Castle and savoured the elegant surroundings and the swinging jazz band who were entertaining the lively crowd. Andrea and Cain were dancing their hearts out, oblivious to anyone else around them and Lily's two sons looked like they were getting on well with two city girls who had arrived as some of the very few singletons.

Ryan was propping up the bar by now, no doubt serenading the bar staff with his smutty jokes. They looked as if they were enjoying his company and he looked as if he was treating everyone who stood near him to a drink.

The song ended to rapturous applause and Ella faced the dance floor once more, clapping along in appreciation of the wonderful music. She kicked her shoes off beneath the table, giving her feet some well-earned breathing-space, and relaxed back in her chair. Perhaps she could treat herself to a small glass of wine now, she thought. She had been so tense all afternoon and wanted to remain totally sober in case of any arguments amongst her children or her husband. But as the evening went on she began to relax and she did so even more at the sight of Jessie approaching her with a huge smile on her face. At that, Ella called for table service and a waiter had a bottle of wine from his tray and onto the table by the time Jessie found her way over.

"Mum," she said, almost falling into the chair opposite Lily, "I am so sorry for all the upset I've caused. All week I've been such a pain in the arse, moaning and disappearing and causing arguments." She took a large gulp from her glass and then refilled it, gulped again and plonked the glass down on the table.

"Jessie, go easy," said Ella, her eyes skirting around to make sure no one witnessed how Jessie was downing her drink so quickly.

"No, no, no, I will not go easy," Jessie said, shaking her head so her dark, newly styled curls shook around her face. "I have no intention of taking it easy. I almost ruined my sister's wedding – I almost ruined my sister's life – and now I'm going to make it up to her. I am going to show her just how sorry I really am."

"By getting drunk?" said Ella through a fake, gritted smile. "Jessie, really, I just think you should slow down. People are watching."

"People are watching? Who cares!" said Jessie. "I don't care any more, Mum. I don't care what people say. From now on, I'm going to live my life exactly how I want to. Not how you, or Dad, or David, or the law firm or anyone else says!"

Jessie stumbled up from the chair and almost fell onto her Aunt Lily's lap, before steadying herself again.

"Whoops!" she giggled. "Sorry, Aunt Lil! Right, now I'm off to enjoy myself. Today is the first day of the rest of my life!"

Ella watched as her daughter weaved her way through the crowd, dancing sloppily off the beat of the music as she crossed the floor, and she didn't take her eyes off her until she disappeared outside through the folding French doors where a small crowd of smokers and those who couldn't stand the heat of the ballroom had gathered.

Jessie bumped her way through the revellers and slumped down onto a picnic bench outside, glancing around for someone she might know.

She quite fancied a cigarette even though she hadn't smoked since she was a teenager. She squinted and looked around the small gathered party, a mixture of tall, skinny model types (Cain's friends, she gathered), literary buffs who were looking at her strangely (Andrea's friends) and a huddle of young men who had loosened their bow ties and opened their top buttons and were laughing like baboons.

"Hey, you're that hot-shot lawyer!" one called to her and she held her hands up.

"Hot shot? Haven't heard that in a while," she said, quite pleased at the compliment. The rest of the gathering stopped to listen. "But if you insist . . ."

"Well, you probably won't hear it again, will you?" laughed the man. "Not when you're going to try and clear the name of that drug-dealing scum-bucket, O'Donnell!"

The group laughed and mocked her and she threw them the middle finger.

"*Wooo*!" jeered the sour-faced reveller. "So, you're not as classy as they say you are, then?" His friends cheered.

"Get out of my fuckin' face!" said Jessie, and she leaned on the table to help herself get up, but she slipped on its wet surface and lost her balance, then fell backwards onto the grassy bank. One of the model types raced to her rescue and helped brush off her dress which was now stained with an unsightly grass mark.

The men looked the other way, realising that Jessie O'Neill was not in any fit state to enjoy a bit of banter, and the literary buffs whispered and pointed.

"I'm fine, I'm fine," she said, holding her hands up in surrender. "I think I'll just get out of your way. I didn't come here to take insults from you lot. I'm the bridesmaid. I'm the fucking stupid drunk bridesmaid. That's who I am."

The strangers watched in pity and shock as the stunning girl in the scarlet bridesmaid dress stumbled back inside the hotel, too drunk to feel as humiliated as she should be.

She dodged other wedding guests as she made her

way through the bar and was doing well at avoiding attention until she felt a cold hand on her bare arm.

"You're Jessie, right?"

Jessie squinted in an attempt to focus on the girl with the platinum bob who had stood in her way. She had never seen her before in her life.

"Who's asking?" she said. "Sorry, but do I know you?"

"Oh, do excuse my ignorance," said the girl, her grip on Jessie's arm tightening as she spoke, and she wore an icy stare. "I'm Bernice. A good friend of Cain's. I made your sister's wedding dress."

Jessie was confused and the girl was hurting her arm.

"No, you didn't," she slurred. "Andrea bought her dress months ago, off the peg. From one of her own very good friends."

"Well," said Bernice, "ask her then. It's just a pity I wasn't able to get my hands on the design of the bridesmaid dresses too. That shade of red, well, it's a bit scarlet, isn't it?"

Bernice let go of Jessie's arm and stood with her hip jutted out as she sipped from a long-stemmed champagne glass which was stained with deep-red lipstick.

"Well, you can't please everyone," said Jessie and she made a move to step away from the blonde stranger with the high opinions. "I like it, scarlet or not."

"But then again, if the cap fits."

"What exactly are you on about?" asked Jessie. "Who are you?"

"I suppose I'm much the same as you really," she

said, smacking her red lips. "A bit of a scarlet lady. Well, at least I am where the lovely Cain is concerned."

She let out a cackle and Jessie stumbled a bit, blinked heavily and again made an attempt to walk past but Bernice grabbed her wrist and held it waist high so no one else could see. She sank her red nails deep into Jessie's skin, so hard that they drew blood instantly.

"Take it from me," she hissed into Jessie's ear, a pearly white smile painted on her face at all times, "I've been watching you."

"What are you doing? Let go of me now!" said Jessie but Bernice's knowing stare was shaking her.

"I know your every nasty move, Jessie O'Neill," said Bernice. "And I know people who can ruin you, so stay away from Cain or I'll fucking kill you, bitch!"

"What are you saying? I don't even know you!"

"I'm saying I've been watching you for a long time. I know everything and there's only room for one mistress in Cain's life. And that will be me. *Not* you. Okay?"

Bernice snapped Jessie's wrist free and shoved past her so that Jessie, dazed and shocked with her wrist throbbing, bumped right into her brother Ryan, knocking his pint of Guinness straight down her front.

"Hey, watch where you're going!" said Ryan and he looked at Jessie in deep disgust. Her make-up was blotchy, mascara hung under her normally immaculate eyes like black spiders and her lips were pursed on her pale face, highlighting her last feeble attempt to apply her red lipstick when under the influence of too much wine.

"I'd better go and get changed," she mumbled.

"Stupid asshole!" he retorted and pulled her back by the arm when she tried to walk past him.

"*Ow!* Ryan, that's sore!" said Jessie and he let her go. "What the hell is your problem? What have I done to you? Let go of my arm."

Ryan's eyes darted around the room and then he stared right into his sister's bloodshot eyes.

"You know, I didn't want to do this here," he said, his teeth grinding in sheer temper. "But you make me so, so sick and I think it's time I told you exactly what I know about you. I just can't keep it to myself any more."

He pushed her towards the doorway she had come through only moments before, a hand at the small of her back and her arm grasped firmly with his other hand. Some of the smokers had gone back inside, but the group of ignoramus media boys were still huddled around, laughing and insulting anyone who came their way.

Ryan pulled Jessie around the side of the gable of the hotel and steadied her against the wall. He fished his hand into the inside pocket of his jacket, all the time focusing on his sister's pitiful face. He didn't want to miss one flicker of expression when he showed her what he had wanted to for days now.

"Do you remember, Jess, when you were sixteen and Andrea had a huge crush on . . . em, who was it?" He was searching in his pocket still, his breathing moving into an unsteady pant. "Colin someone? Come on, help me out here, Sis. Who was it? Colin . . . ?"

"Downey," said Jessie and she winced at the memory.

"Downey! Colin Downey! That's the one – yeah, the soccer player with the flashy car and the whiter than white teeth. Andrea really did have the hots for him, didn't she?"

He laughed at the memory of the sixteen-year-old crush but Jessie's face began to change as she sensed what was coming.

"Ryan, I –"

"Shut up!" he said, so close to her face that she could feel his breath on hers and the light spit escaping his mouth. "You stole him from her, didn't you? Didn't you! You targeted him and made sure he asked you out and ignored your little sister's feelings. What an absolute bitch!"

Jessie felt her eyes burn and her mouth drooped as she fought back tears. She hung her head but Ryan lifted her chin back up again and continued.

"She cried for weeks over that, remember?" he said. "I would hear her every night, sobbing her heart out because, as always, you took what was hers right from under her nose."

"It wasn't like that," sobbed Jessie. "It wasn't –"

"Oh yes it was, Jessie! Everything she did, everything I did, you always swiped it away or made sure you went one better. If Andrea came second place in music, you made it first place – if I got a commendation in sport, you got a medal. All down the years it was the same. But, now! Now you have really pushed the boat out, haven't you?" Ryan's eyes narrowed and he threw his head back in a mocking laugh. "Now, when Andrea is getting married to the man of her dreams, what did you do, Jessie? Despite having your own husband who adored you, what did you do?"

He was shouting now and Jessie feared that some of Andrea's wedding guests were within earshot. She couldn't control her crying now and her tears dripped off her face like a river of guilt and shame and fear.

"Ryan, please! Keep your voice down. This isn't the time . . . I'll tell you everything if you just –"

"*No!* That's the thing, darling sister – you don't need to tell me anything because I know it all. I know all of your dirty little secrets and I have enough evidence right here to break your ass once and for all!"

He held up his mobile phone and Jessie went to grab for it but missed. He smirked and laughed as he dodged her, holding it high, then low, then behind his back like a teenage boy wrestling and teasing a younger relative.

"It was *you*," said Jessie, out of breath now. "It was *you* in my house, wasn't it? *You* left me those notes. *You've* been terrorising me! How brave!"

"I have no idea what you're talking about," he said, pressing 'play' on his mobile video player. "Oh, listen to this. Now, here is my favourite bit. Oh, how romantic!"

Jessie's insides churned as she heard the playback of her night with Cain Daniels and it made her feel so dirty again. So used, so damn foolish. The distinctive sounds of their lovemaking in her house and then the whirr of the water bouncing off the shower-tray swam around her head and she blocked her ears, pleading with her brother, almost on her knees now.

"Cinema at its best," he said. "A bit pornographic but the love story behind it makes it so much more watchable. I'd say it would make an eighteen certificate, wouldn't you? The shower bit is my favourite."

"Turn it off, Ryan! Please, turn it off! Someone might hear it. Andrea might hear it. Please don't ruin her day."

Ryan stopped the video and folded his arms.

"Ruin her day? Huh, Jessie? Ruin her day? This video would ruin her *life*. You could ruin your sister's whole life but I won't let you. No, no, no. It's *your* life that should be ruined, not Andrea's."

Jessie thought she was going to be sick. Bile rose from the pit of her stomach, burning her throat, and her head was spinning more than ever now. She had sobered up quite a lot since Ryan's revelations but the effects of the alcohol still lurked in her system. In the cold light of day, this physical evidence and her brother's in-depth knowledge of her sordid fling with her brother-in-law would have driven her totally over the edge.

She had to say something to settle him down and to end this argument that would change her life forever. She was a solicitor, for God's sake. She should be able to come up with something to challenge him.

"So, tell me this, Ryan," she said, eventually finding a possible avenue. "If you knew all of this and if you love Andrea so much after all I've supposedly done to you both, why didn't you tell her about me and Cain?

200

Why did you let her go ahead and marry that smarmy, egotistical bastard that I was stupid enough to fall for, the same way she has? Why?"

Ryan licked his lips and smirked as if he knew this very question would be coming his way. "Oh, believe me I did consider that. In fact, I was this close to telling all only days ago. This close." He pinched his fingers into Jessie's face. "I didn't want her to marry that asshole!" he spat. "There is no way I wanted to watch what I had to today. I hated the thought of Andrea believing his every stinking word and I prayed he would choke on his vows today!"

"But you did nothing to prevent it!" cried Jessie.

"I turned over every single possible option I could think of to stop this wedding without having to tell Andrea your sordid truth. But now that it has gone ahead and Andrea has married him, it's you who has to suffer." Ryan looked calmer now, as if he had planned every single part of this in finest detail. "I was going to tell her and then I realised that if Andrea found out about you and her fiancé, not only would she would be forced into ditching Cain, but you would have won again. You would have ruined her again. Possibly forever. And I wasn't going to let you do that. Not a chance."

Now it was Jessie's turn to mock her opposition with a snigger. "So, Andrea got her man, and you protected her from humiliation. How noble of you, Ryan! You should be so proud of yourself!"

Ryan's smug expression drooped slightly as Jessie turned her defence argument into attack.

"Don't you think I've wanted to tell Andrea the truth?" said Jessie. "Don't you think I've thought of the same things as you? It has tortured me for months as to how I could stop her marrying him and still avoid her pain of knowing what he was like, but like you I couldn't do it. And in return, he'll probably screw around for years on her, long after children come along and then she'll be tied into him much deeper than she was yesterday or the day before. And that sickens me to the core. To the very core, along with the guilt, the deep-down rotten guilt that I feel every time I look at her."

"I will never feel sorry for you and your guilt, Jessie," said Ryan and a rush of anger spread over his face again. "You can rot in hell for all I care!"

Jessie acknowledged his hatred for her with good grace. She didn't blame him in the slightest but the thought of what he had put her through lately gave her the urge to fight back.

"I'm your sister too, Ryan. I'm not asking you to forgive me. All I am saying is that I am beating myself up inside. Don't push this or it will ruin Andrea. My life is already ruined."

Ryan looked confused now. "You're playing mind games with me. You're playing mind games with your false guilt and your 'I'm suffering too' lecture. Save it for the courtroom, Jessie! If you were so concerned about your sister's future, why the hell did you jump into bed with her man in the first place? Why didn't you tell her then? Why did you let it go this far?"

"I am the one who has gone too far," said Jessie and she pointed to her chest. "After all, I'm as bad as Cain Daniels is. You're the good guy here. Well, you could have been the good guy but just like me, you have let it go too far."

Ryan took a step backwards onto the damp garden grass that surrounded the hotel.

"You're sick. You're playing with my head. Don't think that by turning this round on me you can stop me from ousting you as the dirty slut you are."

Jessie knew she was making him think, despite his bravado. He grabbed her arm again and she pulled away, banging her head off the pebbledash wall, so hard her head stung immediately and she could feel the damp blood seep from under her hair.

"You could have nursed Andrea through the pain of cancelling her wedding and mopped up all her tears, Ryan," said Jessie above the pain. "Hell, you could have been the hero you've always wanted to be in Mum and Dad's eyes and you blew it. You let her go ahead and marry him, all the while knowing what you know. That he's a two-timing, good-for-nothing rat who can't even keep his hands off his fiancée's sister! Good work, Ryan. You're almost as guilty as I am."

Ryan's breathing was so heavy that Jessie could hear his every gasp as he thought about what she had said. She had thrown the ball back in his court and now he didn't know how to react.

"Like I said, why don't you save your monologue for the courtroom?" he blustered. "Save your speeches for protecting scum like Jack O'Donnell, you selfish bitch! Don't make me out to be the loser. You're the slut of the family. I just happen to be the only one who knows that. For now."

The word 'slut' was like a scalding knife-wound to Jessie and she could feel every ounce of Ryan's hatred for her at that moment. She lifted her hand to slap his face but instead her nails caught his cheek and in a fit of drunken temper Ryan retaliated and hit her so hard her nose burst into a sea of red blood.

Years of feeling like the black sheep had come to the surface in Ryan and Jessie was petrified as to how far her brother might go.

She stumbled past him, kicked off her sandals, bent over to pick them up, then headed across the wet grass and down towards the riverbank.

She didn't know where she was going and she didn't know how she was going to escape, but she could feel herself sober up as she wiped the blood from her nose. She glanced behind her and had a feeling her real troubles had only just begun as Ryan came running after her. She glanced back and saw that girl again – the blonde one who warned her to stay away from Cain. Who had dug her nails into her wrist so hard that she still bled. She was standing at the top of the hill outside the hotel, staring at her, still sipping her champagne. Jessie kept running until she came to the river which swirled deep below her. Her head throbbed and blood seeped deep into the fibres of her dress.

Then she heard a second voice echo in the background, arguing with her brother as they tussled between them, saying her name and insisting on just how much they hated everything she stood for.

Chapter 16

"Mum, Dad, come on! It's our last song." Andrea pulled her mother onto the dance floor while her father followed suit and the DJ called for the bride and groom to stand in the centre of the floor.

"Where are Jessie and Ryan?" Ella whispered to her husband when they joined the other guests. "It's important they join in on this. It looks extremely bad otherwise."

Tom hushed her and leaned to whisper in her ear. "Leave it," he said. "Believe me, those two have had way too much to drink so it may be for the best that they're missing. It's almost over and we don't want ny rows." He slipped his arm around his wife's slender waist as the music began. The sounds of *Auld Lang Syne* filled the room and Cain and Andrea laughed and hugged in the middle of the dance floor, much to the delight of the guests who had formed a haphazard circle around them.

Andrea joined her parents at their table as soon as the song ended.

"What a day!" she said, flopping down and pretending to fan her face with her hands. "I have had an absolute ball, even better than I expected."

Tom leaned over and hugged his daughter. "It was an absolute pleasure. The whole day was magnificent. Didn't I tell you it would all work out in the end, Mrs Daniels?"

Andrea held out her left hand to show her wedding ring again to her mother. "Gosh, that makes me sound so old! I'll never get used to changing my name. Maybe I should be like Jessie and keep O'Neill or use both. Andrea O'Neill Daniels has a nice ring to it," she gushed.

At the sound of Jessie's name, Ella's spirits dampened slightly as she thought of the pain her daughter must have been going through all day. She'd heard a few whispers from far-out relatives and friends who were wondering, naturally, why David had missed the wedding.

"He's away on essential business," had been the official line of the O'Neills and it had filtered through their side of the family, with a discreet nod and a wink that was enough to convince concerned enquirers and simmer down the inevitable whispers. Despite the more peaceful times in their part of the world, being a detective in the police force was still quite a taboo subject.

"Yes, you have your whole life ahead of you, darling," said Tom. "Where is the lucky man? I have to lay down some ground rules with him." He winked at his wife who gave him a playful nudge in return.

"Tom, I'm sure Cain knows how to look after our precious girl. I don't think he needs any lessons from you or anyone else."

"I'm kidding," said Tom. "I just wanted to buy my new son-in-law a drink now that all the madness has settled. Should we have a quiet get-together in the residents' bar?"

Andrea was still admiring her wedding ring but listening to her father's cheerful voice. "That's a lovely idea, Dad. Let's wait until some of the guests move on and until Cain comes back. He's just away to freshen up a bit. I couldn't find him for ages before our first dance and now he's off to 'freshen up' again. Gosh, sometimes I think he's more concerned with his appearance today than I am of mine!"

"Impossible," said Tom with a hearty laugh. "Totally impossible. Between you and your sister, there is no man who could ever beat you in a competition for fashion and beauty. And that's a fact."

Andrea waved at some of her old school-friends who were finishing up their champagne at a nearby table and signalled for them to wait for her so she could thank them and say goodbye.

"Where is Jessie?" she asked casually. "I hope she hasn't scarpered off to bed without saying so."

"I wouldn't think so," said Ella. "I'm sure she isn't too far away. Remember as we celebrate for you, love, your sister is going through terrible turmoil."

"I know," said Andrea. "I noticed her shed more than one tear during the ceremony. It must have been so tough for her to think that only this time last year she had the same hopes and dreams as I have now. I feel so sorry for her."

"Me too," said Ella, and her daughter clasped her hand in support. "In fact, if you don't mind I'll just go and take a look for her. Just to make sure she is holding up okay."

Ella said her goodbyes to several of the wedding guests as she made her way towards the grand hotel foyer in search of Jessie. But despite her casual enquiries about her eldest girl on her way past friends and family, no one had seen her in quite a while.

Ella's cousin cornered her for at least ten minutes, ignoring Ella's increasing insistence that she must go and find her daughter, expressing admiration of everything from the flowers to the church music to the favours on the tables, while another friend of Tom's delayed her for what felt like twice that time, complimenting the entire O'Neill connection for putting on yet another stunning day of entertainment and celebration.

She was relieved to finally get through the sea of people into the more sparse surroundings of the foyer, where just a handful of revellers stood waiting for taxis and laughing heartily after too many glasses of complimentary champagne.

"Ah, Donna," said Ella when she spotted one of Jessie's fellow bridesmaids, "did you have a nice day?"

"It was so much fun," said Donna, the sixteen-year-old redhead who had inherited her uncle's charm and confidence. "I think Cain has found the girl of his dreams at last. God knows he has had enough women. He never really was a one-woman guy."

Ella raised an eyebrow and then decided to ignore the young girl's comment on noticing that she had a rather bubbly liquid in her glass. Least said, soonest mended, she thought.

"I was wondering – by any chance have you seen Jessie?" she said. "I'm going to call it a night and I wanted to see her first."

Donna squinted and thought for a moment. "I've no idea, sorry. The last I saw of her, she was draped all over that gorgeous priest – what's-his-name – Father Christopher over by the bar. What a waste of a gorgeous hunk!"

Donna and her friends giggled in agreement but Ella was unimpressed at their loose talk about Father Christopher. No wonder young girls got themselves into so much trouble.

"Okay, thanks anyway," said Ella and she made her way back into the dance hall and across the floor to where the double doors led outside. This was, after all, the last direction she had seen her daughter taking.

Outside, she stalled in shock when she noticed her son slumped on a picnic bench, a cigarette in his hand almost burned to the butt and blood spattered down the front of his shirt.

"Ryan! What on earth happened to you?"

She pulled him up straight and noticed a trickle of fresh blood drip from the corner of his lip. Reaching into her handbag, she felt around for a tissue and then dabbed it dry, while taking the cigarette from him with her other hand and stubbing it out on the ground.

"Ryan, who did this to you?"

Ryan sniffed hard and looked up at his mother from heavy, bloodshot eyes.

"Me," he said, wiping the latest trickle of blood from his mouth with the white sleeve of his shirt. "I did it, Mum. Me, me me!"

He banged his fist on the bench so that the metal ashtray bounced up a few inches into the air and then settled into a cloud of ash and dust.

Ella sat opposite her son and held his hands in hers.

"Tell me, son. Did you get into an argument with someone? Do you want to talk about it?"

Ryan wrestled his hands from his mother's gentle grasp and pushed himself up from the table. With one sweep of his hand, he knocked over a row of empty pint glasses and one rolled off the wooden table and smashed into smithereens all over the ground.

"No, mother dearest, I do not want to talk about it!" he shouted. "Talking sucks! Every one of our family is a two-faced, shit-talking, let's-all-push-the-dirt-under-the-carpet-and-never-talk-about-it-again asshole and I'm sick of it!"

Ella walked around to where her son stood kicking pieces of glass onto the nearby lawn and grabbed his arm.

"Ryan, I am your mother and you will not speak to me like that. Now, you will walk with me back inside and up to your room to clean yourself up so that you

211

show some goddamned respect to your sister and your family on her wedding day. Now!"

Ryan threw his head back and let out a nasty cackle. "Oh, that's right," he roared. "How could I forget? We have to play a game of 'let's pretend', that's right! Let's pretend to the world that we are all a happy family and we are all just elated that Andrea has married the wonderful Cain Daniels and that Jessie is the perfect creature that everyone believes she is!"

"Ryan! That's enough. Keep your voice down!"

"Oh, but I didn't tell you how the world sees me! Well, I get a fool's pardon most of the time, don't I? So the big, dripping blob of blood on my face won't really be a great surprise to our guests at all!"

Ella wondered was it possible to fear one of your own children. For all her years of showering her children with all the love she could find in her body to give them, this was what she got in return. Was it her fault?

She could see her husband inside the hotel, mingling with the last few guests and she wondered why she couldn't be beside him, thanking everyone for their wonderful gifts and sighing at how marvellous a send-off they had given their youngest girl.

Instead, she was standing in the cold, watching her bloodied son rant about how false an existence she had brought onto her children and, on top of that, in the back of her mind she was worried sick about the whereabouts of her suddenly single eldest girl who was so drunk that she could be slumped in any corner of the hotel fast asleep or unconscious.

Ryan wiped his nose on his sleeve this time and Ella noticed for the first time that he was crying. Her big, grown-up son was crying and had no idea what to do. Her precious son – her own flesh and blood – stood before her, pleading for her help and all along she had been numbed to his agonising pain. His erratic behaviour, his neediness, all of his cries for attention down the years were all her fault. She had brushed over all his faults and now it had come bubbling to the forefront, all his anger frothing now and bursting from his mind.

She watched the damage she had caused unfold before her eyes, the competition she had created between her children, the unconscious battle they had fought for just a fraction more of her love and attention. And all the time she had pushed herself to give each of them more than one hundred per cent.

Now, as she tried in vain to comfort her only son as he stood bloodied in the pouring rain, Ella wondered was it possible that she loved her children too much.

And deep in her heart, she knew it was true.

Chapter 17

At one thirty-five, Ella could stand the festivities no more. She was exhausted from her argument with Ryan and had given in to Andrea's belief that Jessie had slipped off to bed without telling anyone, even though it was so out of character.

She was on her way to ask the hotel receptionist for a key to Jessie's room when she met Andrea who by now had changed out of her wedding dress into a short, white linen shift dress which flattered her figure.

"Mum, you are being psychotic at this stage," she said, handing her mother a glass of wine. "Jessie is an adult who has had too much to drink, way too early, and she has slipped off to bed so that you wouldn't fuss. Now, come on!" Taking her mother's arm, she led her firmly into the residents' bar.

On Ella's insistence Tom had taken Ryan to his room to settle him into bed before coming back downstairs to the residents' bar to join in with a selected audience who were up for another few songs and a few more drinks for good measure.

"He's sleeping like a baby," he said to Ella who was sitting at a round table with Andrea. He patted her shoulder in reassurance. "You don't need to worry any more."

"He's been behaving like a baby all day," said Andrea. "I'll be having a firm word in his ear tomorrow and I mean it."

Ella gave her a weary look from where she sat in a high-backed wing chair.

"No, Mum. Here we are, at the end of a wonderful day, and my own brother and sister are in no fit state to join us. It's a disgrace."

Cain approached and rubbed his new wife's shoulders, then whispered something in her ear which Ella didn't hear, but Andrea nodded obediently and Ella felt uneasy at her reaction. Cain then walked towards the bar, with Andrea watching his every move in adoration.

"Yes, I know they should be here," said Ella to her daughter. "But it's been a great day, love. Don't get too annoyed at Ryan and Jessie. We all know they're both having problems at the moment."

Andrea leaned towards her mother, her dark eyes glazed in temper. "Mum, I don't really want to listen to you defending Jessie again," she said under her breath. "Just accept that she has messed up, will you? It's quite suffocating, you know, when you come over with all your 'buts' and 'maybes'. She's can't possibly be as perfect as you think. No one could be as perfect as that."

Ella was shocked at Andrea's no-nonsense response and she glanced around to make sure no one had overheard. It didn't appear that they had, but she could feel Cain's eyes on them, taking in their every move.

"I am simply trying to defuse any arguments between the three of my children, that's all," she whispered back. "It's not about me defending one over the other."

Andrea shrugged her shoulders and swept back her hair. "Well, it looks like that to me. And Ryan. In fact, Cain has even mentioned it to me too. It's not easy always trying to live up to someone else, Mum. I'm sick of it. Why can't you accept each of us for who we are instead of always measuring us against her!"

Andrea dabbed a tear from the inside of her eyes and took a deep breath to compose her appearance again. She dabbed her nose with a tissue and licked her lips, then painted on a wide smile as she realised a few of Cain's relatives were watching her from another table.

"Well, I don't really appreciate Cain's opinion, Andrea," said Ella, feeling automatically defensive when she heard that her new son-in-law had already expressed a view on how she felt about her own family. "And I refuse to argue with you about this on your wedding day. It's obviously another thing we as a family are going to have to address in the very near future. We have a lot to sort out but we can get through it. We will."

"I hope we can," said Andrea with a bitter twist of her mouth. "I hope what has been said and done can be forgotten and we can work on getting back to normal. We used to be so happy."

Ella patted her daughter's arm and looked at her sadly. "You're right," she said. "And we still can be happy, love. We'll fix all of this. Don't worry." She stifled a yawn. "Really, folks, I think I'll call it a night. It's been a wonderful day but now I'm well and truly shattered."

Andrea yawned in response. "Oh Mum, don't start me yawning! I'm not ready for bed yet, unless my new husband has other ideas!"

She glanced over at Cain and he gave her a nod from the bar where he swirled a glass of brandy. His eyes darted around the room and his left hand looked clenched in his pocket, like he was watching for someone, or aware of someone watching him.

Ella caught his eye and he flashed a grin that made her stir. She knew she was being edgy and uneasy but as she remembered his niece's drunken comments from earlier it soured her towards him, no matter how much she tried to push the silly youngster's cheap remarks out of her head.

"Well, tomorrow is another day," she said and she lifted her bag and jacket from the arm of the chair. She gave her daughter a kiss on each cheek and when she pulled away Cain Daniels was beside her.

His towering presence and wholesome smile chilled her to the bone and when he leaned in to kiss her goodnight she winced under his touch. He smelled of brandy, cigars and rich cologne and Ella avoided his eye. He had changed from his wedding attire into a second sharply tailored suit.

"Thanks for everything," he said but Ella couldn't bring herself to reply.

Tom thankfully interrupted the awkward moment and shook Cain's hand, then patted his shoulder in a warm, welcoming gesture.

"You'll look after my girl," he said and Ella could sense his deep emotion. "I know you will, Cain. I trust you will. My girls deserve nothing but the best."

Ella was sure Tom's words almost knocked Cain's smarmy confidence but she wasn't sure why. He looked deeply uncomfortable within Tom's manly grasp and gave a forced laugh, nodding his head.

"You bet they do," he said. "You bet."

"Come on," said Ella, leading her husband gently away. "Let's get you to bed before we all turn soppy."

The hotel lobby was eerily quiet now, and Ella opted to take the lift to the third floor where most of the O'Neills' and Daniels' wedding guests were staying. The long corridor of royal blue carpet was empty of noise too, apart from Tom's occasional outburst of pride as he recollected moments from the day as they strolled along towards their room.

"And then it's all over," he said, clearly sentimental from adrenaline, emotion and alcohol. "All the preparation, all the tears and tantrums and excitement and in the blink of an eye it's over. What on earth do we do now? Get back to normal?"

"Too right," said Ella in a more hushed tone. She didn't want to stir any guests. "I don't know what Andrea will have to talk about now. She has been engrossed in all of this for the past few months. What we do now is aim to enjoy these fantastic surroundings.

218

I'm looking forward to the beginning of reality from tomorrow."

The castle hotel certainly did not disappoint, with its luxurious rooms and efficient service, and she was already planning her next visit. Perhaps with her two daughters, she thought. Yes, a nice, relaxing pamper session would go down a treat when Andrea returned from honeymoon. That would give her something to look forward to.

"We still have plenty to talk about and plenty to focus on," said Tom, in a matter-of-fact tone that brought Ella back to her senses. "Jessie and Ryan still have some explaining to do and, of course, I have other things to address from the last few days. No one tampers with my life or any of my family and gets away with it."

He searched in his pockets as he spoke for the hotel key card and handed it to Ella to manoeuvre. The alcohol had gone to his head now and she felt a bit of a rant coming on.

She opened the bedroom door and its huge neatly pressed bed called to her, the pillows freshly fluffed and the bed sheets turned down to greet them. Andrea's wedding dress and any family arguments were too much to deal with right now and all she could worry about was getting a good night's sleep.

"In fact," said Tom, removing his bow tie and shaking off his shoes at the same time, "I want a full explanation from that girl on the state of her marriage and I want to know what exactly happened that made David Chambers stay away from this wedding. His absence was highly embarrassing and it's simply not good enough. Jessie's behaviour of late has been a downright disgrace."

"Tom, for goodness sake keep your voice down," whispered Ella. "We can talk about this in the morning. You know there's no point now when we've both had a few drinks. Let's get some sleep."

Tom sat on the edge of the bed and stared out the window into the black night. The room backed onto the nearby river which glistened under the light of the moon but as it was raining again the drizzle blurred his view. Ella knew he wasn't ready for sleep now. Too many thoughts spun through his head and she could almost hear them battling in his mind for attention.

"You know, I really fear for Jessie at the moment, no matter what you may think," he said, still staring at the window. "I warned her about the O'Donnell case right from the start but she wouldn't listen. Jack O'Donnell is a treacherous man and in most people's minds he deserved everything he got, brutal as it may sound. But if I thought any of his campaigners had broken into my house on the eve of my daughter's wedding, I would do time myself to make them pay for it."

Ella sighed and her head throbbed as all of her worries of recent days flooded back to haunt her. To see her husband in such a state of worry was even more disturbing. He was always the strong one, always the first to tell her she was overreacting when she expressed her opinion on one of the children.

"Jessie is going to drop the case, I know she is," said Ella in a bid to reassure him, wishing fervently that

Jessie would. "She knows now that seeking justice for that man is only going to bring trouble upon herself and I think she's realised she's not as tough on the inside as she'd like to believe. I think she's terrified, Tom. But we will get her through it. We have to."

Tom shook his head and pursed his lips together. "But there has to be more to it than the case," he said. "I have a feeling there's a lot more trouble going on in Jessie's world than we know of and, first thing in the morning, I'll be making sure I know every single detail. She can't expect us to help her if she won't tell us the truth."

He got up and pulled the heavy curtains, then switched off the light.

"Perhaps we should have reported what happened to the police," she whispered. "I've hardly slept since and neither have you."

Tom turned his back to her and pulled the covers up around his neck.

"No police. I don't need the police to tell me what's going on in my own family. I will find out all of my answers in the morning."

"Yes, in the morning," said Ella and she closed her weary eyes and fell straight into a tipsy sleep.

Chapter 18

Sunday . . .

Ella knocked on Jessie's door for the second time that morning, just after ten. She knew it was exceedingly early after such a heavy night but Tom had insisted they have breakfast at a reasonable hour to keep up appearances with the Daniels family and Tom's own extended guests who had travelled from near and far for the wedding.

"Jessie! Jessie, love? Are you joining us for breakfast?" she called through the heavy mahogany for the second time but there was no reply.

Tom paced the corridor, rubbing his head at the temples. He needed painkillers and he needed them now and his daughter's silence at the other side of the door was beginning to irritate him.

"Did you try phoning her again?" he said and he took out his own mobile phone from his pocket. "The whole Daniels family will be down there by now. It doesn't look good for us to always be so damned disjointed."

Ella continued to knock the door and tried to ignore her husband's impatience. He was a nightmare when he was hung-over and the slightest disruption could send him over the edge. He had been grumpy and irritable all night and her own sleep had been disrupted on more than one occasion as he got in and out of bed and turned on the television at God knows what ridiculous hour of the morning.

"Why don't you go and try Ryan's door to save time?" she suggested. That might distract him. "He should be up and joining us now too. Go on and I'll keep trying here."

Tom disappeared around the corner of the corridor that led to the adjoining wing of the hotel and then Ella could let herself panic at the lack of response from Jessie's room.

Andrea seemed to think it was perfectly probable that Jessie had called it quits due to too much alcohol and Lily had rolled her eyes when Ella had expressed her concern.

Now, a sea of regret washed over her as she realised how flippant she had been the night before in accepting that Jessie had gone to bed without telling anyone. She knew her children more than anyone else, of that she was sure. Jessie had been terribly drunk and if anything happened to her, Ella would never forgive herself.

"She's probably still fast asleep," came a booming voice from down the corridor. "How many times do I have to tell you to leave the girl alone?"

It was Lily and Ella felt like she had been caught doing something she shouldn't as she held her hand up to knock again. Lily was followed by her own children who looked fresh and well slept, in comparison to each of the O'Neills who were too hung-over or in too deep a sleep to make breakfast. For a brief second, Ella was embarrassed but then the panic returned.

"I'm more than a bit worried now," she said.

Lily threw her eyes up, then linked her arm and gently pulled her away from the door. "Now, *there's* something I have never heard you say before."

"I know she had a bit too much last night but surely she would answer her phone? I mean, she's asleep, not deaf!"

"She's a grown woman, Ella," said Lily. "If she wants to sleep off the effects of the night before and ignore the rest of the world around her, then she is quite entitled to do so. Sometimes I wish my boys would let their hair down a bit more. It's healthy and it's normal. Now, come on and enjoy your breakfast."

The hotel dining-room was buzzing with tales of the day before when Ella led Lily and their family inside. Its long banquet-style layout and gold and cream décor gave a palatial feel to the room and Ella felt her tummy rumble at the delicious smell of sizzling bacon and warm toast.

Ella gazed across the room for any signs of her family and the maître d' found Lily a table for her own party of three. There was no sign of Andrea and Cain as yet, and then at the window she saw a dark-haired girl alone, facing the floor-to-ceiling window that overlooked the lake and the manicured lawns outside.

"Jessie!" she called, hurrying over and putting her hand on the girl's shoulder, but the girl started and shook her head, unable to speak as she tried to swallow a mouthful of cereal. "Oh, I'm sorry. I thought you were . . ."

Ella walked away, dizzy now from worry, and she felt her heart sink with disappointment. Why was her beautiful girl ignoring everyone? She wouldn't settle until she saw her face to face.

Her husband waved at her from the far corner of the room and she made her way across, excusing herself to waiting staff as she crossed their path, the smell of hot breakfast wafting past each time.

Tom and Ryan were already nestled in a corner table, well out of the way, and Ella wondered if they had taken that table out of choice or availability. But when she approached them she could see why.

"I found him in the lobby. Wide awake," said Tom with a hint of sarcasm.

Ella gasped at the appalling sight of her son's normally handsome face which had worsened more than considerably overnight. His left eye had swollen so much that it was fully closed and a rainbow of yellows, blues, greens and purples were starting to appear while his right cheek wore a fine scrape that screamed bright red and sore.

"I didn't want to come in here like this," he said. "Dad didn't want me to either but I think it's my right to be here."

Despite his obvious pain, Ryan sat up straight in his seat and his discomfort was only noticeable by his fiddling with a fork in his hand, up and down, up and down. He twisted a napkin in his hands and then let it go, all the while focusing a solemn stare at the table.

"Who did this to you, Ryan? You have to tell us," said Ella. "Your face! Are you in pain?"

Tom O'Neill shifted in his seat.

"Good morning, Mick," he said to Cain Daniels's father who took his seat at the adjacent table and who was obviously aghast at the sight of Ryan's face.

"Everything okay?" he asked and Ryan turned his head towards the window.

"Bit of a scuffle, that's all," said Tom. "Wrong place at the wrong time. He'll be fine." He guffawed at the other man who gave a wide-eyed nod, unsure of the explanation but happy enough to pass it on to save face.

"You don't have to lie for me," said Ryan quietly and he went back to playing with the fork. "I will tell him the truth if he really wants."

"Tell *me* the truth," said Ella and she sat down, fighting back tears as she looked at her son's pathetic appearance. His normally styled hair was flat and lifeless and he had a defiant, almost sinister air about him. Ella felt like she was in the company of a stranger.

"I could ruin all this now," said Ryan as Andrea and Cain made a grand entrance to raised glasses and congratulatory cheers. "I could burst everyone's bubble right now if I wanted to."

He stared at Andrea and Cain as they shook hands with their friends and family, Cain with his usual cocky bluntness working the crowd. Andrea was in stunning form in a lime-green Fran & Jane dress, belted at the waist in shiny black leather. Her matching bracelet and huge hoop earrings accentuated her natural beauty, while Cain looked like her dapper equal in a smart black Paul Costello suit.

Ella shot a glance towards her husband who looked as if he was concentrating on his breathing and nothing else. His jaw was jutted and his mouth was tense and Ella could have sworn that he was pinning his son down to the chair with his right hand.

"What does he mean by that?" she asked, her voice quivering so much she felt a high-pitched squeal might escape, like a child who was told to stop crying but couldn't control themselves. "I don't think I can take any more of this."

Tom eyeballed his son and then looked back at Ella again. There was a dull look in his eyes and his face was pale and dry-looking – a far cry from the slightly crinkled, tanned and healthy complexion he was often complimented on.

"When we've had our breakfast, we will waken Jessie and then we will leave for home," he said and then raised his arm for a waitress.

"But . . ."

"Ella, I will explain when we are on our way home, I said."

Ella felt her hands shake and she clasped them together. Her palms were sweaty and her legs felt cold and suddenly she felt stupidly false as she smiled at passers-by. To others she was the epitome of effortless

227

glamour, dressed in her matching Jackie O-style ruffled jacket and skirt, high-heeled matching shoes and expensive jewellery but inside she felt claustrophobic and a fake.

"Tom, I want to go home now. I want to know what the hell is going on once and for all," she said, wringing her hands together under the table and resisting the urge to scream from the top of her lungs.

"Andrea is coming over," said Tom and transformed his grey appearance into a convincing smile as his daughter made her way to the table.

"Good morning, everyone – oh holy shit, what the hell happened to you?" she said.

Ryan went to speak but Tom took over.

"Don't you remember Rambo here arguing with a barman last night? Turns out he had picked on the wrong guy to mess over a pint of Guinness with."

Andrea folded her arms and raised an eyebrow. "Honestly, I am so embarrassed. Look at the state of him. This is humiliating! And where is Jessie?"

Ryan pointed his finger and looked at his sister. "Bonus point question," he said. "That is the mystery of all mysteries. Where is Jessie?"

"She's in her room," said Ella. "I tried to wake her twice but she was still asleep."

"Positive?" said Ryan. "Did you see her there?"

Ella felt the room spin and she looked from her son to her husband to her daughter who had the grace to look as confused as she was. She felt sick now. She couldn't figure this out at all. Was Jessie in her room? And if not, where the hell was she?

She scraped back her chair and ignored the stares of the fellow diners, who listened to the clipping of her heels and watched her even strides as she made her way through, ignoring any greetings that came her way. Andrea followed her more sheepishly with her head down and on tiptoes so as not to attract any attention, giving wry smiles to her college friends at the far end of the room when she caught their eye.

Her mother swung the door behind her, not realising that Andrea was on her tail. She marched across the marble foyer of the hotel and banged on the reception bell in demand for attention.

"Mum, I think he heard you. He is checking someone in," said Andrea, pushing Ella's hand off the ringer.

Ella prised her hand free and stood her finger on the bell again.

"Well, my request is much more urgent. Sir, please!" she cried.

Andrea rubbed her forehead and then put her hand on her mother's arm in a show of support as the pinched-faced porter shot disapproving glances at them.

He strode over towards them, his eyes squinted and his mouth pursed.

"Really, madam, I will be with you in –" Then his manner changed and his face transformed, like an actor switching from one character to another in a one-man show. "Mrs Daniels, isn't it?"

It took Andrea a few seconds to recognise her new name.

"Oh, yes. That's right."

"Please, I do apologise. What can I do for you and your, er, sister?"

This was no time for charming bullshit. Ella ignored his comment. She didn't need his compliments or time-wasting customer-service jargon.

"I need a room key for Number 347," she said. "Now! Please."

Andrea smiled at the man and stepped in to explain. "It's my sister's room," she said softly. "This is my mother. We need to get in because she was very ill last night and we're a bit concerned."

"Why of course," said the man, whose name badge said *Jeff* in royal blue letters to match the royal blue carpet of the function halls and bedrooms.

Ella wondered how, in her frantic state, she could even absorb such a meaningless fact.

Jeff walked to an adjoining cupboard-sized room and emerged with a small plastic card. He swiped it and entered a code.

"Ms Jessie O'Neill?" he asked, his efficiency waning now under the weight of Ella's stare.

"That's her," she said and she reached forward for the card. "Please, I'm really very worried. Thank you."

Ella clutched the card and, leaving Andrea to deliver her thanks to Jeff, pounded towards the stairwell. She didn't have the patience to wait for the lift to the third floor and was already one floor up by the time Andrea reached the bottom of the flight.

"Mum, wait for me!" shouted Andrea and she dodged other hotel guests on her way up, who each stopped in wonder at the elegant lady from the celebrity wedding and the beautiful newly wed O'Neill girl who was rushing frantically to keep up.

When they reached the miles of carpet on the third floor, Ella raced ahead again, and then Andrea called to her.

"It's here, Mum! Stop here. This is Jessie's room. Give me the key."

Andrea slipped the white card into the brass plate on the front of the wooden door and then pushed it open when the green light indicated they could enter.

She could hear her mother whispering as they walked into the room, met by the same smell of new furniture and cleanliness that each of the other rooms featured so heavily. The dark curtains were still drawn, allowing only speckles of light to fall onto the bed and the adjacent chair and sideboard.

"Jessie?"

Both their voices overlapped and were absorbed into the rich tones of the bedroom's interior and Ella reached for Andrea's arm.

The bed was crisp, pristine and un-slept in and Ella clung to her youngest daughter for strength – but Andrea pulled away and looked in the bathroom before drawing the curtains, allowing the daylight to give the room an altogether different look.

They stood in a muffled silence of whispers and disbelief as they took in their surroundings.

Jessie's suitcase lay opened at the bottom of the bed. Her make-up, her change of clothes, her nightwear, her toiletries, her legal drama novel, her underwear all lay untouched, just as she had left them when she checked in on arrival to the wedding reception the day before. Jessie was gone.

Chapter 19

Tom O'Neill burst into the room minutes later with Ryan trailing behind.

"What do you mean she's gone? Close that damn door, Ryan, and come in here now!"

Ryan let the heavy door swing automatically shut and he sauntered into the room where his mother sat on the bed, sorting through Jessie's belongings for clues that might tell her of her daughter's whereabouts.

"Well, she's not here, is she?" said Andrea. "She must have gone home. Can we call someone to check?"

Ella dialled Jessie's cleaner's number immediately.

"She's not there," said Ella when she hung up. "Charlotte was over there just now with her boyfriend. They were keeping an eye on the house because Jessie thought someone had been lurking around lately. I can't believe she didn't tell us this. She must have been so frightened."

Tom paced the floor, anger bubbling with fear for his family's safety. There was a host of possibilities swirling through his head and he couldn't settle on any one.

"Ryan, I want you to tell me everything you know. Starting from *now*! When did you last see your sister?"

"She's probably shacked up with one of the male guests in another room," said Ryan. "Knowing Jessie."

"What the hell are you on about?" said Andrea. There was a chance Jessie had found her way home, even though it was so far away, but Jessie would never stoop to casual sex!

"I want you to call the police, Tom," said Ella. "This has gone way too far. First an intruder breaks into our family home and reduces Andrea's wedding dress to shreds, then David mysteriously leaves Jessie, and Ryan is beaten to a pulp and now Jessie has been living in fear too! How long are you going to play detective on this, Tom? Call the police now!"

Tom leaned one arm against the wall and concentrated his mind, breathing consciously to prevent his temper snapping through fear. "I think Ryan can tell us more of what has been going on before we get to that stage. Start talking, son, or you'll have more than a busted face to contend with."

His voice was red raw and Ryan held up his hands.

"Hold on, are you threatening me? Why do I have to be key witness in your little Cluedo game? I got into a drunken scuffle, that's all, and I've the bruises to show for it. After that, leave me out of this."

Tom marched towards his son and grabbed him by the throat.

"*Start talking, I said!* Tell me now where you think your sister is!"

"I have no idea where she is," Ryan gasped and he glanced towards his mother and sister for help.

They both looked away.

"Tell me now or I will call the police!" said Tom. "And you know if it gets to that stage, you'll be in trouble. Talk!"

He let go of Ryan's neck and threw him onto the bed.

"Look, I don't want to be the one who . . ." said Ryan. "Hey, have you tried David? Did anyone even think to ring Jessie's own husband? She could be with him and all this just a big spectacle over nothing!"

Andrea was already dialling David's number.

"You said earlier you could ruin everything if you wanted," said Ella. "What did you mean by that?"

Ryan shook his head and then winced at the pain the movement caused him.

"I meant, look . . ." He waited until Andrea walked out onto the corridor to talk to David away from all the frenzy and then he whispered. "I just don't like Cain Daniels, okay? I heard a few things that I didn't like and sometimes it just eats me up inside so much and I . . . well, I'd love to tell him so. You don't know how much it kills me to watch his smarmy ways and his sleazy advances. He makes me so fucking sick!"

Ella perked up. She'd had the same thoughts, of

course, but had stopped herself from slating Andrea's new husband just yet.

"What sort of things have you heard about him?" said Tom. "What exactly do you know about Cain that I don't?"

Ryan held up his hands for mercy. "Nothing too serious," he said. "Just, well, he's a ladies' man, okay? I just don't like his reputation as a womaniser or the way he brags about all the women he's been with. That girl who came to our house with him – what's her name?"

"Bernice?" said Ella.

"Yeah, that's the one. Bernice. I saw him fondle her when Andrea wasn't looking and it drove me mad. I think Andrea is in for a hard time from him. I didn't have the nerve to break her heart but –"

The conversation cut short when Andrea came back into the room.

"David had a missed call from Jessie last night but he hasn't spoken to her since Thursday," said Andrea. "He's been in Dublin all week. He's on his way here now."

Ella noticed Tom do a double-take.

"What?" he roared. "What do you mean he's on his way here now? He's a bit too late coming to this hotel now! Put him on the phone to me immediately! If it wasn't for David Chambers and his quick flit from our daughter's life this wouldn't be happening!"

No one acted on Tom's request and the silence drove through his mind like a hot nail. He sat down on the bed and held his head in his hands, rubbing his face as if by doing so he could erase all the events of the week gone by.

He looked at his family, or what was left of it. His youngest daughter whose wedding dream was in tatters, his son with his bleeding, broken face and buckets of hidden anger and his wife whose only fault was to love her children with an unconditional blindness that was leading her to despair.

Where had it all gone wrong? He had to do something, say something to fix it all. But most of all, he had to find his missing daughter.

David Chambers arrived at Bromley Castle well over an hour later and Andrea met him at the main doors. He looked different, she thought. Awkward perhaps, and not as self-assured as the David she had spoken to only weeks ago when he made a spontaneous lunch for her when Jessie was too busy to talk on one of her random visits.

He was unshaven and his normally pristine clothing had been replaced with an old T-shirt and a pair of jeans that had seen better days.

David leaned down to embrace his sister-in-law and she hugged him back, neither of them speaking at first, then David broke the silence, his strong South London accent wrapping around her like a well-worn familiar blanket.

"We'll find Jessie," he said. "She's okay. I just know it."

"I certainly hope so."

emma louise jordan

Andrea led him through the foyer where a few guests whispered in their direction, already privy to the drama that was slowly unfolding. She ignored their whispering and silent nudges as some of them realised that Jessie's husband had arrived. Aunt Lily was under instruction to keep rumours to a minimum and so far she was doing a great job despite her own anxiety and questioning from her children and many relatives.

"I just wish she would call or text or do something to let us know what the hell is going on, David," said Andrea. "My dad is about to have a breakdown and Mum can't even speak to anyone. This is such a nightmare."

David followed Andrea past the reception desk which was operating with business as usual, around the corner that led to the function room where only hours ago she had danced the night away with her new husband and down past the residents' bar where she and some of her nearest and dearest had sung into the small hours.

"I'm really sorry I couldn't have been here for your big day," said David when they stepped into the elevator. The doors shut and they began their brief journey to the third floor. "We'd been getting it tough for quite a while, as I'm sure you've heard. Jessie had lost all interest in our marriage and I couldn't live a lie any more. I'm really sorry our timing was so off."

Andrea grimaced but couldn't bring herself to accept his apology.

The elevator opened and they made their way to her parents' room. Jessie's room had been vacated on David's instruction by telephone earlier and they had assembled as a family in the larger room which Ella and Tom were sharing

"A word of warning," said Andrea to her brother-in-law. "Dad is full of questions as you can imagine but be prepared to take the brunt of all this for the first while. He's just really upset about you and Jessie breaking up, and now that we can't find her, well . . . "

David shrugged and placed a comforting hand on Andrea's shoulder. "I can handle it, don't worry. Finding Jessie is our ultimate priority and arguing amongst each other won't help us do that."

They waited until Ryan opened the door.

"David, man!" said Ryan, his face brightening for the first time that morning. "It's good to see you. Come in."

"My God, I hope the other guy looks as bad as you do," said David, noticing Ryan's battered face. "Are you okay, mate?"

Ryan nodded. "The other guy hasn't as much as a scrape. But you know me by now, David. Some day I'll learn to keep my big mouth shut."

Tom O'Neill was on the phone to hotel reception when they entered the bedroom suite. He turned his back to finish his conversation and Andrea noticed how Ella's hands shook as she accepted a cup of coffee from Cain in the far corner.

Cain and David exchanged nervous glances and Andrea sensed David's obvious discomfort.

"Hi, everyone," said David.

His greeting was met with light anonymous grunts from the rest of the O'Neills and Andrea saw his face flush with embarrassment.

"David is here to help," she said. "He knows Jessie as well as we do."

David acknowledged Andrea's support but Tom continued his conversation on the phone without glancing in his direction and Ella stared at her coffee cup. She was forlorn and tired and understandably confused about the break-up of her daughter's young marriage and erratic behaviour.

"Look, I know I'm probably the last person you want to see right now," said David, "but believe me, I'm as concerned about Jessie's whereabouts as you all are."

Tom hung up the phone and shot David an accusing look.

"Oh, that's right," he said. "You are so concerned about my daughter that you walked out on her weeks before your first wedding anniversary like a bolt out of the blue! You didn't even give us as much as a hint that there was anything wrong. You just left! I thought you had more backbone in you, David Chambers, but obviously not!" Tom slammed a fist down on a nearby table and clenched his hands tight.

"Dad, really," said Andrea, "you are going to have to calm down or we will get nowhere at all. David is here to help. My God, he's still her husband!"

Tom shook his fist in David's direction. "I don't need you swaggering in here after all the damage you've done to my family! Couldn't you have at least waited until after Andrea's wedding before you decided to throw your own marriage down the tubes? If you hadn't been so hasty in your big exit from her life, my daughter wouldn't be in the mental state she has been in all week. You've almost torn us apart, David!"

David tried to speak but Tom's accusing rant continued.

"And I don't want any of your colleagues snooping around here either, digging up dirt on my family and trying to make out there is something sinister going on here. We can find our daughter ourselves. You gave up your right to be concerned when you walked out on her only five days ago, so go back to where you came from right now. I don't want you here!"

David took off his jacket in defiance and pulled out a chair. In his job he had dealt with angrier men than Tom O'Neill and he wasn't going to be turned away so easily. If Jessie was in trouble, he would do his utmost to help. It was the least he could do.

"Look, Tom. I'm not here to argue or fight with you on this. But Andrea contacted me and said you feared for Jessie's safety. I have a missed call from her from late last night which I have to admit I didn't answer. I was too angry at the time. But it's almost fifteen hours now since she was last seen and no matter what you think of me right now, I think we should save it for later and concentrate on the job at hand. And that is, to find Jessie."

"The job at hand?" roared Tom. "Is that how you see this? A job? My daughter was devastated that you left her. She was at her lowest ebb this week and now she is gone, so save your detective jargon for the cop shop, David, and leave me and my family to deal with this! We don't need your help!"

"Tom, I think we should hear what David has to say," said Ella. Her voice was low and she squeezed a tissue in her shaking hands. "The clock is ticking and my daughter is nowhere to be found and that's all I care about, not what has happened in the past. I think we need all the help we can get and there is no room for pig ignorance or anger right now!"

Andrea rubbed her mother's shoulders and surveyed the scene around her. Ryan was fiddling with a hotel brochure in the corner of the room and Cain stood with his arms folded in silence while David and Tom took centre stage in a battle for authority. They were all going around in circles.

"David," she said, "we've contacted all of Jessie's friends. We've contacted her work colleagues and I've tried to retrace her last known steps with the hotel staff but they can't tell us much until the evening shift comes back on at six. Can you think of anywhere else she might be or of anyone else that she might be with?"

David thought for a moment. "I take it you've rung the house – our house?"

"Yes, of course," said Andrea.

"But has anyone actually gone there to check?" David asked.

"Yes," said Ella wearily. "I thought she might have got a taxi home so I rang her cleaner, Charlotte, who checked for me at the house but there was no sign of her. Anyway, she would probably have taken her case with her if she'd done that. She was terribly drunk but if she was sober enough to call a taxi she would have taken her belongings – or at least a jacket."

"Well, she might have hitched a lift on the spur of the moment," said David.

Ella blanched at the thought and Tom shifted uneasily.

Cain looked at his watch and Andrea noticed he was becoming edgy and anxious. He had already expressed his concern about the guests from his side of the family who were waiting for the new bride and groom to join them for afternoon tea and since David's arrival he had gone very quiet. His parents were jetting off on holiday to the States later that evening and he would want to spend a little time with them before they left. Andrea felt like some breathing space too.

"I'll walk downstairs with you now if you want, honey," she whispered to her husband. "I need some time out." She turned to the others. "Mum, Dad, we're going to see Cain's parents before they leave. We'll be back as soon as we can and while we're down there we'll see what else we can suss out discreetly from the guests."

She kissed her mother's cheek and then left the room with her new husband, carrying a deep weight in her heart and an itch in her soul that told her that Cain was holding back something from her. Something that might help put a final piece of this dreadful jigsaw together.

Chapter 20

"I'm going to drive to Glencuan and take a look around," said Tom, unable to settle any longer in the hotel room. "This place is suffocating me and I can't think straight. We'll never find Jessie as long as we sit here staring at each other and drinking coffee."

Ella put her cup down and watched as her husband gathered his belongings.

"But Tom, it's two hours away. You don't really think Jessie would have headed in that direction and not contacted us by now? I really would rather call the police and let them handle it."

The room was much emptier now without Andrea's presence and her ability to keep conversation flowing, suggesting angles and people they could contact until she could think no more.

Ella watched Tom glare at David who was making notes on a sheet of hotel-branded notepaper.

"So," said David, looking up, "we need to check hospitals, taxi firms, check with all the wedding guests to make sure that Jessie didn't take a ride home with one of them."

Tom had always despised the police force and it had been a bugbear with him ever since David Chambers came into Jessie's life. Ella realised the irony now as Tom came to realise that he was not a law onto himself, and that he might have to give in and let the authorities take over.

David was still scribbling on the notepad.

"The police won't do much unless we have good reason to believe Jessie is in danger," said David. "She's a twenty-eight-year-old woman and she hasn't been missing for long enough yet. I need more information before we make the call so that they will act more quickly. I need you all to think about her state of mind when you last saw her."

"Oh for God's sake, we were at a wedding!" said Tom. "There was alcohol involved. How do you think her mood was?" His frustration was reaching its heights and he found David's questioning tiresome and repetitive.

"Yes, you say she was drunk but what was her mood like?" said David. "Which of you spoke to her last? How was her form? We need to go right back to that moment and take it from there. Ella, when did you last see her?"

Ella pursed her lips and allowed her tears to fall as she recapped her last conversation with her precious daughter.

"She was in a determined mood, I guess," she

whispered. "She was apologetic too. She was saying how no one would tell her how to live her life any more. She walked away from me and made her way outside but when I went looking for her there was no sign. That was the last time I saw her."

"And did you look for her again, after that?" asked David.

"Did I look for her?" asked Ella. "Of course, I looked for her. I searched for her until I was told to stop. When I wanted to check on her late last night in her room, everyone told me to stop fussing. Everyone always tells me to stop fussing but my God!" She slammed the cup on to the table. "My God, I think I know my children better than anyone else! I am her mother! I knew something was wrong but everyone stopped me from following my gut instinct. I went to bed last night convinced by all of you that I was being overprotective but I was right. She may be a twenty-eight-year-old woman to everyone else but to me she's still my child and if I wanted to look for her I should have been allowed to! I should have been allowed to look for my own child and now she's gone!"

Tom O'Neill's breathing could be heard from the far side of the room. His silver hair framed his grey face and his eyes were heavy and sore. He looked around him and then he spoke.

"We all had a bit of a row the night before the wedding," he said.

"Dad!" said Ryan. "What has that got to do with it?"

"I think it explains Jessie's state of mind," he replied and then turned back to David. "Tensions were running high and I barely spoke to Jessie yesterday because I was so mad at her for all the heartache she had brought on her mother and sister at what should have been such a happy time for all of us. I was angry. We all were and we said things we shouldn't have. God, but I am sorry for that now and if anything has happened to my girl, I will never forgive myself."

Ella could barely look at her husband right now. She felt a wall between them that she had never experienced before and for the first time in her life he looked like a stranger to her.

He was part of the reason she hadn't made sure Jessie was in her room the night before. So was Andrea, so was Lily. She felt the room closing in on her and she wanted to scream. Something bad had happened to Jessie and she knew it.

"Ryan," said David gently, "I have to ask you too. When did you last speak to your sister?"

Ryan rubbed his forehead and didn't look up. "Outside. It was quite late. About twelve or so. I suppose it was after Mum had last spoken to her."

The room fell silent. Ryan was the last immediate family member – possibly the last person – who had seen Jessie. Ella's stomach gave a leap which brought her back to the morning that Andrea's wedding dress was ruined and she thought of all the misery Ryan had caused Jessie in the run-up to the wedding. She fought with the urge to point any blame.

"And how was she then?" asked David.

"Look, I really don't remember much," he said. "I'd

had a shit-load to drink. We all had. It's all a bit of a blur. Can't remember what we talked about."

Ella could see her husband's temper rise but David held a hand up in a signal for him to be quiet.

"Ryan, you have to tell us. You may have been one of the last people to see your sister. What did she say to you? Did you have a row?"

Ryan sniggered and looked at his family. "What? This?" He pointed at the swollen bruise around his eye which was becoming progressively worse as the day went on. "Oh, don't make me laugh! It hurts when I laugh."

"Ryan!" Tom O'Neill charged towards his son. "This is no time for games! What did you talk to your sister about? What did you say to her? Don't give me this I-can't-remember fucking nonsense! Think harder. What did you say to her? Tell me now!"

David grabbed Tom before he managed to lunge at Ryan but the older man's strength pulled him free and he clipped his son across the chin. He raised his fist again but this time David caught him before he could follow through.

"I called her a slut!" said Ryan. "I called her a dirty rotten whore! I told her exactly what I thought of her at long last."

"Ryan, no, please stop!" said Ella, horrified by what she was hearing and the brutal scene of her husband and only son physically fighting.

Ryan lunged towards Tom and David, his face demonic with temper.

"I didn't want to be the one to have to tell you this,"

248

he said, "because as always I turn out to be the bad guy. But tough fucking shit, Mum and Dad! Your precious Jessie wasn't as pure as you all thought she was."

"What do you mean?" cried Ella.

"She *wasn't* as pure? You mean she *isn't*?" said David. "Ryan, what have you done?" His words highlighted Ella's fears and a cold shiver ran through her.

"She was seeing Cain Daniels behind your back, David," said Ryan. "She was shagging her own fucking sister's fiancé and I was the only one who knew about it. I saw them together and it made me sick!"

"Cain?" said Tom. "Ryan, I hope you know what you are talking about here. I hope this isn't one of your silly stunts because we all know exactly what you are capable of."

Ryan laughed out loud again. "See!" he said to David. "It's always my fault in this family. The tearaway son. The clichéd black sheep. The only one who didn't go to university, who hasn't got a proper job, who dabbles in trouble with the cops now and then, who crashes his brand-new car, who hangs out boozing with his mates in the park. That's me, that is!" His veins stood out on his neck and he kicked a chair out of his way before going right into David's face. "But I've always really liked you, David. Do you know how hard it has been for me to hold this in for so long? Do you know how long I've been itching to tell you that your precious, beautiful wife took her sister's fiancé into her ivory tower and was sleeping with him for over a month?"

David looked away.

"But you beat me to it, didn't you?" said Ryan. "You left her before I even got the guts to tell you. I knew the silly bitch was lying when she told us you had gone away on business. I thought with your super intuition and detective skills that you had caught her out, but you hadn't and now that she has run away from all of the shit she has caused, you've come running back to find her. I can't believe you didn't know."

Tom and Ella froze and watched as David's world crashed around him. They looked at each other, unable to speak, and Ryan spun round in the middle of the room, eyeing each of them in turn.

"You still don't believe me, do you?" he said and he broke into a nervous laugh. "You can't believe that Little Miss Perfect with her top grades and top-notch manners and first place at everything could possibly have stepped out of line like this! You were all fooled by her, especially David and Andrea, and all along I've been made to feel like the outcast, just because I knew what a dirty rotten little slag she really was!"

David steadied himself and sat down on one of the small sofas in the hotel room's lounge area. He swallowed hard and Ella watched his face break from the practical police officer he had been when he first came into the room to the betrayed husband, the last to know of his wife's sordid affair.

Inside she crumbled too as everything she believed in, everything she had built up in her whole family life was spat back in her face by Ryan's accusations.

"Ryan, this is not the time to carry out a character-assassination on your missing sister," said Ella, eyeballing her son in steely determination. No matter how she tried to absorb what he was saying, it just didn't add up to her. Jessie loved her sister. She would never do something like that to her. Plus Ella's thoughts would not be distracted from the fact that her daughter was nowhere to be found.

"Oh for Christ's sake!" said Ryan.

"I don't know where you've got this silly notion from but it's downright disgusting and I don't want to hear of this ever again," Ella continued. "Your sister is missing and you have the damn audacity to come out with this filth in her absence when she hasn't the chance to defend herself. It doesn't make sense. It's not true. It can't be!"

Ryan continued, centre stage in the middle of the room, as Tom and David backed into the wings in dismay and defeat.

"You are so pathetic, Mum! How pathetic can you be? Don't believe me, then. Believe Jessie as you always have done. No matter what I say against her, you will take her part on every occasion. In your eyes she can do no wrong. What the hell is it about her that has you so blind?"

"Don't you dare question me about how I feel for my children, Ryan!" said Ella. "We have been down this road a million times and I will not withstand this nonsense any longer. I love each and every one of you equally. Jessie is a good girl. She has always been a good girl and you will not tarnish her name to me just because you don't like Cain Daniels!"

She looked at her son who was almost dancing now with bad temper and anger.

"Dad! Say you believe me!" said Ryan. "Surely you can't be so blind as to think that Jessie was beyond sin? David, do you think I'm telling lies?"

David's face was ashen and as much as Ella was hurting inside, she couldn't imagine how this might be making him feel. Despite his brief separation from Jessie, Ella was in no doubt that he still had a deep love for her.

"I really can't take this in right now," he said. "I have no reason to disbelieve you, Ryan, but you'll have to forgive the rest of us as we try to get our heads around all of this. It's more than shocking and as you'll have to agree, totally out of character."

"Ryan, I hope you have strong evidence to back up everything you have just told us," said Tom. "Because should this be true, I will go down to Cain Daniels right now and wipe that smug smile right off his Prince Charming face."

"No!" said David. "Let's just think a moment. I want to let this sink in before any of us approaches him. Do you know how much I too want to smash his face right now? Can you imagine how stupid I feel having been oblivious to this all along? I thought Jessie was drifting away from me because of her obsession with work, or that I was pressurising her into having a baby, but never ever did I think it was because she was seeing someone else."

"So you *do* believe me!" said Ryan.

Tom leaned on the window-sill and stared outside.

Another wedding party was arriving at the hotel full of joy and celebration. He could see the bride and groom pose for photos and his insides burned.

"You should have told us this before," he said to Ryan. "Why did you let it get this far? Why did you let the wedding go ahead? Why did you wait until now?"

"My God, Tom! Do you really think this is true?" Ella cried. "Surely there is some mistake. Maybe Ryan is just jumping to conclusions. You know what Cain is like. He's so flirty and charming with everyone he meets and Jessie –"

"Oh, for Christ's sake, that's enough, woman!" said Tom. "Don't you see things are at last starting to make sense? Jessie was having an affair with Cain which led to her break-up with David even though he is just finding out about this now. It explains why she and Ryan were at loggerheads and it also tells us why she didn't get too excited about this wedding and why she was dodging all the last-minute preparations this week. What it doesn't tell us just yet is where she has decided to disappear to but something tells me she's found it all too much to bear and is running scared. We have to put all our energies into finding her, and then we can deal with this."

David was silent, unable even to string a sentence together to respond to Tom as the last few months slotted into place.

He thought of their holiday together in France last May – of the night that he'd gone to bed early after one too many and left Jessie and Cain in the bar when Andrea had already left because she was feeling unwell.

He recalled how touchy and edgy Jessie became on the last few days of the holiday. She became withdrawn and made excuses to go for walks alone, saying she needed thinking time. And that was why.

Things had gone downhill between them since then but he had always blamed her job and her obsessive ambition for her coldness towards him. He thought she'd been too wrapped up in her job when she shut him out, taking to her study day in, day out and he recalled how she stopped looking sorry when he said he had to go away on business each time. Again, he thought it was so she could have more time to delve into the past life of O'Donnell and his gang.

But never, ever would he have dreamed that all the time she would have been weak enough to fall for the charm of that arrogant bastard Daniels with his fan club and celebrity friends. He felt so used, cheated and bruised at finding out in this public way in front of Jessie's own parents and to be told of how blind he had been by her own brother.

Yet, as angry as he felt towards her now, his fear for Jessie's wellbeing was stronger and until he found out where she was hiding from all of this, he would have to curb his anger and make sure she was out of harm's way.

"So, what do we do now, David?" asked Tom. "Does this change our direction? I can't find answers to the questions in my head. You're the expert. You're the cop. What the hell do we do now?"

David chewed his lip and paced the floor, all the time

fighting the rising fury that bubbled from every inch of his body.

"Yes, of course, it changes things. It makes me think that if she was carrying either a love for that bastard, or a heavy guilt for what she has done, then she may have decided in her alcohol-fuelled mind . . . My God, I just hope she hasn't done anything stupid!"

"Don't say that," said Ella.

"We have to consider all possibilities," said David, "as hard as it is to swallow. If she was very drunk and carrying a lot of guilt, well, we can't rule it out." He forced himself to say it. "We can't deny that Jessie might have taken her own life."

Tom looked wretched at the very thought. "And we've already tried all her friends. Ryan, can you think of anyone else?"

Ryan wiped a speck of blood from the scrape on his face with a tissue and then grabbed his jacket from the back of the chair.

"Ryan!" said Tom again.

"I'm going to my room," he said. "I've had enough of all of this. I'll see you all at home in Glencuan. I hope Jessie knows she's caught, wherever she is. She's been caught out at last. But still you all sit here and pity her for her poor mental state and the possibility that she topped herself. She wouldn't have the guts."

Tom started after him but David pulled him back.

"Let him stew," he said. "Just leave him for now. He feels like the bad guy at the moment so give him some space."

"So, what do we do now?" asked Tom. "Start looking for my daughter's body?"

Ella left the room, unable to take any more.

"We have to look around the grounds," said David, "And I think by now we should call in the police. But we do not discuss one more thing about Jessie or her whereabouts with that Daniels bastard. As hard as this is going to be, for the next few hours we are going to stay out of his way, or else pretend that we know nothing of his alleged affair with my wife."

Chapter 21

Father Christopher's head throbbed as he stood in the vestry of the old church in Glencuan.

As he said two Sunday Masses and chatted to the parishioners that morning, all they wanted to know was the nitty-gritty of the O'Neill wedding reception which had taken place in the grand surroundings of Bromley Castle.

Was it true that Andrea's dress had been hand-designed in London? Was it true that Ireland's top boy band had provided the musical entertainment? Did Cain Daniels really have a surprise chartered plane arranged to take them on honeymoon?

He was strolling through the grounds of the parochial house in the early evening sunshine, on his way to the gate lodge where he was dabbling in some DIY, when he got the phone call to inform him of Jessie's disappearance.

"Father Christopher, it's . . . it's Tom O'Neill here."

"Oh, hello, Tom. How did the rest of the wedding go? Sorry I had to rush off so soon –"

"Look, Father, I'll cut to the chase," interrupted Tom. "We can't find Jessie. I'm trying every angle here and I wonder did you see her today? At Mass?"

Father Christopher stopped dead along the windy gravel path that was framed with cherry blossoms and he waited for Tom to continue.

"She hasn't been seen since around midnight to be honest," said Tom, "and, as you can imagine, we are becoming increasingly concerned."

"Mass? I don't think she was there. No, I definitely don't think so. Jessie normally waits to say hello when she attends Sunday Mass. Didn't she stay at the hotel? I believed that was the plan?"

He could sense Tom's fear from the other end of the line and the older man stuttered before giving him a response.

"No, it doesn't look like it. We are all still at the hotel and we're just trying all angles really. You know, we often joked that Jessie got the religious gene of each of our children, and most of mine and Ella's too, so we thought . . ."

Father Christopher squinted in the sunshine. After conducting his first wedding in Glencuan, he was now preparing for his first funeral having given last rites to an elderly villager in the early hours of the morning and he was extremely tired.

"I'm sorry but no, Tom. I didn't see Jessie this morning at either of my morning Masses, nor have I seen her since I spoke to her briefly after the wedding supper last night, just around nine or so. She was in great form though. I'm sure she'll turn up soon."

"Father," said Tom, slight desperation in his voice, "we have tried almost every avenue we can think of at this stage. We have wrecked our minds as to where our daughter can be. Her mother and her husband and I are scrambling with every inch of our brains to figure out where she is, so if there is anything, and I mean *anything* that you might know or that you may have noticed with her yesterday evening, please, please let me know."

Father Christopher looked out over the valley of Glencuan as he listened to Tom's plea. There was a mist over the village, yet where he stood in the gardens of the parish headquarters and the place he now called home, the afternoon sun was glistening off the grass and flowers and a peaceful mood was reflected all around him.

Yes, Tom's frame of mind from some miles away at Bromley Castle was alien to what Father Christopher could see.

"Of course, Tom," he said. "Please do keep in touch. Good afternoon, sir."

He hung up the phone and inhaled so much he thought his chest might explode.

"Jessie, Jessie, Jessie!" he said aloud. "What the hell have you done now?"

He walked inside the parochial house where his eyes took a moment to adjust from the strong sunshine.

Rosie was in the kitchen as usual and she was

scurrying around with added vigour. He walked towards the kettle and flicked it on, then changing his mind he passed through the kitchen and went to his drawing-room where he reached for a brandy glass and poured himself a large helping of his favourite medicine.

His hands shook as he gulped down the soothing golden liquid which burned his throat at first but then lined his gullet and warmed his stomach and calmed his fears a notch just as he had hoped.

His sense of relaxation and comfort was disturbed by the rattle of the huge brass doorknob and Rosie shuffled in, unable to contain her excitement

"Father, you'll never believe it," she said, removing her yellow rubber gloves from her tiny pink hands, "Maggie McKenna is just off the phone. Her daughter is just back from Bromley Castle. From the O'Neill wedding –"

"And?" said Father Christopher. "I hope this isn't more about boy bands or flowers or the cost of the limousine, is it?"

Rosie could barely breathe and she let the words tumble out of her mouth, her eyes blinking in time with them as they spilled into Father Christopher's ears.

"No, no, not at all," she gasped. "This is much more interesting than that. There's a rumour swimming all throughout the hotel that the bridesmaid girl, you know, the one that was here a few nights ago to see you about the readings, Jessie, yes, that's her, well, they're saying that she was terribly drunk last night, making a show of herself and –"

260

"Rosie, I've told you before. I don't listen to idle gossip around here. I thought you were the same. Only days ago you were warning me against the rumour-mill of a small village like this."

Again, Rosie gasped for breath, unable to get to the juiciest part of her story. "But Father, she hasn't been seen since!"

"How do you mean?" he asked, unwilling to let Rosie or anyone else know of his previous contact with Tom O'Neill. That would really feed the gossip.

"She has disappeared! They say her room wasn't slept in. Her suitcase is unpacked and all of her belongings intact. She must be still wearing her bridesmaid dress, poor thing. She's gone, Father. The police are crawling all over the place now, they say. Jessie O'Neill has disappeared."

Father Christopher reached behind him for the arm of the nearest chair and leaned his other arm on the sideboard while he steadied himself. He tried to brush his fear away, to present a neutral, strong front for what was potentially a very personal nightmare now for him

"Jessie," he whispered and he stared at the floor, watching as the carpet swirled in front of his eyes.

"Father, are you all right? Father, can you believe it? Didn't I tell you they had troubles like everyone else, despite the way they flaunt their riches? Father?"

The priest's handsome brow was furrowed and his eyes were glazed. He pushed his black hair back, gripping it as he moved his hand across his head and then he looked at Rosie, while his heart tore to pieces inside him.

"Say a prayer for her, Rosie," he said and, as Jessie's beautiful face haunted his mind, he knew he couldn't deny his feelings any more. Jessie O'Neill had crept right under his skin and he had fallen for her in a way he had never, ever felt before.

Having dealt with the in-laws through gritted teeth and avoided the stares of lingering wedding guests who were more than concerned at the rumours now flooding the hotel of Jessie's disappearance, Andrea had suggested she and Cain return to their room for a breather. She felt like a hormonal teenager on the verge of tears at every turn.

Cain made for the drinks cabinet when they reached their room, much to her disbelief and frustration.

"Really, love, do you have to start drinking when all this is going on?"

Cain glanced back over his shoulder at her and grunted. He was suffering from the hangover from hell and Andrea's constant yapping was grating on his dehydrated brain.

"I mean I'd love to have a drink too," she went on. "Hell, I'd love to get totally pissed right now and forget about everything but we all need to keep a clear head to deal with this. My God, drinking is part of the reason why none of us knows where Jessie might have gone to last night!"

Cain ignored his wife and poured a whiskey measure and downed it in one.

"Jesus Christ, Andrea," he said, filling the glass

again, "give me a break! We should be leaving for our honeymoon shortly, not conducting a damned search party for a woman who knows her own mind and is big enough to look after herself. We are due to leave in two hours and now everything's all up in the air."

Andrea stared at him in disbelief. His sandy hair was tousled and his normally immaculate appearance looked more dishevelled than she had ever seen it before. But no matter how unkempt he looked, nothing could have prepared her for his sudden outburst about missing their honeymoon.

"That holiday cost my parents almost five grand," he said. "And because of your sister's little Houdini act, we might not even make it at all!"

Andrea bundled a pile of clothes on top of their bed, firing dirty laundry into a basket and folding clean clothes in a bid to keep her mind occupied and hold on to some control.

"Money! Is that all you ever think of, Cain? My sister could be lying in a ditch somewhere and all you can think of is how much money we might waste by not going on fucking honeymoon!" She threw the clothes more forcefully around her as she spoke. "I couldn't give a shit about the Bahamas or the sun or the beach at this very moment. All I want is my sister back! Can't you understand that?"

Cain swirled the whiskey in its glass and tightened his mouth. Andrea could hear him sucking his teeth, an unconscious trait that told the world of his bad temper and it made her even angrier at his selfish antics. He obviously had no idea what her family were going through.

"Christ, but you've changed your tune!" he said. "Days ago you were cursing your sister up and down as she flitted in and out of your best-laid plans and now that she takes it upon herself to play a disappearing game because for once the spotlight shifts off her pretty little face, you are jumping to her attention just like you've always done!"

The phone rang from the bedside locker and Cain reached for it ahead of his wife.

Andrea stopped arranging the clothing and clasped her hands together. She watched her husband's face pale more and more by the second as he gave a series of 'yes' and 'no' replies to the caller. Then he hung up and his mouth twisted into an angry contour and his eyes went dead.

"What is it? What is it, Cain? Have they found her? Talk to me!"

Cain walked to the bathroom and Andrea followed.

"Cain, who was it on the phone? Please, Cain. What's wrong?"

He splashed his face with cold water, ran his wrists under the tap, dabbed his hands and face with a towel and then turned towards Andrea.

"I have to phone Mick Morris and get him here right away," he said and pushed past her back into the main bedroom and put on his jacket. Then he fixed his tie in the mirror and splashed some Armani under his jaw-line.

"Mick Morris? What the hell do you need your lawyer for? He'll be in Belfast by now. He left here early this morning and it's Sunday. Cain?"

He walked towards the door and stepped out into the corridor, then stopped to face her.

"The honeymoon is over, Andrea," he said, his green eyes slanted and full of fear. "So you can cancel it for definite now. I've been asked to report to the police station immediately in connection with the disappearance of one Miss Jessie O'Neill."

Chapter 22

Ella waited as Tom's lengthy conversation with Charles Bradley, Bromley Castle's Managing Director continued.

She didn't have the strength to take part but in her mind she could think of so much she would want to say to the pompous young man whose beady eyes shifted around the walls as he spoke, his nerves unable to cope with the sudden negative public focus on his establishment.

"The Press are having a field day," he said. "I have had to pull in a top PR firm to deal with the enquiries."

Jessie's law firm had confirmed her stepping down from the O'Donnell case and they had released a statement to the Press and now the media were crawling with whispers that the O'Neill-Daniels wedding had turned into a circus with her 'alleged' disappearance.

Ella stared at the weedy, faceless man who had spent too long behind a desk and computer to give sympathy when it was needed. His office was modern and airy, but his clothing made him look much older than his years. He pushed back his glasses and sat back in his chair, his arms folded one second, then flapping around the next.

"Once the police confirm that Jessie is not with anyone here," said Tom, "or anywhere on the castle estate, we will be moving on swiftly so your PR people don't have much longer to keep the wolves from the door." His panic had lessened now and he felt more at ease, despite his initial fears of involving the police. So far, they had been most courteous and professional and Martin Cooper, the Detective Inspector on duty for the evening, had managed to keep everything at a level pace, casually asking around for information without raising the alarm to frantic levels.

Charles Bradley, on the other hand, was having his own panic attack.

"My management team have spent ten years building this venue to the reputation it has today," said Charles, "and I do not want TV cameras crawling around and insinuating that something sinister is going on in my hotel. Do you realise how many high-profile weddings I could lose over this?"

Tom stood up and gently led Ella in the direction of the door.

"Like I said, Mr Bradley, that is your problem," he said. "Mine is to find my missing daughter who has not been seen or heard of for almost twenty-four hours now."

"Why, of course, sir. I know how –"

"And I'm sure that when you take a moment out to think about the torment that my wife and family are going through right now, you'll find that I don't really give a fuck about your hotel's reputation or how many so-called jumped-up celebrities decide to make other plans!"

Charles Bradley ran around his desk and walked with the O'Neills to the door, stuttering all the way in recognition of the PR disaster he may just have fed. He changed his approach immediately, almost bowing to Tom's every word.

"Of course, all of my staff are on hand for anything you need for as long as you are here," he stammered. "Tea, coffee, meals and I'd like to offer you your room for the night with no charge."

"We can pay our way, thank you. My family will be co-operating with the police for as long as this takes," said Tom. "And I would assume that you and your staff will do the same."

He led his wife out of Bradley's office and they took the lift in silence to the ground floor where Detective Cooper was on his mobile phone in Reception. They were met immediately by a plain-clothes detective who extended her hand in introduction.

"Mr and Mrs O'Neill, my name is Detective Inspector Sandra Millar," she said. "I'm a colleague of David's and I'm leading the home side of the investigation into Jessie's whereabouts. Can I have a quick word?"

Redheaded Sandra Millar spoke in a light Derry accent and her heels clipped along the hotel's marble floor when she walked ahead of the O'Neills towards a door that said '*Conference Room 1B*' on a brass plaque.

She was dressed impeccably in a navy pin-striped suit and crisp white shirt and she pushed open the door that led to a small airy room. The sensor lights flickered on automatically and they lit up the room so brightly they made Ella squint her tired eyes.

"Take a seat," said Sandra, gesturing towards a row of navy-blue velvet and gold-rimmed chairs. The room had a flipchart, a whiteboard and was laid out for a business meeting, but this was anything but normal business for the O'Neill family.

Ella sat down, dwarfed by the formality and the empty feeling of the room. It was almost eleven and she felt like a zombie, being led from pillar to post, room to room and answering the same questions over and over again.

"First of all, I would like to say that at this stage we are confident we will find your daughter safely," said Sandra. Her voice was clipped and to the point, but it had a soft tone in parts that conveyed feeling and empathy. "It is only with the highly sensitive nature of Jessie's job and, of course, through David's influence, that we are reacting as quickly as this. Most missing persons over the age of eighteen are not investigated within twenty-four hours, but David has emphasised that the O'Donnell case brought Jessie extra risk and strain in her everyday life. Can you elaborate on this at all? Did she seem nervous or scared or threatened at all to you?"

Tom coughed and pulled his chair closer to the table, then gestured towards his wife.

He was business-like now too, thought Ella, but perhaps it was the only way he was able to get through this living nightmare.

"Ella and Jessie are extremely close," he explained and turned to Ella. "Did she express any concerns to you that she may have been in any danger?"

Ella shook her head and tried to find her voice. "She was determined to see it through, that's all," she whispered. "David was more concerned than she was, from what I could see, but Jessie is a headstrong girl and if she wanted to see it through then no one would have stopped her . . ."

"But then she dropped the case on Friday?" said Sandra and produced from her handbag a print-out of an online news bulletin. "Were you aware of this?"

Tom O'Neill reached for the sheet of paper and was taken aback to see a photo of his eldest daughter on the corner of the front page.

"*Fears for Solicitor after Dropping O'Donnell Case,*" read the headline and Ella went cold from head to toe.

Tom recalled that the picture was taken at a charity gala ball they had attended back in March or April as a family. David had been cropped from the side of the image so that it was just Jessie, her dark hair in spiral curls, her head tilted slightly to the side and her lips a deep red colour that complemented her perfect white smile.

He scanned through the article quickly and then threw the newspaper down on the table.

"No, I wasn't aware of it," he said, "but my wife knew she was intending to. Isn't that so, Ella?""

"Not really," Ella confessed. "I just said that to appease you when you were suggesting she might have brought this on herself by being involved with O'Donnell. But she obviously has felt the need to drop it. Oh, God."

"Did you know she had been receiving threatening letters?" asked Sandra. "Did you know she suspected someone was intruding into her house?"

"No, we didn't! Not until today either! My God, how long was this going on? Why didn't she say?"

Ella was as shocked as her husband at the revelations of the journalist who had quoted 'a friend of the family' in their article which speculated that Jessie had pulled out of the O'Donnell case through fear and threats. She pulled the sheet of paper towards her and then traced her finger along Jessie's face as a new sensation of fear washed through her.

"I need some fresh air," said Tom. "Do you mind if we take a moment?

Sandra shook her head and waited until Tom and Ella returned some minutes later. She had poured each of them a glass of fresh water and they took their seats again. Ella's glamour and confidence was totally stripped from her by now, and she was unrecognisable as the woman she had been only days ago before her family's lives were turned upside down.

"Now, is there anything else you can tell me about Jessie's behaviour of the last few days?" said Sandra.

"David tells me she failed to turn up for an appointment with her sister. Is that unusual for Jessie?" Ella perked up slightly. There was a perfect explanation to that. "It was the day David left her, so Andrea and I both understood that she wasn't herself for that reason."

"How late was she?" asked Sandra.

"I think she was about two hours late. We were very concerned but then when she explained . . ."

"That she had to give David his mobile phone?"

"Yes."

Sandra clasped her hands on the table and leaned forward. "David has since informed us that this did not happen. He did not leave his phone behind. He met Ryan in the filling station when he stopped to buy cigarettes but he had not spoken to Jessie or any other member of your family since 9am. Yet when Andrea went to check on her, she wasn't at home. Do you have any idea where she really was?"

Tom and Ella looked confused.

"Do you have any idea why Jessie would have lied about her whereabouts that morning? Was there anything else different that happened at that time?"

Ella shook her head and then Tom spoke up.

"Think hard, Ella," he said. "I was at work while all of this was going on. Was there anything at all which hinted where Jessie was that morning?"

Again Ella shook her head and tightened her hands. "I can't think straight," she said. "What did Andrea say about all of this? She might remember. Have you spoken to her yet?"

"No, not yet. We are piecing together what David has told us and what each of you has already told him. But Andrea's husband has been taken to the station for questioning. So has your son, Ryan."

Tom lunged forward and pointed his finger at Sandra. His business-like approach was coming to an end and he couldn't hide his emotions at the thought of his son sitting in a cold police station.

"My son is *where*? Why wasn't I told this until now?" He stood up, his anger bubbling and threatening to explode.

"Mr O'Neill –"

"My son needs a solicitor. You can't just order him down to a police station on his own. I'm going down there now."

"Mr O'Neill, please sit down," said Sandra, calmly pushing a stray strand of red hair behind her ears. She put on a stylish pair of black-rimmed glasses and calmly continued. "Ryan was given the opportunity to call a solicitor but he refused. He is helping the police with their enquiries so that we can piece enough information together to find your daughter as quickly as possible."

"But what the hell has he got to do with this? I thought you were exploring the O'Donnell connection, not some sibling-rivalry nonsense!"

Sandra remained composed in the face of Tom's anger. She had been warned of his tendency to fly off the handle at a second's notice and she was unscathed by his shouting.

"My colleagues were told that Ryan was the last

family member to speak to Jessie," she said. "Obviously we needed to talk to him."

It was pitch black outside now and the music from the Sunday afternoon wedding party spilled into the small conference room where the O'Neills sat with the young police officer.

On the surface, Bromley Castle seemed oblivious to the torment of Tom and Ella O'Neill as it kept busy, with diners making their way to its award-winning restaurant and wedding guests mingling in the foyer which gave Ella a sense of *déjà vu*. She longed to be back at that moment last night when there was still time to look for Jessie. She wished she had gone after her when she danced away that time, so full of determination and a new attitude. She longed to turn back the clock and start all over again so that she would look after her daughter in the way only she could.

Her eyes were burning from exhaustion and she felt weak and small and so full of regret. She had survived on several cups of coffee but had refused food, despite Charles Bradley's insistence that his chef rustle them up a quick snack to maintain their energies. Tom had drunk water and smoked cigarettes at every opportunity. It had been a long day which was showing no signs of having a quick ending and Ella's surroundings were becoming a haze.

"I've been told that your son suspected Jessie was having an affair with Cain Daniels," said Sandra, swiftly moving on. "Can you tell me anything about that?"

"That it's absolute nonsense," said Ella tartly. The

very suggestion felt like a pinprick which brought her back from her muddled mindset.

"We just heard about it this afternoon," said Tom. He had taken his seat again but Ella could sense his burning desire to race to his son's defence at the nearby village police station. "We're not sure what to believe as we haven't approached Cain on it but I doubt if it has anything to do with her disappearance."

Sandra raised an eyebrow. "And your son's black eye? Has he explained the story behind it?"

"No," said Tom. "Well, yes, I suppose he has. He said it was a drunken brawl and I have no reason to believe it was anything different. Ryan is the same as any other lad. Shoots his mouth off and then pays the price."

Sandra made a note on her filing pad and then sucked the top of her pen. "Is there anyone in your family home right now?" she asked. "It's important that someone you trust is there in case Jessie shows up. And, of course, we've arranged to take a look around Jessie and David's home over the next few hours if she hasn't come forward by then."

"My sister Lily and her family left for Glencuan this afternoon," said Tom. "We have been in contact with her almost every hour. There is absolutely no reason to believe that Jessie has been there within the past twenty-four hours but Lily will keep us informed of any changes."

"Good. It's important we keep all lines of communication open at all times," said Sandra, closing her file. She shuffled her papers into a neat pile, removed her glasses and lifted her handbag from the chair beside her. Then she stood up, cradling her documents to her chest. "I think that's all I need to know for now. Unless there is something we have missed?"

The O'Neills sat in silence, racking their brains for any vital clues that might have slipped their mind. Then Tom remembered something that he couldn't believe had got lost along the way. It might have nothing to do with Jessie but it still was worth putting forward, now that the police were in this up to their necks.

"Andrea's dress!" he said and Sandra sat back down, slipped on her glasses and opened her file.

"Yes?" she said. "Go on."

"On Thursday –"

"It was Wednesday," Ella interrupted. "It happened on Wednesday. It was early evening, about five."

"You tell it," said Tom. "I wasn't home at the time for this one either."

Ella braced herself and then told Sandra of how Andrea's dress was torn to pieces only days before the wedding and of the panic to replace it without causing too much fuss.

"And why didn't you report this at the time?" asked Sandra. "Is it possible someone had broken into your home to do such a thing?"

Tom took over the conversation. "It was my fault we didn't report it. I was thinking of Andrea and Cain. I didn't want the Press to get hold of it and for it to ruin their day so I told everyone to keep it to themselves and I planned to deal with it after the wedding. But then this happened and I suppose today has been so crazy it has just come back to me now."

"It totally left my mind until now as well," said Ella with a feeling they had just signed another black mark against their son. She had never felt so torn in all her life.

Sandra noted furiously in her file block, and then lifted her head.

"I need to know who was in your house when this happened," she said. "Then you are free to go."

"Well, my sister Lily, Andrea and Ella were there. Lily's children were out at the time. But that's all."

"And –" Ella stopped herself before she went too far. "Yes, to my knowledge that's all was there. Just us girls."

Ella hooked her husband's arm to show solidarity and Tom patted her hand in support.

"So, what now?" he said. "What are we supposed to do now? Wait? Go home? Stay here at the hotel? What do we do?"

Sandra sensed their frustration. Glencuan was a two-hour drive away but the fact that Jessie's belongings were still at Bromley Castle gave hope that she might return for them, if she was going to return at all.

"Obviously I will return to Glencuan tonight and follow up any lines of enquiry my colleagues have from your home village," she said. "You should know we are also chasing up alibis for both Jack O'Donnell and some of the well-known locals who would have been against Jessie's involvement in the case. In the meantime, I suggest you get some sleep, Mr and Mrs O'Neill. Oh, just out of curiosity, what happened to the dress?"

"Sorry?" said Ella.

"Your daughter's wedding dress. You said it was destroyed. How did she find another so quickly? I can only imagine the stress."

Ella nodded. Yes, stress was one word for it. "We had it remade by a friend of Cain's," she said. "Bernice Bradshaw was her name. Lovely girl she was too. Very willing to help."

"Right. I was just wondering," said Sandra and she opened the door of the conference room. "Good night. I'll be in touch in the morning."

Chapter 23

"I think we should go home," said Ella as they walked up to their bedroom. "This place is haunting me and I feel like we're getting in the way right now. Yet, at the same time I'm so scared to leave in case she comes back here."

Tom knew exactly where his wife was coming from. He could sense the stares of pity from staff and other hotel guests as the word filtered out and it was suffocating. A number of police officers had carried out an extensive search for clues in Jessie's room taking her belongings with them for evidence.

It was now over twenty-four hours since Jessie's disappearance and the police had agreed to formally declare her missing at that point and begin an extensive search of Bromley Castle and its surrounding gardens.

Tom's insides burned with fear.

His daughter was an intelligent, loveable girl who

had always been extremely close to her mother and sister. Her behaviour of late was poles apart from the girl he knew and loved so much and, deep in the pit of his soul, Tom was beginning to fear the worst.

Jessie would have been in contact by now if she was in any way able to do so. She would have called her mother no matter how much she felt threatened or scared by whoever had been taunting her. She would never, ever leave her sister's wedding party and deliberately disappear like that. There was simply no way any of it made sense to Tom and he was petrified.

Ella opened the door of the room and the now familiar smell of new furniture and coffee met her instantly. She would never look at a hotel room in the same way after this weekend. She had always loved the anonymity and the neat simplicity of hotel rooms. She would make note of their interior and marvel at their simple luxury and could recite her top five favourites which she would often update and recommend to her friends on the Daffodil Ball Committee.

Her phone bleeped a text message and Ella didn't need to search for it as she normally did. Since Jessie's disappearance she had kept her phone in her jacket pocket and randomly felt for it in panic in case it had fallen out or in case she had missed a call from her daughter at any point of the day.

The text was from Lily. "*Any news?*" it read and Ella handed it to her husband to reply.

He too had several messages from some of his closer family members who had heard various rumours and who wondered if there was anything they could do to help. He sent each of them a courteous reply and then tried to call his son but Ryan's phone went to voicemail.

He then dialled Andrea's number and she answered immediately, her voice dry and full of despair.

"Daddy, I need you to come down here to the station," she said. "They won't let me in with Cain, and Ryan is waiting to be called but he won't talk to me. Cain has been in for ages now. What are they talking to him for?"

Tom listened to his poor innocent daughter and remembered that no matter how this panned out, she was going to suffer terribly over the next few hours as Cain's alleged affair with Jessie came to the forefront of the investigation. Andrea would crumble at such a double betrayal and Tom prayed in his heart that Ryan had made a terrible mistake. But despite his hope and longing for it to be a false accusation, Tom knew that it all made sense.

"I don't like to leave your mother," he said. "She wouldn't be fit to sit in a police station at this hour after all the shocks she has encountered today but I'll try my best, love. Tell Ryan I will do my very best to get over there soon for him too. This will all work out, sweetie. Everything will be all right soon."

He hung up the phone and dropped it on the bed, then noticed that Ella had unwillingly fallen asleep in the armchair by the window. He pondered a moment. If she woke up she would panic at being alone but his children needed him too. He was torn and confused as to what to do and he fought an uncontrollable urge to sink a double brandy from the drinks cabinet to settle his nerves.

The phone startled him again and he answered it in a whisper.

"Tom O'Neill," he said, since he didn't recognise the mobile number that appeared on the screen.

"Inspector Martin Cooper," said the voice. "We've managed to track down the friend of the family who was quoted in the newspaper. A Miss Charlotte Quinn. Sound familiar?"

Tom rubbed his head. Yes, of course. "She did some cleaning for Jessie around the house. Jessie spoke highly of her. Why? What has she got to say?"

Cooper cleared his throat and flicked his phone to loudspeaker.

"I'm on my way to see her now. She says Jessie was petrified when she last saw her but that she had sworn her to secrecy. The Press nailed her at Jessie's house yesterday when she went to collect a purse she thought she'd left behind. She says Jessie was sure there had been an intruder in her house and she says that she was too."

"My God," said Tom. "Charlotte mentioned this to Ella on the phone yesterday but what made her so sure? An intruder?"

He walked towards the window and his heart sank as he saw in the distance, under the floodlights of the garden, that the police had begun combing the area for any sign of his missing girl.

"Miss Quinn says that when she had arrived on Friday to clean Jessie's house, someone had written the word 'slut' in lipstick on her bathroom mirror and all over the shower cubicle. Our forensic team are on their way to the house. David has given them a key."

Tom leaned one hand on the windowsill to prevent himself from falling down. This was serious now. He was glad his wife hadn't heard what Cooper had just told him

"Tom, we need a copy of the wedding-guest list faxed for my attention as quickly as you can. David is on his way back to the hotel with some photos of Jessie he has developed from your wife's camera from yesterday. He plans to show every member of staff her picture in the clothes she was wearing to see if any of them noticed anything suspicious or anyone lingering around who caught their attention. As you can imagine, these findings shed a very different light on our bid to find Jessie."

David knocked on the door twenty minutes later and Tom tried to disguise the fact that he had been crying since he hung up the phone from Martin Cooper, but David sensed it immediately.

"Cooper is the best man for the job," said David, lowering his voice when he saw that Ella was asleep at the far side of the suite.

Tom had gently manoeuvred her into bed and had sobbed like a baby as he watched his wife sleep.

"He is totally on the ball and has assured me he won't waste any time or leave any stone unturned until he finds out exactly what has happened to Jess."

"I just can't take all this in," said Tom, nodding for David to take a seat in the small lounge area. "Everything is moving at lightning pace and I can't keep up. My daughter is gone, my son is in being questioned over her disappearance and my other daughter's husband is in the firing line too. This is crazy. I mean, I feel like I don't know my own family any more."

David leaned forward and looked Tom in the eye. He was feeling the exact same pain and had wept for Jessie's safe return on his way to the hotel but he refused to let his emotions take over until he knew where she was or who had harmed her.

"Try to be strong, Tom," he whispered. "Your family is not broken. Like you say this is all crazy. I'm clinging on to the hope that Jessie has run away from all her troubles. Until we know any different, I urge you to try and do the same. For Ella's sake as much as your own."

Tom's eyes were blurred again with tears and he wiped under them, slightly embarrassed at showing any sign of weakness in front of his son-in-law. He rubbed his thighs and took several deep breaths, still fighting the knowledge that a stiff drink would steady him like nothing else could.

"Cooper mentioned photos," he said, sniffing back emotion and trying to keep focused on what had to be done. "He said you had them. Do you mind?"

David lifted an envelope from his inside pocket and handed them to Tom across the coffee table that separated the two small sofas. Tom slowly opened the sleeve and removed a set of glossy photos that painted a colourful picture of family life as it was. In just twenty-four hours, the colour had been drained and his whole world had turned to black and white and grey.

Ella was radiant in her pale blue Mother of the Bride ensemble, complete with matching twinkling eyes that creased at the sides as she laughed in the picture. Andrea was striking and rich in her full ivory gown and Tom stood proud beside her while Ryan looked slightly awkward and clumsy in his wedding attire. But it was Jessie who he couldn't take his eyes off. Sweet, beautiful, gentle Jessie – his first-born child who had never given him a moment of worry in all her years.

Now, all of the normal worry or concerns that any parent carries as their child moves through early school days, teenage trauma, career uncertainties and relationship ups and downs had been snowballed into one, multiplied to extreme levels and fired in the direction of Tom and Ella O'Neill.

Tom quickly flicked by a few photos and then handed them back to David, unable to look at them any longer.

"I've copied this one," said David, holding up a stunning solo photo of Jessie giving a light smile at her mother through the lens of the camera. "I've given copies to all staff here tonight to see if it will jog any memories of when, where or if they remember seeing her. It's worth a try, but in the meantime I think you should pop down to the police station and show some support to Andrea. I think she's going to need her dad right now."

On instinct, Tom's first reaction was to race for the door and cosset his youngest girl whose life was also falling apart, but then he remembered Ella asleep and he sat back down again.

"I can't leave Ella," he said. "She'll wake up soon and she'll panic if she finds herself alone in this place. Oh God, I've been trying to convince myself that Ryan will look after Andrea as she waits for Cain, but she says he won't talk to her."

Putting the envelope of photos back into his pocket, David hunkered down at the side of the chair where Tom sat.

"Look, Tom, I know Ryan and I know he is riddled with guilt because he was the one who told us all about Jessie and Cain. He's terrified that he was the last person to see her last night and he's holding back from talking to Andrea, knowing that she too will learn of her husband and her sister's betrayal soon enough." He placed his hand on the older man's shoulder and spoke softly. "Your children need you, Tom. I will stay with Ella until you come back, but don't expect that Ryan will be coming back here with you tonight."

Tom looked back at David and his face was grey and lifeless.

"Why do you say that?" Tom asked, knowing the answer before David even spoke.

"Because right now he isn't in a good position. O'Donnell and his crew have an alibi for the past two days but Ryan has already put himself right at the top of the list of suspects by confirming that he and Jessie had a vicious row possibly moments before she disappeared."

"No! You're wrong!" said Tom, pulling away from

David. He stood up and looked out the window again, then dropped his voice into a lower but steely, determined tone. "My son would never harm his sister, no matter how much he argued with her or no matter what was said. Damn cops! I knew I shouldn't have let them meddle in our family problems. No!" He turned to face David defiantly.

"Listen to me, Tom," said David and he stood up to match his father-in-law. "Get down to the station now and make sure you get Ryan the best lawyer you can find, because unless Cain Daniels makes a cock-up and admits that he knows where Jessie might be or might have run to, Ryan is in the firing line on this one."

Tom opened the drinks cabinet and poured a large brandy, the bottle clinking off the glass as his hands shook with fear and nervous tension.

"I'm not leaving my wife with anyone when all this is going on. I don't trust anyone!"

"For Christ's sake, Tom, are you saying you don't trust me to sit here for an hour so you can go and see to your two children who are cooped up in a cop shop?" He paused. "Tom, what did Cooper tell you had been written on the shower wall by Jessie's intruder?"

Tom gulped down the brandy and then cowered as he recalled the word that had been used to describe his daughter.

"'Slut'," he said and his blood ran cold so that he could feel every vein in his body. "They wrote 'slut' all over her bathroom mirror and on the shower wall. Bastards."

"And how did Ryan last describe his sister?" asked David, then he watched Tom as the true fear for his son's actions clicked into place. "What did he call her in this very room earlier today? What did he tell us were his last words to Jessie?"

"Oh, Jesus Christ!" said Tom and he reached for his jacket. "He called her a slut."

"Exactly," said David. "Exactly."

Chapter 24

Andrea could feel her eyes grow heavier and heavier and she felt extremely uncomfortable on the horrible plastic chair she had sat on for over two hours now.

She looked at the clock on the pale-blue wall and it reminded her of one that used to hang in the school dinner hall when she was small. Its white face and fine black numbers had a cold, clinical look and the red hand that spun around without pausing at all seemed to go in slow motion.

They had told her she wasn't needed. Not yet, anyway, but that later in the night they might feel the need to ask her questions about her sister. She closed her eyes and allowed herself to pretend that this had all been a bad dream.

She pictured her sister, smiling and confident in her smart business suit on the way to court, chatting on the phone to a client as she made her way in to fight another law case. She placed herself back in her cosy little bookshop, surrounded by bright colours and soft carpets and low lighting. She imagined her mother with her slogan-clad aprons at the stove, looking like someone from a magazine cookery feature, all glamorous and domesticated. She saw Ryan on his motorbike, zooming along the coastline in his leathers that always made him look so handsome. And she thought of her father, strong and self-assured, negotiating deals with construction workers and architects as he built his latest property empire to the awe of all around him.

"Andrea, love," said a voice and she peeled open her weary eyes. It took her a moment to focus and then she widened them and sat up straight.

"Oh Daddy!" she said and she wrapped her arms around him and rested there.

It was her father, yet he looked like a diluted version of the man she had just pictured in her head. This man's hair was lank and grey, not glossy and silver. His skin was blotchy and pale, not rosy and glowing and his face was sad and full of concern, not smiling or powerful at all. This was her father but it didn't look like her dad at all.

"Are you okay? Where's Ryan?" he asked, glancing around the empty, spartan waiting room with its cold green lino and light blue walls. A drinks machine that had seen better days was propped in the corner and a coffee table that was stained and scarred with graffiti bore a scattered collection of magazines all dated from Christmas and springtime the year before. Tom O'Neill guessed this was a police station that had rarely been put to use – for all the right reasons, of course.

"I'm okay, I suppose," said Andrea. She spoke incoherently almost, like she had been silent and without conversation for so long that she was afraid to stop talking now. "Ryan must have gone to the bathroom but Cain has been in there for ages. Sometimes I can hear the raised voices of Mick Morris and that policeman but I don't know what they're saying, Dad. I mean, why are they questioning Cain? What has he got to do with all this? I keep asking Ryan but he won't answer me. He just keeps staring at the TV or flicking through magazines even though I know he isn't reading a word."

Tom sat down on a chair beside his daughter and put his arm around her, almost hushing her as he would have done when she was a baby. He looked up at the white ceiling and then blinked from the bright fluorescent light bulb that ran across its centre. Prayers didn't come easily to Tom O'Neill but he closed his eyes and quickly asked God to help his family get through this torture they had been suddenly subjected to.

"Andrea, I think it's time we started to prepare ourselves for what's ahead," he said, his voice low and husky from exhaustion and grief.

Andrea sat up straight. Her face was blank as she waited for her father to continue.

"I don't know what to expect any more, love, but I fear that something terrible may have happened to your sister. Someone was lurking around her house, taunting her and calling her names."

Tom watched his daughter's mood change to one of anger at the thought of anyone attempting to harm Jessie.

"Why didn't she listen to David? He warned her she was putting her life in danger by meddling with those gangs and their –"

"We don't know if Jessie's disappearance has anything to do with the O'Donnell case yet," said Tom and then he closed his eyes and rested his head back on the cold cement wall. "In fact, the cops seem to think that Cain or Ryan may know more than they have told us to date. I have asked Bert McManus to make his way down here now, because Ryan especially is going to need all the help he can get to pull himself out of trouble this time."

Andrea reached for her father's arm and she held on to it and let her heavy eyes close until she dozed off, back into a dream where everything in her life was as picture-perfect as it was before.

Bert McManus reminded Andrea of her father in more ways than one when he entered the station over an hour later. His powerful stature, the way he walked tall and his commanding presence when he came into a room gave him the ultimate respect of everyone he came across.

His hair was greying at the sides, he wore a light beard that gave away his age and his cheeks were flushed. His pale grey suit was dapper and tailored and he greeted each of the O'Neills with a firm handshake and a slight bow of his head.

Andrea gave him a welcoming smile but Ryan barely

acknowledged the man's presence, much to his father's and sister's distress, an expression of defeat all over his face. He pulled his baseball cap down on his forehead

McManus scraped a chair across the floor, set it directly under Ryan's nose and sat down.

"You and I will need to have a lengthy chat in private, Ryan," he said in his rich, bellowing voice, chewing gum between sentences. "I am here for two reasons. First of all, to make sure you are given every reasonable opportunity to tell exactly what has been going on in your family over the past few days, and secondly I am here in hope that what you and I can tell the police may help them find out where your sister is."

He reminded Andrea of a football manager on the sideline of a big game who knew that every decision he made could affect his team's outcome, but emphasising that he needed everyone involved to pull their weight or the team would go nowhere.

He got up and, taking Ryan by the arm, led him into a side room which was flanked by a uniformed officer but, when Tom and Andrea got up to follow, McManus signalled for them to stay put. Tom was aggrieved at first but then he settled down in the knowledge that Ryan might open up to a stranger more quickly than he would if his father were present.

"I've been thinking," said Tom to Andrea, "well, not thinking straight but thinking nonetheless. I would be happier if you would stay with your mother and me tonight. At the hotel of course. There is a spare room in our suite and I'd be much more content if you came back with me as soon as Ryan has finished answering any questions the police may have for him. I will ask him to stay with us too. I want us to be together at all times."

Andrea looked back in disgust at her father. Her forehead creased and she held her hair back with both hands, a habit she had developed as a young child which indicated frustration and disbelief.

"Why on earth do you say that, Dad? Why wouldn't I go back to the hotel with my husband? Isn't he considered family?"

Tom bit his lip and his eyes welled up as he stared at the pretty girl before him. Her heart was about to be broken and he dreaded her feelings and reaction. The poor girl had been through enough, yet it was better she heard it from him than during an aggressive police enquiry.

"Sit down, love," he said and he patted the chair beside him.

Andrea did so, still playing with her hair, still staring back at him in bewilderment.

"I – I don't know how to tell you this – but – well, we have just learned today that – well, Ryan is completely sure – he says that Cain and Jessie were . . . Andrea, he swears to us that they were having an affair."

Andrea's pale face turned to stone. Her hands slipped from her hair and fell onto her lap. Slowly, she began to shake her head, and then as if her whole body had been invaded she screamed back at her father.

"You are all *sick*!" she roared, spitting with bad

temper and disbelief. She stood up and held her hands to her head. "Don't you dare say that ever again! She is my sister! He is my husband! No, I don't believe it. Ryan is a monster for saying such a thing. No!"

The door behind her clicked open and Cain Daniels and his solicitor emerged, followed by two uniformed officers and Martin Cooper who nodded at Tom and then turned to Andrea.

"Cain, it's not true!" Andrea cried. "I know it's not true!"

"Andrea," said Detective Cooper, "how about we settle down, eh? Come on, love."

Tears pumped from Andrea's eyes and Cooper handed her a tissue from a box on the coffee table.

"Settle down? How the hell can I settle down? My sister is missing, I'm supposed to be on honeymoon and now my brother is making terrible accusations! No, I will not settle down. I am sick of this shit. Can I have my husband and my sister and my family back and then I'll fucking settle down? I suppose you're going to tell me my husband is a suspect now, is that it? I suppose you believe all the bullshit my brother is coming out with?"

Cooper smacked his lips. "Em, that's all for tonight," he said, rubbing his hands together. "Tom, you can take your family home now and we'll resume any questions we may have in the morning. I've had a long day and I can only imagine what it must be like for you. Good night."

Detective Cooper marched down the hallway out of sight and Tom O'Neill stared at Cain Daniels who tilted his head with a smile and matched Tom's glare.

"Come on, love," Cain said, putting his arm around Andrea's waist. "I think I've had just about enough of all this slander and bullshit. I quite fancy a drink. You look like you could do with one too. For shock. You and I have both had a nasty shock."

As Andrea walked away with her husband and his lawyer, she glanced back a number of times at her father. She knew he was confused and frustrated with Jessie's disappearance but why was he trying to bring Cain into it? Why was Ryan out to ruin everything for her?

Her dad looked forlorn and confused and alone in the empty corridor and Andrea's heart felt as if it was torn in two when she saw him sit back down on the cold, hard, orange chair and sink his head into his hands. She wanted to go back and tell him that Ryan was wrong. She wanted to reach up and turn back that horrible clock on the wall and start all over again, last week, yesterday, today. But most of all she wanted to go back and give her father a hug and tell him Jessie would be back soon.

"Dad!" she called but Tom didn't hear her. She was just about to let go of Cain's strong grasp and run back to her father when Cooper came spinning around the corner of the corridor, his voice echoing as he called to them.

"Cain, Andrea. The Press are outside," he said, a tad breathless. "They're waiting for you, Cain."

"Shit!" said Cain and he kicked the wall. "Fuck! Fuck! Fuck! What the hell am I supposed to do now? Jesus!"

Andrea felt faint. This was all a big misunderstanding. It had to be.

"Do you expect me to stand back and watch my career go down the pan just because you listened to that spoilt little fuck claim I was out to ruin his game of happy families!" roared Cain.

"I suggest you calm down," said Cooper. "It is up to you and your lawyer to think of something to say, but for God's sake don't be putting on a show. I have no time for circus acts and by God I've seen enough of those in my day. Keep it short and snappy."

Cooper strode away again and Mick Morris took over, his short stubby legs apart while he spoke with his hands.

"Let me deal with this," he said and he looked up at the couple, his bald head shining under the stark light of the police station. "Cain and Andrea, neither of you will respond to any questions, do you hear? I will dissolve this as quickly as it started. Walk together, hold hands and keep your heads held high. You have nothing to hide. Now let's go!"

When Mick Morris pushed open the double doors of Bromley Police Station, cameras flashed and voices overlapped as a sea of questions was fired at Cain and Andrea.

"Mrs Daniels?" they called and she barely recognised it as her own name. She did recognise the names of a radio station from a labelled microphone and she looked up at her husband for reassurance but he was doing exactly as he had been instructed, holding his chin high and staring straight ahead as if the gathered journalists were invisible.

Andrea felt her chin wobble and her eyes fill up as she was led by Cain into an awaiting car. He slammed the door and she watched through the window as Mick Morris delivered a matter-of-fact response into the journalists' microphones and then he joined them in the car, a light smell of perspiration filling the back seat when he closed the door and they sped away.

As they pounded down the road it started to rain again and Andrea looked back at the small, isolated country police station as the journalists gathered their gear and made their way into cars and vans. She sobbed silently for the sorry mess of her precious family while her heart mourned for her normally private and extremely proud father who was sitting inside the station waiting for his only son, totally unaware of the media frenzy that had just scraped the surface of their lives.

Chapter 25

Monday . . .

Father Christopher heard the hum of the morning news in the background and he cursed himself for falling asleep again with the television on. He lifted the alarm clock from his bedside locker and squinted to see the time but the clock had stopped somewhere during the night around three.

His bedroom smelled of stale whiskey and his stomach heaved from his over-indulgence the night before. He would have to stop drinking his way through every problem that came his way but so far the alcohol was doing a great job, if only at the time, of blocking out his feelings and getting him through the night. Jessic O'Neill never left his mind and it was keeping him awake every hour God sent.

The very look of the bedroom and the fusty house he had so tried to make a home frustrated him now. He had begun two nights ago to scrape some of the horrible sticky woodchip wallpaper from the walls but it made his mood much worse and he gave up, sinking another bottle instead.

No one warned him of the lonely life associated with the priesthood. He thought the north would be like his tiny home village, all stone walls and cottages and people who dropped in for tea with hearty conversation.

Instead he had found the village of Glencuan to be modern, fast-moving and riddled with gossip, jealousy, envy and greed. People had nothing good to say about their neighbour and they begrudged those who did well. Those who had so much more than the average person failed to appreciate what they had and still strove for fulfilment when their greed and lust were so overpowering they would never know true happiness. He had preached on that very subject at Sunday Mass the day before and had stunned his parishioners who knew what he was getting at.

The more he thought of their petty, false, two-faced ways the angrier he became. Why did everyone want more? More money, more work, more lovers, more . . .

He stopped himself right there, realising that what he was thinking was quite hypocritical. He was guilty of sin too, of course he was, and how could he be so judgemental of others when he had let the weaknesses of his own heart rule his head so much of late?

His heart had almost burst open when he first saw Jessie O'Neill that night when she turned up on his doorstep. At first sight, he turned into protector, confidant and best friend and only that he had fought the idea every step of the way, he knew that behind it all, more than anything else, he wanted to be her lover.

He pictured her sweet face, the way she listened to him, laughed with him and the way she cried to him. God, but he was only human! He had chosen a vocation that he knew would involve sacrifice and loneliness and longing and here he was, falling at almost the first hurdle. And deep inside it killed him even more because he was convinced she really felt the same about him.

He climbed out of bed, unable to fight for much longer the heavy thoughts he was juggling in his hungover state and he made his way to the bathroom where he splashed his face with cold water and looked in the mirror. He rubbed his stubbly jaw, its sandpaper touch feeling rough on his soft hands, and stared at his reflection but all he could see was her beautiful face.

He walked through the hallway and saw the open bedroom door and the bed where she had spent the night when she was so distressed and sad.

How he had longed then to hold her and make all her worries go away!

How he longed for her now.

How he wanted to tell her and ask her to hear him out, to see if she felt the same as he did. He wanted to put his fears aside and to help her put her life back together – and she could do the same for him. With Jessie by his side he could take on the world as he never was able to before. He might even look up his mother again and show her how well he had turned out despite all the trauma and bullshit she had put him through as a boy.

But that would be so wrong. He would make his vocation work to prove his mother wrong and he would never, ever admit to anyone the love he had in his lonely heart for Jessie O'Neill.

He jumped in the shower and let the hot steam ease his pumping head while he soaped his body, all the while urging any thoughts of her out of his mind. He put his handsome face back and closed his eyes, allowing the water to trickle off his jawline, down his shoulders and listened to it splash on the tray below him. The zesty smell of the shower cream brought him around and he rinsed off, then wrapped a towel around his lean waist and walked across the threadbare patch of carpet into the bedroom.

He reached for his clothing from the wardrobe and then he froze when he heard Jessie's name from the television news that was still on in the corner. He closed the wardrobe door and made his way across to the TV and a cold shiver ran through him, giving his naked arms and back goose bumps. It was Andrea O'Neill and Cain and a lawyer who was speaking on their behalf.

"My client and his wife are determined to do everything possible to help find Jessie O'Neill as quickly as possible. Of course, my client is more than happy to have helped the police with their enquiries in any way."

He stood in the middle of the bedroom, unable to move as the bulletin cut back to the newsreader in the studio.

"The fear for the safety of solicitor Jessie O'Neill continues as police continue to search the grounds of

Bromley Castle, Co Fermanagh, and retrace the last-known steps of a well-respected young lady whom her family have described as 'gentle, talented and beautiful'. Police say they are following several lines of enquiry in connection with the disappearance of the twenty-eight-year-old from a family wedding, just before midnight on Saturday."

Father Christopher pounded down the stairs and across the hallway as the reality of Jessie's disappearance hit him like a slap in the face. It was ten minutes to eight and he was due to give a Funeral Mass in just over half an hour. He ran back upstairs, unsure of what he should do next and then threw himself on the bed and wept sore for the girl he had fallen in love with. He had no idea what to do, and had lost all track of what was right and what was wrong but he knew above anything else that Jessie would want him to save her.

Daylight filled the room at Bromley Castle when Ella pulled the heavy curtains. "Tom, love – Tom?" she nudged her husband. "It's almost eight."

Tom was huddled on the armchair of the hotel suite, while David was sitting on the chair opposite, both sound asleep now having talked and racked their brains until after one that morning. Ella hated disturbing either of them now but she knew her husband had to take Ryan back to the police station for nine.

She had first woken up at three, disorientated and wretched, when the horrors of the day before flooded her mind again. She had heard sniffles from the opposite side of the room and she had assumed it was Tom as his side of the bed was empty, but as she looked closer she recognised her son-in-law, his hand covering his mouth as he sobbed over a photo of Jessie that was now used as an officially released picture in connection with her disappearance. Seeing David cry was like a knife through Ella's already bruised heart. In his career with the police he had witnessed bombs and bullets and murder cases in his specialised area of crime operations, and he had given talks to police-college students and at conferences all over the UK and Ireland. But this was different. He had been ordered to take additional leave because of the emotional involvement he inevitably had with Jessie's case. He had bottled up all his feelings over the loss of his marriage and in addition he knew that if Jessie didn't show up very soon, he might find himself being vigorously questioned as well.

Eventually his sobs had quietened and Ella had slid back into a troubled sleep. But now, it was time for all of them to face another day of worry and new findings about the last steps Jessie took on that fateful night.

"My God, what time is it?" said Tom, pushing the woollen blanket off him and hoisting his weary body up on the chair. He rubbed his eyes and looked at his watch before Ella had a chance to remind him. "Christ! Ryan! I'd better get down there now."

David stirred as well and stretched on his chair and Ella put on the kettle. A good strong cup of coffee would at least wake everyone up properly before they faced the day ahead.

"I didn't sleep for long," said David. "I woke around three and went out for a walk about an hour later. It was almost daylight so I went down along the riverbank but there isn't a sign of anything to suggest Jessie may have headed in that direction."

Ella shuddered at the very thought of her daughter wandering alone by the river, cold and afraid and –

"*Ow!*" She had scalded her hand with the water from the kettle. She ran to the sink and closed her eyes as the cold water stung at first and then cooled down the throbbing burn on her left hand.

"Here, let me see," said Tom and he turned his wife's hand around to examine the damage.

She could feel David look on with sorrow and Ella thanked God that she had her husband to stand beside her through all of this horror. Poor David was so alone and since his last words with Jessie were to say he was leaving, she could only imagine the sense of regret he was now going through as time ticked on.

"I think I'll go and get freshened up," he said. "And then I'll go and phone Cooper to see what the latest is. That's if he'll tell me."

Ella watched him stride into the bathroom and she lifted her suitcase and plonked it on the bed.

"There isn't much point us hanging around here all day again," she said. "I'm determined that we pack up and make our way home as soon as we get Ryan out of that goddamned police station."

Tom wrapped his arms around her waist and held her tight.

"Oh, when is this nightmare going to end?" she said.

David came out of the bathroom and looked at his in-laws awkwardly as they embraced. He gathered his jacket and phone from the table and lifted his coffee, took a few sips and then made his way for the door.

"You okay?" said Tom. "Are you going to the station?"

"No," said David. "They don't think it is ethical for me to be around so I'm going to check downstairs again to see if there's anything I've missed that might point us in the right direction. I'll keep in touch."

He walked out and shut the door and when Ella went to go after him, Tom called her back.

"He needs some space, Ella. Can you imagine what he must be going through? Cooper doesn't want him hanging around and he feels like an outsider now to us too. Leave him be and let him sort his thoughts out for a while."

Ella folded her clothes and began to place them neatly into the suitcase. "I know, but I just feel for him. Imagine his regrets and his what-ifs? Jessie is still his wife and he is tormented as much as we are. He was crying here last night when I woke up."

"Really? He must be so scared."

David's cheery voice and jokes and smile had been so endearing down the years and he was always the first to put a positive spin on everything no matter what went on in the O'Neill household, yet now it had been drained from him. The spirit had been drained from them all.

"Any word from Andrea?" asked Tom. "I don't think I'm flavour of the month in that camp either."

"No, not a thing," said Ella, and she checked her mobile phone just to be sure. "I'll call her while you are down at the station. Make sure she knows we still care."

"Good idea. Right, I'll be off then. Do you want to see Ryan before we leave? He might be in there for quite a while?"

Ella walked towards the window and folded her arms. Images of Andrea's strewn wedding dress and the names and accusations Ryan fired at Jessie turned her stomach sour.

"No, I don't," she said. "I don't think I could deal with seeing him right now."

Tom gulped a rage of temper back at his wife's indifference to Ryan. "Ella! He's your son! I know Jessie is first priority here but Ryan needs our support. They all do. You don't honestly think —"

"I don't know what to think!" said Ella. "Silly things, silly moments are racing through my mind all morning, all night and I don't know what is right and what is wrong. I just don't know what to do! I keep getting these images of her in my head and the idea that she may have taken her own life is lingering at the back of my head. It's torture, Tom. I just want her back so much."

Tom eased towards his wife as she fought back tears, a rush of adrenaline and anger pulsing through her body.

"Ella, Ryan may have caused trouble in the past but he would never hurt his sister, would he?"

Ella wiped her nose, shaking her head.

"Or is there something you know that I don't? We have to stick together on this, Ella. If you know anything, then I deserve to know it too."

Ella tried to find the words but each time she tried to speak, her mouth wouldn't allow the spitting accusation to follow through.

Tom walked for the door and as he turned the handle Ella closed her eyes. Then she spoke.

"Wednesday. When Andrea's dress was destroyed . . . I told you that Lily and I were the only people in the house."

Tom let go of the handle and turned towards his wife.

"I lied," she said. "I lied to you."

"What? How?"

"Ryan was there too," said Ella. "He was in his bedroom and he had been in his bedroom all along. He was upstairs the whole time. Why didn't he hear someone in her room? He was right next door. I just can't get it out of my head that he might have done it himself."

Ella watched her husband's face twitch and his expression move from shock to denial.

"What the hell are you playing at, woman? Are you trying to pull our family apart by coming out with such things?"

"It's true, Tom. Ask Lily. She was there. She saw him."

"But that doesn't mean anything! Just because Ryan was in the house at the time. You were in the house too. Lily was there. And Andrea. Why didn't any of *you* hear something? That's ridiculous! Don't let me hear you bad-mouthing our son ever again!"

"And I don't want Ryan to be connected with this as much as you don't but you know he's been acting strange. You said it yourself. You grabbed him by the throat and you made him say what he thought about Jessie and Cain. You said it . . ."

Tom opened the hotel room door and then closed it again as a chambermaid walked past. His voice dropped. "I said those things when I thought Jessie was going to walk back through the door and tell us all we were stark raving mad. I said those things because I was convinced she'd had a silly row with her brother," said Tom. "I never, ever thought it would come to this with the police and the questioning and the searching of fucking hotel grounds for our missing daughter. I never, ever thought Jessie would have let her sister and her own husband down like that. And I never, ever thought that we'd be sitting here now wondering if she was missing, murdered or if she'd taken her own life! Ryan's involvement has fallen way down the pecking order in my book."

"But you can't deny it," said Ella. "I can't deny it. Ryan *is* involved. He did have a row with Jessie and it looks like it was a pretty bad one to me. He knew about Cain. He called her a slut. "

Tom's mouth tightened and he clenched his fists by his sides.

"If you think for one second I am going to give those cops a solitary inch of information that might write off this search and record it as a domestic row, just so they can then shove it in a file where it will gather dust and Jessie will never be found, well, then you don't know me very well at all."

He slammed the door and left Ella alone in the room, listening to the clatter of delph from outside the door and the chit-chat of the domestic staff of the hotel.

Her husband's words echoed in her head.

'You don't know me at all,' he had said to her. And maybe she didn't.

In fact, Ella wondered just how much she really knew any of her precious family at all.

Chapter 26

Ryan's co-operation with the police left a lot to be desired. He repeatedly looked at his watch and sighed in between answering questions that had been going on for over an hour now.

"So, you believed your sister was having an affair with Cain Daniels?"

"I know she was. She slept with him at least once."

"Yet last night when we spoke to Mr Daniels, he categorically denied anything of the sort."

Ryan's arrogance was getting right up his nose and he planned to pull every piece of information from this jumped-up little rich kid in one session.

"I know everything," said Ryan.

"Everything?"

"Everything."

"Elaborate. How long have you known everything?"

"Forever," he snorted.

"Ryan, we are on a road to nowhere here. What else did you know?"

"Everything." Then he added with a snigger, "And they had no idea at all."

"Since when?"

"Since I overheard their conversation one afternoon."

"When?"

"In May, I think. Yes, it was in May. I used to do odd jobs for David around the house and he'd asked me to cut the lawns back then."

"And?"

"And I was coming around the side of the house one day when I heard Cain's laughter."

"Go on."

"Nothing unusual there, of course, but then when I came around the corner, I saw them. They were snogging like teenagers. It was sick."

"And what did you do then?"

"I did nothing," said Ryan and he sat back and swung on the back legs of the chair, his arms folded. "I was going to interrupt but then I thought, no. This could be fun."

"Fun?" roared Cooper. "You thought it was fun that Jessie and Cain were playing around behind your other sister's back? And not to mention how they were doing the dirt on your good old buddy, David?"

Ryan put his hands behind his head. "It was fun at the start. You see, I really couldn't believe it. You don't know what it has been like growing up in her shadow. Jessie has always been a hard act to follow. Yes, I got my share of attention for being the only son but my

312

mess-ups in life meant I could never sit anywhere near the height of my big sister's pedestal."

Cooper paced the room, chewing a pen as he spoke. "So you decided to torment your sister with a few games. Fun, right?"

"Damn right I did," said Ryan and he slammed his fist on the table. "I felt sorry for Andrea more, though. She had always lurked in Jessie's shadow, pushing herself to keep up with the way Jessie just slid through life with everything so perfect. Poor Andrea was always at least two steps behind despite her efforts and here she was playing second fiddle again." Ryan upped his monologue. "Pretty, yes, but not quite as beautiful as Jess – bright but not top-notch-lawyer clever – bubbly and fun, but not nearly as endearing as her big sister. And now poor Andrea is a victim of Jessie's horrible game. We all are."

Cooper smacked his lips, a trait that Ryan had noticed from the start. "I don't know your sister," Cooper said. "But from what I'm told I don't think she is the type to play deliberate games with anyone. Why do you think she was having an affair with someone like Cain Daniels?"

Ryan drummed his hands on the table and Bert McManus gave him a look that told him to stop.

"Well, let's face it," Ryan said. "She's a bigger sucker than we all gave her credit for. She was always so ambitious so a celebrity broadcaster with oodles of charm didn't have much competition with old hapless copper Dave who wanted to settle down with two point four children and a white picket fence. Like you say, you don't know my sister. I did. I know her very well indeed."

Cooper pulled out a chair and sat down, crossing his legs, the pen still in his mouth. He took it out and waved it in the air as he spoke. "So, you saw Jessie and Cain have a bit of a fumble in the garden and then it turned into an illicit affair which he denies and Jessie isn't here to give her side of the story. Why on earth should we believe you?"

Ryan leaned across the table. "You don't have to believe me," he said. "But take a fucking look at this and then tell me I'm making this all up!"

He swivelled his mobile phone across the table and Cooper caught it before it fell on the floor. He opened it and followed Ryan's instructions, then closed it again when he had seen enough.

"For the benefit of the tape, Mr O'Neill has presented a video recording on a mobile phone of his sister Jessie and Cain Daniels having sex in a shower."

Cooper threw the phone at his colleague who caught it with both hands and Ryan gave him a cheeky nod.

"Have fun," he said with a wink.

"Mr O'Neill, do you have any idea where your sister is right now?" asked Cooper.

"No."

"Do you have any idea who she might be with?"

"God knows."

"You're nothing only a dirty little pervert, aren't you, Ryan?" said Cooper, leaning across so that Ryan could smell his smoky breath. "You had no intentions of doing anything to stop the affair. You were getting such kicks from following your sister and her lover around that you forgot that there was a big wedding coming up, didn't you? You forgot that you had another sister whose life would be ruined by all of this but you didn't even think of her because you were having too much fun!"

Ryan leaned away from the detective and fanned his face. "Watching my sister and Cain Daniels made me sick. The fun went straight out the window when I realised just how fucking far they were prepared to take it. My own sister. My own sister was behaving like a star-struck teenager, fucking around with her sister's fiancé. Do you know how mad that made me feel? How sorry that made me feel for Andrea? But I couldn't hurt Andrea like that. She would have been devastated if I told her the truth."

"No, you didn't want to hurt her!" said Cooper and he kicked a chair out of his path. "You decided to let her marry the bastard instead!"

"I tried to stop it!" said Ryan and he scraped back his own chair and stood up. "I didn't want her to marry him at all. I hate him and I hate Jessie! I hate them for what they have done."

"I want some time with my client," said Bert McManus, pulling Ryan to his seat again.

"Where is your sister?" shouted Cooper, holding his hand to signal McManus to stay quiet.

"I don't know!"

"Where is your sister?"

"I said I don't know where she is!"

315

"I request time out now," said McManus, taking to his feet.

"Who punched your face in, Ryan?" shouted Cooper. "Who gave you the kicking that so many men in Glencuan have always longed to, little rich kid?"

"You bastard!" said Ryan. "I told Jess that I knew about it. That's why she flipped and scraped my face."

He pointed at the fine slither of dried blood that ran down his cheek.

"Your sister did that to you?"

"Yes, she did! She scraped me with her nails and then she walked away towards the river. But, but –"

McManus held up his hand to stop Ryan but Cooper blanked him. "Keep going Ryan. But what?"

"But then – then – he came out of nowhere," Ryan slumped back into his chair and his voice lowered. "And he went for me from behind. I was drunk. I didn't stand a chance. He shoved me on the ground and punched me so hard I thought he broke my nose. When I came round she was gone. And so was he."

"Now, we're getting somewhere! Now, we're kicking ass, Ryan! Who was gone? Who?"

Ryan gripped his hair as he held his head and then looked up.

"I don't know," he said.

"What?" yelled Cooper. "What do you mean you don't know? Who the fuck was the last person with your sister? Who?"

"I can't really remember! I – I –"

Cooper sat opposite Ryan and softened his tone,

316

meeting the young man's eye. "Ryan, this is important. Who hit you?"

"I – it was down by the river bank. He came out of nowhere. I was so drunk. I – I think it was Cain Daniels who did this to me. And I think he knows where Jessie is too."

"Interview aborted at eleven twenty-three am," said Cooper and he nodded to his colleague who clicked off the tape.

He then turned to Ryan who was a shadow of the cocky, arrogant young man who had come to the station that morning. Now, he looked like a wounded animal, riddled with guilt and shame that he might have played even a minor role in his sister's disappearance.

"Don't think for one second that I feel sorry for you," said Cooper. "You're not off the hook yet."

Bert McManus shot a dirty look at Cooper and led Ryan out of the room and into an adjoining waiting area.

"Get that lying bastard Daniels down here right now," said Cooper and he marched out behind them and almost took the door off the hinges.

He was met in the corridor by Sandra Millar who was carrying a bundle of files and balancing a coffee in her other hand. He bumped into her and she almost spilled her drink, shook her head in despair at his haste and then she spoke to him at lightning speed.

"I've just had David on the phone," she said, trying to keep up with her boss's pace as he walked towards the coffee machine.

"I told David Chambers to keep his fucking nose out of this," said Cooper.

"What? Why?" said Sandra. "The man's distraught, sir. What do you expect him to do? Sit back and wait until his wife says, 'Honey, I'm home!'"

Cooper punched the drinks machine and his money fell out and onto the floor. He slotted it back in and pressed a different coffee type, then sighed with relief as the polystyrene cup popped out and filled with hot, frothy liquid.

"We'll have to talk to him again," said Cooper. "Officially this time."

"Why? What's happened?"

"Well, it looks like his wife *was* having an affair after all and he claims he didn't know about it."

"Oh . . ."

"Yes. Oh, indeed. And he left her only days before she disappeared. Funny that. Get him in here again for a chat."

"Okay, okay I will," said Sandra, a tad disappointed for David.

"And what have *you* to report," said Cooper, "apart from feeling sorry for your colleague though all this?"

Sandra became animated again at the opportunity to tell of her recent findings. "Well, I actually do have something. Could be interesting."

"Go on," said Cooper, blowing the hot coffee.

"One of the barmen at Bromley Castle was off sick last night. He was back on duty this morning and hadn't been around the hotel since the wedding, hadn't seen the news etc. Then when David showed him the photo of Jessie this morning he recognised her instantly."

Cooper made his way back up the corridor with Sandra on his tail.

"And he said he saw her chatting to a priest. The priest who had officiated at the wedding. I've tracked him down and his name is Father Christopher Lennon. The barman said they seemed really friendly."

"So what? Haven't we already been told that Jessie is the type to eat the altar rails? Of course, she would know her priest. Even I know my local minister and that's saying something."

Sandra stopped, frustrated at how Cooper was brushing her off. She'd expected him to at least stop to hear her out but instead he marched on.

"She was holding his hand, sir!" she shouted after her boss. "She kissed him on the cheek too. Do you know your minister as well as that?"

Sandra watched as Cooper stopped in his tracks, then turned and marched towards her.

"No. No, I don't. Reverend Hall just isn't my type, funnily enough. Okay, then. Find out more about him. In fact, go and call in on him and suss out if there's any reason to drag him down here for questioning. That's all we fucking need – a God-fearing preacher man in the middle of all this!"

Cooper walked away again and Sandra smiled and clicked her fingers, delighted that she had found one possible trail.

"My God," said Cooper, ranting on as he walked as

if Sandra was still beside him. "Quite a handful is this Miss Jessie O'Neill. It's just surprises all fucking over the show with this family."

David Chambers met Cain Daniels on the steps of the police station as both of them arrived and deliberately avoided eye contact.

Daniels had always been a thorn in his side, ever since he arrived on Andrea's arm what seemed like only weeks ago. Before any of the O'Neills could question it, he had moulded himself into part of the family.

"Well, if it isn't the prodigal son," said Cain but David didn't answer. Cain's arrogance didn't surprise him at all. Cain Daniels was the type of man who knew everything about everyone and would argue his point prolifically with anyone who dared question him. He was a name-dropping arselicker in David's eyes and there was a suave coolness to his persona that David couldn't warm to. Andrea was always a more fickle girl than her older sister, or so he had always thought, and he wasn't surprised at all that she had fallen for this charming snake's celebrity and glossy lifestyle. But Jessie? He would never have thought it.

David wasn't at all shocked at having been called back in for official questioning, but Daniels, despite his glossy attempts at making conversation, looked stunned like a naughty schoolboy on his way to see his headmaster.

"Looks like we're all under the big bad spotlight," he said and he brushed past David, making his way through the double doors of the station.

David stopped and let Cain walk a few steps ahead of him. He didn't want any idle conversation with this man right now. In fact he believed that if it wasn't for Daniels and his filthy antics, Jessie wouldn't be missing. He didn't doubt that for a second.

The station was cool inside and David hunched up the hood of his fleecy jacket to block the draught he felt on his neck as he waited to be called.

Unlike Cain who was flanked by his lawyer, David sat alone, unfazed by the procedures that he dealt with on a daily basis as part of his working life.

He knew the process inside out.

Questioning, interrogation, the right to remain silent, prosecution, prison . . .

But he had no intention of getting that far, of course.

Until Jessie was found, they were all just accessories in one big unsolved jigsaw puzzle.

Until Jessie was found, they were simply helping police with their enquiries. He kept chanting this over and over again in his head. The more he remembered that he knew these cops inside out, the longer he could remain calm about being on the other side of the table when he was finally called into the interrogation room.

Chapter 27

Rosie Sheehan was daydreaming about Jessie O'Neill's disappearance when the doorbell of the parochial house rang later that afternoon.

She peeped out through the Venetian blinds and wondered if she had imagined the bell ringing, she had been so lost in thought.

It was a glorious day at last and she really should open the windows and air the place but she couldn't concentrate on work with her phone bleeping and her regular updating of friends and neighbours on news as she heard it. There had been nothing like this in town since – well, never really.

Speculation said that the O'Neill family were due back home today and already there were a few journalists waiting around the gates of their mansion on the hilltop of Glencuan.

Maggie McKenna said she'd heard that the only son,

Ryan, was in a terrible row with his sister before she disappeared and they were even suspecting the husband now too.

Of course, the people at North FM were keeping the whole story out of their news bulletins or mid-morning discussions on account of Cain Daniels's connections and the so-called rumours of his affair with Jessie.

Yes, that was Rosie's favourite part of it all. The affair.

Who would have thought that the gorgeous Cain Daniels, the housewife's hunk, he of the velvet voice, would have been such a bad boy beneath it all?

The front doorbell rang again and Rosie made her way to answer it, hoping it would be her daughter or maybe even Maggie with more titbits of news.

"Good morning. Oh!" said Rosie, quite taken aback.

"Sorry to call on you unannounced like this."

"But Father isn't in at the moment. Can I take a message? There's no point waiting because I don't know how long he will be."

The girl was dressed in a smart suit and her neatly cut red hair skimmed her shoulders, framing her heart-shaped face and almond eyes.

"I'm Detective Inspector Sandra Millar," said the lady and she held up a badge that showed a picture of her with much longer hair and a nervous smile.

"Oh!" said Rosie and she put her hand to her chest. "Oh, well, do come in then. I suppose you're doing the rounds about the O'Neill fiasco, are you? Such a tragedy. Such a worry for that poor family."

She stood back and signalled the police officer to come inside.

"Yes, that's it," said Sandra taking in her surroundings. "Such a worry, but like you said – I'm just doing the rounds."

"Well, Father is tending the village sick but he should be back in half an hour or so," said Rosie, leading the way into the drawing-room. "I normally don't like people hanging around and waiting for him without an appointment, but we can make an exception on this important occasion. Have a seat in here and I'll fetch us some tea. It's a terrible situation altogether, isn't it? Terrible altogether."

Sandra looked around the old-fashioned drawing-room that had been modernised with new furniture and trendy sofas and she wondered what on earth she should expect from her meeting with Father Christopher Lennon. She had never met a Catholic priest before and the whole mystery of a different religion engulfed her as she took in the rosary beads on the table, the picture of Our Lady on the far wall, the Sacred Heart picture with its red glow by the door.

A clock ticked in the background and through the back window she could see the beautiful gardens that surrounded the old house and the long-stemmed flowers as they waved in the light breeze.

The silence of the whole house all amazed her. How disciplined and lonely a life it must be to live in such a huge place all alone, with rituals and Masses and virtual strangers calling on you every hour with births, deaths, marriages, confessions, troubles and tales of woe.

Sandra shuddered. What type of a man would choose a life like this? What type of man took a vow of celibacy and stuck with it forever?

She glanced at the door and listened but she could only hear Rosie humming a made-up tune in the distance so she took the liberty of having a quick look around the room.

The mantelpiece was as tall as she was and she gazed along the peppered display of photographs, in frames of all different shapes and sizes, of men who she presumed to be different priests who had lived in the house before Father Christopher. Their black and white stares shook her slightly and she wondered how many of them were dead now and were watching over her, watching her watching them. She shivered.

And then she recognised him. She gulped hard when she came to his photo, a stunning picture of the man she presumed she was about to meet. The date on the bottom of the photo showed it was taken only a year ago and it was of a very handsome young priest with his arm draped around an older woman who wasn't looking at the camera. His companion looked like she had been momentarily distracted, or else she was totally unaware that the picture was being taken.

He on the other hand was seducing the lens with his gorgeous brown eyes and swarthy skin and the way his black hair fell down around his temples made Sandra want to see more. She looked closer, holding the photo by the bottom edge of the frame as she stood on her tip-toes, desperate to get a better look.

The click of the door took her breath away and she jumped back, embarrassed at being caught snooping.

"He didn't want to keep those older photos up at all," said Rosie, and she placed a tray of tea and biscuits on the coffee table. "He's obsessed with modernising this place and giving it a complete makeover." She gave a high-pitched laugh which illustrated her gripe with his views. "I mean, tradition is tradition. He can't change that."

"Of course. Who is the lady in the photograph?" asked Sandra, and Rosie's silence told her it was none of her business. "It's just that the others are photographed alone."

"Oh, it's his mother," said Rosie, throwing her eyes up. "She lives in Athlone now. They're originally from Cork."

"Oh. And how do you find him? He's very young, isn't he?"

Rosie knew what the young lady was thinking. She saw it in every female visitor to the house.

"He's a real gentleman," said Rosie. "He treats me very well. But you know, what gets to me is that he just can't seem to stick to the way things were around here. Mind, I'm not one to complain. I suppose he's a young man and that's just the way it is . . ."

Sandra smiled inwardly as Rosie struck off into a rant.

"I mean, he even tried to scrape the old wallpaper upstairs himself," said Rosie, taking her voice down into a whisper. "That was, until he realised he doesn't have the time for such petty issues and just when I think he's starting to settle, he announces that he's changing one of the rooms or outhouses into a gym! A gym, I say! Father Jones before him would never have worried about such materialistic nonsense. What would a priest want a gym for?"

Sandra blinked and glanced back at the gallery of clerics, then sat down on her seat again.

Yes, Father Jones looked at least forty years older than Father Lennon for a start, she thought, and she resisted a giggle. Father Lennon on the other hand looked like he kept himself in pretty fine shape.

"Like you say, he's a young man," said Sandra, still looking at the photo in admiration. "Most men of his age do go to the gym, I guess. Why do you think he should be any different? Is it because he's a priest?"

"Exactly," said Rosie, watching the young woman's every move. "He is a priest. Oh, it *is* hard to get used to his modern ideas. And he is so busy. Being a priest is a twenty-four-hour job, you know. There's hardly such thing as an hour off."

"I can imagine." Sandra looked back at the other photos on the mantel again. "Well, I don't think I would want the faces of people who used to live in my house watching my every move. I'd find it a bit spooky."

She lifted a cup of freshly poured tea and sipped from it, revelling in its sweet taste. There was something particularly old-fashioned about Rosie in her presentation and in her beliefs and Sandra could see how she was suited to her job.

"Had you worked for some of the others, too?" she asked.

"Oh yes!" said Rosie with great pride. She spoke as she chewed a biscuit but managed to do it quite discreetly. "I've lived in this village all of my life, long before many of these blow-ins who just use it to commute to and from the city. Faceless people, really. No, I'm one of the original villagers, you might say. There are very few of us left."

Sandra watched Rosie chomp through biscuit after biscuit and her tongue loosened with every top-up of tea. She doubted she would need to talk to anyone else in Glencuan after this visit. Rosie was a real fount of information, from days gone by right up until what happened in the village that very morning.

"So, the O'Neills arrived in the village about thirty years ago, I gather?" asked Sandra.

"No, well, Jessie is twenty-eight, right?" said Rosie. "That's what the papers say anyway. Well, I do remember that when they arrived she was just a tiny baby and Mrs O'Neill had this minute, neat baby bump which would have been the second girl. She was always so glamorous. Then there was a bit of a gap before their son was born. Rascal of a boy he is too."

Sandra had heard enough about Ryan on her travels. A few scrapes with the law over biking and speeding were obviously enough to scar him with everyone in this village.

"What about the girls? How do you find them?"

"I've always found Andrea to be quite polite and sweet but Jessie was a quiet type," said Rosie. "Even as a child she hid behind her beauty and she didn't bother much with us townsfolk. Ella O'Neill adored each of them in what they said was an obsessive manner. So they say. They say she was getting help for her nerves. Huh! I never heard the like of it – all these'uns who claim to be bad with their nerves!"

Sandra heard the front door close and she brushed crumbs off her lap, fixed her hair and sat up straight.

Rosie gave her a knowing smile, as if she had seen that reaction before in young ladies who were preparing to meet Father Lennon for the first time and each and every time after that. She found it quite entertaining that anyone should fancy a parish priest.

When Father Christopher opened the drawing-room door, Sandra tried to introduce herself but words failed her.

He was much, much more handsome than his photo suggested, but he looked tired and worn around the edges. When he smiled at her, his eyes crinkled at the sides and she sensed he had a lot on his mind.

"Father, this is Detective Sandra Millar," said Rosie as if she was speaking to a child. "She is here to speak to you about Jessie O'Neill. She's just doing the rounds."

Rosie hesitated for a moment and then eventually left the room.

Father Christopher sat down without properly introducing himself to Sandra.

"Has something happened to her? Have you found her?" he asked.

"I'm afraid we haven't yet, Father," said Sandra. "I'm

trying to trace Jessie's last few days and well, I'm led to believe that you and Jessie had become quite close . . ."

"I'm new to the village," he said. "Jessie had called here to do with the wedding and we got talking."

"Of course . . ."

"I've really only known her for over a week now, but I suppose you could say we were . . . well, we were on the way to becoming good friends."

"Good friends?"

"Yes. Good friends. Even people like me need friends, you know."

He raised an eyebrow as he said it and Sandra couldn't take her eyes off him. He was like nothing she had ever seen before. She could feel her whole body melt when he spoke and she braced herself in the line of duty.

"And how did er, how did Jessie seem to you then? Was she worried about anything in particular? You do know her husband had left her quite recently?"

"Well, yes I do," said the priest. "We discussed a lot of things actually, but it is my duty not to disclose a parishioner's confession or private conversation. Not unless, of course, you feel it may be relevant to finding her. I will obviously do anything at all to help."

Sandra felt she could drown in his eyes. She could see them filling up as he thought of Jessie and she sensed that, although he was trying his best to seem neutral and professional, he had grown very close to this young lady indeed.

"Did she tell you of her affair?"

Father Christopher looked startled for the first time. He paused.

"Yes. Yes, she did," he said and then he looked at the floor as he spoke. "I wouldn't call it an affair as such. More a half-hearted fling and it was breaking her heart to have betrayed her husband and her sister. She is a good girl, no matter what it may seem."

Sandra watched as he clasped and unclasped his hands. His voice was mellow and full of worry for the beautiful O'Neill girl.

"Did Jessie acknowledge your support?"

"How do you mean?"

"I mean, did she feel that you helped her to move on from her worries, or to make decisions about how to deal with her guilt?"

The priest nodded and he let out a sigh. "Yes, she did." He smiled at the memory. "That's my job after all. She thanked me over and over again for helping her to find some direction on how to deal with her sin. In fact it was the last conversation I had with her at the hotel. She thanked me again and . . . and then she danced away. She seemed so happy. So content at last."

Sandra sat in silence and for the first time in the last two days, she felt like she really knew Jessie O'Neill.

She was just a girl who had done wrong, who was confused with her feelings for an arrogant, cheap celebrity but who had paid the price for her sins by losing her husband and destroying her marriage. She shivered at the thought that Jessie might be lying somewhere alone and hurt, or even worse.

"Can I ask you more about your last conversation? Anything else?"

"Yes. She thanked me for being there for her. She was smiling, happy. Happier than I've ever seen her."

"And you left the wedding after that conversation?"

"Yes, I did. It was well after nine and I drove home, stopping by the grocery store outside the village. Am I to justify my whereabouts?"

"Well, this is an investigation. It might be a good idea." Sandra hadn't thought of it that way, but since he'd mentioned it.

Father Christopher shrugged. "I stopped off at the grocery store. The local Spar. And then I came home and went to bed. I was wakened with a call around midnight to give last rites to an elderly man. I spent most of the night with the family. He was buried yesterday."

"Oh," said Sandra. Well you couldn't really argue with that. "And the family of the man – "

"Joe Roberts."

"Joe Roberts," she said, writing it down as she spoke. "The Roberts family can vouch for that of course?"

"Of course," said Father Christopher, with a gentle smile. "Now, would you like more tea?"

"Yes. I would, I'd love some, thank you," said Sandra and he left her alone in the drawing-room again.

As she waited for him to return, Sandra thought with empathy about the O'Neill family who were probably on their way home now, back to this village where everyone was hungry for information and updates on the disappearance of Jessie.

Everywhere she had visited – the local shop, the pub, the post office, all had a varied opinion of the family that had moved in and taken over their village some years ago with their wealth and grandeur and lofty approach to making friends among the commoners.

"This is a beautiful house," she called to him through the hallway. "Do you mind if I take a look around?"

"Go ahead," he said and Sandra wandered around the stark entrance to the house, lifting Mass bulletins and religious pamphlets. She could hear the housekeeper muffle around upstairs and when she stepped backwards to admire a statue she accidentally knocked a vase over, spilling water all over a side table. She closed her eyes as it crashed onto the floor and Father Christopher rushed out into the hallway, looking flustered.

"I'm so, so sorry," she muttered, mopping up the water with a hanky. "I'm so clumsy."

Her hands were shaking with embarrassment and she fumbled with the fresh flowers that were strewn all over the floor.

"It's okay," said Father Christopher. "Really, don't worry."

He bent down beside her and swept up the remainder of the flowers, so close to her she could smell his sweet cologne. "Rosie?" he called. "Can you bring a mop? And a bill for a broken vase?"

Sandra looked embarrassed.

"I'm kidding," he said and he walked back into the drawing-room. Sandra felt hot and she fanned her face behind him. He was mesmerising, gorgeous *and* he had a sense of humour. And he's a priest, she reminded herself. And you're a cop. Now focus. What else did she need to know?

"So you've only known Jessie for a week really?" she asked eventually. "You seem have got to know her quite well. How did that come around? The wedding?"

Father Christopher sat down on the seat in the far corner of the room. He relaxed into the chair and smiled as he recalled his knowledge of Jessie.

"Well, not only the wedding. She had troubles. She asked for my help and I was happy to try and advise her."

"Of course," said Sandra. "You obviously were – I mean, you obviously are very fond of the girl."

Sandra sensed that she had hit a nerve at his reaction.

"Like I said, it's my job. And most people seem to be fond of Jessie. That's what I gather. She is a very endearing, gentle person who I listened to in my line of duty," he said, jumping to the defence of his true feelings. "Perhaps I've said too much. Like I said, I really can only tell you what is relevant to your enquiry."

"Of course," said Sandra. "But did you sense from her at all that she was under any threat? I'm sure you've read in the papers that Jessie was very vulnerable lately."

"She was in a terrible state when she came to see me first," he said. "She was so afraid, so worried about her family and how she had betrayed them."

"So she confessed to you?"

"You know I cannot tell you every detail of that, but yes. She asked for absolution. She has great faith."

"And what of her vulnerability?"

"She was so afraid. She – oh!" He suddenly looked stricken, almost shocked as he stared ahead of him unseeingly.

"What is it?" asked Sandra eagerly.

"I've just remembered something. Something important." He set his cup down and it splashed onto the table, then he jumped to his feet and went out.

He returned a minute later, smoothing out a scrunched-up page of notepaper with his hand.

"How could I have forgotten? This could be a vital clue! Here, read it. I do apologise. Someone left this for Jessie and she gave it to me."

Sandra read aloud.

"Your time is running out. I am watching your every move. So it's a priest next then? First you're whoring with a gangster, then your sister's boyfriend and now you're throwing yourself at a priest. Dirty bitch. Dirty rotten whore. What would David say? What would your sister say?"

"She gave it to me just last week. Look, she was terrified. Someone had left it in her house but I didn't let her see it."

"Father, you really should have given this to us before now."

"I should have. I'm sorry. I put it in my pocket at the time and by chance it was still upstairs. It totally escaped my mind that I might still have it. I really didn't want Jessie to ever know what it said. I didn't want to fuel her fears."

Sandra read the note again and then she looked up at Father Christopher.

"Your relationship with Jessie. It's – it's not how this note suggests, is it?"

Father Lennon looked deeply insulted and Sandra wished she didn't have to ask him.

"No, it's not," he said. "Contrary to what the author of that note says, she respects my position as a priest. And I would never, ever jeopardise our friendship, no matter – no matter how much I enjoy her company. I pray that she has come to no harm. I really do."

Sandra felt like she was on the verge of hearing a confession of undying love from this handsome man. She had never met Jessie O'Neill but now she wished she had. Whatever her secret was, she must be able to transfix every person she came into contact with. Well, almost everyone considering the venom behind the note.

"Thank you, Father," she said. "Thank you for this. You have been most helpful. I pray too that Jessie has come to no harm. I wish you well."

Sandra put the note into a clear plastic folder, zipped it up the side and stood up, finding herself lost again in this gorgeous, untouchable man's eyes. She shook his hand and left the house, then she watched in her rear-view mirror as he walked back into his magnificent home, alone and full of love for a girl he could never claim as his own.

Chapter 28

Bert McManus braced himself for the bad news he was about to break to the O'Neill family who had packed up their car and were ready to depart Bromley Castle for Glencuan.

The Mercedes was full of cases and McManus sensed their eagerness to leave Bromley and all that it represented far behind them.

"We had planned to be away an hour ago," said Tom O'Neill to his lawyer and he looked at his watch. "I was going to come straight back here when I made sure Andrea and Ella were settled at home. They just can't handle this place any more."

"I know," said McManus. "I'm sorry to delay you."

He swallowed hard and then pulled Tom to the side, out of the earshot of the two women who were waiting in the car in the hotel carpark.

"It's not good, Tom. I'm sorry but it doesn't look

good for Ryan at the moment. Bring your family back inside and I'll ask the hotel to give us a room for some privacy, and then I can tell you everything."

Tom felt bile burn his stomach and his heart bled at the thought of the news he was about to hear. He looked back at his wife and daughter who waited in the car.

Poor Andrea who should have been living it up on a sandy beach, full of happiness and hope for the future, and Ella who was just a shadow of her former self. She hadn't eaten in two days now and it was evident in her frail, bony structure.

Each step he took felt like he was carrying lead and he could feel his body was stooped over as though already in mourning in preparation for the new heartache that was only seconds away.

He opened the car door while McManus went ahead into the hotel and he tried to find his voice. His wife and daughter looked back at him in bewilderment, already exhausted with all of the revelations to date and longing to get home to the comfort of their own surroundings.

"Change of plans, ladies," he said, trying to stifle the panic in his throat and wanting with all his strength to delay the inevitable. "There is some news. Bert has some news. I'm not sure what to expect but we have been asked to go inside for a quick word."

Ella and Andrea both went pale and Tom helped them from the car. The two women linked arms as they walked along the tarmac and then onto the paved walkway that Andrea had made her grand entrance along just two days ago full of hopes and dreams and promises.

He led them into the bright conference room that McManus had been allocated and Ella put her head on her daughter's shoulder when she went inside, longing for the nightmare to be over but knowing that they still had a long way to go by the look on their lawyer's face.

"It's not looking good," he said, trying his best to appear stoic but he was obviously heartbroken by the news he was about to impart. "Ryan has been arrested in connection with Jessie's disappearance."

The O'Neill family held onto one another and Ella closed her eyes, wanting to shut out the world and all the words that Bert McManus was saying to her.

"He has made a full confession to breaking and entering your daughter's home, to defacing her property and to sending hate mail which we have traced a copy of and bears his fingerprints as well as those of Father Christopher Lennon who disclosed the sample."

"Father Lennon? How did he have it?"

"Jessie showed it to him a number of days ago. He was sure he had disposed of it but handed it in to Detective Millar when she spoke to him this morning."

Ella's and Andrea sat emotionless, stunned by what they were hearing.

"Where do they think Jessie is? Are they suggesting Ryan . . .?"

"They found her dress and shoes about two miles from here just over two hours ago. They were spattered in blood and forensics have confirmed that traces of

Ryan's blood were also seeped into the fibres. Ryan confessed to the notes just after Detective Millar phoned through saying she had tracked one of them from the priest. He has been taunting his sister for weeks now. He has admitted it himself."

Andrea's arm hung limp around her mother's shoulders as she grasped her and clung into her side.

She couldn't think of anything to say. She had no response to McManus's announcement or to her brother's arrest or to her sister's possible death which was what McManus was obviously suggesting.

"So they have arrested him on suspicion of what exactly?" said Tom, teetering between great anger and grief. "Are you saying they think Jessie is dead? That Ryan killed her?"

"Not necessarily, no," said McManus. "Yes, there is evidence of a scuffle but we knew that Ryan had been involved in that all along. But Jessie has obviously been hurt badly too and they couldn't hold Ryan any longer without arresting him. I'm afraid the evidence is well stacked against him."

"The boy is in a mess. He doesn't know what he is saying!" said Tom.

"I'm sorry, but I did all I can. I plan to go back down to the station now, but I felt it was important you knew of this before you decide to go back to Glencuan."

Again, the O'Neills sat silent, unable to take in all they had heard.

"Why did he feel he had to deal with this for me?" said Andrea, her voice building until she eventually found herself shouting at the man across from her, and then at her parents. "Who the hell gave Ryan the right to fight my battles? It was up to me how to deal with their ugly fling or affair or whatever it was! I could have handled it. It was my problem. It's up to me to hate Jessie, not Ryan! He should have stayed out of this!"

"I know, love," said McManus. "It's a lot for you to accept right now."

"I should hate her! I should want to hit her and hate her!" she cried. "Yet, I don't hate her at all! Why can't I find it in me to hate her? Why?"

She broke down and fell into her mother's arms. Ella held her tight but Tom's mind was in overdrive, refusing to believe for one second that his son was guilty of assaulting his own sister.

He held his head in his hands and wiped his eyes, breathing slowly so as to curb what he was about to say. He knew that when he said it, he would never be able to take his words back but his veins were throbbing with adrenaline and anger.

"How could you hate her, Andrea?" he said. "How could anyone ever as much as dislike Jessie? Your mother had her so wrapped up in cotton wool and you looked up to her in such awe that she could never do wrong in either of your eyes."

"Tom!" said Ella. "Please, don't start this now. Please!"

"Yes, Andrea, you tried to air your opinions on feeling second best," he continued. "But it was always shunned, always brushed under the carpet with a courtesy hug or a kiss on the cheek for reassurance."

"Tom, tensions are running high," said Bert McManus, trying his best to settle his old friend down. "You've all had quite a shock. It's not the time to point the finger of blame –"

"Don't tell me how to speak to my family!" said Tom and he rose to his feet. "I know what that boy has been through down the years. He was always fussed over so much and smothered by his mother that, of course, he began to rebel. Well, that wasn't good enough for you, Ella, was it? So you started comparing him to Jessie. Jessie would never have made such silly mistakes, Jessie always did her homework, Jessie never crashed her car, Jessie, Jessie, Jessie!! Now, look what you've done!" Tom's nostrils flared and his eyes were bloodshot with rage and he knew he had lost control of his senses.

He made for the door and Andrea called after him in desperation.

"Daddy, please. You don't mean that. Where are you going? We need you."

Tom stopped at the door and glared at his wife and daughter.

"I'm going to see my son," he said. "I'm going to find out what the fuck is going on in his head, once and for all."

Ryan looked pitiful in the small holding cell at Bromley Police Barracks. He seemed small and fragile in comparison to the stocky, confident lad that Tom had been so proud of down the years.

His baseball hat disguised the extent of the injury on his face and he sat on the narrow white bed with his arms around his knees, huddled like a naughty schoolboy who was exasperated at being punished for his actions.

Tom waited for the cell to open and a police officer accompanied him inside, checked his watch and told him sternly that he had five minutes. The man then stood at the door of the cell and Tom sat beside his son who turned his face into the wall and refused to speak.

"I know you didn't do this," said Tom but Ryan didn't flinch. "I know your sister is still alive and that this has all been one big mistake after another. We are going to find her – you know that too, don't you?"

Ryan buried his face further into his chest and shrugged.

"Ryan, I am on your side, son. I don't believe for a second you would do anything to harm Jessie. Yes, you had a row – yes, you may have felt like you hated her for what she was doing but my God you wouldn't hurt her, would you? You were only trying to scare her for betraying her family, isn't that right? "

The policeman at the door checked his watch and Tom ignored him. But Ryan was refusing to communicate, just as Bert McManus had warned him.

"I've been through the whole story with McManus. He told me you think Cain Daniels hit you after you had a row with Jess. You say that was the last you saw of her and I believe you. Now, think hard, Ryan. Think about where she headed to after that. Did Daniels take her somewhere? Did she run away? Was there anyone else around at that time? *Think*, Ryan. *Think* before it's too late."

Ryan turned around and faced his father, though he didn't lift his head. Tom could hear him cry. Then he whispered softly, "I'm not sure." His sobs became heavier. "I don't know, Dad."

"What? Come *on*, Ryan. Just tell me what you're thinking so I can help you."

Tom lifted the cap back from his son's face and he prayed like he never had before that Ryan would tell him something that might lead to Jessie and would get him out of this mess.

"I don't remember a thing," said Ryan. "After Jessie scraped my face, I don't remember a thing."

"But you said Cain hit you after that. Wasn't that the last thing you remember before your mother found you outside? Did Cain hit you, Ryan?"

"I think it was him. I think it was."

"But he was in the hall all evening," said Tom. "He never left Andrea's side, except . . . except, that's right, the last dance!"

Tom remembered how Cain had gone missing and had to be waited for before the last dance of the evening. That was around the same time that Ryan was outside with Jessie.

"He must have been the last one to see her then. Is that it? Did Cain Daniels hit you and then do something to Jessie?"

"I don't know!" said Ryan, shouting now.

344

The policeman at the door turned to face them and Tom shouted at him to give them one more minute.

Tom pleaded with God to give his son an answer, but Ryan turned to the wall again.

"I don't know, I said! I can't remember if it was Cain or if it was me."

"What the hell do you mean you can't remember? You *have* to remember," said Tom. "Come on, Ryan. I'm here for you. Think about what happened. Think hard."

"I had too much to drink, Dad," said Ryan and he turned towards his father again. "I hit her. I may have hit her too hard. I don't deserve your help because I can't remember what happened after that. I can't remember what I have done to Jessie. I can't remember if Cain Daniels was there at all. I can't really remember anything."

Chapter 29

Andrea's mobile phone rang as she and her mother walked around the gardens of the hotel, not sure where to go or what to do next.

It was almost five now and as the evening sun split through the trees at Bromley Castle, a bridal party were by the river bank happily posing for photographs with friends and family.

"If it's him, don't answer it," said Ella. "It will only annoy you and God knows you've had enough annoyance today."

Andrea toyed with the phone in her hand and then pressed the answer button, hushing her mother who looked exasperated at Andrea's defiance.

"Yes?" said Andrea.

"I just wanted to hear your voice," said Cain. "I'm on my way to Glencuan and I wondered if you'd got home yet. We could meet up. We could go for a walk or how about to the bookshop, back to where it all began. I know you're upset but . . . "

Andrea sighed and let him ramble on, infuriated at his gall to actually contact her.

"My sister is still missing," she said in a matter-of-fact tone. "You screwed around with her and you screwed around with me, Cain. What on earth is there left to talk about?"

"Everyone makes mistakes, Andy," he said.

Her blood curdled. She hated when he shortened her name. It was a sure sign of a suck-up.

"We can move on, just the two of us. We can work this out, me and you."

"You mean, now that Jessie is out of the equation, is that it?" said Andrea, almost spitting down the phone. "Now that my sister is conveniently off the radar, you can settle back with little old me and we'll go back to the bookshop where you can woo me with your charm and empty promises? I don't think so. Blood is thicker than water, perhaps you forgot that, Cain?"

"But I'm your husband! Doesn't that count for anything?" he muttered. "Come on babes, at least meet with me and see how you feel then. We took vows together, remember. Just a few days ago."

Andrea resisted the urge to laugh at how pathetic he sounded, grovelling to her and insinuating that meeting him face to face would change her opinion of him.

"Cain, darling, you will never be anyone's husband," she said. "You can't even stick to the boyfriend game without groping and sniffing around every unfortunate woman who comes your way. I'm sure Jessie wasn't your only little plaything. That Bernice bitch who made my dress? What was the story with her?"

"Bernice? She was nothing. That was history."

Cain continued to stammer his answer but Andrea spoke over him.

"My priority at the minute is to support my family through this horrendous experience and you are not my family. You never will be. So from now on, please contact me only through my solicitor. Goodbye, Cain."

Andrea hung up the phone and breathed out, then in again and felt an overwhelming sense of release.

"I can see now why you had to do that," said her mother. "Well done, love. You are bearing up so well. I'm so proud of you."

Andrea linked her mum's arm and they walked in silence through pathways lined with the white flowers of Japanese Snowbells and heart-shaped leaves of mulberry trees.

Summer was here at last and Andrea couldn't help but think that the weather had been trying to tell her something when it rained on her wedding day.

"Isn't that David?" said Ella and Andrea squinted in the sun as a flock of birds swarmed overhead. David stood in the distance, down by the river bank.

"So it is," she said and they made their way towards him. He was still wearing the same clothes from the day before and he was smoking a cigarette as he walked along the grassy river's edge.

"He just won't give up," said Ella sadly as she

watched his handsome figure climb back up the slight hill that led down to the river and towards them. "He refuses to go home until he knows that Jessie has been found."

David's eyes were hidden behind sunglasses and his arms bore a light tan. Andrea hugged him on approach and he welcomed the gesture, his broad chest heaving up and down, unable to say a word.

"They found her dress and shoes," he said, sniffing as he spoke, unable to contain his angst for his lost wife. Ella nodded and Andrea stared at the ground.

"We know," said Andrea.

"I just can't believe this," said David. "I'm trying so hard not to imagine what has become of her but these pictures keep flashing in my mind. Who would want to hurt her like this? Who would want to do this to us?"

Ella didn't have an answer, nor did Andrea but they were both thinking the same thing.

"Ryan has been arrested," said Andrea. "Cain is on his way back home."

"I heard," said David in his strong English accent. "It's so hard to digest, isn't it? Ryan admitted to sending her all those notes and to writing those things in our home to frighten her. It really is such a shock to think he would do that much, but would he go so far as to . . ."

"No!" said Ella. "No one has any evidence of that yet. We have to remain in hope, don't we?"

David held his fist to his face and nodded.

"Why don't you come home with us?" asked Andrea. "It won't do any of us any good to hang around here and the whole place is giving me the creeps right now."

David looked at her, puzzled, yet she could see his delight at being included still as part of the family, despite his brief separation from Jessie before she disappeared.

"I think that would be a good idea," he said and they walked together towards the carpark and then made the long journey back in convoy to Glencuan.

Aunt Lily met them at the door when they arrived back home and Ella almost collapsed onto the couch when she was greeted by the warm familiarity of home.

She hadn't spoken to Tom since his outburst at the hotel but in a way she was settled in the knowledge that Ryan had someone nearby. Somewhere inside she had found a shield of disbelief that he was any way involved and she was holding on to it tight, knowing that if she let go she would crumble.

"Now, I've made a nice salad and I've some fresh carrot and coriander soup on the boil. David? You look like you haven't eaten a bite in days."

"Try weeks," he said and held up a packet of cigarettes. "Since Jessie and I split up, these little cancer sticks have been keeping me going though I don't know for how much longer. I haven't had the stomach for food at all."

Lily tutted and laid out some places at the table.

"It will do you all the power of good to have a decent meal in your bellies and then we can have a quiet evening and hope and pray for some good news."

Ella and Andrea nibbled through the leafy salad

350

prepared by Lily while David seemed glad of the bowl of soup and went back for more.

This was his first time in the O'Neill family home without Jessie by his side and he missed her sorely. His feelings were on a rollercoaster as they went from acceptance that Jessie didn't love him enough, to toying with the idea that she had made a silly mistake, to the realisation that she might never be back for him to find out. His mind was in turmoil but he knew he would never be able to settle in the company of her family. He had to believe he was looking for her. He had to try. It was the least he could do. It was his job after all.

He was a first-class policeman but, above all else, he was her husband.

They ate in virtual silence with Aunt Lily trying to stir up conversation about well-wishing neighbours and how she was questioned every time she went to the local shop for groceries.

"My boys went for a walk this morning, just before they caught their flight back home and they were stopped by the local newspaper," she said, toying with her salad. "They are running a feature in this evening's paper and are going to put Jessie's photo on the front page."

"That's good," said Andrea, unable to find the words to discuss it any further.

"And I believe that the police have a profile on their web site appealing for any sightings or of anyone who might have heard from Jessie in the past week or so. It's important they piece together every piece of information they have."

Andrea swallowed her food but it felt as if she was swallowing razor blades, while Ella chased her salad around the plate, not having the energy or the inclination to eat it at all. Pictures of Jessie flashed through her mind and she couldn't get the image of her bloodied shoes out of her head at all.

"She's not coming back, is she?" she said, staring at the plate in front of her. "I mean, we can talk and we can pray and we can piece all her conversations and movements together all we want, but she isn't coming back. I think it's about time we realised that. Jessie is never coming home. She's gone."

Ella's face was stoic and her outburst was met by a lengthy silence.

"Mum, don't say that! You can't think like that. We have to keep the faith. We will find her."

Ella threw her cutlery onto the plate and its clanking sound made the others jump. "Faith? I have no faith left in me, Andrea! My son is in a police station, my daughter's blood-stained shoes bear his fingerprints and your marriage is over before it even began! And to top it all off, my husband is now blaming *me*."

"What?" said Lily. "Where did that come from?"

"Oh yes," said Ella. "According to Tom, I drove Ryan to hating his sister by always boosting her up so much above everyone else. According to my husband, I loved my daughter so much that it made my son feel isolated and has turned him into a living psychopath!"

David excused himself from the table, unable to cope with Ella's outburst any longer. He placed his soup bowl in the dishwasher and washed his hands and then he lifted his jacket and car keys.

"Thanks for dinner," he said. "I'm going to make my way home now."

"Oh David, please don't go! I'm sorry," said Ella.

She ran after him and he stopped, unsure whether he wanted to be alone at all.

"It's okay," he mumbled. "I think I might go back to work tomorrow if there still is no more news. They won't let me officially work on Jessie's case, but maybe when I'm in the station environment I may be able to do some of my own probing when they think I'm working on something else. It will keep my mind occupied too."

Ella and Andrea glanced at each other.

"I think that's a great idea," said Andrea. "But why don't you stay here tonight with us? I don't imagine Dad is coming home and it would make us girls feel a lot safer if we had a man about the house."

David pondered their suggestion but his heart and head were pulling him in the direction of his own marital home.

"I know you mean well but if you don't mind I'll make my way back home. I want to make sure the house is in one piece and maybe turn on the heating and tidy up for . . . I was going to say for Jessie coming home. God, I really hope she comes home."

David buried his head in his hands and cried like a baby, all of his fears and grief pouring out like a dam had been lifted inside him.

"I'm so sorry for walking away from her! We should

have tried harder," he sobbed. "All our years together can't be thrown away because that bastard came into our lives and ripped us all apart. I just hope and pray that we are given a second chance."

Andrea felt a lump in her throat at the sight of David, so handsome and strong and proud, crying for her sister and she allowed herself to shed a tear for him, as well as for Jessie.

"You will get a second chance," said Andrea. "Everyone deserves a second chance."

"And Cain?" he said. "Will you give him a second chance?"

Andrea shook her head and looked at the floor. "I have a feeling he has already used up all his chances with this family," she said. "Please stay here tonight, David. I want us to keep together in case there is any news. We need each other more than ever now."

David put his jacket on and made his way towards the back door.

"Okay then," he said. "I'll be back soon. I just want to go home for a while. I need some time alone."

He leaned forward and kissed Andrea on the cheek, said a brisk goodbye to the others and left the O'Neill family home before he could change his mind.

Chapter 30

David lay on his marital bed and stared at the ceiling. He noticed the beginning of a tiny crack in the centre, just beside where the silver metal light fitting hung that matched the silver and black décor of the bedroom. He remembered the day they had chosen the entire fittings for their new bedroom. How Jessie sketched out a plan of the room, then gathered samples of material and colour swatches. She and Andrea had sat on this bed, cross-legged with the plan between them, toying over colours while David got on with painting the banister a rich ivory. They were so close, those two girls. So, so close. David sighed at the memory of their giggles and disagreements on texture and colour, on wall lights or ceiling lights, on lampshades and rugs. Andrea had stayed the night before and they were both in their dressing-gowns – Andrea in a glamorous satin red and Jessie in her favourite fluffy pink one.

She loved that bathrobe and would often work in her home office for hours in the winter with it wrapped around her like a comfort. She loved to spend cosy nights in front of the fire, snuggled up beside him on the sofa, watching rented movies and then she would fall asleep before they finished and he would carry her, still wearing the dressing-gown, into bed where she would ask a muffled question about how the movie ended.

David closed his eyes and racked his mind for any other clues that might lead him in the right direction to finding her. If Cain Daniels, or Ryan, had hurt her badly he would serve his own time for them. If either of them were behind this, he would take life into his own hands. For that he had no doubt.

David opened his eyes again, unable to settle now and he sat up on the bed. He stood up and stretched his arms, then walked towards the landing and closed the door behind him, expecting as always that Jessie's infamous dressing-gown would catch on the door from where it hung on a hook so that she could find it always when she needed it.

But the door closed with ease and David did a double-take. He opened the door and looked behind it to where the robe always hung. But it wasn't there.

"So, Daniels goes missing at the end of the night for about half an hour or so," said Bert McManus. "He goes outside, hears the commotion between Jessie and Ryan, feels threatened by the hard evidence Ryan has at hand, then he punches Ryan and in blind panic he either says something that scares the hell out of Jessie or else he has done something much worse. Is that what you're saying?"

Tom O'Neill scratched his head and looked his lawyer in the eye.

"It's as good as I can come up with," he said. "Is there any way we can have Daniels questioned again?"

McManus shrugged. "Depends what forensics say. If Daniels did manhandle Jessie in any way, his prints will be all over her dress. Until the report comes back, we will have to hope that either Ryan's memory lapse comes to an end, or that Jessie is found and can tell us what really happened."

The room was cold and Tom's stomach grumbled. He realised he hadn't eaten in over twenty-four hours now and his sugar levels were running low.

"Talk to Cooper again," he said. "I want every single possible angle covered on this. If there's the slightest chance that Daniels was the last to see Jessie, I want him outed and I want to know why he has kept it to himself until now."

McManus's mobile phone rang and he answered it straight away.

"It's for you – Cooper."

Tom grabbed the phone. "Speak of the devil – Detective Cooper," he said, his voice raspy from lack of sleep. "Please tell me you've got some good news for me."

Cooper coughed and then spoke in a business-like tone. "I tried you on your own line but couldn't get through, so I figured you'd be with McManus. I think we may be a step closer to finding your daughter, Tom."

"What? Where?"

"Don't get your hopes up but David has just called me. He's back at his house and he had a look around. This could turn us right round again, Tom. He says he is sure that Jessie, or someone on Jessie's behalf, paid a visit home recently."

Tom's heart leapt in his chest and he pulled a chair. "Go on . . ."

"He says there's something missing from the house. Something that Jessie loved. A dressing-gown or bathrobe or something of that sort? It's not something that any of my men would have ever picked up on, but he's adamant it's a sign."

Tom closed his eyes and gripped the table tight. A rush of adrenaline burst through his veins and he could barely contain his new sense of hope.

"So what does this mean? What do we do now? Does this mean that Ryan is out of the spotlight?"

"No, no, not just yet," said Cooper. "But we're sending a team over to the house now to see what they can pick up from David's claims. Let's just hope, for your daughter's sake and for your son's that David is on the right trail on this one."

Andrea swerved her car through the gates and up the drive that led to Jessie and David's house. She parked alongside David's Saab and yanked the handbrake, then ran to the front door, barely taking the time to close the car door behind her. The house seemed lonely and dark and David was evidently keeping a low profile but she couldn't wait to hear what he had to say.

She knocked hard on the door and David opened it immediately. He marched across the hallway into the kitchen where he had a low lamp on and he pulled out a stool and sat down, gesturing for Andrea to do the same.

"Tell me," she said. "Please tell me why you believe she was here."

"*Someone* was here," said David. "Someone who knew what to look for. I am totally sure of that. I don't know that it was Jessie, though. I just have a sense that someone has been here recently and they have been going through her stuff."

Andrea could see a new spark of life in David's eyes as she spoke to her. He had found energy again and she knew he truly believed he was on the scent of something.

"Do you think it's the same person who was taunting her with the notes and graffiti in the bathroom?" asked Andrea. "Does this mean that Ryan . . .?"

"No," said David. "Ryan has already admitted to sending those notes and to the whole shower story. He's guilty of that, that's for sure but if Jessie was here, or if someone else was here for her, then it means Ryan's involvement ends with the row at the wedding reception."

Andrea closed her eyes for a moment and concentrated on her breathing. She couldn't understand why Jessie would be missing on purpose. It wasn't her form at all to disappear.

"But how would she have got here from the hotel? It's two hours away and she was drunk and she had no car."

"She could have hitched a ride," he said. "I don't know. But let's see what the other cops say. I have a real hunch that she came through this village at some stage either yesterday or the night of the wedding."

"I hope you're right, David," she said. "I really do."

"Well, when I came in here at first, everything seemed quite normal I suppose. I was looking for any sort of clue at all but nothing stood out. Everything was in its place, just as Jessie would have left it. But then I was lying on the bed trying to get some sleep and my mind was racing. It just wouldn't switch off. The goddam thing always catches on the door from where it hangs and it was then I noticed it was missing."

"Are you sure?"

David stood up and Andrea followed him upstairs. He talked as he walked, his energy and belief so evident as he explained his rationale.

"She wore that old thing as she worked some days. It was like a comfort to her, like an old blanket and it always hung on the back of the bedroom door. I've searched high and low to see if it is lying around and it isn't. I've asked Cooper if she had brought it to the hotel with her, but no."

"I don't get it," said Andrea. "Why on earth would she take that old thing with her if she was doing a flit? Why not take clothes?"

David stopped on the stairs as the doorbell rang.

"Because I don't honestly think it was her," he said. "I don't think Jessie was here at all. I think that someone else was here on her behalf and that wherever she is, she doesn't need anything more than her dressing-gown.

And we've already checked every hospital on both sides of the border. It's a wild shot, but one I believe in. Someone was here to get this for her. It didn't walk out of the house itself and with just two of us living here, there's no way anything like that can really get lost."

Andrea raced down the stairs again after David who was approaching the door.

"Oh my God, David. Do you think she's still alive?" she asked, her voice quivering now. "Or could this mean someone has killed her?"

"I don't know," said David. "I don't even want to think about that right now."

David opened the door and Sandra Millar walked inside.

"You know these guys," she said, nodding at her two colleagues who entered the house behind her. "No need for introductions, I take it?"

"No need at all," said David. "Hi."

David shook hands with the two officers and they both gave him a supportive pat on the arm.

"Right, go on," said Sandra. She chewed gum like a man, thought Andrea as she watched the detective survey her sister's house like it was a crime scene itself.

David explained his theory and Sandra took it all in without stopping him once.

"I don't think it was Jessie," he said. "I think it was someone else."

"Guys, get looking again for some prints around the house – anything at all to indicate who may have been here since Saturday."

The police officers took off in different directions and Sandra went to the kitchen and flicked on the kettle.

"You look like you need one," she said to David. "Sugar?"

"Two," said David, and he smirked at his colleague's familiarity. "I think Andrea could use one too."

"Is this a good sign?" asked Andrea. "What do you think, Officer?"

Sandra paced the floor as she waited for the kettle to boil. She tapped a spoon against her hand as she thought.

"Not sure," she said. "David knows what he's talking about but I can't see why a girl of her age would want to take an old dressing-gown with her if it was a matter of choice. Surely she would have taken clothes, jewellery, make-up?"

"Like most women would," said Andrea, not sure that she liked the way the detective's line of thought was travelling. Her hopes had climbed when she got the call from David but now they were hurtling downwards again.

"Exactly. So her dress was found about two hours from here. She has no money, no clothes and her phone is either dead or she's lost it."

"I've got a print," said the young detective through the kitchen door. "But it's the same as when we first checked over the place yesterday. About size eleven, smart shoes – it's at the top of the stairs, on the way to the bedroom."

"Well, that's probably mine then," said David. "Sorry. Maybe I'm totally off the mark. I just thought –"

Sandra filled five cups of coffee and handed them out to her colleagues and one to Andrea whose blood had run so cold she let out a shiver.

"Unless someone else wears that shoe size?" asked Sandra. "Andrea, you look like you've seen a ghost."

Andrea felt tears of anger and fear prick her eyes and her hands shook so much that she had to set her coffee cup on the table.

"My – my husband," she said, her lip quivering with humiliation and fear. "My so-called husband Cain wears that shoe size. Oh my God. Oh my God, what on earth has he done to her?"

Andrea listened as Detective Sandra Millar spoke to her boss on the phone and relayed the information to him.

"Yes, I can get him in here," she was saying. "He still hasn't admitted to hitting Ryan, or that he was the last one to possibly see Jessie so I want to go over that with him too. I think he scared the shit out of her on Saturday night and she's running from him. The only question now is why the hell was he in her house? Why was he upstairs? Where has he hidden Jessie? There's still something missing."

The sound of Sandra's voice turned to a muffled hum as Andrea tried her best to make sense of it all in her own mind. Cain could have threatened Jessie, there's no doubt about that. He wasn't admitting to having seen her before she went missing, yet he strangely left to 'freshen up' around the same time.

He did seem edgy after that, distracted even, and

when she'd asked him what was wrong he brushed it off, saying she was fussing and that he was fine.

"Officer," said Andrea, "I have something else you may want to ask my husband to explain."

"Yes?" said Sandra and she clicked off her phone.

"A few days before the wedding, remember we said that Jessie was acting really strange? Well, she told us she was late for her make-up trial because she had to give David his mobile phone. I remember now that Cain was off air for about half an hour around that time and when I asked him later he changed the subject. I'd hoped all along he wouldn't be connected to this but maybe he was with Jessie then. It was the day David left her and she may have called on him. I don't know, maybe it's stupid but I thought you should know."

Sandra nodded and made a few notes, then packed up her briefcase.

"I think we have enough to justify a little chat with Mr Daniels. Where would we find him at this time of day?"

Andrea lifted her phone from her handbag and dialled Cain's number.

"Here you are," she said, her hands trembling with trepidation. "Why not chat to him now?"

Chapter 31

Tuesday . . .

Rosie Sheehan watched the very handsome Father Christopher carry his latest set of gym weights down through the gardens on his way to the gate lodge and she threw her eyes up to the heavens. There was still no word on Jessie O'Neill and she knew it was devastating for the whole village, but Father Christopher – well – she almost felt like he was heartbroken. He was struggling to carry the box, the third one that had arrived since yesterday and he was spending more and more time at the gate lodge, eager to turn it into a place where he could relax and keep his fitness levels up.

He started each morning now with a cycle around the village and then morning Mass followed by some home visits and then paperwork and schools talks most afternoons. His weekends were centred around Sunday Mass, of course, and weddings, funerals and christenings popped up here and there, but every other moment of his time was spent at the gate lodge turning it into his dream gym, or scouring newspapers for news on Jessie. She had caught him one day, staring at her photo in one of the articles and she was sure she saw tears in his eyes. "Jessie. My poor Jessie," she heard him say. "What on earth have they done to you?"

Of course, she shouldn't jump to conclusions, but Rosie Sheehan was sure that Father Christopher Lennon was more devastated than anyone ever knew over the O'Neill girl's disappearance. And as the days went by, she could sense it was stressing him more and more as the likelihood of her ever returning home safe became more and more impossible.

Rosie shuffled through to the drawing-room with her polishing rag and spray in her hand and she carefully removed each of the photographs of the former clerics one by one from the mantelpiece.

Father Brian McMenemy with his cheery smile, the more serious-looking Father Eamonn Christie, the very frail and elderly Father Jones and then the young, striking face of Father Christopher Lennon.

Rosie had tried to mention that the O'Neills were back in town and that Ryan had been arrested on suspicion but he didn't want to know.

"I've been in contact with Tom O'Neill and I would prefer to hear updates from the horse's mouth and not through idle gossip," he had told her and Rosie vowed not to bring up the subject in his presence again, no matter what the latest gossip in town was. She had seen with her own two eyes, after all, how much he devoured every news bulletin and how he wiped his eyes as he stared at her photo.

Her thoughts were interrupted by a knock on the door and she sighed and set down her polishing tools. It was only nine thirty and already parishioners were calling with this and that – anniversary mass requests, bookings and invitations to local events.

It never stopped and Rosie was determined she would eventually convince Father Christopher to adopt some sort of appointment system instead of this haphazard open-house approach.

She opened the front door and her heart stopped in a mixture of excitement and sorrow. It was Ella O'Neill but she looked at least ten years older with her face scraped of make-up and her hair tied back. Even her clothes looked baggy and careless and her face wore a frown that spelt loss and fear.

"Come in, Mrs O'Neill," said Rosie. "Gosh, you poor thing1 I can't tell you how much the whole village is praying and hoping for Jessie's safe return. Your family must be climbing the walls with worry."

Ella walked through the hallway without speaking at all and she followed Rosie into the drawing-room.

"Father isn't too far away," said Rosie, pulling out a comfy chair for Mrs O'Neill to sit on. "I'll just go and get him, shall I? Then I'll make you both a nice strong cup of tea."

Ella heard the young priest's voice and she straightened up on the chair. She hadn't wanted to come to him, but something told her she might find some answers or at least keep her strength up by finding some faith in God.

She hadn't slept at all last night and when Andrea had arrived home full of possibilities that Jessie might have passed through the village at some stage, it had set her mind racing.

She had spoken to Tom as well and he had high hopes that Ryan was slipping further from suspicion. Cooper was begging him for answers but so far his memory stopped at the point where Jessie hit him and he hit her back and the image of that was haunting Ella.

"Mrs O'Neill, I'm so sorry for keeping you."

Father Christopher Lennon looked almost as weary as she did. His dark eyes were glazed and his swarthy skin was paler than usual.

"That's okay," said Ella in a small voice. "I don't know why I'm here really."

The young priest sat down opposite Ella and he clasped his hands in front of him, leaning forward on his knees.

"You're worried, right? Of course, you are and you don't know where to turn."

"That's right," said Ella. "I was feeling claustrophobic and yet terribly alone at home so I went for a walk. I've never been in this house before. I'm not a churchgoer, Father, so I feel quite hypocritical for landing in on you like this, but I feel that if I don't turn to God I'll crack up. I need something or someone to lean on."

Father Christopher listened to her as if she was the most important person on the planet.

"Where do you think your daughter is, Mrs O'Neill?"

"I have no idea," said Ella and she felt her eyes well up. "I just hope she's safe, that's all."

"I pray she is too," said Father Christopher. "She is a strong woman but I know that is not much comfort to you now. A mother's love is the deepest, they say."

He glanced up at the photograph on the mantelpiece and Ella followed his gaze. The woman in the picture was blonde and pretty but she looked distant in comparison to her son's enthusiastic smile.

"You don't look like your mother at all, do you?" she said, glad to have the chance to change the subject. "Where do your dark looks come from? Your father's side?"

"So I'm told," said Father Christopher. "My father was an Italian man, but I've never met him. It was always just me and my mother."

"Ah, I'm sure you are very close then?"

"We were, I suppose. As much as we could be. We were very close."

"Oh, I'm sorry," said Ella and she could feel her face flush. "I didn't think . . . I'm so sorry."

The priest laughed lightly, and held up his hands. "Oh, no, it's not like that. My mother is alive and well and living in Athlone now. We just aren't in touch any more. She's not like you."

Ella pricked up at his comment. What was that supposed to mean?

"How do you know she's not like me?" she asked.

This was only her third encounter with this young man, yet he was claiming now to know her?

"Well, you seem so loyal to your children. You wouldn't single one of them out over the other, would you? You wouldn't make differences in them? I'd say you love each of your children so much that no matter what they did in life, no matter how badly they behaved, you'd see a reason for it. Am I right?"

Ella felt her body go intensely warm at his questioning. Was he getting at her? Did he mean Ryan? Or Andrea? Was he referring to Jessie?

"I'm not sure you know me at all," she said. "How could you possibly know me?"

"No, I don't," he said. Of course, Jessie had told him so much about her mother that he felt he did know her, but Ella didn't know just how close the two of them had become. "I was just guessing. You see, my mother isn't like that at all. She's more of a 'one strike and you're out' type of person. We didn't have much when I was growing up in Cork and she was determined that I made something of myself."

"And so you did," said Ella. "She must be so proud."

Again, the priest laughed and Ella sensed she was wrong for the second time.

"I'm afraid not," he said gently. "All she ever wanted was me to be a doctor or a lawyer or anything that guaranteed big money. She wanted a daughter-in-law, she wanted grandchildren, she wanted what we never had together. A family."

"Oh. I see." Ella shuddered when he spoke of family as she realised what a mess hers had turned out to be. The reality of her own family situation swamped her again and she stood up and made for the door, then she turned towards Father Christopher.

"Thank you for your time, Father. Like I said, I'm not a holy person at all, but I do love my family. Please remember us all in your prayers. That's all I came here for."

"I will. Of course, I will," said Father Christopher and he watched with deep sorrow as Ella O'Neill walked out of his sightline. Whoever had hurt her daughter had a hell of a lot to answer for.

"Oh, has Mrs O'Neill gone already?" said Rosie, balancing a tray with tea and scones on it. "She didn't even stay for tea."

Father Christopher was in some sort of a trance and she racked her brain for a way to ask him what had been said without sounding nosey or like she was gossiping again.

"How is she bearing up, poor mite?" she asked, opting for the concerned route. Surely he wouldn't deny her some information when she was merely concerned for the lady's wellbeing at such a difficult time.

The priest looked back at her. "She seems to be . . . well, you know. I'd say she has done a lot of thinking of late. It can't be easy, I'm sure. Right, I'd better get changed and ready for some home visits. See you at lunch-time."

"Okay, Father. As you wish." Rosie remembered she

hadn't finished her dusting so she put the tea tray back in the kitchen, tutting to herself about the waste of time and good teabags, and then she came back into the drawing-room to finish her chores.

She lifted each of the photographs back onto the mantel, then wiped around the bookcase and Father's extensive CD collection. Carefully, she lifted the CD box from its shelf and wiped underneath it, only to knock over the entire library of CDs so that they scattered over the floor.

She could hear him walk around upstairs and she bent down immediately, trying to catch some of the discs as they sprang from their covers and spun across the floor. She gathered them up hastily and shoved them back in the box.

"Darn," she muttered and she reached her hand under the gap beneath the sofa and the floor to fish the last one out but she couldn't grasp it. She heard his footsteps come down the stairs and she quickly put the CD box back on the shelf, and waited until she heard the front door close before she moved back the sofa to find the missing disc. He was a music fanatic and the last thing she wanted to do was to ruin his U2 collection or whoever young men listened to these days.

She lifted the CD out, blew a fine layer of dust off its surface and wiped it with her sleeve then clicked it back into its box and moved the sofa back into place. Then something caught her eye.

A fine silver bracelet with encrusted rubies lay on the

floor. It must have been under the sofa and was pushed out when she moved it back. Rosie bent down again and picked it up – it was light and fine and delicate and as she held it in her hand.

"How beautiful," she muttered, fingering the light metal which was Celtic in design but with the most beautiful modern twist. It must belong to Mrs O'Neill, she thought. It looked terribly expensive.

Then Rosie froze.

No, she thought. No, how could it be?

She rummaged in the wastepaper bin for the newspaper from the day before where it described in detail what Jessie had been wearing on the day of the wedding. A red satin dress, matching shoes and a handmade silver bracelet encrusted in rubies which had been a gift from her sister, the bride. Her heart thumping, Rosie reached for her glasses which she wore on a chain around her neck. She studied the picture of Jessie in her full wedding attire, and she held the newspaper closer, examining the bracelet in the photo, and then the one in her hand.

"Jesus, God in heaven, preserve us!" she said and she blessed herself. What was going on? It didn't make sense

"Everything okay, Rosie?"

She gasped when she realised that Father Christopher was watching her. His voice startled her and she looked around to see him at the doorway of the room, watching her stare at the bracelet, the newspaper in her hand and her glasses on the end of her nose.

"Father! I was just . . ." She swept off her glasses.

"Cleaning around? Yeah, so I see. Let me see what you found? Goodness knows what slips under that sofa. You could find all sorts of trinkets under there."

His voice was gentle, calm and his attitude shook Rosie from inside. Didn't he know what this meant? Didn't he know who it belonged to?

"Oh, look," he said. "Isn't that pretty? Perhaps Mrs O'Neill dropped it when she was here earlier. Let me take it to her. In fact, I'll do it straight away."

He held out his hand and Rosie let the fine sliver of silver slip out of her hand onto his and she wiped her hands on her apron, as if she wanted to remove all traces of having come across it in the first place.

Her head spun with possibilities when he left her in the room. Perhaps he was right. Maybe it did belong to Mrs O'Neill. Maybe she had exactly the same bracelet as a mother-of-the-bride gift? Maybe she was jumping to conclusions. Her daughter always accused her of as much. She wiped around the coffee table and listened again for the front door, then she ran into the hallway and watched Father Christopher walk confidently down the lane, his fine black figure disappearing into the distance in the morning sun.

Rosie could still feel the sensation of the bracelet in her hand and she felt shivery again. He had been so calm and cool about her finding the piece of jewellery and now he had taken it away with him. What should she do?

She stood frozen at the window, waiting to make up her mind. She lifted the phone and dialled her friend Mamie's number. Mamie would know what to do. Rosie didn't like to gossip, of course, but in this instance she simply didn't have a choice.

Chapter 32

Ella was in the garden when the telephone rang, but Andrea reached it before she could make her way inside.

It was a glorious morning and the weather forecast confirmed that the summer season had finally arrived. The garden was a sea of colour under the hazy sunshine and Ella found its silence comforting and a welcome break from sitting indoors waiting on news and living on coffee and light conversation.

"Any word from David?" asked Tom O'Neill from his hotel room at Bromley Castle. "I heard that Cain was taken back in last night for more questioning."

Andrea handed the phone to her mother who had by now reached the kitchen from her spell outside.

"Tom, you must understand how difficult this is for Andrea," she said. "Just two days ago she married a man who is now public enemy number one. You can't expect her to discuss him the way that we do. She's still in shock with all this. She's grieving for her marriage as well as for –"

As expected, Tom's answer was a barking defensive tone. "Oh, so you'd rather your own son was harassed and questioned instead, is that it? I just don't understand you at all. Who's side are you on?"

Ella rubbed her forehead. The fresh air had relaxed her somewhat and now after just seconds on the phone to her husband, all her tensions had returned again.

"Ryan's of course. How dare you insinuate that I want Ryan banged up in a police cell! But my God I'm trying to think of everyone in this mess. David, Andrea, Ryan, you, me – we're all cut up over Jessie and I don't think pulling punches at each other is going to help matters. Not at all!"

Tom's spoke after a few seconds of silence and his tone was settled a bit. "I know, I know. But Ryan is breaking my heart here, Ella. Looking at him is tearing me apart. He is huddled up in the corner of a room and he won't speak at all, except to say he doesn't remember anything. And it's eating at him. He is devastated just like we are, yet he has this huge ball of guilt inside him like he feels this may be his fault."

Ella sat down on Tom's chair and she could imagine him sitting there with his newspaper, waiting on dinner and flicking through the pages as he commented on the day's news around the world. How she wished she could go back to all that! How had her whole family taken what they had together so much for granted.

"Should I come down to see him?" asked Ella. "I haven't had the strength to even look at him in that state, but if I thought it would help him?"

"No," said Tom. "He is riddled with shame and I don't think he could cope with seeing you or Andrea. Leave it to me. I'll tell him you are all thinking of him, but stay where you are and we'll keep in touch."

Ella nodded and tried not to picture her baby boy in such a state of despair. She wanted to hold him, to tell him it would be okay. Her whole world had been rocked to the core in just one weekend that should have been lodged in her memory forever for more joyous reasons.

"Okay," she whispered to her husband. "Tell him we are thinking of him. Oh, and Tom?"

"Yes?"

"Please . . . please tell Ryan I do love him dearly. Tell him that from me, please."

But Tom didn't reply. He just hung up the phone and left Ella clinging to the receiver, feeling like her heart was ripped to shreds and wondering how much longer she could deal with its pain.

David arrived at the O'Neill home at lunch-time with a new-found spring in his step. He knocked on the door and entered the house carrying a paper bag full of coffee and muffins and he set them on the kitchen table but neither Andrea nor Ella noticed them or passed any comment on his gift.

"I've heard he's in with Detective Millar," said David, plonking down on one of the softer seats in the corner of the room.

"Who's he?" said Andrea. "I take it you mean Cain?"

David twitched in his seat, sensing a very different attitude in Andrea from the hope she felt the night before.

"Yes, of course, I mean Cain," he said. "He's in the station now. God, I hope he can give us some answers. I went into work this morning but they told me to take the week off on sympathy leave. They don't want me around at all."

Andrea was reading a magazine and she barely lifted her head while Ella flicked through a photo album. David could see Lily in the garden, pottering around through the flowers and he realised that none of them was in the mood to talk much.

"Perhaps I'll go for a walk," he said. "I've left coffee and muffins on the table. That's if you feel like them, of course. No pressure, I won't be offended."

"I'm sorry, David," said Ella. She removed her glasses and closed the photo album over. "I think we're all just suffering from fatigue at this stage and maybe for some of us the shock of it all is just kicking in."

Ella nodded across at Andrea who was ignoring the conversation or doing her best to block it out.

"Oh, of course," said David. "Well, like I said, I'll go for a walk or something just to have a think about things. I can't stand this sitting around waiting."

"Do you know, I think I'll join you," said Ella and she left the photo album and her glasses on the coffee table. "Andrea? Do you fancy a walk?"

Andrea shook her head. "I'll stay here in case the phone rings. I want to be first to know if my husband has anything to do with my sister's disappearance. It's all fun and games this, isn't it?"

She kept her nose in the magazine and Ella patted her shoulder on her way past.

"I know, baby," said Ella. "I know this is so hard for you. We'll get through this. I know we will."

The village was quiet as David and Ella walked around the outskirts on a well-known route called 'Duck's Parade'.

It was a man-made walkway, with laurel trees and cherry blossoms waving alongside a busy main road that led out of Glencuan to the nearby town and on to the motorway to Belfast city.

Ella had fond memories of pushing her girls in a double buggy around Duck's Parade and they would stop at the riverbank and look out for fish and squeal with delight when they saw a mother duck and her family come hurtling downstream.

When Ryan was a baby, Ella would take all three for a picnic and they would while away hours on the riverbank, waiting for something to tell Tom about when they would make their way home in time for tea.

"Will you ever forgive her?" asked Ella and she linked her son-in-law's arm as they walked.

She looked up at David's face which was lost in deep thought and she knew he had pondered this very question himself on many occasions lately.

"I don't know. I can't think straight at all right now," he said and he kicked a fallen branch from their pathway. "I've tried to imagine talking to her about it, asking her why and searching for answers but then this rising panic comes over me that I might never get the chance to even have that conversation with her and it squeezes the life from me inside so hard that I cannot breathe. I want to find her first, and then I'll worry about what she has done to all of us later."

They walked in silence along the riverbank, the only sounds being the faint hum of a tractor in the distance and light birdsong from the trees overhead.

They turned the corner that led back onto the village green where their route had begun and both agreed the change of scenery and the fresh air had made them feel just a bit better.

Ella's headache had lifted and David's mind was clearer and more focused and he looked forward to hearing an update from the station with less impatience now.

Ella spotted Rosie Sheehan at the grocery store on the corner and she waved sheepishly at the older lady. She could almost hear her whisper to her friend about how frail she was looking and how she had visited the priest earlier that morning and she crossed the street to avoid any small talk from the women who were rife with gossip at any time of year, let alone when a scandal like this one hung over the village.

"Mrs O'Neill!" called Rosie, and Ella stopped, knowing that it would only feed rumours if it seemed like she was too busy or too upset to hold a brief conversation. The O'Neills already held an aloof reputation amongst the villagers and Ella didn't want to appear distant, despite her instant desire to run in the opposite direction from her.

"Mrs Sheehan, how are you?" asked Ella, realising that it was only a matter of hours since they had last laid eyes on each other and therefore not a very appropriate base for small talk.

"Oh, I won't keep you," said Rosie and she nodded in acknowledgement of David with a look of pity and regret. "I was just wondering if Father gave it back to you yet."

"What's that?" asked Ella. "Sorry, I don't understand."

"Your bracelet?" said Rosie and she looked like she had said too much already.

Ella looked at her wrist which bore a silver chunky bangle that she had kept on since the wedding. "But . . ."

"He thought you must have dropped it earlier when you were around. I found it under the sofa after you left and he said he would give it to you later but perhaps he hasn't found the time yet. He's very busy."

Ella looked at David in confusion and then she placed her hand on the older woman's arm.

"There must be some mistake," she said. "I wasn't wearing any other jewellery this morning so it must belong to another visitor, but thank you anyway."

Rosie's face drained and she scuttled away, back to where her friend stood, and Ella linked David's arm again and they walked towards the edge of the village.

"Hold on," said David. "What was that lady's name again?"

"Mrs Sheehan," said Ella. "Rosie Sheehan. She's known as the village gossip so I'd take what she says with a pinch of salt."

"Mrs Sheehan!" called David and he let go of Ella's arm and sprinted back down the hill to where the two ladies were huddled in conversation.

Rosie braced herself, as if she knew what he was going to ask her.

"What did the bracelet look like?" he said.

She glanced at her elderly friend for support and then frowned at her lack of response.

"I'm not sure," she said and the other lady gave her a nudge.

"It's important," said David. "It's important you tell me what it looks like. Ella has just realised it may be hers after all. I could go and get it for her."

He darted his eyes from one lady to the other and eventually Mrs Sheehan's friend folded her arms.

"Okay, *I'll* tell him then," she said. "She says it was silver, very fine and it was encrusted with –"

"Red rubies," said Rosie Sheehan and her eyes dropped to the floor. "It had a tiny row of red rubies on it. Just as it said in the newspaper about . . . That's why I thought . . . look, we'd better be off then."

"Oh," said David, and he steadied himself on the wall of the shop.

"I'm going to go now and light a candle," said Rosie. "And then I'd better get back to work. Father will be back soon for his tea. Good day."

Chapter 33

Father Christopher fingered the bracelet in his pocket and he knew right then it was time for him to go.

He already had his car packed up with enough clothes and some light snacks and although he would have preferred to have waited until dark, he imagined he didn't have time to hang around.

He closed the boot and locked the door of his house, and then he drove his car around the back and walked through the garden to the gate lodge.

Jessie was awake as he had hoped but her face hadn't cleared up as much as he would have liked it. Her cheek was still bruised and the scrapes down her neck where she had fallen were still quite raw but he had dressed them and cared for them as best he could.

"Are you ready?" he asked and she stretched her arms out for him to come to her.

He knelt at her side and rubbed her forehead.

"My ankle really hurts," she said. "Where are we going?"

She was still drowsy from the heavy dosage of painkillers he had given her and the dark curtains in the room made it difficult for her to tell if it was night or day.

"We are going for a short break, just me and you," said Christopher and he kissed her lightly on her bruised knuckles. "They'll never hurt you again. I'll take you far away so that no one will ever do this to you again."

He peeped out through the window of the gate lodge and the sight of Rosie slumping down the pathway irritated him.

"I'll be right back," he said to Jessie and her eyes began to droop again. "Don't be scared. I'll just be a moment."

The bright sunshine in the garden made him blink as he made his way towards his housekeeper who was carrying a tray of sandwiches and soup, just as he had told her to prepare for him earlier that morning.

"Your tea, Father. I thought you may prefer to eat it down here since you've been keeping so busy."

The priest raised an eyebrow at Rosie and he could see the doubt and fear in her eyes.

"Thank you," he said gently. "You really are very thoughtful. Are you off then?"

She stared back at him, her green eyes squinting in the evening sun and she appeared lost for words.

"I – I met Mrs O'Neill and her son-in-law just now," she stuttered.

He broke into a smile which unnerved her. "And?" he asked, lifting the tray from her shaking hands.

"It's not her bracelet," she said.

Again, he looked at her with a handsome grin and he walked backwards, towards the gate lodge.

"What bracelet?" he asked and then he turned in the right direction. "Good evening, Rosie. I'll see you . . . well, I'll see you around."

He casually opened the door of the gate lodge without looking back, and then when he got inside he left the tray on the sideboard and watched until Rosie disappeared around the side of the house.

He quickly stepped over the stack of cardboard boxes he had been using to block anyone's view of where he had made a bed for Jessie and he leaned over her, watching her breathe in and out and wince in pain as she did so.

"Come on, Jess," he said. "It's time to go. Come on."

He scooped her up in his strong arms and wrapped her cosy dressing-gown around her more tightly, then he made his way back out of the gate lodge, closed the door behind him and he clicked open his car.

He glanced around him to make sure no one was around, but the bottom of the garden and the old gate lodge were so secluded amongst the greenery of the grounds that no one could possibly have seen them.

He had a blanket in the car for her and a pillow for her head and he laid her in the back seat, tucked her in and then got into the front seat of the car and drove along the bumpy country lane which led out onto the main road in Glencuan.

"It's okay now, Jessie," he said. "We're on a smoother road now. Just rest your eyes and tell me if you need anything."

He looked in the rear-view mirror of the car and in the distance he could see a flashy silver Saab swerve through the front gates of the parochial house.

"Too late," he smiled and he put his foot down on the accelerator. "She's safe with me now. You can never hurt her again."

David Chambers yelled at Sandra Millar down the phone. He was banging on the door of the parochial house as he spoke to her, ignoring her pleas for him to step back.

"I don't give a fuck what you say, Detective! I am not waiting. I will not take any chances on this!"

He could hear the clip of Millar's heels down the line as she paced the corridor at the station.

"I have already spoken to the priest," she said. "How many times must you be told to let us get on with this? You are way too emotionally involved to start investigating. Go home and let me get on with my job."

"Well, I'm here now. I just want to ask him about the bracelet. It's Jessie's. I know it is. Plus I've traced the number of the landline she called me from the other night. It was his. She was in his house, late at night."

"Look, David," said Millar. "They were friendly. I've already established that. Get into your car and get yourself out of there right now. You can't just storm in there and question a man when you're not officially on the case. We have Daniels by the balls in here right now. He has confessed to not only beating the face off Ryan but it looks like he gave Jessie a nasty blow too. We have him. I swear we do. Bear with me."

David looked in through the windows of the huge Georgian house and then kicked the wall in bad temper. There was no sign of life about the place at all and he was becoming more and more angry at being held at arm's length in the search for his wife.

"I need to find her," he said and he threw his back against the wall. "I just need to find her."

Father Christopher felt a huge weight off his shoulders when he crossed the border into Ireland's Republic. He checked his watch. They had only been on the road for over thirty minutes but until now it had seemed like hours. Now that they were in a different jurisdiction he could relax and enjoy the journey.

He flicked through his CD collection and slid a smooth disc into the player, and then he leaned back, turned up the volume and hummed along to the music.

"This is our song," he said, glancing from the road to Jessie who, apart from a few sleepy muffles, had been totally silent all along the way. "Do you hear it, Jess?"

He smiled to himself and breathed in deeply as a rich sense of contentment filled his heart and lungs. He had never felt like this before and he thanked God to have brought Jessie to him just when he needed her most and more importantly, just as she needed him.

What would have become of her if he hadn't answered her call that fateful night? She would have been dead. She would have bled to death in the cold and rain.

He had just climbed into bed when his phone had rung and he knew she was in trouble when he'd heard her trembling voice on the other end of the line.

"Father, please. I need your help again," she had said. "I need you now. I'm bleeding. I'm so sore. Please come and get me. Quickly!"

He had driven along the windy roads at breathtaking speeds, having heard the panic in her voice which was almost unrecognisable.

For over an hour she had waited for him, but he'd made the journey in record time.

She sat huddled in a bus shelter on the side of a lonely country road where the last cars would have passed ages ago.

She was barefoot and her skin was scraped from head to toe, her beautiful black hair was matted with blood and debris and she was already sporting bruises from where she had fallen after Cain Daniels had dragged her to the riverside and left her there to bleed in the rain and cold.

"Who did this to you?" he had shouted at first, surveying her bloodied body which had been further injured when she had fallen in a ditch as she walked along the lonely, empty road.

She had been delirious with cold and pain and he was glad of the rug he kept in the back window to keep her warm when he tore off her ragged dress to protect his car from bloodstains.

He felt like a Good Samaritan but his feelings for Jessie ran much deeper than that and at that moment when he watched her in so much pain and full of heartbreak at her guilt and fear of what her family might do when they found her out, he knew he was the only one who could protect her.

His initial premonitions had been for a reason, he realised.

It was God's message to him that he would help this young woman in her hour of need. She had confessed to him, she had confided to him, she had run to him when she felt that she had no one else in this world and now he was fulfilling her every request by taking her away from her sins.

She didn't tell her husband, nor her sister, nor her mother nor anyone else in her close circle of her troubles.

She had come only to him and now he would make sure he finished the job she had asked him to do.

He would take her to a new life where she would

never have to go through such physical and emotional damage again. He had saved her life from people who were riddled with evil and it felt so good.

Andrea answered David's call before the phone hardly had a chance to ring. It was dark now and her father and Ryan were on their way home, due to some U-turn in the investigation. They didn't have much information then, but her father's joy would be her own husband's nightmare and she dreaded what David had to say.

She hated the fact the Cain was now her husband. When she said the word, it stumbled on her tongue like a bad taste.

"They won't listen to me," said David down the phone and Andrea realised that her train of thought was running in the opposite direction from her brother-in-law's. "She was in the priest's house. She had to be. Her bracelet was found there this afternoon."

Andrea's head spun as David ranted on but she picked up on the instruction to meet him on the village Main Street and to bring the matching bracelet she had worn on her wedding day to help him prove his point.

The street was quiet as always at that time of the evening and David was already standing on the kerbside waiting for her when she arrived just minutes later.

"What is this all about?" said Andrea, slamming the door of her Mini Cooper. "They've got him now. They've got a confession to beating Jessie so what more do you need?"

"I need to rule this out," he said, marching ahead of her. "Where is it? Where is the bracelet?"

Andrea reached out her wrist and David unclipped the fastener and then laid it across his hand.

"I haven't taken it off since the wedding until now," said Andrea. "It sort of gave me hope, you know. I thought of her wearing the same one, wherever she is, and I can't forget the words she said to me when I gave it to her. It all makes sense now."

But David wasn't listening. He was looking along the row of terraced houses, up and down as they strode along the street and eventually he stopped at the house with the yellow door.

He looked behind him at the stone wall of the Church and he knew he was at the right place. Ella's directions were spot on.

"Mrs Sheehan," he said when the lady opened the door.

She looked petrified to see him and she closed the door over and hooked a chain across, then peered out.

"What do you want? I told you, I can't help you any further. It was a mistake," she said.

David held out his hand and showed her the fragile piece of silver that crossed his palm. The rubies glistened under the street lamps and he held it up, closer to where Rosie peeped out at him.

"I just need you to tell me one thing and then I'm gone," he said, his voice shaking and time ticking away in his head. "Is this the same bracelet you found in Father Christopher Lennon's house this afternoon?"

He waited for her to answer, his breathing so loud that Andrea could hear him from where she stood a few feet away.

Rosie glanced at the bracelet and then looked David straight in the eye.

"Yes, it is. I have no doubt about it," she said. "That's the one."

Chapter 34

Andrea and David burst through the doors of Glencuan Police Station and David rang the bell consistently until his colleague and friend, Detective Inspector Mark Redmond, came to the glass that looked out onto reception.

"I need to speak to Cooper right now," said David. "I don't think we have much time to hang around. Where is he?"

Cooper appeared in a flash, a broad smile pasted across his face. He folded his arms and gave a haughty laugh.

"For Christ's sake, Chambers! All this running around after clergymen will give you a heart attack. Either that or you'll go straight for hell for pointing the finger in the wrong direction."

He sniggered at his own joke but his laughter trailed off when he witnessed the stony faces on David Chambers and Andrea O'Neill in front of him.

David held up the bracelet under Cooper's nose.

"She's out there," he said, his lips dry with the heat of the stuffy station. "The exact same bracelet as this was found in that priest's house this afternoon. How likely is it that it belongs to anyone else?"

Sandra Millar's piercing voice could be heard from far down the corridor. She stopped dead when she saw David and Andrea standing with Cooper.

"David, don't tell me you're still on about Father Lennon, are you? I said I'd contact you if I thought it was worth pursuing and at this moment we have enough information to crush Daniels. It's all coming together nicely."

David approached Sandra with a look of venom and he pointed his finger in her face and then pointed back at Cooper.

"This is my wife we are talking about!" he shouted. "You can't push me away from this no matter what you say. Prove me wrong! Go round there now and talk to him. Prove he has nothing to do with this, but my guess is that he has done a runner and if Jessie is harmed because of your arrogance and sheer insistence on policy and protocol when it comes to my interests, then fuck you all!"

He signalled to Andrea to follow him outside and they marched in sync out through the double doors, down the concrete steps and towards his car.

He bleeped the car open, mumbling under his breath as they got inside and he turned the ignition. He had just put the car into reverse gear when there was a knock on the window.

"Let me in," said Cooper. "Let me in so we can check this out to put your fucking mind at rest."

Cooper jumped into the back seat and David put his foot on the pedal, not slacking until he came to the leafy driveway that led to Glencuan's Parochial House.

The house was dark and just as David had predicted, Father Lennon's car was gone. He felt a mixture of trepidation and anxiety as they went to the front door and just as he had done on his earlier visit, they peered through the windows but there was definitely no one there.

"What do you say we have a look around the back?"

Cooper rolled his eyes and followed, while Andrea held on to David's arm in the darkness. She had been told to sit in the car and wait but the fear she felt inside wouldn't let her. She didn't want to be alone.

David grabbed a torch from the boot of his car and they made their way along the gable of the redbrick house, past a row of hedges that had seen better days and eventually they came to the lush greenery of the parochial gardens.

Andrea imagined how pretty the garden would be in daylight but now, as evening fell the plants and trees dropped a sea of shadows onto the walls and windows of the house that made heightened her fears.

"There's no one home, that's for sure," said Cooper. "Spooky enough around here at night, eh?"

He let out a raspy laugh and Andrea clung on to David tighter.

"Hold on," said David as he whooshed the torch

around the doors and windows and then onto the gardens. "What's that down there?"

They squinted and followed the beam of light that David held high above the greenery and could make out the roof of the gate lodge in the distance.

"Looks like a garden shed to me," said Cooper. "Oh for God's sake, Chambers, let's go! You don't think she is in there, do you?"

David followed his instincts and followed the beam of light down through the garden, leaving Andrea with Cooper at the back door of the house. She had never felt so terrified in her life and when she saw David pause to light up a cigarette on his way down through the garden, she knew he was as nervous as she felt right at that moment.

"I can't believe we're standing here," said Cooper, shaking his head. "What the hell would your sister have been here for? How would she have made it here at that time of night when the goddamn priest left the wedding hours before her? Unless . . ."

He scooped his mobile phone from his hip belt and pressed Sandra Millar's number.

"Millar," he said when she answered, "we're waiting for Chambers outside the priest's house here and I just want to know one thing."

"Go on," said Millar.

Andrea could hear her every word from where she stood and Cooper continued.

"He says he left the wedding at around nine, right?"

"Yes, he did," said Millar. "He stopped off in the

village grocery store at about ten thirty. I did check it out."

Cooper drew a sharp breath which told Andrea he felt he was clutching straws.

"Well, what are the chances he would have turned his car and gone back for Jessie if she had asked him to? Would he have done it for her? Or more to the point, would she have asked him to come and get her if she was in trouble?"

Millar took her time and recalled the conversation with Father Christopher, the way his voice changed when he spoke of Jessie, the way he avoided her eye when he said Jessie's name and then she knew.

But before she answered, David ran back up through the garden, panting and swirling the torch around as he moved. His eyes were electric and his voice was dry.

"I think I see a bed inside," he shouted. "Lots of boxes, lots of gym gear, but I'll swear there is a makeshift bed in that place and I have a hunch it might have been made for Jessie."

Cooper put up his hand in David's direction and held his eye contact. "What do you think, Millar? Was he close enough for her to ask him to come for her? Quickly."

"Yes, I think she might have. It's possible," she said. "It's very possible. But he was giving last rites to a Joe Roberts. He stayed with the family most of the night. They can vouch for him he said. "

"And did you?"

"Well, no. But the man *did* die. His funeral was yesterday. I'll check with the family now."

"Yes, do that now! And then get your ass over here, Millar!" said Cooper. "We have some talking to do."

Ella sat in the living-room with Andrea and Lily and watched the phone, just as she had been doing since they had got home the day before. David had been gone for over an hour now and the waiting was killing them, plus Tom was due home any second with Ryan.

The click of the back door brought the three of them to their feet and Ella wrung her hands, her nerves in tatters as to how she should greet her son. She had so many questions for him, yet she wanted to first of all hold him in her arms and remove all his fears. He had done wrong but he had believed at the time that his actions were right and Ella would try to understand that, as difficult as it might be.

He was home now, and that was a positive step in the right direction for all of them.

Ella looked at her baby boy and took in his frail appearance. His jeans were grubby and baggy and his jacket hung on his shoulders, loose and untidy. He looked smaller now, more boyish than manly and in comparison his father beside him looked as if he had aged ten years in just three days.

"Oh Ryan!" said Ella and she instinctively ran for him and wrapped her arms around his feeble shoulders. She hugged him so tight she thought he might break under her force but he stood statuesque in response, his hands in his pockets and his head facing the floor.

"I just want to go to bed, Mum," he mumbled. "I'm tired and I don't think I can talk much right now."

"Of course not, honey," said Ella, holding his face in both of her hands. "You just take your time, son. Now that you're back at home with us, you can take all the time you need. And when Jessie comes home everything will get back to the way we were. The good times are just around the corner, son. You'll see."

Tom led Ryan upstairs, his arm never leaving his shoulders and Ella collapsed on the couch in the sitting-room. She couldn't speak as she watched her husband take their son up to bed.

"Come on, love," said Lily and she put her arm around her friend. "He's home now. Ryan's home and, like you say, the good times are just around the corner. Let's get you up to bed too and hope that the morning brings us the news we've all been waiting for."

Lily hoisted Ella up from the seat and turned to her niece.

"How about you, love? An early night is what you need too."

"I'll stay up for another little while," said Andrea, staring at the silent flicker of the television in the corner. "I'll just make Dad some tea and we'll wait for news from David. Just in case, you know . . ."

"If you're sure," said Aunt Lily. She paused at the door and looked at Andrea who was huddled up in the corner of the huge sofa, television remote in one hand and mobile phone in the other.

"I'm sure," said Andrea, giving her aunt a small but reassuring smile.

Aunt Lily pursed her lips.

"Goodnight, love," she whispered. "We're all very, very proud of you, you do know that. You've been so, so brave."

Andrea nodded. "I only wish she was home. That's all I want right now."

Chapter 35

"Joe Roberts – the dead guy – has no fuckin' family! How the hell did you miss that one?"

Sandra knew she would never live it down so she had to take the blame for missing out on something so simple.

"So his alibi is a guy who is now six feet under, is that what you're saying?"

"There was a neighbour there too," said Sandra. "He rang for the priest but then left them to it. I'm sorry, sir."

"So you fuckin' should be," said Cooper to Sandra who sat in the back seat of the Saab as they headed out of the village. "So this Rosie woman – the housekeeper – she is adamant the priest had no appointments this evening? Are you at least sure of that?"

"Yes," said Sandra. "She told me he was spending every spare hour at the gate lodge. He was turning it into a gym. He even ate his meals down there on occasion but he seemed reluctant to let her inside."

Sandra held on tight to the handles above the windows of the car and almost bounced off the glass when David took a corner at death-defying high speed.

"Christ, would you slow down, David! Do you want to kill us all?"

"She's right, Chambers," said Cooper. "This A-Team car chase speed is unnecessary. We aren't even sure we're going in the right direction yet and you're about to land us in a ditch."

David slacked off the accelerator and the tension in the car eased. It was almost ten o'clock and he could hear every second tick by in his head like a time bomb.

"Right," said Cooper. "Now that I have the brain space to think properly and I'm not competing with the speed of light, Cain Daniels has admitted to hitting Jessie at least with a slap after he punched her brother, but he says that she stumbled away in her drunken state towards the river bank."

"And yet her bracelet ends up in Father Lennon's house," said Sandra. "The bracelet she wore to the wedding which Andrea says was specially made. So, how did she get to the priest's house at that hour?"

"She must have called him to come get her," said Cooper. "She tried David first who missed her call –"

"Rub it in, man! This is killing me, you know!"

"I'm just recapping the facts. So, she is in a bad state and she calls her new friend, Father Christopher, who takes her to his house and either against her will, or with her consent, he sets up a mini base for her –"

"In the gate lodge," said David. "The perfect hiding place. No one would ever have thought of heading down there."

They drove for a few minutes in silence, digesting the information they had pieced together so far and then Sandra piped up from the back seat.

"He wouldn't harm her though," she said adamantly. "I have no reason to believe he would harm her. He seemed nervous to me, but gentle and –"

"Oh, cut the shit, Millar," said Cooper, straining his neck to see his colleague's reaction. "If he wasn't so young and handsome you'd have him down as a psycho cleric and have him banged up in no time. This is no time for romance. If he has taken Jessie and deliberately kept her from her family, then he's a nutter, full stop."

"Oh, you just know everything, don't you? You've never even met the man."

"Well, he may look like a movie star, but he's a psychotic freak who knew there was a top-drawer search going on. Where would he have stopped? Would he let Ryan be banged up in the wrong or even Daniels?"

"But he believes that *they* are in the wrong," said Millar. "He is protecting Jessie from them. I just know it."

The roads were dark and quite busy as they left Glencuan and they drove onto the dual carriageway that led to Belfast City.

"Oh, my God! Oh, my God, we're going the wrong way!" said Millar and she clicked off her seatbelt and perched up between the two front seats of the car. "I think he's taking her south."

"Oh, so you're Mystic fucking Meg now too, into the bargain!" yelled Cooper. "Where the hell did this revelation come from?"

"It's not a revelation, it's –"

"Well, what is it then? Because I reckon when you went to talk to the gorgeous Father Almighty, you were too busy ogling him to remember that you were in fact on official business and not on a hot date!"

"You bastard!"

"In fact, only for that nosey old housekeeper of his, we would be still be staring across a table at Cain Daniels or hauling answers from Ryan O'Neill. Explain yourself, Millar! How did you miss out on him? You were too busy batting your eyelids at him, that's why!"

Millar sat back on the seat again and clicked her seat belt back on. She folded her arms and stared out the window as cars zoomed past them and she watched as the white lines on the road faded into each other.

"Sandra, don't listen to the big bad boss and his tactics," said David, looking at her in the rear-view. "I believe you. I'm listening. Now why do you think we are going the wrong way? Where do you think he might run to?"

Sandra licked her lips and slowly blinked her weary eyes.

"I have a feeling he might take her to see his mother," she said. "That's all I was going to say."

"In fucking Cork?" said Cooper, hoisting his body round in her direction again. "Jesus! This is getting worse!"

"No, not in fucking Cork," Sandra roared back at him. "You see, Detective Cooper, I did manage to listen to him while I was ogling his fine beauty yesterday. It's called multi-tasking and we women are known to be exceptionally good at it, whereas men on the other hand can't multi-task worth a shit!"

David managed to laugh when he glanced at Cooper's face. Millar had him good on that one.

"His mother lives in the Republic, near Athlone, and she's the one person he wants to impress most in the world. I think if he wanted to keep Jessie safe, it's the first place he would run to. So he could live out his dream to have a family unit. Rosie told me that too. She heard him say it to Ella O'Neill when she visited earlier today."

David didn't wait for Cooper's approval.

He indicated at the next gap on the carriageway and headed back in the direction of Glencuan, then down towards Monaghan and across the border where he headed south for the two-hour journey to Athlone.

Father Christopher had never been to the town of Athlone before but he spoke to his mother on the phone every Sunday and she would talk about how wonderful it was and how much it had lived up to her expectations.

She had always intended to settle there, having traced her own ancestors back to the town on the River Shannon that was known as the heart of Ireland. She spoke of boat trips on Lough Ree and of walks around the castle and the colourful selection of bistros and craft shops and alternative boutiques she loved to browse around.

She promised that when he would settle into his new parish, she would come to Glencuan to visit him and see how all of his hard work had paid off for him. She was a proud woman but in her heart she had always hoped that her only son would have settled with a nice girl and given her a few grandchildren to while away her later years with. She had always pined for a daughter to keep her company, and now, Christopher was going to give her the best of both worlds.

Not only had he played the role of the Good Samaritan, but he had rescued Jessie from a life of misery and blame and he had kept his vocational vows despite his deep love for her. He would let his mother look after her and she would thrive in her new life, away from the stresses and strains of courts and law and a family who could never grant her forgiveness as he could.

And then, when Jessie decided she loved him as much as he loved her, he would discuss his options with his mother and he would reassess his future and take one step at a time.

"Are you hungry?" he asked but there was no reply

from his fellow passenger. Instead she just groaned a bit and shifted from the back seat bed he had made for her.

He checked the clock on the dashboard of the car and its green digital symbols told him it was way after eleven. He wondered when he had last given her medication and he frowned at the thought that she should be still so drowsy.

She had asked him only an hour ago if her mother had called yet, but when he told her not to stress over her family, she had heeded his every word and settled back down again. She didn't even know what day it was, poor thing, but then he had given her just enough sedation to keep her mind at ease, but to quietly let him know when she needed anything like the bathroom, or extra blankets or a drink or if she would like some music in the background.

Of course, her parents would be welcome in Athlone from time to time, eventually. It would be wrong for him to insist that she sacrifice her relationship with her parents but the rest of the family would deservedly be kept at a distance.

Her husband had left her on a whim when she was obviously deeply troubled and confused, her sister would always be tied up with that nasty Daniels fellow who had seduced Jessie and then left her to rot by a riverbank, and her own brother had made her life a living misery by taunting her and breaking into her home with his sordid notes and slanderous graffiti.

No, they would never receive an invitation to Jessie's new home.

"Not long now, Jess," he said as he took a turn onto the last leg of the N55 that led straight to their destination. "You warm enough?"

Again, Jessie didn't answer and he tried not to panic. He would have liked her to be making more conversation at this point. The journey was long without proper company and Christopher kicked himself for giving her that last sedative.

Then he imagined her poor broken face and how it would light up when she realised all he had done for her. He had lied, yes, but it was for the overall good and he would convince the O'Neill family that he was right to help out his friend in this way, just as other strangers had helped him and his mother in their desperate hour of need.

A blue light in the distance made him squint through the windscreen and he rolled his eyes when he realised it was a police checkpoint. He waited in line in the queue of cars and sighed at the disruption to his journey which was so far taking longer than he anticipated.

Drink drivers he supposed, and he glanced back at his patient who was sleeping like a baby, her pink dressing gown tucked up under her chin and a fleecy blanket around her shoulders. She looked so peaceful and happy and he was so glad to help her, but he knew her presence might stir up some questions so he reached into the back window and tugged down the dark blue car rug

410

and fixed it over her so that unless someone was looking for her, she wouldn't be seen in the dark of night.

He flicked the car radio on to Classic FM and relaxed his shoulders, breathing along to the relaxing tone of the music so that he wouldn't appear in any way that he had something to hide.

"Good evening, sir," said the Garda as Christopher put down the window at the checkpoint. He held up a thin torchlight which shone in Christopher's face and then he pointed it across to the empty passenger seat. "Can I see your driving licence, please?"

Christopher scrambled in the visor pocket and handed the Garda his licence, wearing a charming smile the whole time. His collar often got him through police checkpoints quite quickly.

"Nice night," he said, wondering if small talk might allow him some grace and the instruction to move on.

"Sure is," said the Garda in a strong South Cavan accent. "Pull in to the side of the road, Father. Now."

"I – I'm in a bit of a hurry actually, Constable," said Christopher, already finding first gear in the car. "I'm expected at a wake in Athlone and I'm running late as it is. Is this necessary?"

The cop reached into the car and turned the ignition off.

"Yes, it is necessary," he said. "Now, just forget about pulling the car over. Just get out, Father. Get out of the fucking car right now and I'll see to your passenger in the back."

The Garda radioed through to the car in front and his two colleagues ran to the car and pulled Father Christopher out of his seat, then pushed him against the cool exterior of the vehicle and handcuffed him, then read him his rights.

"Father Christopher Lennon, I arrest you in connection with the unlawful kidnapping of Ms Jessie O'Neill-Chambers. You do not have to say anything, but it may harm your defence if you do not mention, when questioned, something which you later rely on in court. Anything you do say may be given in evidence."

"No, this is all wrong. You are wrong! They will hurt her again. She needs me. Please listen. Jessie! Jessie, don't worry!"

They pushed his head down into the awaiting marked car and he shouted out of the back seat.

"Please don't hurt her," he shouted. "She's been hurt enough already. Be careful! Please be careful. Her medication is in the bag on the back seat. She needs it. She needs me."

A sea of paramedics surrounded his car and he watched them lift Jessie out from the back seat and lay her on a stretcher, then they lifted her into the back of the ambulance.

"I love you, Jessie!" he shouted as the ambulance drove away into the distance towards Athlone Hospital. "I only wanted the best for you. I did my very best to protect you from them. I'm so, so sorry."

Chapter 36

Six months later . . .

Jessie sat in her study, watching the splodges of heavy snow fall on the window pane.

It was freezing outside but in her bedroom she was warm and toasty. She sucked the top of her pen, then began to write her letter and then stopped again, a tugging in her heart not letting her say exactly how she felt.

She could hear her family whisper downstairs, discussing when she might find the strength to face them all together and how they would have to be patient. Jessie hated to keep them all waiting on such a special occasion, but writing this letter was something she had to do first.

She lifted her pen again and pressed out the cream notepaper, then cursed as a tear blobbed onto its embossed surface.

He never left her mind. Every day when she woke

413

up, his was the first name that crossed her lips, the first face her mind saw and the first voice she heard in her own head. She had to contact him, despite what everyone said. Despite what he might want. She had to let him know she cared.

"Dear Christopher," she wrote.

I just heard the good news and I wanted to let you know how delighted I am that you will be home in time for Christmas.

I really wanted to visit you in hospital but they didn't think it would do either of us any good. We all have to move on, they say.

I hope you are finding the strength and understanding from others to move on.

We are all finding it very difficult, but Mum is keeping up a very brave front and is making any excuse to keep us together, even inventing little occasions when we can have dinner or just hang out in the same room or same place.

Today is one of those occasions. She had invited everyone to my house for Thanksgiving even though we have never celebrated such an occasion here in our lives.

I suppose it has real meaning though. We have a lot to be sorry for, but we also have a lot to give thanks for in our family.

Mum has really surprised everyone on how she is fully focused on the future and on making everything better for all of us. She is a strong, amazing woman and we are very lucky (as a good friend once told me) to

have such a force behind us and someone who believes in each of us with her heart and soul. She is spending lots of time with Andrea and Ryan now, and I'm glad she is taking the time to slowly get to know each of us again.

Dad is putting on a fair show of bravery but I can see he has lost his spark inside, but he is an ox behind it all and I know that it won't be long until he commands the same respect that he always has in this village. His pride has taken a fall, but there are times when he lets himself go and I see him looking at Mum, or Andrea, or Ryan, or even me and I recognise that same old glint of pleasure that he used to have.

Ryan is going to need a lot of help to 'move on'. It will take a long time, but we will get there. He and I have had some long, gut-wrenching talks and there have been tears and a lot of words spilled, but we both accept we have done wrong and we have to allow each other to breathe it out, and to grieve as well. There has been a lot of faith and trust lost in our family, but we will fight hard until it comes back.

They've suggested counselling for all of us and maybe in time we will consider that route. At the moment, we are taking baby steps to heal the wounds we all have suffered lately.

Andrea is my hero and I feel humbled and yet sore every time I look at her.

She has lost her path in life and yet she has turned it into a positive, joking that she would have been in for a life of misery if Cain hadn't made his dirty advances on me (of course, I have been given plenty of wry comments on how 'it takes two' but I'm up for them. It's the least I deserve).

He may have beaten me physically but I don't think his actions against my sister managed to wound her emotionally as we would have thought. He asked her to come visit him as he serves his sentence but she answered in true Andrea style – I'll let you imagine the literary way she put it!

Even David has been in touch with me on a regular basis and he reckons in time we will be able to put this all in the past and make a future together.

I'm not sure yet, but he is a wonderful man who deserves the very best of me, and when I know I can give him my best, I will make the commitment that I should have made when I married him. But until then, I have to get to know myself inside and out and every day I feel as if I'm learning and taking notes on how to be a better person.

My wrist is well healed now and the scars on my arms and face have begun to fade, but the scars on the inside are still raw and bleeding. I have tried to blank a lot of what happened out of my mind but I know that eventually I will have to face up to every minute detail and stop punishing myself for the part I played in my own downfall.

I want to thank you again, Christopher. From the bottom of my heart I want to thank you for saving me in more ways than one. I told them all you never meant to hurt me. I called you in my hour of need and you came running.

Now, because you answered my call and did what you felt was best for me, your life will never be the same.

Mine will never be the same because of you, Father Christopher Lennon. You will remain forever in my heart – my friend and my saviour.

God bless,

Jessie xxx

Jessie sealed the envelope and addressed it to Christopher, care of the hospital he had been assigned to since his nervous breakdown after his arrest.

She placed the letter in front of her computer and fixed her hair, then she walked down the stairs of her house and into the sea of laughter in her living-room and she felt alive again.

She heard David's voice and his signature laugh above the others and then she caught her sister's eye at the far end of the room.

"Ryan for a song!" said Andrea and she snuggled up to her father's side.

"Yes," said Jessie and she sat on the arm of the chair beside her brother. "Ryan for a song."

At the far side of the room, Ella smiled and a warm glow of hope filled her from her head to her toes.

Happiness is just around the corner she thought, and for the first time, she actually believed that it might be true.

THE END